MICHAEL ASHER

Michael Asher has served in the Parachute Regiment and the SAS, and studied English at the University of Leeds. He has made expeditions in many countries, always preferring to travel on foot or with animal transport. He lived for three years with a Bedu tribe totally unaffected by the outside world and, with his wife, Arabist and Photographer Mariantonietta Peru, made the first west–east crossing of the Sahara on foot and with camels – a distance of 4,500 miles – without technology or back-up of any kind.

Michael Asher is the author of nine books and has travelled a total of 16,000 miles by camel.

D1369107

THE
EYE
OF
RA

MICHAEL
ASHER

HarperCollins*Publishers*

HarperCollins*Publishers*
77–85 Fulham Palace Road,
Hammersmith, London W6 8JB

www.**fire**and**water**.com

This paperback edition 2000
1 3 5 7 9 8 6 4 2

First published in Great Britain by
HarperCollins*Publishers* 1999

ISBN 0 00 651317 4

Set in Times New Roman by
Rowland Phototypesetting Ltd,
Bury St Edmunds, Suffolk

Printed and bound in Great Britain by
Clays Ltd, St Ives plc

To the memory of my father-in-law,
General Pasquale Peru, Soldier and Traveller
And to Mariantonietta and Burton, again

ACKNOWLEDGEMENTS

I am most grateful to my agent, Anthony Goff, of David Higham Associates, probably the best literary agent working in London today. Without his tireless work this book would probably never have seen the light. I am also very grateful to Susan Watt of HarperCollins for her great faith and boundless enthusiasm which have meant a great deal to me. Of course, this book could not have been written without the help and suggestions of my wife, Mariantonietta Peru and my son, Burton, to whom I offer my sincere thanks. I very much appreciate the help of my parents-in-law Prof. Italia Peru and the late General Pasquale Peru, to whom this book is partly dedicated.

Michael Asher
Nairobi and Frazione Agnata, Sardinia

PRELUDE

VALLEY OF THE KINGS, EGYPT

L ONG AFTER IT WAS OVER, a friend sent me a cutting he'd found while rummaging through newly released files at Reuters. It appeared to be part of a report by Walter Morrison, who'd been sent to Luxor in 1923 as correspondent on the Tutankhamen story. At that time exclusive rights on the opening of the burial-chamber had been given to *The Times*, but Morrison, a seasoned hack, was so determined that Reuters should get the scoop that he actually bought a Model-T Ford and hired a felucca and a team of donkeys to carry the news to the nearest telegraph station. The problem that remained was how to get into the tomb. Rumour has it that he bribed an Egyptian pasha and posed as a guest. It appears, anyway, that he was among the spectators when Howard Carter opened the chamber. Whether the following was intended as the beginning of a book or a follow-up article will never be known, for Morrison was found dead in unexplained circumstances in his London club in the summer of 1923. Incidentally, the fragment bore no resemblance to the report actually published on the day under his byline:

Valley of the Kings, Egypt. 16th February, 1923

It was stifling in the tomb, and the air was made fouler by the crush of onlookers and the heat of the two giant arc-lamps brought in to illuminate the final act of penetration. Howard Carter, stripped down to his neatly laundered shirt, rolled up his sleeves, and hefted the sledge-hammer, testing its weight against the palm of his left hand. Lord Carnarvon looked on imperturbably, betraying no sign of the discomfort he must have felt dressed in the tweed uniform of the British aristocracy. Carter gave the hammer an experimental swing, and almost at once trickles of sweat beaded his brow. He could easily have got one of his team of *guftis* to do the manual work, but this was the crowning moment of years of excavation in the Nile Valley, and no doubt he was justified in feeling that the honour belonged to him alone. There was an expectant hush in the tomb. Someone coughed uneasily. I had to repress the disturbing sense that we were all intruders here in the grave of a lost king. Carter glanced at Carnarvon. This was the moment they had waited for. His Lordship nodded, and Carter swung the hammer in earnest, punching a hole in the wall which had guarded its secrets for almost three and a half thousand years.

It was four months since Carter's foreman, Rais Ahmad, had run to his house at Luxor with the news that his *guftis* had unearthed three stone steps under the debris of an ancient workman's hut in the Valley of the Kings. Carter rushed to the necropolis, examined the steps, and ordered the *guftis* to dig down into what he thought was the beginning of an underground passage. The workmen shovelled frantically and in ninety minutes uncovered ten steps. After another ninety they came to a sealed door, on which Carter found two seals: the Jackal-god Anubis – ancient Egyptian symbol of the dead – and a cartouche containing the Eye of Ra, the seal of the guardians of the royal necropolis. To his astonishment, the seals seemed undisturbed and for the first time he dared hope that he had discovered an intact pharaonic tomb – a unique window into the heart of the ancient Egyptian world. The workmen named the place 'The Tomb of the Bird' after Carter's goldcoloured canary, which they believed had brought him luck. Carter could have appeased his curiosity there and then by tearing down the door. But after thirty years of hope and disillusion, he was not the man to rush things. Instead he had his labourers fill up the passage, and posted a guard on the site. Then he returned calmly to Luxor and despatched a telegram to his sponsor, Lord Carnarvon, in England: 'Wonderful discovery in the Valley at last,' he wrote. 'A tomb with undamaged seals. Everything covered in until your arrival. Congratulations.'

It was not until Carnarvon arrived at the beginning of November that Carter found the seal of Tutankhamen hidden under a pile of debris, and realised that he'd found the tomb of one of the two major lost pharaohs of the 18th Dynasty. On the first day his workmen broke through the sealed door and cut into it a passage twenty feet long, filled with rubble and shards of terracotta and alabaster vessels. At the end of the passage was a second door, closed with twin seals. On 25th November, Carter put an iron spike through the door and passed his candle inside. Peering into the darkness, he caught a glimpse of strange objects: animals, statues, caskets, chariots and pressed flowers.

'Can you see anything?' Carnarvon asked.

'Yes,' Carter replied, 'Wonderful things!'

The tomb of Tutankhamen turned out to be the most sensational discovery in archaeological history – its treasures exceeded its finders' wildest dreams. For the first ten weeks Carter and his team worked on the objects they found in the antechamber, artefacts of astounding beauty and craftsmanship – drawing, measuring, photographing and removing them piece by piece. The University of Chicago hieroglypher James Henry Breasted translated the wall seals, and confirmed that this was indeed the tomb of the lost pharaoh Tutankhamen. All that remained was the discovery of the mummy itself. They found a secret door in the antechamber wall guarded by two life-size wooden statues, and guessed that the sarcophagus of Tutankhamen lay beyond. All was prepared for the final triumph – the unsealing of the burial-chamber, set for 16th February.

Carter swung the sledge-hammer again and again, the blows reverberating around the walls of the small chamber. Within ten minutes his shirt was soaked with perspiration, and he had knocked out the remaining plaster, opening a slit wide enough for him to squeeze through. He shone his torch into the breach and the spectators gasped as the beam flashed back from what appeared to be a solid wall of gold. He hesitated for a moment. He was about to step into the grave of a king who had been dead for thirty-five centuries, the first human being to cross that threshold since pharaonic times. If the idea of sacrilege crossed his mind, he suppressed it well; he'd been preparing for this moment for three decades, after all, and it was too late to stop now. He plunged through the gap, out of sight. He was gone five minutes, then ten, fifteen, twenty. Lord Carnarvon stood stock still: a single track of sweat decorated his forehead. The onlookers fidgeted impatiently. Suddenly Carter's face appeared in the glare of the spotlights, smeared with dust and deadly pale.

'What did you see?' Carnarvon demanded, his voice thick with excitement.

Carter seemed to be shaking uncontrollably. 'My God!' he was muttering in a faint voice, almost to himself. 'Lord Carnarvon, I think you'd better come and look at this . . .'

By the time I saw this fragment, of course, I already knew about Morrison, and how he'd sneaked into the tomb uninvited. I often wonder whether, if I'd come across it before I received Julian Cranwell's call for help, it would have made any difference. Perhaps I might have guessed what lay in store for me – then again, perhaps not . . .

PART I

LONDON
& CAIRO
1995

1

LONDON

A RAINY MARCH NIGHT ON THE Clapham omnibus. Streets passing out of focus, a smear of white and orange lights through fogged window panes. I cleared myself a little wet patch on the window, stared out into the undifferentiated urban night, and swore under my breath. I was on my way home from my talk on 'The Origins & Construction of the Giza Pyramids' to the Society of Antiquarians, and the evening hadn't exactly been a successful one. In fact it had been a disaster. The moment I stood at the lectern I knew they'd gathered for a human sacrifice – mine.

All the most distinguished and most vitriolic Egyptologists in Britain, and many from elsewhere, had been present. Of course, they knew I'd been sacked from my post with the Egyptian Antiquities Service two years earlier for my supposedly 'irrational' opinions on the origin of Egyptian civilisation. Word gets around. To the high priesthood of science 'irrational' means what medieval Christians meant by 'heretical' – that you have views different from the currently accepted canon. They can excommunicate you, too, just as they did with Heyerdahl and Velikovsky. The irony is that I've always prided myself on being a logical thinker, and here I was, typecast as an inhabitant of the lunatic fringe. To tell the truth, I'm not a great speaker at the best of times. I can expound my views clearly enough in private, but crowds give me the jitters. That night, the baleful stares and the cold silence would have been enough to unnerve even an expert pedagogue. As I stood up, surveying the rows of venerable heads, I half expected them to heckle me before I'd even started speaking. That had happened to me more than once in the previous two years. To give the Antiquarians their due, they'd heard me out for the first half-hour. It was only when I suggested that the Great Pyramid hadn't been built by Pharaoh Khufu of the 4th Dynasty, but by an unknown race of immigrants, centuries earlier, that the murmuring began. A man with a face so florid it looked like it'd been steeped all night in brandy, a walrus moustache and unkempt silver hair, stood up and cleared his throat ominously. It was Giles Garstang, professor of Egyptology at Cambridge University, author of a notable book on the dating sequence of ancient Egypt. The Lord High Executioner, I thought.

'Forgive me for interrupting, Mr Ross,' Garstang opened pleasantly, as if he wanted to clear up a trifling, minor point that puzzled him. His voice had the same brandy-marinated quality as his face. 'If my memory is correct, and of course it's not what it used to be.' He turned and smiled at the audience – jolly, erudite chuckles from both sides. 'If I remember rightly, a series of semi-hieratic symbols, actually quarry marks, referring to the Pharaoh Khufu were found painted on certain stone blocks inside several of the chambers of the Great Pyramid, by Colonel Howard Vyse, in 1837. They are, I believe, and *do* correct me if I'm wrong, the only epigraphic records ever found inside the structure.' His amiable expression hardened, and I saw his eyes fix on the tiny silver earring I was wearing on the upper fold of my right ear. I shouldn't have worn it tonight, of course, but it had a special significance for me that Garstang couldn't have guessed. 'Now, to me, Mr Ross,' he went on, 'and I'm sure to most Fellows of the Society, that suggests strongly that Khufu – a Pharaoh of the 4th Dynasty – was associated with the building of the Great Pyramid . . .' Murmurs of well-educated assent from the audience, growing steadily in volume. 'Certainly,' Garstang went on, 'there is no record of the "unknown race" which you suggest built the pyramid thousands of years before Khufu – when, I might add, the ancient Egyptians were still running about the desert naked hunting wild auroch.' More snickers from the audience. 'My questions are simple: Who was this mystery race? Why is there no record of it? And most important of all, where did it come from?'

'Out of Chingford!' A bass voice rang out from the back.

'No! No!' some other bright spark tittered, 'Elephant and Castle!'

Guffaws of laughter from the assembly. I struggled to make myself heard over the uproar. 'They probably came from an older civilisation,' I said, 'one that was lost because of some physical disaster.'

'You mean like Atlantis?' Garstang enquired, narrowing his eyes to slits of disbelief.

The roars and hoots increased in volume. 'Get that half-wit off the stage!' somebody shouted. Garstang was struggling to look solemn. I clutched the microphone with my left hand. A knot was tightening in my stomach and I fought to keep my temper under control. I waved the laser-pointer at Garstang. 'Howard Vyse was an impostor and a fraud,' I bawled, 'who painted the marks himself and enjoyed international acclaim for it!'

More cries, this time suspiciously like boos. 'Vyse was an officer in the Guards, dammit!' Garstang snapped.

I wrenched off my glasses. 'I don't give a toss if he was a Beefeater,' I shouted back. 'He lied. You know how I know he painted those marks himself? Because he used hieratic – a script that wasn't even invented in Khufu's day – and what's more, *he made a spelling mistake*!'

This was too much. I knew it. People started to stand up. For a moment I thought they were going to pelt me with rotten fruit. 'Bloody lunatic!' someone yelled.

'Disgrace!' someone else jeered. 'Shouldn't allow charlatans in the Society.'

They began to file out.

My cheeks were burning. They hadn't even let me finish my argument. Suddenly I couldn't hold my temper any longer. 'Why bother to study Egyptology!' I found myself bellowing after the retreating backs. 'You have nothing more to learn. You know it all already!' I let go of the microphone, flung the laser-pointer in a chair, gathered my notes and walked out amid the caustic comments with as much dignity as I could muster.

I was still shaking when I got on the bus. My views had been mocked before, of course, but never by so distinguished a gathering. I swore to myself again at the ignominy of it. The academic establishment claims to deal in 'proven scientific fact', but actually they accept only the facts that suit their view of the world. The 'fact' is that there is nothing in the Great Pyramid to tie it to the Pharaoh Khufu in the 4th Dynasty. The hieratic symbols or 'quarry marks' Howard Vyse claimed to have found in 1837 are certainly forgeries, for not only are they in hieratic, a developed form of script not known in Khufu's day, but they were also copied from the only book on the subject available to Vyse – Gardiner-Wilkinson. Or is it a coincidence that the symbol for Khufu in the book is misspelled in exactly the same way it's misspelled in Vyse's 'discoveries'? Actually, there isn't a shred of evidence to prove that the pyramids weren't standing on the plateau at Giza thousands of years before the reign of Khufu, millennia before ancient Egyptian civilisation is supposed to have existed. Neither is there any real evidence to suggest who built them. The Sphinx, which stands on the same plateau, shows signs of deep erosion by water, yet we know there haven't been heavy rains in that area since about 10,000 BC. The people who built the Sphinx were certainly capable of building the pyramids, too. The thing that really irritated me was that they hadn't even allowed me to get to the real core of my argument: the actual building of the pyramids. The concept currently popular was that the builders dragged the great monoliths up a series of temporary ramps made of earth and stones. Some simple calculations show this is impossible. To reach the top of the Great Pyramid, a ramp would have required 17.5 million cubic yards of material – seven times more than the amount of material needed to build the pyramid itself. It would have taken a workforce of at least half a million men longer than Khufu's entire reign to construct and dismantle such a ramp. If this vast army of labour, with all its logistics and supply problems, food, water, shelter, administration, ever concentrated on the Giza plateau there is no archaeological trace of it, neither is there any remnant of the millions of cubic yards of debris which were supposedly used. The ramp theory was a myth. All right, I admit that I didn't know for certain how the pyramids were constructed, but I reckoned they were a lot older than suspected, and were probably built with an advanced technology which subsequent ages lost. It's a habit of mine — probably a habit of all poor speakers – to formulate a devastating argument when it's too late. You know what Schopenhauer said about the truth? That it will first be ridiculed, then violently opposed, and finally accepted as self-evident. My truth was obviously still in the ridicule stage.

I walked the last hundred metres from the bus-stop, turning my collar up to the drizzle. My house is part of a Victorian terrace overlooking the common, with a patch of garden at the back and enough room for my Honda Gold Wing. Some people think I'm mad to run a 1000cc motor-bike – the same people who raise an eyebrow when they notice my earring. I'm a researcher for the British Museum's Ancient Near East Department, and I suppose, to most people, these things don't really go with the job. You expect a BM researcher to be a cobwebby old don with elbow-patches on his tweed jacket and corduroy trousers, not an earring and full racing leathers. We all think in such stereotypes, that's one of our major problems. We've been trained from birth in the technique of dividing nature into discrete compartments, each with its own characteristics. I'm as bad as the next man – or I was, until I started to realise that there are no compartments really, the universe is all one piece. Anyhow, as far as motor-cycles are concerned, I grew up in the seventies with *Easy Rider* and *Zen and the Art of Motorcycle Maintenance*, and I've always had a special place in my heart for fast bikes. It's speed I enjoy. Speed transcends – at ninety miles an hour you seem to be hurled into an alternative dimension, beyond your physical body. I love opening up the throttle on a fast road, but I don't use the bike for trotting round to the supermarket, or even going to work unless I happen to be late. That would be disrespectful to such a piece of precision engineering.

I bought both the house and the bike with the money I inherited from my father when he died of cancer in 1990. Actually, he left me well provided for – my grandfather was what you might call a self-made man, who founded an empire on Starlight Soap. He was the son of a Liverpool docker with nothing but a basic education and a genius for making money and, I suppose, making soap. He ended up selling the business for a tidy sum, retired to an estate in Dorset and spent the rest of his life pretending to be a country squire. My father didn't exactly squander the money, but he used it to do the things he wanted to do and inevitably it was whittled down. While he left me enough to have avoided working at all if I hadn't felt like it, the great fortune my grandfather bequeathed was gone.

I tabbed up the path feeling as though I was shifting a hundred-pound rucksack, aiming only to throw myself in an armchair, light my pipe, pour myself a stiff whisky and catch the evening news on TV. As soon as I opened the door I heard the answering-machine bleep. I didn't rush to play it back. Actually, my attention was distracted by a picture postcard of Brighton pier standing on the table by the telephone. I turned it over and found the note scrawled in Monica's almost indecipherable hand: 'Dear Jamie, Came to get the rest of my things,' it read. 'Have taken everything and am leaving the keys. So this is goodbye. Love Monica.'

I looked around for the keys, but they weren't there. This must have been about the fourth 'So this is goodbye' note I'd had from Monica in a month. It was like the story of Mustafa's old shoes – every time you thought you'd heard the last of them, they kept on turning up. I suppose I should have had the locks changed, but somehow I'd never got round to it. Monica was a minor annoyance, like a mosquito in the ear; that's more or less all she'd been for most of our six-month relationship. It was entirely my fault, of course. She was as stunningly pretty as she was cerebrally vacant, and I'd fallen for the beauty trap. Maybe I just hadn't given her enough attention. I should have been more suspicious of those late nights 'clubbing with the girls' when she arrived home in the wee small hours and tiptoed to bed. As it was I didn't even think about it until she told me she'd been seeing someone else. I really believe she thought I'd get jealous and possessive, but I didn't. I just laughed and threw her out. That had been a month ago, and since then she'd phoned, left messages, and let herself in 'for the last time' more times than I could count.

I swore, tore up the card, flung it in the waste-paper basket and made a bee-line for the drinks cabinet. It wasn't until I'd tossed off a large Scotch that I became aware of the answering-machine again. They deliberately program them with a sound that's so irritating you *have* to do something about it. I was tempted just to switch it off. It would probably be Monica, I thought, ringing to say she'd forgotten to leave the keys, and when could she come round again. Instead I assumed a mental posture of absolute complacency and pressed the play button. It wasn't Monica, it was Julian Cranwell.

His voice cut through my assumed attitude like a knife. 'Ross,' he said, 'it's me, Julian. If you're there pick up the receiver, if you're not get back to me *pronto*. Listen, I've come across some-thing – something important.'

There was a shakiness about his voice that I'd never heard before.

'I can't go into it now,' he said, 'but believe me, I'm in deep shit. I don't know how much time I've got. Jesus Christ, I think they're coming right now. Ross, you've got to help me. These devils are dangerous. They killed George Herbert, Orde Wingate and Tutankhamen! I think it's the Akhnaton *ushabtis* they're after . . .'

The line went dead – fizzles of static burning across the emp-tiness.

For a moment I think I just stood there stunned. Then I pulled off my glasses, rubbed them slowly on my sleeve and took three deep breaths. I hadn't heard from Julian in six months, and now this. Out of the blue. I checked the message timer: 'Seven fifty-two,' the automatic voice said: almost half an hour ago, eight minutes before ten in Egypt.

I grabbed the phone and punched through the number to Julian's flat in Cairo. I heard the engaged tone and hung up straight away. I hit the digits again. Still no reply. Again and again I tried, bashing the keys down, getting more and more frustrated. In the end I punched through to the international operator and gave him the number. There was a pause, and the polite male voice came back, 'I'm sorry. That number appears to be out of service.' I slammed the phone down and tried again. This time there was a whining tone, as if the line had been disconnected.

I replayed the tape on the answering-machine, and as I listened I felt a surge of anxiety for Julian Cranwell that wasn't altogether unfamiliar. Crises hadn't been rare in his life, and I'd often been the one called in to deal with them. Yet I'd never complained. That was how Julian was. It was his undisciplined, neurotic side that made him such a brilliant Egyptologist. Like that celebrated time he'd sprung out of bed one morning at Luxor declaring that he'd had a dream about a lost pharaonic temple at Bahriyya in the Western Desert. Rude scoffs from all the experts. No major archaeological sites had ever been found in the area, it was pointed out. Julian ignored them. He took a jeep, a barrel of petrol, two jerrycans of water and a carton of Scotch, slung in his surveying equipment, and with me as assistant, drove off to Bahriyya oasis. Within a week we'd sunk not only the Scotch but also a six-foot trench revealing the girdle wall of a temple dating back to 2000 BC – a temple dedicated to the god Ptah. It turned out to be one of the most important finds of the decade. Julian's ecstatic jig the night we found it was something I've never forgotten.

Anyway, I owed Julian. In spite of his erratic nature, he'd always been loyal to me. He'd stuck his neck out for me when they gave me the heave-ho from the Egyptian Antiquities Service – he'd actually had the nerve to accuse the director of 'intellectual fascism', even at the risk of losing his own job, while the others turned their backs cravenly and minded their own business. When the EAS stuck to its guns, Julian offered to take me on as his private assistant. 'I'll pay you out of my own pocket,' he said, 'the bastards can't stop me doing that!' It was sour grapes that prevented me from taking him up on it. I came back home – inasmuch as England is really home – and tried to follow up my research, but my heart wasn't in it; I'm a fieldman to the core, and my sense of purpose had somehow deserted me. Any attraction the country had seemed to offer, even running the Gold Wing, had quickly palled. My few attempts with women had reached their climax in Monica. I regretted the decision to return. I found my work at the museum boring, and no one wanted to listen to my theories. At first I'd just caught myself hanging round the Egyptian exhibition more and more frequently. Time after time I'd tagged along with the guided tours, even if they were in Japanese, just as an excuse to look at the exhibits. In the end I'd spent long periods staring out of the window thinking of Egypt, completely absorbed, until one of my colleagues came and yelled, 'Ross!' right in my ear. Most of all I wondered what had happened to the Siriun Stela, and why I'd come across no references to it in the literature. There was unfinished business in Egypt. For months, in fact, I'd been looking for an excuse to go back. And this was it. I mulled over Julian's message all night, and the more I turned it over, the more apprehensive I became. This wasn't like Julian. The Julian I knew was fearless to the point of bravado. I had a bad feeling from the start, and by the time the light was creeping through the window I felt thoroughly alarmed. Later that morning I handed in my notice to the BM. I locked the Gold Wing in the house, cleaned out my current account at Barclays, and flew to Cairo the same day.

2

CAIRO

I<small>T TOOK ME THREE DAYS TO</small> find Julian, and then it certainly wasn't the fond reunion I'd imagined. He wasn't at his flat. I found out that much from Doc Barrington, an old friend of mine who knew him well. She'd been phoning him for a couple of days, she said, and the line seemed to have been disconnected. In the end she'd sent a man round who'd been told by the *ghaffir* that he hadn't been home for some time. I rang the office of the Antiquities Service and a brusque secretary said he was supposed to be at his dig at Siwa, but when I phoned, the site foreman said he hadn't seen him in a week. Finally I dropped in at the British Embassy in Garden City and asked to talk to the Consul. They made me sign a form, asked for my passport and let me wait for half an hour in a room among battered old copies of *The Times* and *Country Life*. The wall was covered in a corkboard on which were pinned photos of missing persons. Julian's wasn't among them, I noticed. Finally, they showed me behind the glass booths to a white-walled room with an opaque window, where I was introduced to the British Consul, Melvin Renner.

Renner looked like a man playing out a fantasy of what he thought a British Consul should be – an image that belonged to the colonial era. He wore a white blazer, white ducks, club tie, monogrammed shirt, and I'd have bet money there was a panama hat hanging on a hook somewhere near by. He was a lightly built, athletic-looking man in his late twenties – the kind that runs with the Hash House Harriers every Monday and boasts about it *ad nauseam* in the bar afterwards. You might have said he was an entrant for some Mister-Middle-England contest – cornflower-blue eyes and a long fringe of straw-coloured hair which he kept on flicking out of his face, and he spoke with an Oxford accent that was almost certainly assumed. He looked me up and down, and his eyes lingered on my earring. He didn't ask me to sit, so I sat down anyway.

'Mr Ross?' he said, examining my passport. 'So you're after Dr Cranwell, are you?'

'He's missing,' I said. 'He phoned me in London three days ago scared stiff, saying his life was in danger. Now he's vanished.'

'Men like Dr Cranwell don't just vanish, Mr Ross,' Renner said, flicking aside his wayward lock languidly. 'Not even in Egypt.'

'OK, where is he then?'

'He could be anywhere – taken off with a Ghawazi dancing-girl, gone on some crazy jaunt into the Western Desert, maybe even stashed himself in one of those tombs he's always turning up.'

'You know Julian, then.'

He gritted his teeth theatrically, then grinned. 'I have had the pleasure, and I must say nothing that man could do would surprise me. Between you and me, he's hardly the full pack of cards. That's why I'm inclined to believe you're on a wild-goose chase, Mr Ross.'

I sighed. It was indiscreet of him to have said so, but I had to admit he was right about Julian. 'Well back to the streets, then,' I said.

'Sorry not to be more help,' he said, beaming to show he didn't really give a damn, 'just leave your name and phone number at the reception and I'll let you know if something *does* come up. But knowing old Cranners, I wouldn't bank on it.'

The next morning I was woken at daybreak by a telephone bell that bored into my head like a drill-bit. I slapped on my glasses, grabbed the receiver, and found myself talking to Renner.

'Isn't this a bit early?' I groaned.

'I'm sorry, Mr Ross,' he said. His voice sounded less well-oiled and more sombre this morning and I noticed it had clicked a couple of degrees down the social scale. 'I was wrong about Dr Cranwell. Something *has* come up. His body was found on the Giza plateau at first light this morning. The police identified him from his passport.'

3

WHEN I GOT THERE IT WAS still quite early, and you could feel the latent heat swelling out of the desert – a heat that would lay the city flat under its weight by high noon. In the raw sun the pyramids looked like three ceremonial blades presented to the heavens, and already there were groups of tourists in shorts and sunhats patrolling the necropolis wearing cameras and expressions of awe. Julian's body had been found almost within the shadow of the Great Pyramid, but now it lay at the very apex of the shadow, as if the wedge of darkness was a giant arrow pointing at the broken thing in the sand beneath. From the top of the pyramid, I thought, the knot of police officers gathering around the dead man would have appeared like a squad of black ants on the edge of an amber infinity: the Western Desert – *Ament* – the ancient Egyptian Country of the Dead.

The detective from the Investigation Department had thrown expanding circles of black-jackets around the corpse, with bayonets fixed. I suppose they'd been ordered to keep the tourists' noses out, but I managed to slip through them magically by repeating, '*Ana sadiq al-mayyit!*' – 'I'm a friend of the dead!' – which cleared a swathe like some secret password. An oblong area had been sealed off with white tape on sticks pushed into the sand, and in the centre of it lay Julian's body, fully clothed. No blood. No apparent sign of injury. The left leg was slightly raised, the sole of his desert boot resting squarely in the sand. His clothes –

khaki slacks and blue cotton shirt – looked untorn, but his bulky torso was twisted sideways and the arms flung back as if at the moment of death he'd been trying to stave off a blow. It was the look on his face, though, that really gave me the shivers. I mean, you could hardly tell it was Julian at all. His eyes bulged out of their sockets, the black pupils contracted to specks, the lips drawn back from bared teeth in a rictus of primeval fear.

The detective was tall for an Egyptian – a seventeen-stone bruiser, six-foot-three, broad-shouldered, with a domed forehead, a cropped sliver of moustache and ferret-like black eyes. His suit was too small for him, showing off his torpedo-like figure, and the jacket hung open revealing the handle of a Ruger .44 Magnum revolver protruding from his waistband. A giant's weapon, I thought. When he looked at me I recognised bafflement in his eyes. That wasn't unusual. He was asking himself the same question that people in Egypt always asked themselves about me: is he one of *us* or one of *them*?

'Who the hell are you?' he asked, at last.

'I'm a friend of the dead.'

'Well, stay on that side of the line. I shall personally flay alive anyone who crosses the line before the tracker's done his work.'

He turned to a plum-faced uniformed sergeant and a gaggle of assistants at his elbow. 'Where *is* the bloody tracker?' he demanded.

A frail man in a black suit, with a long, sour face was nudged forward. The big detective shook his head in derision. 'Oh, Lord, save us,' he sneered. 'Last time I looked, that was the pathologist. Don't they teach you anything at the Academy? First we have the photographer, then the tracker, *then* the pathologist. You dunderheads couldn't organise an orgy in a bordello!'

The sergeant beckoned and an old Bedouin sheikh, dressed in a ragged *jibba* of russet-coloured cloth and a lump of *shamagh*, sidled out of the crowd. He placed a hard brown hand on the young sergeant's shoulder, and spoke to him in a low voice. Even before I noticed the earring, I recognised him from the cut of his *jibba* and headcloth as a Hazmi, one of the despised 'Ghosts of the Desert' – despised, but regarded with awe even by the so-called 'noble' Bedouin for their almost supernatural ability as trackers. It was the earring that clinched it, though – like me, the tracker was wearing a tiny silver ring on the upper fold of his right ear. All Hawazim boys have their upper right ears pierced at circumcision. The silver ring – the Hawazim call it *fidwa* – is a kind of recognition symbol of the tribe, but it's also a personal seal, because each one is different. The old man's face reminded me of my childhood, of the unkempt elfish figures smelling of milk and dust and goatskin that drifted like phantoms through my earliest years.

The Hazmi finished talking. The sergeant turned to the big detective. 'He claims *Jinns* have done it, Captain Hammoudi,' he said, smirking. 'He won't go near the body.'

A slight flush warmed the big man's cheeks. His eyes narrowed to black dots. Suddenly his massive, lanky frame jerked and a long arm slashed out with incredible speed, catching the old Hazmi with an open hand across the side of the face. There was a sickening slap of flesh that made me wince. The old man staggered forwards momentarily, then regained his balance. He glared defiantly at the detective, rubbing his livid cheek, and I saw his right hand linger momentarily against his left sleeve, where I knew the small but razor-sharp Hawazim *khanjar* would be concealed. Then he straightened, turned and walked away with perfect dignity. 'Your mother!' the captain spat after him. 'We have trained staff, modern equipment and proper procedures for investigation, and your solution to our problem is that he was killed by an *evil spirit*! Oh Mary and Jesus preserve us, we're still in the bloody dark ages.'

I could quite happily have punched him. I whipped off my glasses, wiped them solemnly on my shirt, took several more gulps of air and then replaced them carefully, squinting at the scuffed and churned-loose sand around Julian's body, forcing myself to concentrate. There were eight sets of footprints. Two sets were Fellahs' tracks, probably belonging to a father and son who'd been taking produce to the market by donkey and who'd come across the body. The donkey's tracks were cut deep, indicating that it was fully laden and on its way to market. Two sets of tracks belonged to Bedouin – I'd have bet camel-men who gave tourists rides at the pyramids. They were easy to spot – they didn't often wear shoes and their soles were calloused from walking about on hot stones and sand all their lives. I saw four sets of tracks belonging to policemen, three of them to the Tourist Police who'd probably been first on the scene. They wore hobnailed boots – they'd have been nearer at hand than the regular police, and the fact that they'd trailed round and round the body aimlessly showed they weren't used to the procedure at a crime scene. Then, last of all, came Hammoudi's – the tracks of a big man, size eleven or twelve. City shoes, used to hard streets. A very determined stride, straight up to the body. No squeamishness there. This was a man quite accustomed to seeing gruesome things. None of these tracks was made by a killer. They belonged to people who were clearly reacting to the body they found in the sand. I was tempted to tell Hammoudi so, but I divined from his aggressive glare that my intrusion wouldn't be welcomed.

'OK, bring on the pathologist,' Hammoudi drawled, and I suddenly identified his accent. He was a *Sa'idi*: a southerner, and the reference to Jesus and Mary made it certain that he was a Copt, despite his name. Probably from Asyut, where the majority of Copts are concentrated. No one seems to know exactly how many Copts there are in Egypt – the official estimate is ten per cent of the population, while the Copts themselves put it at twenty per cent. The Muslims look down on them as unbelievers. The Copts despise the Muslims as Johnny-come-latelys and consider themselves the direct lineal descendants of the ancient pharaohs. At first sight Hammoudi seemed beef-witted, but one thing I was sure of: a Copt from the south didn't get to be an investigator in Cairo without showing powers of cunning and ruthlessness way above normal.

The pathologist scurried forward carrying a leather bag and a stethoscope. 'Ah, Dr Amin,' Hammoudi said, 'I hope *you're* not afraid of *Jinns*.'

'It doesn't pay in my profession, Captain,' the doctor replied, 'but *Jinns* exist. It says so in the Quran. There are three kinds of beings mentioned there: angels, *Jinns* and human beings.'

Hammoudi grasped his own throat as if he was about to vomit, then fixed his eyes on me. 'All right, Mr Friend-of-the-Dead,' he said, 'can you confirm that this is Dr Julian Cranwell, the British Egyptologist?'

'Yes, I suppose so.'

'What do you mean, suppose so?'

'The features are distorted, but yes, I'd say it's him.'

I watched the pathologist as he pulled on rubber gloves and went about his work, examining the body nervously. 'There are no external wounds,' he commented, 'and no sign of a struggle. The lips and face are purple. It looks to me very much like a simple cardiac arrest. Was he a healthy man?'

'I think so,' I said, 'but I haven't seen him for two years.'

'Two years is a long time. Drinking man, was he?'

'He enjoyed the odd tot, yes.'

'Did he ever complain of angina? We'll have to check the medical record, I suppose. See the face – bright purple – that means dilation of the capillaries consistent with cardiac arrest. He was probably just strolling around the pyramids late yesterday afternoon, overtaxed himself and dropped dead. We're nearly into the summer season, I mean it was about thirty-six degrees in the shade yesterday. The late afternoon heat is worse than midday – you don't notice how hot it is until it's too late. I'd say cause of death was a heart attack. I don't see any sign of suspicious circumstances.'

'Really,' I said, an angry tightness creeping into my stomach. 'I see plenty. Like how come nobody saw him collapse? The place is full of tourists in the late afternoon, it's the ideal time to see the pyramids because of the light. Then you've got hordes of camel and horsemen, guides, the Tourist Police, yet you're saying no one notices a man collapse and die? He must have been screaming in agony – look at the face, you'd think he'd seen a ghost.'

The troopers within earshot eyed each other uneasily, shifting the slings of their automatics. I even saw one or two making the sign for protection against evil spirits.

Hammoudi noticed the gestures and turned sand-bagged eyes like blasting-lasers on the men who'd made them. 'What do you think this is?' he growled accusingly. 'The Mummy's Curse?'

'There's nothing abnormal here,' Amin cut in soberly. 'The bulging eyes and the distorted expression are caused by the severe chest pain that comes with cardiac arrest.'

I removed my glasses, wiped them on my shirt, replaced them again, and took two slow, well-spaced breaths. I stared at Hammoudi, wondering if he knew that Julian had been missing for three days. Three days. And now here he was suddenly, lying in a heap beneath the Great Pyramid, apparently dead from a heart attack, having collapsed on a walk round the plateau? I didn't swallow it. Julian had been in Egypt for twenty years. He'd even excavated at Giza. He was eccentric, certainly, but he wasn't the type to have visited the pyramids for an afternoon stroll.

A sudden thought struck me. 'Did he have a ticket?' I asked.

'Oh, listen to Mr *Sherlock Holmes*!' Hammoudi chuckled, holding up a plastic bag with a blue and white card inside. 'With the official stamp too. That means he must have come through the gate at before four yesterday afternoon.'

I shook my head, prepared to speak, then thought better of it. Hammoudi brought out a disposable lighter and a pack of Cleopatra cigarettes. He flicked the corner of the pack so that a single stick emerged, then placed it in his mouth and lit it slowly. He didn't offer them round.

'I can't go any further until the autopsy,' Amin said, 'but I don't think there's any need to go round pulling in suspects at this stage, Captain Hammoudi.'

'That wraps it up for now, then,' Hammoudi said with obvious relief. 'No need for the press to print crap about Islamic terrorists this time. This death is an act of God and nothing else. No knives in the back. No machine-guns. Nothing. If any of you men is caught breathing a word to the newspapers, I shall *personally* castrate him. This is death by misadventure. No suspects. No ulterior motives. Terrorism is definitely *not* involved.'

He pulled out his notebook and turned to me. 'Name and address?' he demanded.

'My name is Omar James Ross.'

'Omar? So you *are* an Arab?'

'Actually I am half-Egyptian. My mother was Egyptian, my father British and I have dual nationality. I'm staying at the Shepheard's Hotel.'

'Don't leave the city without letting me know. I might want to ask you some questions.'

4

BY THE TIME THE AMBULANCE HAD left, scouring up mustard-powder dust across the plateau of Giza, the pyramid's shadow had melted away, and the three great points of stone stood gleaming in sunlight like burnished brass. Already the tourists had thinned out, driven off by the heat, and the camel-men had couched their animals in cracks and clefts of shade awaiting the afternoon shift. A sudden buffet of wind, squalling off the desert, brought a moment of relief from the stagnant air. As I walked back towards the pyramid, I realised that I was more shocked by Julian's death than I'd first thought. In front of Hammoudi it'd seemed easy enough to put on a show of nonchalance. Away from public scrutiny, though, the delayed reaction set in, and my eyes filled with tears which I swept away angrily. My mother had disappeared when I was a child. My father had been distant. Julian Cranwell had filled the gap, had been the mentor I lacked, had supported me in public even when he disagreed privately. He was generous, kind and wise – a man who laughed at convention and got things done in his own way. I admired him. When I'd first arrived in Egypt twelve years earlier, awkward, aggressive, uncertain but opinionated, with a chip on my shoulder, I'd queered the pitch with almost everyone who might have taught me something. Only Julian had put up with me, because Julian himself was an erratic loner who didn't give a damn what the establishment thought, and who saw me as a younger version of himself. Colleagues in the

Antiquities Service sucked in their breath with theatrical derision when they heard I'd been appointed as Julian's assistant: 'He's a nut!' one told me. 'Drinks like a bloody grouper! Three sheets to the wind five nights a week and has "insights" while he's pissed. Hates women. Hates children. Hates Gyppos. Hates Brits. Hates Yanks. Hates everybody. His last assistant left after three weeks with a broken nose. They had a fist-fight apparently. You won't find him easy company.'

The tales proved to be exaggerated, the prediction entirely false. I'd found Julian perfect company. Under his tutelage I'd done some of my best work – blossomed from an amateur into a decent field Egyptologist in five years. Even when we'd parted two years before, when they booted me out of the Antiquities Service, I'd comforted myself with the thought that we'd work together again some day. Now there were no 'some days' left, only a terrible vacuum which I knew I'd never be able to fill.

There was a touch on my arm and I looked up to see the old Hazmi tracker, his face puckered as a prune from a lifetime in the high sun. 'I'll kill that policeman,' he said earnestly, massaging my wrist.

'I know,' I said.

'God give me the strength!'

He released my arm and searched my face. 'I'm Sulayman wald Haamid of the Hawazim,' he said. 'Are you one of us?'

'My mother was Hawazim, yes. I'm Omar, the son of Maryam bint Salim.'

'I knew it!' he said, touching my earring lightly. 'I knew from this. I knew your face, your speech – the blood shows through even if you're wearing foreign clothes. I know who you are now, your father was *Abu Sibaahi* – the Englishman who lived with our tribe. I've heard of you. Your mother was the sister of the *amnir* of al-Maqs.'

'That's right.'

'She was lost, they say, taken by the *ghibli* wind, in the Year of the Great Red Dust. Your grandfather, Salim, was lost in the desert, too. Runs in your family. Take care you aren't lost, Omar. Don't have anything to do with the police or that dead man.'

'Why?'

'I know a *Jinn*'s work when I see it. There were only eight sets of tracks around that body: two Fellahs, two Bedouin, four policemen – eight.'

'That's right. I saw them myself.'

'Yes, but there should have been nine. Where were the dead man's tracks? And his face! Did you ever see a face like that on a corpse? Keep away from it, Omar. Don't get involved.'

'I'm already involved,' I said. 'The dead man was my friend.'

'What kind of friend?'

'The kind that's like a brother.'

'Then I pity you.'

We shook hands. Then I worked my way thoughtfully along the side of the Great Pyramid. Sulayman was right, of course. I hadn't even thought of a ninth set of prints. There I was, taking secret pleasure in my ability to read tracks, and I wasn't even in the same league as the Hawazim tribesmen who'd taught me as a boy. All night it had been deathly still. The wind had not stirred since the previous morning. If Julian had been walking around and simply dropped dead, as Amin had suggested, where were his own footprints? Sand reveals everything. The Hawazim read it like a book. Everyone else's prints were clearly visible on the surface – but the dead man had left no tracks.

5

A S I WALKED ALONG THE PYRAMID'S base, I ran my hand
along the polished stone blocks, relearning their texture,
wondering again as I'd wondered for many years, at their precision. Ever since I lost my mother in childhood, I've had the
ability to switch off painful emotions and lose myself in facts and
figures, and especially in architectural forms. This pyramid has
remained unchanged for at least forty-five centuries, and if I'm
correct, much longer. It has retained its form while millions of
human lives have flicked on and off like candles. Its concept is
immense. Some of these limestone blocks are thirty feet long and
weigh fifteen tons. More than two million of them are incorporated
in the structure, making up a staggering total of eighty-five million
cubic feet of stone. The pyramid is a masterpiece of mathematical
exactitude. Its four faces are aligned almost perfectly to the car-
dinal points of the compass, with an average error of only three
minutes of arc, a deviation from true of only 0.015%. That's an
almost unbelievable feat of accuracy for the engineers of any age,
but especially for those of the dawn of civilisation. And there is
more. The four sides of the pyramid are almost exactly the same
length at the base, showing an error of less than 1 per cent, a
flaw smaller than a modern architect would be allowed in the
construction of a large building, and the corners are almost perfect
right-angles, a perfection denied many of the most modern struc-
tures. In sum, the Great Pyramid, one of the oldest and largest

buildings on earth, represents a mathematical precision only equalled and not surpassed in the modern age. Was this mathematical precision simply to satisfy the vanity of a single man, the pharaoh Khufu, who wanted to triumph over death and live a million million years? I'd come back full circle, I realised suddenly – back, inevitably to death, the great mystery, the great obsession of the ancient Egyptians, the great taboo of the twentieth century. Was the pyramid intended simply as a huge and vulgar tombstone, or was it something else, a vast cosmic clock, a machine for measuring time? Death and time are, anyway, just aspects of the same thing, examples of entropy, that quality of the universe which is always degrading and running down. Life flows against them, defying the laws of thermodynamics, expanding eternally in the opposite direction. To the ancient Egyptians death was a journey into an alternative dimension, a shadow realm of endless possibilities. But if the pyramids were intended just as monuments, why were they built with such precision? And how did the ancient Egyptians develop such accurate engineering techniques – apparently very suddenly – when the rest of the world was still living in the stone age?

I screwed up my eyes at the incredible brightness of the sun. Not a single pad of cloud remained in the unforgiving sky. I remember my childhood like that. The long holidays spent with my cousins in an oasis in the Western Desert: the unbearable infinity of the desert sky. Out there in the wastes the sun stands so high in midsummer that you have almost no shadow at all. In the Western Desert it might rain once in forty years and the meteorologists have discovered that there is cloud-cover there for only four per cent of daylight hours. That means that for ninety-six per cent of the day, summer and winter, you're getting pure, unadulterated, high octane ultraviolet. No wonder the ancient Egyptians worshipped Ra, the sun-god, above all others. No wonder they chose the west bank of the Nile to bury their dead. On the fringes of the Western Desert it's so hot and dry that a body left in the sand will mummify naturally within hours. They're still pulling pre-dynastic corpses out of the earth, buried two thousand years before the pharaohs in the Valley of the Kings, complete with hair and skin. When I was eight or nine, I rode with my older cousins on camels into the Western Desert, far beyond the outlying villages of the oases. Nobody lived out there, and after two days we were into frightening sand-sheets which trembled with heat-haze around the edges and which seemed to have no beginning and no end. The sand-sheets were featureless: not a single stone, not a tree, not a blade of grass. The emptiness played havoc with your sense of scale, and the dark hump on the sand-sheet in front of us seemed a mountain at first, until we came right up to it and realised it was a dead person. I was scared: I'd never seen anyone mummified before. The corpse was curled up in a foetal position, its flesh melted but its skin and bones intact. Strips of a *jibba* fluttered like faded pennants from the cadaver. My cousin searched the corpse's pockets and found inside a pouch full of silver coins. We discovered later that the coins were of Turkish origin and hadn't been in use for a hundred years. That was how long the corpse had lain there, undiscovered, perfectly mummified by the dry heat. A little farther on, we found a severed camel's leg, and further on still, the carcass of a three-legged camel, completely preserved. We concluded that the man had been riding towards the oases when his camel had died of thirst. He'd cut off its leg for food and tried to walk on. Soon the leg had proved too cumbersome and he'd dropped it, and not far away he'd given up, laid down on the sand and died. No one had disturbed the body until we'd come by a century later.

I stood outside the gates of the Mena House Oberoi. Gharry drivers, working their lunch-hour, pestered me to take a ride. Ordinarily, I enjoyed the tranquillity of a gharry, but today I wanted to get out of the noise and heat of the city quickly. I stopped a black-and-white taxi and got in. The plastic seat burned my legs. The driver smelt of perspiration and bad breath. I gave him Doc Barrington's address on the Gezira, and asked if the meter was working, knowing that in Cairo the meter is never working.

'Don't dare charge me tourist fare,' I said.

'Are you Egyptian or foreign?' the driver asked.

'What does it matter?' I said. 'The distance to Gezira is still the same.'

The traffic riffled on, jerking, slowing, halting, the sunlight flipped back blindingly from windscreens and mirrors and chromium bumpers. It was like floating in a stream of hot sauce, smelling of sweat, petrol fumes, burned rubber and stale tobacco, with horns dementedly honking and drivers shaking their pressed thumbs and forefingers, and swearing savagely. The traffic thinned as we turned left before the Giza Bridge and drove along Shari' an-Nil with the choppy waters of the river beside us, catching the highlights of the noon sun. Across the Nile at Gala'a Bridge: past the concrete pagoda of Cairo Tower, past the worn-out buildings of the once fashionable Gezira Sporting Club, its oblong of unkempt turf now hemmed in narrowly by new cement blocks, and into the relative tranquillity of Zamalek.

I paid off the driver outside Doc's block. The *ghaffir*, a sullen old man with a drooping neck, was new: at least I didn't remember his face from the years when I had been a lodger with Doc. I wished him '*as salaam 'alaykum*', but the man only scowled miserably and mumbled at me: '*al-assensir baayiz*: the lift is out of order.' I groaned and hurried up the winding stairs, gasping in the oven-like heat. I hoped Doc would be in. I'd phoned her the previous night to say I'd be over, but now I was hours late for our appointment. I passed down a corridor straddled with bars of light and shade and halted before a carved wood door on which Doc had painted a large coloured version of the Wedjet Eye, the Eye of Ra. It was a fine example of Doc's Gothic humour. The Eye of Ra symbolised the eye of consciousness peering into the void. I pressed the bell and waited, feeling a prickle of uneasiness: the Eye of Ra seemed to be studying me, blinking at me balefully. I peered at it and realised with a mild start that in the very centre of the eye a peep-hole had been opened. I could now see a real eye beyond, a fish eye eerily distorted by the magnification of the lens. Then Doc opened the door and a cool breeze from her open balcony hit me in the face. She flung both arms around me. 'I told you you'd be back!' she said.

She wore a loose cotton blouse and pants and as she squeezed me I could feel the bearish bulk of her body. She'd lost a bit of weight, perhaps, but she still looked like a trainee sumo-wrestler who would knock you down for tuppence. In the days when she'd taught judo at the British Embassy, it had been a brave man indeed who'd been ready to square up to Doc.

'Did you find Julian?' she asked.

'Julian's dead, Doc.'

'Jesus Christ. No. I don't believe it. Where?'

'On the Giza plateau right plonk under the Great Pyramid. A couple of Fellahs came across the body at sunrise and reported it to the police. They found his passport on him and phoned the Consulate. The Consul let me know first thing.'

'God, Jamie,' Doc said, shaking her head in disbelief, 'God, I'm dreadfully sorry.'

I nodded and glanced around at the vast, austere apartment with its statuettes and dark draperies, its corners full of purple shadows, its computer hardware and its overstuffed bookshelves lining every wall. Evelyn 'Doc' Barrington had been a real doctor in a far-off, antediluvian era, but at some stage she'd been recruited by the British Secret Intelligence Service, MI6. Years ago, she'd been the mainstay of their Cairo office, an accomplished investigator and inquisitor who spoke fluent Arabic and knew everyone and everything that went on in the city. That was until her husband Ronnie, also MI6, had died in a motor accident. Murdered, Doc always claimed. Their son David had been at university in the States at the time and hardly ever visited, and Ronnie was all Doc had. She'd taken it very hard, broken down for a while, and suffered fits of melancholy and paranoia, manifested in a tendency to see conspiracies everywhere. Doc had become a liability to the office, or so rumour had it. They'd given her counselling, helped her back to normal, but she'd never been returned to the active list.

I'd first met Doc not long after Ronnie died. I think it was the loneliness that had made her put out feelers for a lodger. Anyway, I'd heard about the room through the British Embassy. Of course I couldn't spend all my time at Doc's because I was often out up country on digs, but it had been very convenient to have a comfortable room and a warm welcome whenever I got back. I was more than happy to spend boozy evenings with her over grilled Nile perch or shrimps and a couple of bottles of local wine, listening to Umm Kalthum or Fairuz, and talking remorselessly. Conversations with Doc were a feast of quite a different order from the ones I enjoyed with Julian. She and I were alike – precise, analytical, intense, but my range of knowledge was pygmy-sized compared with hers. We would debate anything and everything: philosophy, politics and history, French literature, Italian wine, ancient Greek ceramics, pre-Islamic Arabic verse. Often, Doc would simply rattle on while I listened, entranced by the new world that she'd just opened up for me. Doc looked like a cross between a gone-to-seed English rose and a bulldog with attitude: a big woman, as tall as me, with close-cropped hair that suited the sensuous face. There was a touch of something almost Mongolian about its broadness and flatness, the high cheekbones, intense dark eyes, full lips. Doc could look ferocious, but actually she was very up front and warm blooded, and I liked her the more for that. Her mother was Italian, a Roman – 'the wrong half of Italy', Doc used to say, not without pride – and her father British. She'd been brought up in Uganda, though, where her people owned some kind of plantation. Wattle, I think. Anyway, those nights had been oases of pleasure for me and slowly we'd grown attached to each other. David, Doc's son, was more or less lost to her; he'd dropped out of university and become some sort of hippie. 'Sod never even came to Ronnie's funeral,' she would tell me mournfully after a few drinks. 'That was just about the end for me.' I noticed, though, that David's photo still featured on her desk. As time went on, I felt Doc pressing me into the role David had vacated. There were little tell-tale things like always making sure I had a clean shirt, always getting in the food I liked, tut-tutting if I came in late or had too much to drink, giving me maternal advice about girls. Our relationship had never been an equal one, but I'd accepted that. Doc was bossy and opinionated and sometimes, with a hangover, a bully and a martinet, but she was a woman who knew everything, a hundred degree-proof intellect that cut through problems like a knife.

The flat reeked of tobacco smoke, despite the open balcony and the creaking fans. I saw that Doc had been working at her desk on an Apple computer when I arrived: files and booklets were scattered across the Persian carpet and an ash-tray full of cigarette butts stood on the bare floor. Doc ushered me to the balcony where there were two wicker chairs and a low wooden table. Tumblers and a half-full bottle of Johnny Walker Black Label already stood on the table. I sat down and took in the view: the massed buildings of central Cairo across the Nile, the great monoliths of hotels with their windows blazing sunlight like whirls of fire. The growl and honk of traffic was more distant from here. I watched a convoy of black barges moving down the Nile as silently as a camel caravan. Doc eased gracefully into a chair, folded her legs, and picked up the whisky bottle: 'Time for a little snifter, I think, don't you, darling?' she said. Nothing had changed, I thought. Any time was time for a little snifter as far as Doc was concerned. It didn't require the death of an old friend to bring out the Scotch. She poured two fingers of whisky into my glass and into hers and added ice from a carafe. 'Cheers!' she said, dismally. I took a gulp, feeling the rich liquid burning in my throat. I coughed.

'Jamie, it's ghastly,' she said. 'Really awful.'

'The pathologist swore he'd dropped dead of a heart attack on a stroll round the necropolis,' I said, 'but Julian wasn't the kind of guy who went to the pyramids for an afternoon out. I mean, he knew every stone of the bloody place and lost interest in it years ago. I got the feeling they wanted to sweep the whole thing under the carpet in double-quick time. The word "terrorism" was mooted obliquely.'

'It makes sense, Jamie. They get the jitters when there's any sniff of the dreaded "T" word. You can't blame them when the entire economy rests on tourism. Couldn't handle another trauma like the Groppi's blast. When some poor bugger gets his leg shredded, it's not exactly brilliant PR. If there's anything guaranteed to put off tourists it's violent death or permanent mutilation, and no tourists means no hotel trade, empty restaurants and tea-shops, no fares for the cabbies, no souvenir-trade, no jobs, no nothing. Luxor and Aswan would just fold up. The Groppi's fiasco cost the government about fifty million, they reckon.' She paused, sipped her drink and stared at me appraisingly. 'Why? *Was* there anything suspicious?'

'My nose tells me something's not kosher. I mean, Julian looked like shit, as if he'd pegged out in absolute agony or terror or both, but no one heard or saw anything. They put the time of death at late afternoon; just the time when the place is jam-packed, yet no one sees a blind thing till first light today.'

'Interesting.'

'And there was another thing. Eight sets of tracks round the body, but none of them his.'

'Couldn't the breeze have obliterated them?'

'Wasn't a breath of it last night. All the tracks around him were intact.'

'That's weird!'

'I thought so too. Yet the investigator's all for wrapping it up as misadventure.'

'They try to sell you any crock of shit, darling. They tried to tell me Ronnie's death was an accident. Going too fast, they said, and when the tyre burst he hit the brakes too quickly. I ask you! *Ronnie?* He used to drive the Monte Carlo!'

I sighed. I'd heard the story before.

Doc lit a Rothmans with a silver pocket lighter, inhaled, and expelled the smoke across the balcony. 'Who was the investigator?' she enquired.

'Guy called Hammoudi, a big bruiser, built like a brick shithouse. Copt, I think.'

'Oh, my giddy aunts.'

'You know him?'

'Never had the pleasure, but Hammoudi's one of those guys whose name makes grown men wet their pants. He's *Mukhabaraat* – SID branch – and don't be misled by the beef. He might look like Mr Plod, but the guy's got a mind like a stiletto. A bloody one, I should add. Used to be a parachute sergeant in the Yemen in the sixties. Led a patrol called the ''Night Butchers''. They used to go out at night behind enemy lines, slit royalists' throats and come back with their cocks as souvenirs. He's no chicken either – been cited for bravery umpteen times. Hammoudi used to report to a Major called Rasim, a very slippery customer with contacts in the underworld. Looks like a mafioso himself. Rasim's more of a desk man, though. It's Hammoudi who does the foot-slogging.'

We sipped our whisky in silence, and I studied the buildings of Cairo, the new, modern Cairo that had sprung up in the last decade out of the old squalor.

'Thing is, Doc,' I sighed, 'I mean if I'd got here a bit quicker Julian might still be alive.'

'Don't, Jamie,' Doc said. 'You always blame yourself in situations like this. It's a natural reaction. I felt the same way when Ronnie died. Anyway, you got here like a bat out of hell. I doubt if anyone could have done it quicker unless they were beamed across.'

'No, but I'm just thinking that if I'd accepted Julian's offer I'd have been here anyway.'

'He told me he was ready to take you on as his private assistant. Why didn't you accept it?'

'I don't know. He'd got obsessed with the Zerzura Project, which wasn't what you'd call mainstream Egyptology at all.'

'Yeah, Jules was absolutely sold on the legend of the Lost Oasis, wasn't he.'

'He thought it was more than a legend. Used to point out *ad nauseam* that it's mentioned in medieval manuscripts like al-Khalidi's *Book of Lost Treasures*. He was convinced that out there in the Western Desert he'd find a lost city, just as the medieval stories said. He collected all the accounts, everything that was written or told about the place, and when people laughed, he used to call them Philistines and cite Schliemann, who discovered the site of ancient Troy. Jules and I were so different. He fed on dreams and symbols and insights like some kind of modern bloody witch-doctor, and it worked – at least it sometimes did. I always prided myself on cold logic, Occam's Razor. Now they call me "irrational". Can you believe how things turn out!'

'Perhaps you weren't so fundamentally different after all.'

'Maybe. If I had the time over I'd have accepted his offer. See, there was more to it than Zerzura. I knew he didn't really need me as an assistant. What he needed was a friend, a kind of surrogate son he'd never had. You knew Julian; he was a difficult man. Suffered terrible mood-swings: one day scintillating and brilliant and the next so far down in the dumps that he could hardly speak.'

'That's why he never got hitched, not because he was a woman-hater or queer like they said; he just knew no woman would put up with it.'

'Right. He needed a friend to sort of look after him. He didn't really give a shit what I thought about the Zerzura Project, he just wanted me for myself, and the fact is, under it all I knew it, and I let him down.'

'It's all water under the bridge now.'

'Doc, Julian was missing for three days. Where was he?'

'Elementary, Jamie. Either he'd been kidnapped or he was hiding.'

'When he phoned me in London he said someone was trying to kill him: "These devils killed George Herbert, Orde Wingate and Tutankhamen," he said.'

'That's preposterous.'

'Absolutely. Tut died in about 1300 BC, yet three days ago Julian announces quite sincerely he's in danger from someone – or something – that killed both Tut and two twentieth-century Englishmen!'

'Steady on. Herbert wasn't English. If that's George Edward Stanhope Molyneux Herbert, the fifth Earl of Carnarvon, he was Welsh. Snooty Welsh, but Welsh all the same.'

'In any case he wasn't murdered . . . died of a scorpion sting.'

'Cause of death was officially given as an "infected mosquito bite", if I remember rightly. You know he and Carter had been digging for thirty years for Tut, but the poor bugger never lived to see the mummy after all those years of searching and all that dosh he'd shelled out. Died in 1923, not long after they opened the sarcophagus, here in Cairo, actually, at the Grand Continental, which was considered very swish then; a dump now, of course.

Some odd things happened when he died, they reckon: all the lights in the city went out in the same moment, and at home in England his pet terrier suddenly rolled over and croaked.'

'You're joking!'

'In the case of the city lights, it happens to be well authenticated. I've seen the actual report submitted to Allenby, who was High Commissioner in Cairo then, stating that an offical inquiry had failed to find out why all the lights in the city had cut at that time. Don't know about the mutt, but his son, Lord Porchester, used to tell that story, apparently.'

'All right. But scorpion or mosquito, Carnarvon still died a natural death.'

'Yes, but there was another oddity. Apparently the fatal mosquito bite was on his left cheek. And guess what? There was a flaw in the gold of Tutankhamen's funerary mask in the same place. Not only that, when the mummy was unwrapped in 1925, it had a wound in exactly the same place!'

'Good story, Doc.'

'OK, probably a coincidence. But isn't it pretty clear that Tut *was* zapped?'

'It's not absolutely certain. There was a wound on his skull, but it was partly healed. And then there's the third party Julian mentioned, Orde Wingate; he seems to have no connection with the others at all.'

'All I know about Wingate is that he was a gung-ho guerrilla – sort of poor man's T.E. Lawrence of the Second World War. Restored Haile Selassie to his throne in Ethiopia, and led the Chindits in Burma. Offhand, though, I can't think of any link between Wingate and Carnarvon, or Wingate and Tutankhamen.'

I finished my whisky. Doc poured us both another. I took my pipe and pouch of tobacco from an inside pocket. I spent ten minutes cleaning it, filling it and lighting it, while Doc watched with approval. 'Still puffing that dirty old thing,' she said. 'Always liked to watch a man smoke a pipe. So relaxing.'

I filled my mouth with smoke and then blew it out in a ragged circle.

'What else did Julian say?' Doc asked.

'Said he'd come across something important. Didn't say what it was, but he did add something that struck me as wacky. Said he reckoned "they" – whoever "they" were – were after the "Akhnaton *ushabtis*".'

'What's so wacky about that? I mean, *ushabtis* are common enough. Aren't they statuettes meant to represent Osiris?'

'In a way yes, but since Egyptian pharaohs were supposed to be incarnations of Osiris, the *ushabtis* were actually miniature effigies of the pharaoh in whose tomb they were placed. The idea was that if the pharaoh was dragooned into any menial task in the underworld – building the levee against the Nile flood, or shifting sand from east to west were the favourite ones – the *ushabti* would sweat it out on his behalf. There were more than four hundred of them in Tut's tomb, all different, one for every day of the year, plus "supervisors".'

'How come there are no Akhnaton *ushabtis* then? I'd lay a fiver I've actually *seen* one.'

'Akhnaton is the only major pharaoh of the 18th Dynasty whose mummy hasn't yet turned up. He reigned for seventeen years and was probably Tut's father or father-in-law, maybe both. They cut an official tomb for him at Amarna, but there was no trace of the mummy and no evidence his body had ever been there. *Ushabtis* were always placed in tombs; no Akhnaton tomb means no Akhnaton *ushabtis*.'

'Unless they're fakes.'

'That's one possibility. The other is that someone found Akhnaton's tomb and isn't telling.'

'Unless we're dealing with an instance of Julian's periodical bullshit. I mean Julian was a wonderful man, darling. I loved him. But he used to come out with the most appalling shit occasionally.'

'Julian had wild ideas. People took the piss, me and you included, but ninety per cent of the time he turned out to be right. However you look at it, Doc, you've got to admit there's a bad smell about this.'

'Steady on. You sound like you're developing intuition in your old age. Isn't that what you always took the piss out of Julian about?'

'Maybe I'm just getting wiser.'

'Maybe, maybe not. But one thing's certain: Julian's as dead as a bloody doornail. Chapter closed. Brilliant Egyptologist found dead by Great Pyramid. Fitting headline, don't you think?'

I looked up and saw tears welling down Doc's face. 'Sorry, darling,' she said, 'only I can't help thinking about how they got Ronnie. Now Julian. They always seem to take the best, somehow.'

6

I WENT BACK TO SHEPHEARD'S HOTEL on the Nile Corniche. I might have stayed at Doc's; my old room was free, and Doc was willing, but for tonight, anyway, I wanted to be alone. I'd always chosen Shepheard's when I was stuck for a room in Cairo, because it was where my father had stayed as a young officer in the Int. Corps during the war, and I always remembered the sepia-tinted photo of it in his album when I was a boy. It took me a long time to work out that his Shepheard's and the one I stayed at were entirely different places. My room was on the first floor overlooking the Nile, and as I lay on the bed the night sounds of the city crawled in, the constant grating of gears, the clop of gharries, pedestrians shouting to one another. I tossed and turned restlessly. Sleep eluded me. When I closed my eyes I was overwhelmed by images of Julian's dead face.

Finally, I got up, stepped out on to the balcony, and looked at the silent black slick of the Nile, illuminated by a mixture of moonlight and sodium light. A tourist gharry was parked beneath my balcony, its blinkered horse champing the *barseem* which the driver had spread across the pavement. The driver, dressed in a wide-sleeved Fellah's *gallabiyya*, saw me looking: 'You want ride, mister?' he called out in English, 'I take you nice ladies!' I grinned. Cairenes were irrepressible, I thought. They had been conquered by Persians, Greeks, Romans, Mamluks, Turks, French, British, and God knew who else, but their spirit had remained, a deeply embedded subversiveness hidden under a show of conformity. They called their city 'The Mother of the World'. In the dank, cold days in England I thought I'd never return to Egypt. Now I felt a sudden surge of gratitude to Julian, who had brought me back to the country of my birth, and bequeathed me a reason to remain.

At sunrise I slipped out of the hotel and hired the gharry-man to take me to Khan al-Khalili, for a look at Julian's flat. The Corniche was almost empty at that hour, the sun no more than a gleam of redness on a furl of cloud over the Eastern Desert. The gharry creaked through streets like chasms and rifts and valleys, a confusion of designs – romantic, art-deco, Islamic, Turkish, rococo and baroque. We clipped past tenements with rounded balconies and protruding dormer windows, past great urban chateaux blackened by generations of traffic-fumes, their walls a pattern of striations where the dark plaster had fallen away like dead skin to reveal yellowing plaster beneath. Soon we'd left the main thoroughfares behind and entered the sprawling maze of the Khan. It was the place where camel caravans from the Sahara had reached Cairo since medieval times, and still remained a world within itself, a world with its own laws, its own customs and its own traditions. Slowly the streets became narrower as if we were travelling up the tributaries of a great stream, and we were among the smell of *shawarma* grilling on charcoal, of roast fish, fresh horse-dung, apple-tobacco and mint-tea from honeycombs of tea-stalls. Here there were whole streets of workshops caked with oil and soot, from which came the fizz of welding torches and the desperate hammering of metals. There were entire alleys full of poultry, where thousands of chickens, ducks and turkeys squawked and gobbled inside wire cages. There were streets of sawyers where you heard the scuff of saws and smelt sandalwood and cedar, streets of goldsmiths, silversmiths, shoemakers, spice-merchants. We lurched along alleys that can't have changed much since Turkish times, past moresco arches that seemed to open into hidden recesses, past the stone buttresses of ancient mosques, past gnarled doors and crumbling staircases. The alleys were already pullulating with people wearing thick *gallabiyyas* and woollen hats against the morning cool. I left the gharry and walked along The Muski, elbowing my way through the crowds. Someone shouted '*Baalak!*' in my ear, and I jumped to avoid a caravan of donkeys, their pack-saddles laden with sand, clicking past, driven by a sour-faced Fellah in a black *gallabiyya* who periodically whacked the last donkey on the bony rump with a knotted pole. There was a constant stream of bicycles weighed down with enormous loads of fresh fish, or fruit in plastic crates, creaking donkey-carts piled high with disks of bread. I saw one cyclist disappearing into the crowd with a vast tray of bread-loaves actually balanced on his head.

Almost opposite the door of Julian's house, a hunchback was selling cooked sweet potatoes from a mobile oven, a contraption of spouts and chimneys so grotesque that it might have been designed by a Surrealist. The man speared a potato with a toasting fork and held it up for my inspection, 'Very fresh! Very nice!' he grinned. I noticed that he had curly red hair beneath his pointed skullcap, green eyes and freckles – an unusual combination for an Egyptian. The peasants still believed that men with features like his were the descendants of medieval crusaders, and knew secrets of witchcraft and sorcery. I shook my head, stepped over to the gnarled wooden door and rang the bell. After a few minutes I heard the sound of heavy feet on stairs, and the scut of bolts being drawn. The door was opened by a middle-aged man with a pot belly, and arms like hams under a faded Arab shirt. I didn't recognise him from my last visit to the place more than two years ago. The man looked at me with bulging eyes as he wiped greasy hands on his *gallabiyya*. 'What do you want?' he demanded.

'I want to see Dr Cranwell's flat.'

'Dr Cranwell is dead. Found dead at the pyramids yesterday.'

'I know. I was his friend. I'd like to look at his flat.'

The *ghaffir* cocked his head slightly to one side and watched me closely as if he could scarcely believe the impertinence of the request. 'What for?' he enquired.

'That's my business.'

'You won't find anything, not papers or anything like that. The police were here yesterday – went over every corner of the place. They took away everything. "Evidence", they said it was.'

That was a surprise. Why were the police looking for 'evidence' when Hammoudi had insisted that Julian's death was a simple heart attack?

'Who was in charge?' I asked.

'Big detective from the *Mukhabaraat*, the Special Investigations Department. Tall man with a southern accent – might have been a Copt. He left strict instructions not to let anyone in.'

'It would be worth your while.' I said, holding up a fifty Egyptian pound note.

The doorman looked at the money hungrily, but shook his head. 'It's more than my life's worth to go against the *Mukhabaraat*. I couldn't do it, not even for fifty Egyptian pounds.'

I took more notes out of my wallet. 'Not even for seventy?' I enquired.

'Not even seventy. I'm an honest man. It wouldn't be right – you might be a thief or something!'

'Do I look like a thief? I was Dr Cranwell's best friend.'

'How do I know that? I can't do it, by God; I'm an honest man.'

'Not for eighty pounds?'

'Absolutely not: what do you take me for?'

'What about ninety?'

'The very idea of it!'

'Ninety-five?'

'Make it a hundred.'

'Done.'

'And don't take anything away – more than my life's worth if the police come back.'

I closed the door and followed the *ghaffir*'s great haunches as he waddled upstairs. The flat opened off the landing; so did the doorman's quarters, from the door of which came a miasma of oil fumes and the cabbagey odour of boiling *fuul*. The man produced a key, unlocked the flat door and held his fat hand out. I slapped five twenties into it. The *ghaffir* put the cash away quickly. 'I'm telling you now,' he said, 'you won't find anything. So it's no good asking for the money back later.'

I stepped inside and looked around the small study. It was exactly as I remembered it – a cosy, almost Victorian, parlour: open fireplace with a broad mantelpiece on which stood some mementoes: copies of *ushabti* figures of Ramses II and Amenhotep III, a miniature sphinx, a statuette of the cat goddess Bastet, together with Julian's walnut rack of pipes and a jar of his favourite tobacco mixture – pipe smoking had been another hobby we'd shared. In the grate there was a brass coal-scuttle and poker-set, and a pair of velvet-upholstered chairs with claw-and-ball wooden legs stood by the hearth. There was a threadbare Persian carpet on the parquet floor, a carved mahogany drinks cabinet, containing half a dozen bottles of Scotch, Vodka and Brandy. An ancient TV stood on a low table near by, next to an old-fashioned black telephone and a set of directories. David Roberts's 1830's prints of Karnak and the Valley of the Kings decorated the wall, together with framed antique posters advertising Cook's Nile Cruises. Along the lower part of the wall ran fitted shelves containing Julian's collection of books on Egypt. There were editions by Wendorf and Schild on the Western Desert, by Breasted on history, and Howard Carter's three-volume work *The Tomb of Tutankhamen*. I also noticed works on Akhnaton by Redford and Aldred, and Petrie's 1894 report on Amarna. I knelt down to examine them, and came across a dozen more titles on Akhnaton, some of them with the label of a well-known second-hand bookshop stuck inside the cover. These works were recently acquired, I realised – a new direction for Julian; the Julian I'd known had shown very little interest in the 18th Dynasty.

In the corner of the room stood a once-elegant Louis Quinze scroll-top writing desk which had been smashed open by the police and was now virtually empty, its shallow drawers gaping sadly. 'Didn't Dr Cranwell have a computer?' I asked the *ghaffir*, who was standing at the door rattling the keys uncertainly in the pocket of his *gallabiyya*.

'Police took it,' he said.

The kitchen was even less yielding than the study: crockery, pots and pans, a cupboard full of tinned food – Heinz Baked Beans, soup, tomato ketchup, a row of little bottles containing spices. A gas-ring and a cylinder, a blackened kettle, plastic jars of sugar, tea and dried milk. In the bedroom, there was a single pinewood bed, a bedside table, a cheap rug on a lino floor, a print of the pyramids. I opened the drawer of the bedside table; it was empty of anything but pens, pencils, a Chinese flashlight. No diary, no notes, not a single sheet of paper. I had a quick look round the tiny bathroom, and examined the built-in airing cupboard – sheets, blankets carefully folded. A small wardrobe in the passage contained safari shirts, pants, socks and tweed jackets, but no sign of any documents. 'I told you,' the doorman said, triumphantly. I returned to the sitting room, and picked up the telephone receiver: there was no dialling tone. I replaced it and pulled on the plaited nylon lead, following it carefully along the parquet to the wall junction, where it had been neatly severed with a knife. I glanced at the *ghaffir*, who was watching intently. 'Did you know about this?'

'*Aiwa*. I thought it was funny the phone didn't ring, and I checked it and found it like that.'

'How long has it been like this?'

'Two or three days.'

'Was it working last Tuesday . . . three days ago?'

'I can't be sure, it might have been. That would have been the day he got the visitors. He quite often had visitors, of course, and a lot of them were unsavoury – hyenas, they were: low-life characters, gangsters, criminals. Dr Cranwell seemed to like them, but he was mad as a hatter anyway. That night there were two of them. It was already dark when they came, and I was a bit annoyed because they let themselves in without knocking. God knows how they did it; Dr Cranwell must have given them a key. Anyway, I heard them shouting – really going at each other hammer and tongs. Only I couldn't understand; it sounded foreign. Then they went quiet and they all left together. I looked out through the crack in my door and saw them from behind. The men were dressed in long black suits and big black hats – you know, like

Hassidic Jews – but they weren't Hassidics because they had no sidelocks. Their hats were pulled down, shadowing their faces, so I couldn't make them out properly, but as they turned to go down the stairs I saw one of them in the light. It gave me quite a shock, I can tell you! I only saw him for a fraction of a second, mind, but his eyes looked yellow like a cat's eyes, with slits, not pupils. A demon, by God! Set me shaking it did! I almost ran out after them, but I thought they might be *Jinns* and I was too scared. Dr Cranwell looked a bit shaken too, but he never shouted at me, so I guessed he wanted me to mind my own business. I never saw him again.'

'Did you tell the police this?'

'Yes.'

'Have you any idea where Dr Cranwell went after he left here?'

'God knows. He never told *me* his movements. Hadn't been here in a week before that night. Only used this place when he was in Cairo, but most of the time he was out in the sticks. Always gallivanting off somewhere, and when he *was* here he was hardly ever sober. Mad as a rabid dog that man was.'

I took a last glance around the room, and began to sniff audibly: 'Have you left something cooking?' I asked.

'My God, the *fuul*!' the *ghaffir* exclaimed, and he rushed out.

I stepped over to the ruined Louis Quinze desk, knelt down, and felt carefully underneath for the catch which opened the secret compartment. 'If there's anything I want only you to find,' Julian once told me, 'I'll leave it here.' That must have been five years ago. It was a long shot, but it was worth a try.

My finger found the catch, and the compartment slid down into my hand with a click. 'Yes!' I hissed to myself. The wooden drawer was nine inches deep, but it contained only a packet of ten computer diskettes and fresh photocopies of two newspaper cuttings, neatly folded. I put the diskettes in the pocket of my jacket and glanced quickly at the two photocopies. One consisted of a very old newspaper photograph and the other of a page from a more recent article. The photograph showed two mustachioed men in dark suits. One of them, wearing a shapeless slouch-hat, was smoking rakishly and pointing to a grey blur which seemed to be the front page of a newspaper. The other man, hatless and wearing a black bow-tie, was looking on ruefully. In the background, holding the newspaper, it appeared, was a third figure, whose features were indistinct. Very close to the figures, someone had drawn the ancient Egyptian hieroglyph for the ibis-headed god, Thoth. The faces of the two men in focus were vaguely familiar, and I unfolded the caption which had been tucked underneath: 'Howard Carter and Lord Carnarvon,' it read. 'Valley of the Kings. February 16th, 1923.' I turned it over and on the back, written in Julian's spidery handwriting, was the name 'Nikolai Kolpos – Dealer in Antiquities', and the address of a shop in Khan al-Khalili. The second photocopy consisted of a page torn from the *Herald Tribune* dated December 1981 – almost sixty years after the first – a piece about the Space Shuttle Columbia's 1981 flight, entitled 'Trouble with SIR-A' by a well-known American science journalist. Another Thoth hieroglyph had been carefully drawn against the headline.

There were footsteps outside. I stuffed the copies hastily into my jacket and pushed the compartment closed, just as the doorman appeared. 'I was having a last look at the cabinet,' I said. 'You were right, there's nothing here.'

The hunchback was still at his sweet-potato machine when I closed the door. As soon as I saw him, he waggled his forked sweet potato at me, and beckoned me with his left hand. 'Had trouble with *Abu Kirsh*?' he rasped. I chuckled; '*Abu Kirsh*' meant 'Father of the Belly', and it was the perfect nickname for Julian's watchman. The hunchback beckoned me closer, and as I leaned towards him, I smelled cooked sweet potato and garlic breath.

'He isn't dead, you know,' the hunchback whispered.

'Who?' I asked.

'The *Englishman*! I saw him yesterday. They said he was dead, but I saw him come back here yesterday night, and let himself in, God strike me down dead if I lie! His face was white as a sheet, and you should have seen the look on his face. You'd think he'd bumped into Satan himself!' The man nodded sagely and his eyes burned into me for a second before he looked away, waving his fragrant sweet potato under the nose of the next customer.

7

A BOLT OF LIGHT SHOT THROUGH Doc's dining room window, illuminating the two photocopies unfolded on the green baize cloth of her large oak table. 'Ah, the god Thoth,' Doc said, leaning over the two texts with a map-lens, 'An old *amico* of mine, aka Tehuti, I believe. He was one of the oldest of the ancient Egyptian gods, usually depicted as a man with the head of an ibis, though sometimes as an ape. They called him ''The Measurer of Time'', and it was Thoth who was supposed to have invented numbers and introduced science, calculation, astronomy, magic, medicine, music and writing to ancient Egyptian civilisation. He was also supposed to be the one who recorded the moral weight of the deceased's heart after death. How did I do, darling?'

'Full marks!' I said.

'The first question,' Doc said, 'is: why should Julian have drawn the hieroglyph for Thoth on the cuttings?'

'That's got to be a message to me,' I said. 'He couldn't write my name on them in case they were found, but he knew Thoth was one of the central figures in my thesis on the origin of Egyptian civilisation, and writing the Thoth hieroglyph on them was just like saying ''Hey, Ross, look at this!'' '

Doc examined the picture gravely with her lens. 'Have you noticed their faces?' she said. 'Carnarvon seems pleased: he's looking directly at the camera, smirking like the cat who got the cream. Carter seems annoyed, as if Carnarvon were doing something he disagreed with. There seems to be a third figure in the background – the one holding the newspaper – but you can't make out if it's a man or a woman.'

'I'd give my right arm to read that headline.'

'Ask and it shall be given, oh my liege. These days there exist such miracles as computer-enhanced imaging.'

'Is it *that* good?'

'I can't promise anything. I mean, this is a photocopy and I'll bet even the original wasn't exactly razor sharp. It'll take time, though. My computer's out of the ark, I don't have scanning facilities, but I can get it done.'

'Did you have a glance at those diskettes?'

'I've had a quick butcher's. Full of all sorts of wondrous fare.'

'What about the name Nikolai Kolpos?'

'I've met Kolpos – plump little Greek fellow with a bald head and hair like a tonsure; he looks like a Trappist monk. He owns a shop in the bazaar, "Osiris Emporium" or some such dull name; you know, the type that sells stone models of the pyramids and copies of statues of Ramses II. I'd call him a third-rate dealer in bric-à-brac.'

'Was he a friend of Julian's?'

'Yes. For some reason they were thick as thieves. I don't know why. Kolpos isn't on Julian's wavelength in any shape or form. In fact a little bird told me that our Mr Kolpos is not altogether squeaky clean in all his dealings.'

'You mean black-market trafficking in antiquities?'

'That's where the real money is. Of course, I might be talking out of my hat, but one thing is for certain: Kolpos has more going for him than that little shop.'

'You don't think Julian was mixed up in flogging *antikas*?'

'Who knows, darling? I mean, I had Julian down as a completely straight eccentric – if you know what I mean. He never kept pieces for himself, not even for sentimental reasons; you know that better than anyone. But just lately – since you left – he started hanging round with the oddest crowd, people you wouldn't want to meet at night in a dark alley.'

'His *ghaffir* called them hyenas.'

'That's not far off it. I still find it hard to swallow that Julian was into anything shady, though. For a time I thought it was Kolpos's girl he was interested in.'

'He has a daughter?'

'No. Elena Anasis is his assistant. She's half Greek, but had a bad time with her pa in Alexandria and legged it to Cairo. She took up with Kolpos, who looked after her, and gave her a job as his assistant. I thought Julian might have a thing for her, which would explain his friendship with Kolpos, but when I saw her I couldn't believe it. She's one of those girls who could have been a model – beautiful dark hair, classic Mediterranean features, great legs. And she's about twenty-five – Julian was fifty-four, and not exactly an oil-painting, after all. You never can tell of course, but on the surface, anyway, Julian and Elena just didn't make sense. It had to be something else, some business he and Kolpos were engaged in.'

'I think I should have a word with Mr Kolpos.'

'Definitely. What about this other copy: the Space Shuttle business? That seems to have no link to anything.'

I picked up the article and read it again:

A serious fire at the Pasadena offices of the Jet Propulsion Laboratory yesterday was the most recent of a series of incidents which has marred the success of the Shuttle Imaging Radar, SIR-A, deployed on the space shuttle Columbia's last test flight, STS-2. The radar, which formed part of NASA's Office of Space and Terrestrial Applications payload (OSTA-1), was designed first to acquire radar images of several different geologic regions and second, to assess the shuttle as a scientific platform for the observation of earth.

The unmanned orbital flight which left Houston on November 12th went badly wrong only an hour after take-off when a fault in the computer navigation system nudged the shuttle off course and sent it spinning around the earth on a different trajectory. Instead of the series of sites NASA had selected to be photographed by SIR-A, the radar snapped a sequence of unscheduled sites, including the Western Desert of Egypt. The test flight was shortened from 4 days to 2½ days as a result of the malfunction, though JPL officials claimed that the experiment had achieved all of its goals, collecting 10 million square kilometres of imagery on a film which runs for eight hours.

After the flight, the mile-long film was analysed by a top geophysicist from the California Institute of Technology, Lynne Regis, who announced that the radar had penetrated almost a hundred feet below the land surface and disclosed some previously unknown features. Ms Regis was tragically killed in a motor accident before publishing her analysis. Yesterday, only a week after her untimely death, her office was one of those gutted by a freak fire which swept through the JPL building in Oak Grove Drive, Pasadena. A spokesman for the Institute of Technology admitted that much of SIR-A's irreplaceable film had been lost . . .

'I see a link,' I said, 'the Western Desert of Egypt, Jules's obsession.'

'Maybe he'd been banking on using the SIR film for his Zerzura Project.'

'Not a chance – the Columbia mission was in '81. Julian didn't get involved in the Western Desert until we found the temple of Ptah at Bahri in '86, four years after the film had been destroyed.'

'Then why his interest in something that happened more than a decade ago?'

I stood up heavily and stretched. I put my pipe down, whipped off my glasses, and took a couple of deep inhalations, expelling the air steadily through my mouth. I hadn't slept a wink last night; Julian's last words had played themselves over and over in my head, and the more they had replayed, the more angry I'd become at my confusion. 'What we need is a pattern,' I told Doc. 'What we've got is a list of anomalies. One, Julian rings me in Britain claiming his life is in danger from the same ''devils'' who killed an ancient Egyptian pharaoh almost three and a half thousand years ago, and two twentieth-century Englishmen – all right, Britons – who themselves seem to be unconnected in any way. Two, he's found dead by the Great Pyramid supposedly of a heart attack, with no tracks and no indication of how he got there. Three,

Julian's flat has been turned over by the SID. Papers and a computer are removed as "evidence" in a case they have already dismissed as misadventure. Four, Julian leaves the name of a contact, and what seems to be a cryptic message for me in the form of an old photograph of Carter and Carnarvon, and a newspaper article about the destruction of some film years before he even started his quest in the Western Desert, and fifth . . .'

'Is there a fifth?'

'There might be – at least one person reports seeing Julian alive since I saw his corpse disappear in the ambulance yesterday morning!'

'Whoever told you that must be off his chump, darling.'

'No doubt. But I'd like to see Julian's body. Where would it be now, in the city morgue?'

'Yes, but they'll never let you in – or give you access to the pathologist's reports. You're not even next of kin.'

'Julian's parents are dead, he never married and he has no brothers or sisters. In fact, I was his *only* kin.'

'I doubt if that will wash.'

'Couldn't you pull some strings at the Embassy?'

'I don't carry much weight there anymore – not since they retired me from the Office. If anyone has to inspect the body it'll be the Consul. They won't see why an unrelated private individual should be allowed to go.' Doc sat down and lit a cigarette, deep in thought. 'I know,' she said, 'Pete Margoulis – Dr Pietro Margoulis. He teaches physical anthropology and genetics at the American University of Cairo and he might be able to get you permission to visit the morgue for academic purposes.'

'I've never heard of him.'

'Pete's a friend of mine from the old days. He's clever but very self-absorbed, you might say. If you weren't so polite you might say egotistical or even narcissistic. He's very fond of young girls, – students mostly – but he's also respectably married to an heiress and occasionally there's what you might call a "conflict of interests". I once helped him out of bother, and he owes me.'

'Sounds charming!'

'OK, Pete's not my favourite person. But he's a brilliant geneticist. He's done surveys of the skull-dimensions on the Nubian population to determine a correlation between them and the ancient Egyptians. Got it all on some kind of computer matrix. He also worked extensively on Tut's mummy, so by chatting him up you can kill two birds with one stone – get a chance to see Julian's body, and find out whether Tutankhamen really was murdered.'

8

MARGOULIS'S OFFICE WAS ON THE first floor of the American University, opening off an outside walkway, and I arrived there at the end of the lunch break when dozens of Egyptian students were milling around in the courtyard beneath, drinking Coke. Margoulis's timetable was pasted on the board outside his room, and I glanced at it. He was anything but hard worked, I noticed: only four hours a week were blocked in. The rest of the time was marked 'free research' – like the period which was beginning now. I leaned on the balustrade. A slender, bearded man in a white lab-coat came swinging along the walkway, hand-in-hand with a pretty girl. He saw me standing there, and released the girl's hand, speaking to her softly. He must have been in his forties: the girl looked about eighteen. She hurried off quickly, and the man glared at me with clear blue eyes. His black hair – bottle-black probably – was cut short and he wore a small gold ring in his left earlobe. Under the lab-coat, I glimpsed jeans and cowboy boots.

'Dr Margoulis?' I asked: the man nodded, 'I'm Omar James Ross, a friend of Evelyn Barrington. She said you might be able to help me.'

'What about'

'Can we talk?'

Margoulis shifted uneasily and glanced, almost wisfully after the girl.

'I suppose so,' he said at last. 'Come in, won't you?'

The room was small and untidy: a desk pushed into one corner, bookshelves, a full-sized skeleton in another corner, and anatomical charts in garish colours on the walls. Two computer terminals blinked at me from the top of a steel work-table. Margoulis brought out a bottle of old sherry and two stemmed glasses from a specimen cabinet that stood in another corner.

'Care for a tot?' he asked, 'Don't normally drink in the office, you understand – hospitality purposes only.'

He filled the two glasses, handed one to me, and sat down in his chair. 'Please,' he said, 'have a seat.'

I sat down in the only other chair and sipped my sherry. Behind Margoulis's desk was a digital shot of Tutankhamen's mummy – a photo of the actual cadaver, stripped of its beaten-gold funerary mask.

Doc said you worked on Tut's body.' I said.

'I did,' Margoulis replied. His accent was mild, Californian perhaps. 'There was already some anatomical analysis done, of course, by Harrison and others, but none of it was very reliable. I thought there was room for some, ah . . . first class work. My speciality is cranio-facial morphology and the hereditary factors affecting it. My particular interest is in malocclusion.'

'Malocclusion?'

Margoulis grinned as if he had scored a point. 'Here,' he said, 'let me show you.' He put his glass down, stood up, and strode over to one of his computer terminals. I followed him. I watched as he dabbled the keyboard for a moment until the multicoloured digital image of a human cranium formed on the screen. He touched the keys again, tweaking the skull from side to side.

'Tutankhamen's cranium,' he said proudly. 'My methodology is to take precise lateral cephalometric X-rays and use the high-speed computer to analyse the data. Each image is traced on acetate and digitised. There are a hundred and seventy-seven coordinate points which are stored on the computer's hard disk.'

'With what result?'

'Well, look at this cranium. Doesn't it strike you as peculiar?'

I examined the image with interest. Tutankhamen's face looked somehow flattened and the back of the skull seemed to project backwards abnormally far.

'It's platycephalic,' Margoulis said, impatiently, 'That is, flattened out on top, and projecting prominently backwards. Actually, there is a marked thickening on the left side and the region behind the brain is depressed.'

'How unusual is that?'

'Most unusual. In all my research I have never come across another specimen quite like it, except for the unidentified mummy from Tomb 55 in the Valley of the Kings, which may be Smenkhare, Tut's brother. That skull is even more remarkable – it's probably the largest human cranium ever found. With regard to Tut, though, there are some other interesting peculiarities.' He tweaked the image of the skull around to produce a frontal view. Tutankhamen's narrow, lopsided face leered at me peevishly from the screen. 'You know that teeth cease to decay after death?' he asked. 'Well, as you can see, the cadaver's canine teeth are prominent – in life they would have protruded above his gums like fangs – that's malocclusion. Despite the beautiful funerary mask, at the time of his death, "King Tut" would have actually have looked something like Dracula.'

I chuckled. 'So what was the cause of death?'

'Well, ah, there is a fracture of the left cranium.' Margoulis said, twisting the image laterally again. 'Oh, there's been a lot of hullabaloo over whether it was made before or after death. My opinion is that it was made before death by a blow from a blunt instrument, probably a club, used at close quarters. The angle of the wound suggests to me that Tutankhamen was hit from behind, which would mean a surprise attack – probably assassination – rather than a death in battle, as would be suggested by a frontal wound.'

'Unless he was running away, of course.'

Margoulis evidently didn't get the joke. 'Ah, quite . . .' he said without smiling, flicking off the image on the screen abruptly. 'Anyhow it's a fascinating pathology. He was an adolescent when he died, you know, and there is every indication that his body was frail. The cadaver was incredibly well preserved. You may not be familiar with the details of the ancient Egyptian practice of mummification, Mr Ross.'

I was tempted to announce that I was an Egyptologist of fourteen years standing, but Margoulis was so obviously enamoured of his own voice, that I decided to let it pass. I forced myself to remember that I was here to ask the man a favour.

Margoulis sat down again behind his desk, motioning me to sit also. He retrieved his glass of sherry and held it up towards the light as if examining the colour of the liquid carefully. 'After death,' he said, 'the brains of the cadaver would be pulled out through a nostril using a special iron hook. The parts that the hook could not reach were removed by an infusion of chemicals. The empty skull was filled with resin. They then made an incision in the cadaver's side with a razor-sharp stone, removed the intestines, and having rinsed the belly with palm-wine, would fill it with cassia and myrrh, sew it up, and steep it in natron – rock salt – solution for forty to seventy days. The process was extremely expensive – it cost about four hundred dollars: a king's ransom in those days – and its practice was probably perpetrated by a professional guild of embalmers: they were highly regarded, but they were principally charlatans. In fact, there are mummies from the 11th Dynasty – six hundred years older than Tutankhamen – in which the intestines and brains were left alone, and these are the best preserved mummies we have. The embalmers were guilding the lily for money: the best work of all was done by nature!'

'Remarkable,' I said with my tongue firmly in my cheek. Margoulis knew his malocclusion, but he was no expert on ancient Egyptian sociology. In fact the desecration of grave robbers had eventually forced them to bury the dead deeper and deeper, and of course the climatic conditions didn't apply dozens of feet underground. I kept quiet, though: I didn't need a discussion on mummification.

Margoulis yawned as if he had suddenly lost interest in the subject and glanced at his watch. 'Enough of this small talk,' he said. 'I'm sure you didn't come here just to ask about Tutankhamen. What can I do for you, Mr Ross?'

'I need to see a body in the city morgue. Doc told me you might be able to help.'

'Are you medical?'

'No.'

'I see. It might be difficult. Which is the body in question?'

'Julian Cranwell, a friend.'

'Ah, I heard about Cranwell's death – heart attack at the pyramids, wasn't it? Should have drunk less whisky from what I hear. Why do you want to see the body?'

'Last respects, you might say. Do you have any pull with the government?'

Margoulis rocked back on his chair. I guessed I had pressed the right button: 'As a matter of fact,' he said, slowly, 'the Minister of the Interior is a personal friend of mine. So is the Minister of Health. My wife and I play bridge with them both.' He stopped himself, realising that he was giving away too much. 'But no need for high-level support. What I can do is give you a note saying that you are an assistant of mine, and that you need to see a recently-dead cadaver. I'll put you down as a "Dr Ross, Assistant Lecturer in Physical Anthropology". How you work it from there is entirely up to you.'

'Thanks,' I said, 'Doc will be very grateful.'

Margoulis reddened slightly, and I wondered what secret hold Doc had on him. I waited while he scribbled the note and sealed it in an envelope.

As I ran down the stairs afterwards, I saw the pretty, dark student, standing in the shadows under the stairwell. 'Free research,' I found myself thinking. The girl looked up sulkily as I hurried past.

9

THE MORTUARY BUILDING MIGHT HAVE been built for Stalinist Russia – a drab, grey, featureless block festooned with greasy windows. The plate-glass doors were cracked and there were crushed flies on the linoleum. A single, unshaded lightbulb dangled from the ceiling among coils of stripped grey paint, and a fan circled ponderously. A receptionist with a two day stubble and a frayed shirt-collar took my note and disappeared silently into the shadows. I sat down on a chair of patched leather and watched a squadron of flies colonising the tea-stains on the receptionist's desk. Ironic, I thought, that in a country where the conditions were perfect for preserving human bodies, they should have to be kept here in refrigerators at enormous cost. I watched the minutes ticking away on a wall clock behind the desk, which was an hour slow.

Ten minutes passed. Footsteps clicked across the lino, and I looked up to see a man in a dark suit coming out of a corridor. As he emerged into the light, I recognised the long, sad face of Dr Amin, the police pathologist, and was suddenly, embarrassingly, aware that I had just presented a letter introducing myself as an assistant lecturer in anthropology at the American University. Amin was walking quickly, deep in thought, his eyes fixed on the ground. He didn't appear to have seen me yet. I looked around frantically for a way of escape – a newspaper to cover my face, anything – but this must have been the only waiting-room in Cairo without reading-material. The door of a broom closet stood almost opposite me. The odds were it would be locked, I knew. But Amin was still advancing, and there was no other way. I leapt up, keeping my face turned away from him, and tried the handle. It stuck.

Amin's steps were nearby now, and suddenly his voice snapped: 'Just a minute, you!'

The handle went down and the door opened. I glanced over my shoulder to see Amin accosting the receptionist, who'd just returned through another door. I pushed myself into the narrow closet amid mops, buckets, and tins of cleaner, and closed the door to a crack. Moments later Amin sauntered past and went through the cracked glass doors leading into the street. I opened the cupboard to find the receptionist standing with his hands on his hips and eyeing me curiously.

'Sorry,' I said, 'I thought it was the toilet.'

He showed me to a filthy, smelly toilet along a corridor, and when I returned to my seat he was wafting away flies with a folder and pretending to read.

Another ten minutes passed. Then twenty. I yawned and shuffled my feet. At that moment a bald man in an off-white lab-coat hurried out of the shadows, carrying my note gingerly, looking round-shouldered and apologetic. I rose to greet him: the man's handshake was limp and his palm damp. He avoided my gaze, his eyes shifting sideways beneath the thick lenses of his spectacles.

'Dr Ross,' he said, 'I'm Dr Rafiq. We always like to welcome our colleagues from the universities, and of course, we know Dr Margoulis well.'

'Hello Dr Rafiq,' I said.

'You wanted see the body of Julian Cranwell, I understand?'

'Yes, he died of a heart attack and was sent here yesterday.'

Rafiq began to tap his feet nervously. He looked away and a spillikin of sweat ran down his brow. 'I'm afraid there's a problem,' he said.

I tensed. I'd waited forty minutes – ample time for Rafiq to check up on me. Or perhaps Amin had spotted me after all. 'I can't see him?' I enquired.

'I'm sorry, but you can't, Dr Ross.'

'Why?'

Rafiq took a deep breath. 'Because according to our records, there were no heart-attack victims from Giza admitted to the morgue yesterday. I've checked thoroughly. I'm afraid the body in question is simply not here!'

$$10$$

THE COFFEE HOUSE ON THE CORNICHE was packed and from the rear came the clack of dominoes being slapped down on tables. From another direction came a heavy, intoxicating rhythm and the wail of Umm Kalthum. I took a table on the pavement and watched the procession of lights that poured like burning oil through the darkness on the bridge of Qasr an-Nil. The waiter brought red tea and the *shisha*-man set up a heavy brass-bound water pipe. I sipped the tea and took a long cool draught of honey-flavoured smoke from the bubbling pipe. I let the smoke dribble out of my nostrils with satisfaction: *shisha* smoking is the most relaxing, most civilised Egyptian custom I know. Cars rumbled by incessantly in a slurry of vapour-trails, but through the pall of city smog I could make out some of the constellations that litter the night sky. It's not as easy to see them in the city as it is in the desert, where the whole dome of the heavens often seems weighted with bright bodies. In the city the stars are cloaked by the glare of a billion sodium lamps and clouds of effluent and motor fumes. There are four hundred million stars in our galaxy alone, but even on a good day only about two thousand are visible to the naked eye. In the city it's far fewer. As my eyes adjusted, though, I managed to make out some old friends: Taurus, Cassiopeia, Orion's belt with Sirius hanging below. Sirius looked lack-lustre in the fumes but actually it's one of the brightest stars in the heavens. Only eight-and-a-half light years from earth, it's among our closest neighbours. In fact, Sirius is a binary star: there are two stars in the system, Sirius A and Sirius B, or Digitaria as it's sometimes called. Sirius A can be seen clearly with the naked eye, but Digitaria is invisible. Lost in the glare of its bright companion, its presence wasn't guessed until the 1830s and not proved until 1862. In 1915 it was identified as a white dwarf, a super-dense star, that orbits Sirius A every fifty years.

Sirius had a special significance for me. Two years earlier, I'd uncovered a narrow shaft on the west bank of the Nile at Madinat Habu near Luxor that descended at an angle forty feet into the cliff. I was only just able to crawl through it on hands and knees, but it opened out into a spacious cave where there was a door sealed with the symbols of the Winged Disc and the Eye of Ra. At first I could hardly believe it. This had some of the features of an 18th Dynasty burial – it might even have been the grave of Akhnaton himself – the proverbial 'Big One' every Egyptologist dreams of. I went back next day with *guftis* and a photographer and unsealed the door. To my disappointment though, there was no tomb behind it, only a stone shelf containing a hoard of artefacts. One of them was a stone stela, which looked as if it had once formed part of a wall-decoration, bearing the ancient Egyptian hieroglyph for Sirius, carved into a circle surrounded by a perfectly elliptical cartouche. The stela was identifiable from its style as 18th Dynasty, about 3400 years ago, and I examined it from every possible point of view. It was obviously making a statement about Sirius – the hieroglyph made that clear. But there was something extraordinary here. The ellipse was formed from circular dots – exactly fifty of them – and I knew it took fifty years for Sirius B to make an *elliptical* orbit of its brighter companion. If the ellipse really showed the orbit of Sirius B, a star invisible to the naked eye, it would mean that the ancient Egyptians had access to advanced optical techniques – telescopes, possibly even a knowledge of spectrum physics. Surely, that was impossible. At least Dr Abbas Rifad, Director General of the EAS, thought so. He entered the cave and examined the 'Siriun Stela' personally. 'I think your theory is far-fetched, Mr Ross,' he told me. 'Sirius B was detected by spectrum analysis in 1915. I doubt if they had that technique in the 14th century BC! Ill-conceived ideas like that bring the Service into disrepute. After all, it's only a circle, an ellipse and the Sirius symbol. To me the find has no significance at all.' I wanted to remove the stela. Rifad said no. He ordered it kept *in situ* until the whole context could be thoroughly studied by a team of 18th-Dynasty experts – extravagant measures, I thought, for a find of 'no significance'. It wasn't long after that Rifad posted me to another dig at Heliopolis, and shortly they threw me out on my ear altogether.

'You're miles away!' a voice said, and I glanced up to see Doc Barrington standing in front of the table, smiling. Tonight she was wearing a knee-length black dress with a wheel design on the chest, and she'd taken the trouble to put on some make-up and gold ear-studs. She took the pipe from me. 'I love a *shisha*,' she said. 'What were you ruminating on?'

'The stars,' I said.

'Did you see Julian?'

'Julian's not in the morgue.'

'You're kidding!'

'Not a sniff of him.'

'It's just a bureaucratic cock-up, must be. Wouldn't be the first time they got the labels muddled.'

'No, I thought of that. I even went over the admissions lists with Dr Rafiq, and no corpse of Julian's age or description was admitted to the mortuary the day before yesterday, at least no one sent from the pyramids. He's just not there, Doc!'

'Well if he's not in the morgue, where the hell is he?'

'Buried already?'

'That would be illegal without Consular permission. Anyway, you said there was going to be an autopsy.'

'That's what they told me. You can't trust anyone in this place!'

Doc sent a nervous glance in my direction, put the *shisha* down, and lit a Rothmans with fingers that were surprisingly shaky. She leaned over towards me. 'Darling,' she said, almost in a whisper, 'the walls have ears. When Ronnie died I told them the same thing – that there's something going on here. Something big. That there were people following us and watching us. You know what they said? They said I was nuts – paranoid delusions caused by the trauma of Ronnie's death. Sent me to a loony-bin and sort of ironed my head out. Now I just keep my mouth shut and try to think rationally. You really do go round the bend if you start thinking about all that. You can read anything into anything, but it's all bunk in the end. Julian's dead. He's not coming back. You saw him at the pyramids. His body might have been misplaced but it will turn up.'

I looked at Doc in surprise. Sometimes she'd come out with this sort of stuff before, and I had the impression of a quick and intelligent mind constrained by fears of wandering into the fearful *terra incognita* of the irrational. I sympathised with her more profoundly than she would ever know.

'OK, Doc,' I said, 'I know you'll say it's crazy, but I can't help thinking about what that hunchback said. That he saw Julian after he was supposed to be dead.'

'Darling, no one rises from the dead except Jesus Christ, and whatever else Julian may have been he was *not* Jesus Christ. You *saw* his corpse at the pyramids. Look, I'll get on to the Consulate tomorrow, they might know something about it. Don't worry, Jamie. I'm certain there's no big mystery. A body can't just vanish. It's some kind of mistake and everything will be explained.'

'Right.'

Doc sat in silence for a few moments, composing herself. The waiter came and she ordered coffee. I turned back to the stars. 'You know Sirius?' I asked after a while.

Doc glanced up. 'Certainly. It's in Canis Major,' she said. 'The brightest star in the sky.'

'Did you know it's a binary star?'

'Of course, darling. It's encircled by Sirius B, a white dwarf so dense that it gives out hardly any light. Its helium and light hydrogen has burned up and the remaining material is so tightly packed that a spoonful of the stuff would weigh tons.'

'Did you know that the ancient Egyptians based their calendar on the heliacal rising of Sirius? They believed it was the home of departed souls. It was immensely important to them.'

'Why?'

'No one knows for certain, but there are strong traditions about Sirius in many ancient civilisations. The Dogon of Mali believe that the starting point of civilisation is the star that revolves around Sirius – the smallest and heaviest of all stars.'

'Who told them?'

'No one – at least not recently. The tradition was discovered by two anthropologists, Griaule and Dieterlen, in the 1930s, and the Dogon shamans claimed it dated back to the remotest antiquity. Apparently they also knew that the star revolved around Sirius with an elliptical orbit, once every fifty years.'

'That's ridiculous, Jamie. How could they possibly have known that in the remotest antiquity?'

'Right. It wasn't known in the West until a century ago, and wasn't even photographed until the 1970s. Some say the Dogon are descendants of Egyptians who fled from their country during the Arab invasion of AD 640. Their ancestors might have brought advanced knowledge with them. In 1993, I found a stela at Madinat Habu dated to the 18th Dynasty, that bore an inscription of the hieroglyph for Sirius, on an engraving of a circle enclosed by an ellipse. The ellipse was portrayed by dots, and there were exactly fifty of them. Was it a coincidence? Or did the ancient Egyptians actually *know* about the white dwarf Sirius B?'

'But how could they? Telescopes weren't invented till Galileo tottered along in the 1500s.'

'Yes, but perhaps their civilisation was descended from a previous one that did have telescopes.'

Doc shrugged. She knew my hobby-horse only too well. 'Well, I hope they were right about one thing,' she said.

'What's that?'

'That Sirius is the home of departed souls. If so, then Julian and Ronnie are up there laughing at us right now.' Doc smiled at the thought and swallowed her coffee.

'Come to the flat, Jamie,' she said. 'I can't see why you want to stay in that awful Shepheard's anyway.'

'I will, Doc, I promise. But not tonight.'

11

IN THE MORNING I TOOK A taxi back to Khan al-Khalili to hunt for Nikolai Kolpos. By the time I arrived in the bazaars it was ten o'clock and the warren of alleys was a surge of movement. I forced my way through the crowds jammed around bakers' stalls and fruit stalls, stalls piled with shoes and second-hand clothes. The address Julian had written on the back of the photocopy – The Osiris Arcade – was tucked into a side-street, entered through a moresco arch and paved with stone flags. The store was draped with a gay-coloured awning and festooned with gaudy goods – gold-lamé pouffes, stuffed camels, onyx scarabs, jade Nefertiti busts, bronze palm-trees, brass coffee-pots with Islamic inscriptions, miniature pyramids. I pushed open the glass door and a bell rang shrilly. At once a woven drapery behind the counter was thrust aside and a fat man in a generously cut grey suit walked out. I recognised him easily from Doc's description – a loop of shaved hair circled his tanned pate and his cheeks were as plump as a cherub's. Thick glasses sat on the end of his nose, and the small black eyes behind them shifted constantly.

'Can I help you, sir?' he asked, with an oily show of helpfulness which was palpably false.

'Aren't you Nikolai Kolpos?' I enquired.

His face clouded over for an instant, but the change of expression was so rapid that I doubted that I'd actually seen it.

'I am, yes,' he said. He opened his mouth in what was evidently meant to be an engaging smile, showing dazzlingly white teeth. 'How can I help?'

'I'm Omar Ross, a friend of Dr Cranwell's.'

'Who?'

'Julian Cranwell?'

'Sorry, never heard of him.'

'My friend Evelyn Barrington assures me you have.'

'I don't know her either. You've got the wrong person. I've no idea what you want, but if you'll excuse me I've got work to do.'

Kolpos had dropped the pretence of friendliness now. He was sidling very cautiously away from me, with fear showing unmistakably in his shifty eyes, fumbling for something hidden by the counter. It's hard to be sure now, looking back, but I'm almost certain that a split second before it happened, I felt cold fingers probing under my skull and clutching the grey matter itself. There was a lash of pain and I had a clear image of a steel blade slicing down towards me. I leapt aside frantically only an instant before Kolpos brought the real meat cleaver out and down, slicing into the wood, splintering it in several places. The movement was so fast I had the impression he'd practised it. I put a choking armlock on the thick neck, caught the hand and twisted it down across the counter, smashing the knuckles against the edge until Kolpos screeched and dropped the blade. 'Elena, Elena,' he choked.

Almost at once the tapestry at the back of the shop was flung open and a slim girl stepped into the room. She moved uncertainly, stretching out with her feet, feeling for the solidity of the floor to maintain her balance, never taking her eyes off me. Her arms were fully extended towards me and in her hands, police-fashion, she held a small black .38 calibre pistol whose muzzle wavered slightly as she pointed it at my chest. Her eyes blazed: 'Leave him alone,' she shouted, 'or I'll kill you.'

I released Kolpos. The man rubbed his neck, then his wrist. 'You hurt me', he said indignantly, panting with exertion. 'You son-of-a-bitch, I'll have your prick flayed off over a slow fire.'

'Nice welcome,' I said.

'What do you want?' the girl demanded, still holding up the pistol.

'Look, there's been a misunderstanding,' I said, turning to face her fully.

'Don't move,' she said.

'Julian Cranwell was my friend. He was found dead two days ago at the pyramids. He left your name and address for me on a paper at his flat.'

'Who are you?' the girl demanded again, still pointing the pistol at me.

'I'm Omar James Ross.'

'Prove it.'

I opened the flap pocket of my bush-shirt carefully and held up my passport. Kolpos took it and flipped through the pages doubtfully. 'Distinguishing marks,' he read out, 'pierced upper lobe of right ear.' He looked at my earring with a flash of recognition.

'Ah, the *fidwa*,' he said, 'Yes, I remember Julian saying you were half Hawazim.' He nodded at the girl. 'He's clean.'

Hesitantly, still watching me like a hawk, she lowered the pistol.

'Pity you didn't think of that before you almost scalped me,' I said, wondering if Kolpos had ever heard of the word 'apology'.

He grinned suddenly, showing his teeth. 'We've been a bit on edge since Julian died.'

'A bit on edge! What would you have done if I hadn't dodged in time?'

Kolpos shrugged. 'There are casualties in every war.'

'That's wonderful! What the hell are you so frightened of?'

He lost his false smile. 'Look, Ross. Julian Cranwell was murdered two days ago. I don't want myself or Elena to be next on the list, OK?'

'The police said Julian's death was caused by a heart attack.'

Kolpos scoffed. 'A heart attack! If you believe that, Ross, you're a bigger fool than you look.'

'Maybe. But I saw his body. There were no marks on him.'

'Hah! There are more ways than one to skin a cat.'

'Right. But I came from London to find Julian, and now I want to know what's going on.'

Kolpos glanced at Elena. 'Shut up shop,' he told her, 'I think perhaps we owe Mr Ross a cup of coffee and an explanation.'

The apartment behind the shop was extensive, but most of the space was taken up with junk. There were crates and cans and cartons piled everywhere, piles of old books and bric-à-brac, imitation Bedouin coffee-pots, beads, Nubian swords, Beja daggers, brass models of the pyramids, brass lamp-stands, tea trays, kettles, desert fossils, bits of ancient saddlery. Kolpos led me into a parlour with a sash-window looking on to the street, beside which an ornate pendulum clock tocked away noisily on the wall. Behind the parlour was a door opening into a kitchenette and another into a small study with a writing desk and a telephone. He removed a pile of newspapers from an armchair and slapped off the dust, inviting me to sit down. Elena knelt and rubbed ointment into his bruised hand where I'd bashed it against the counter, making small sucking noises. I glimpsed the nape of a long neck, a delicate ear with a golden stud, and caught a faint whiff of sandalwood. Then she busied herself in the kitchen with coffee. I sat and studied a photo on the mantelpiece of a middle-aged woman wearing a colourful Arab dress and a floral headcloth. 'My wife,' Kolpos said, catching my glance. 'I am Greek – Alexandria Greek, that is – but my wife was Egyptian – a Catholic. She died in the influenza epidemic five years ago. There was nothing they could do. I said, how is it possible in these days of space flight and computers that people are still dying of influenza? They said it was a new type, Chinese 'flu, that they'd never seen before. Magda came back one day with a high fever, I put her to bed and within forty-eight hours she was dead. My sons are both in America, big businessmen. Elena's been good to me, though – like a daughter. Better than a daughter. I don't think I could have got over Magda's death without her.'

Elena glided in from the kitchenette carrying two brass coffee-jugs on a tray with tiny glasses. Doc had certainly been right about her. She had the kind of long-legged beauty you often found among Israeli *sabras*, a perfect match of the oriental and the Western – jet black hair, velvet-olive skin, eyes like charcoal, slightly hooked nose, slim hips, high breasts. Yet she was distinctly understated. Her hair was brushed back and tied in a pony tail, the true contours of the body not defined but only suggested by the baggy pants and shirt. She set the tray on the table, crouched down and began to pour the coffee carefully. 'Turkish coffee is to be savoured,' she said. 'You only get a little bit.' The aroma of the coffee was delicious. I sipped it and found it very hot, very sweet and very strong. 'If you shoot as well as you make coffee, I'm glad you didn't pull the trigger,' I said.

She looked embarrassed. 'I've never used a gun in my life,' she said.

'Would you really have shot me?'

'If you'd hurt Nikolai any more, yes.'

Kolpos beamed at her benevolently.

I finished the coffee and put the cup back on the tray. 'So how well did you know Julian?' I asked Kolpos.

He hesitated, as if weighing the question carefully. His eyes behind the thick glasses were expressionless and watchful. He put his hand over his mouth and set his cup down, staring at Elena.

She gave me a lingering look. 'Julian said he trusted Mr Ross,' she said. 'Better tell him the whole story.'

'OK,' Kolpos said slowly. 'Let's start at the beginning. This shop isn't much, Ross, but it's not my only resource. In fact, I travel widely looking for antiquities – Aleppo, Damascus, Stamboul, Tashkent, Bokhara, Samarkand – even Beijing. Remarkable what treasures the Communists left intact. About a year ago I was in Samarkand where, in a tiny one-room shop in the bazaar, I found something that I'd been dreaming of for years. It was the original manuscript copy of Al-Khalidi's *Book of Lost Treasures*.'

'I know the book. It's a fifteenth-century Latin translation –'

'Of a twelfth-century Arabic manuscript, yes. But the Arabic manuscript was itself based on another seventh-century Arabic text which was believed lost. What I had stumbled across was the original, or at least a copy of it.'

'Good God.'

'Quite. I think you can imagine my excitement, Ross. This was the find of a lifetime. The book itself was priceless just as a curiosity, of course, but the information it held was of even greater interest to me. The later version listed four hundred treasure troves hidden in Egypt, most, though not all, of which had been well dug-over centuries ago. When I examined the original text, though, I found out that the copyist had omitted the details of at least twenty treasure sites, almost all of them of greater interest than the ones included in the later edition. I could only conclude that the omission had been intentional. The dealer was a poor man – the descendant of an Arab pedlar who'd probably brought the book with him to that far-off place. He couldn't read Arabic, and hadn't much idea of the book's value. Of course, I had no intention of cheating him, you understand, but my resources were limited. I gave him $1000 for it. He was accustomed to a very modest lifestyle, so by his standards it was an excellent deal. At once I began on my own translation of the book, picking out the choice sites of course.'

'Of course.'

'Then I sold it to an anonymous collector in Dubai.'

'For more than $1000, naturally.'

Kolpos gulped with satisfaction. 'Considerably more, yes, but not as much as I could have sold it for had I shopped around. We don't live by bread alone, and as I said it wasn't only the money that interested me. I still had my translation.'

'You had your bread as well as eating it, so to speak.'

'Crudely put, but yes, essentially so. Now, here's the really fascinating bit, Ross. One of the sites mentioned in the book was the Lost Oasis.'

'Zerzura.'

'Yes. Zerzura. Of course Zerzura is also mentioned in the twelfth-century copy, but the directions are so archaic that no one could possibly work out what was intended. The original description was much more detailed: Zerzura was a white city, it said, located in the farthest reaches of the Western Desert, hidden under the sand. In the city lay a dead king and queen on a hoard of priceless treasure. There was a door with the effigy of a bird on it, with a key in its beak. You take the key, open the door and help yourself to the treasure. The directions were detailed but somewhat cryptic.'

'So you're telling me that the Lost Oasis of Zerzura actually existed?'

'According to the book, yes. You know the story of a lost city in the desert has been mentioned as far back as Strabon, the Greek traveller, in the first century BC, and Bedouin folktales are peppered with references to the Lost Oasis.'

'And it was the treasure that was supposed to lie there that interested you?'

'No, it wasn't. You see, Zerzura was of great historical importance. With the laws in this country being what they are it would have been very difficult to sell the bulk of the treasure. Anything found at Zerzura would almost certainly have been government property and ended up in a museum. That was no good to me. There was, however, another site which tickled my fancy: an ancient diamond mine used by Pharaoh Ramses II, which had been covered by an earthquake centuries ago and never rediscovered. This site also lay in the Western Desert, and its prospects excited me much more. Uncut diamonds have no historical value, and can thus be freely traded. However, finding the site would not be at all straightforward. The descriptions were more than a thousand years old and had to be interpreted by someone who knew the desert well and who was skilled in tracing archaeological sites. It had to be someone discreet, preferably a foreigner, who was not well in with the authorities. Moreover, it had to be someone who had a strong motive for uncovering these sites.'

'Julian Cranwell.'

'Julian was the perfect choice. I met him at a party at the British Embassy; your Mrs Barrington was there, too. He was depressed and broke. The EAS had ceased funding his Zerzura Project, which hadn't produced anything of interest. The situation was ideal for me. He was obsessed with finding the Lost Oasis. I had the means of finding it and, thanks to my happy sale in Dubai, I had the funds to finance it. He didn't like the idea of working with me – didn't trust me at first – but I had the goods, and he was hooked. The deal was that Julian would find both the sites using my money and my translations of the manuscript. While Julian would have exclusive rights to excavate Zerzura, I should be entirely free to exploit the Ramses Mine. Julian agreed eventually. We had a deal. He would still continue his work for the EAS of course, but it would be scaled down. Our project had to be kept secret, and he would work on it in his spare time. That was three months ago.'

'What happened?'

'At first nothing. I gave Julian the translation, but it was immensely difficult. As I said, the topography was archaic, some of the directions were encrypted: it was like working with a guide-book from a different planet. Julian was brilliant. He worked by intuition and then fitted the calculations in later, but it was slow work. At least he thought he had a starting-point; that was all important, of course. Then something unexpected happened: Julian returned, very excited, with two figurines.'

'Akhnaton *ushabtis*?'

'You knew about that?'

'Julian mentioned them to me before he died. I just never believed it.'

'Yes, they appeared to be Akhnaton *ushabtis*. At first even I didn't believe they were genuine – as you know, Akhnaton's tomb has never been found. Julian admitted he'd also been sceptical, but now he was convinced they were the real thing. He took them to a friend of his, Robert Rabjohn, an expert on ancient Egyptian artefacts, and Rabjohn agreed they were authentic.'

'I've never heard of Rabjohn. Was he a friend of Julian's?'

'I don't know. Rabjohn's one of these sophisticated loners . . . a bit of a cold fish. I think he helped fund the Zerzura Project. He's absolutely stinking rich – inherited money from his father who built a railway in the States. He's what you might call a pro-fessional dilettante, but he's very well versed in artefacts. He's seen almost everything and he's like a bloodhound when it comes to forgeries. Got a collection of artefacts to die for. I don't know how he gets away with it. I've never had the pleasure of seeing more than a fraction of what he's got, but judging by that, it all ought to be in museums.'

'So Julian accepted his verdict on the *ushabtis*?'

'Yes, he came to see me, very excited. If they were genuine, he said, then the grave of the last undiscovered pharaoh of the 18th Dynasty, Akhnaton, must have been found. Found secretly, of course, but that didn't bother him altogether, because he was confident that he could track it down. The problem was time. What worried him sick was that the place might be cleaned out and even closed before its archaeological significance was known. If Akhnaton's tomb really has been discovered, think of the other treasures it might contain. Akhnaton was a major player. He ruled Egypt for twice as long as Tutankhamen, who was still a boy when he died, yet the treasure in his tomb was reckoned to have been worth £3 million at the time of discovery. It would be worth billions today. Just imagine the value of Akhnaton's treasure! There are plenty of sharks around who would be only too quick to eat the whole lot.'

'You weren't tempted to sell the *ushabtis*?'

'Never! Julian had no interest in personal enrichment and, as I've said, I've always been wary of dealing in genuine antiquities in this country. Sadly, Julian was so taken up with the possibility of Akhnaton's tomb that he no longer seemed interested in my proposition. But there was no question of him selling the pieces. He was all for revealing the discovery to the Antiquities Service. In fact he was just about to do so, when he suddenly got scared.'

'That wasn't like him.'

'No, it wasn't. Normally he was scared of no one and nothing. But this time he was truly terrified. I don't know if he discovered something about Akhnaton's tomb that frightened him, or whether he was actually threatened, but for the first time I saw him terrified. The next thing I knew, Julian had been found dead. That was the end of my diamond mine.'

'But you still have the descriptions?'

'No. There was only ever one copy of the translations. We agreed on that for security reasons. I don't know where the texts are. Only Julian knew that, and he's dead.'

'What about the original text?'

'I don't even know the name of the buyer. I dealt through

middlemen, cash only. No doubt the collector had a reason for keeping his name out of it. No, I don't think he'll ever be found.'

Kolpos paused and looked at me carefully. Elena was also watching me. I removed my glasses and wiped them on my sleeve. The first two fingers of my right hand had gone numb for no apparent reason and there was an almost imperceptible blemish at the edge of my vision. These were the tell-tale signs that a massive migraine attack was on its way. I took a couple of deep breaths, knowing that one thing deep breathing could not cure was a migraine. Then I replaced my glasses.

'OK, you think Julian was murdered,' I said, 'but why should *you* be next on the list?'

'Look, I don't know why Julian was killed,' Kolpos said, 'but if it was for the *ushabtis*, then I might be in trouble. You see, I'm the only one who knows where they are.'

'And where are they?'

Kolpos's face closed up like a camera shutter. 'I can't tell you,' he said, sharply. 'Are you crazy? You don't even want to know. There are crooks in this town who'd kill their own mothers to get their hands on them.'

'How do I know the *ushabtis* even exist?'

'You'll have to take my word – and Julian's.'

I looked at them both. The story had come out too readily somehow. Kolpos seemed too anxious for me to swallow it. It might be part of the truth, but I was certain it wasn't the whole thing. And there were no artefacts to corroborate it. I got up to leave. My vision was already beginning to swim at the periphery; within twenty minutes I knew I'd scarcely be able to see at all. 'You tell a riveting story, Mr Kolpos,' I said, 'but unfortunately without seeing the *ushabtis* I can't even judge whether they are a figment of your – or Julian's – imagination. Here's my number . . .' I gave him a slip of paper with Doc's telephone number on it. 'If you decide you want to tell me any more, perhaps you'd give me a call.'

The mass of whorls and vortices had already begun rolling across my vision by the time I showed myself out.

12

B Y THE TIME I REACHED DOC'S flat my head felt as though someone had shoved a red-hot knitting needle through it. The visual aura which always heralded the attacks had gone, leaving a residue of nausea and the embarrassing inability to articulate a sentence.

'Migraine,' I told Doc as soon as she opened the door.

'Oh, you poor dear,' she said, leading me to my old bedroom and making me comfortable. She shut out the light, helped me pull off my shoes, then hurried off and came back shortly with some disgusting-looking concoction in a glass, like seaweed soup. I shook my head violently, but Doc insisted. 'It's just a herbal infusion,' she said. 'It's the only thing that really works. They always recommend paracetamol, but it's no good. No one knows what causes migraine, but it's probably stress-related. Attacks the optic nerve, and your brainwaves go haywire – almost like a miniature epileptic fit. Had a bad day, darling?'

I tried to explain that I'd narrowly escaped being sliced up with a meat cleaver and shot, but the words failed to materialise. Instead, a stream of gibberish came out. The oral effect is the most frightening aspect of migraine; it usually lasts only minutes, but while it lasts it's a glimpse of madness I can well do without.

'Don't try, darling,' Doc said. 'It'll be gone in twenty minutes. You know that.'

I lay back on the pillow. It was good to be doctored by Doc.

There was a comforting, nursy, air of competence and warmth about her which made you feel instantly at ease. She settled down on the armchair while I swallowed the infusion. It tasted as vile as it smelt.

'I've got some news for you,' Doc said. 'This morning I rang up the Consulate to find out what they knew about Julian's body. At first I couldn't get through to Melvin – Melvin Renner, HMC. I said to the girl, "Look, I know him, he's a personal friend of mine." Did no good. Anyway about ten calls later they put Melvin on. I explained the problem about Julian and he said, "I'm sorry, Evelyn, but I don't know anything about it, and even if I did I wouldn't tell you. It's not your affair, and I can only advise the next of kin." Then he hung up, the shit. I've known Melvin since he was posted here – always was a supercilious prick. Anyway, that's him off the Christmas card list, for a start. But it still leaves us with no body. The only thing we can do now is contact the police.'

Doc smoothed the pillow for me and flicked on a red night-light. 'Does that bother you, Jamie?' she asked.

I grunted.

'By the way,' she said, 'I started looking at the diskettes you found at Julian's. There's all sorts of weird shit, including a file on Orde Wingate. I found out why Julian was so interested in him. As a young officer in the Royal Artillery, he was stationed in Khartoum in the 1930s. It's certain that he visited Tut's tomb in the Valley of the Kings, and possible, though not confirmed, that he met Howard Carter. But that's not the most intriguing thing. In 1933 he organised an expedition in search of the Lost Oasis of Zerzura . . .'

I sat up and tried to speak, my jaw working like a goldfish. 'No, lie back, dear,' Doc said, soothingly. 'Just listen. In 1933, Wingate tramps off into the Western Desert – *terra incognita* in those days – to look for Julian's favourite Lost Oasis, with a caravan of about fifteen Bedouin. The Bedouin are never seen again. Wingate and his headman totter out of the dunes after three weeks, so shaken they can hardly talk. The headman cracks up properly and has to be put away, and Wingate claims to be suffering from amnesia. He recovers slowly and writes a milk-and-water report which reveals nothing. There are plenty of rumours, but nothing concrete, and Wingate himself begins to behave strangely, as if he's hiding some big secret. Seems everybody regarded Wingate as a real asshole, but they all agreed he was a military genius. He organised the Gideon Mission in Ethiopia in 1941, drove the Italians out and put Haile Selassie back on the throne. After it was over he tried to top himself here in Cairo by sticking a bowie knife in his throat – twice. Someone rescued him before he bled to death.'

'Good God,' I said. The oral distortion was passing; the herbal infusion was spreading a comforting blanket of warmth across my body.

'Sounds like it's working,' said Doc.

'Feels like a hot needle in my head.'

'Just lie still, Jamie. Let it pass. Where was I . . . Oh, yes . . . they gave him fourteen pints of blood and he pulled through. Then they made him a general and trotted him off to lead the Chindits in Burma. Another brilliant campaign. No one believed the British could outfight the Japs in the jungle, but under Wingate they did it. He croaked in 1944.'

'How?'

'His plane crashed in the bush. No one knows what happened. Took off from a place called Imphal and didn't come back. Next day they sent out a foot patrol and found it nose-down in the *ulu*. The bodies were unrecognisable, but they discovered Wingate's Wolseley helmet, and assumed he was among the dead. Ironically enough, all his life he'd been terrified of flying.'

Doc paused and lit a cigarette with her silver lighter. 'So of the three men Julian mentioned it seems only one of them, Tutankhamen, could have been murdered. Lord Carnarvon died of a mosquito-bite, 1923, and Orde Wingate died in a plane crash, 1944. All died in different ways, and the only link between them is that they'd all been in Tut's tomb. It's very shaky ground for anything – I mean, millions have been there. But what *is* interesting is that there's a connection between Orde Wingate and Julian Cranwell: the Lost Oasis of Zerzura.'

'You're great, Doc,' I said. 'My favourite doctor.'

'And you *will* stay tonight, Jamie.'

'All right. I don't think I could move now anyway. I'll collect my things from the hotel tomorrow.'

I woke up to find beams of sunlight trickling through the open window. The herbal infusion had done the trick, and there remained only a muzziness in my head where the pain had been. I opened the small wardrobe in the room to find that Doc had actually kept some of my things from ancient times. There was a white cotton suit, some jeans, pants, socks, sandals, baggy *sirwal*, and a couple of spare shirts. There was even a washing and shaving bag and an old pair of glasses. Doc really *was* a wonder; there's nothing so pleasant as rediscovering a hoard of possessions you've completely forgotten about. It's almost like finding buried treasure. Doc was already humped over her computer-desk in a towelling dressing-gown when I emerged, her long fingers working over the keys deftly with blinding speed. She looked as though she had been at it already for hours. I tiptoed past her and entered the bathroom and removed the clothes I'd slept in. Doc had laid out some fresh pine soap, shaving gear and a new toothbrush with a squiggle of striped toothpaste on it, all ready for me, just like in the old days. Little considerations like that had always endeared Doc to me. I stepped into a hot shower. The steam rinsed away the heaviness, and when I emerged, dressed in two clean towels, she was waiting for me on the balcony with fresh croissants, coffee and orange juice. This morning her face looked pale and drawn: 'I've been up since sparrowfart,' she said. 'Sometimes I don't sleep well these days.'

I drank the juice in two gulps and described my encounter with Kolpos while eating the croissants and drinking the coffee. 'Sounds like something out of *Aladdin and the Magic Lamp*,' Doc said finally.

'Yeah, but the weirdest thing was when Kolpos tried to dice me with the cleaver. I mean, it was as if I *knew* what was going to happen just a split second before. It saved my life.'

'Maybe you just divined it unconsciously from his expression; that happens.'

'No. I actually saw the blade flash in my head a moment before it appeared.'

'That is weird, Jamie, but memory plays tricks. Perhaps it didn't really come in that sequence at all.'

'You're probably right, Doc.'

'Did it ever happen to you before?'

'No,' I lied. I was starting to feel uncomfortable. If I went on like this Doc would soon be thinking I was cuckoo. 'What about the parallel between Julian and Wingate, though?' I said, deliberately changing the subject.

'Very interesting. In 1933 Wingate trogs off to find Zerzura with fifteen men, none of whom return. He himself is never the same again and his headman is so crazy he has to be put away. In 1995, sixty years later, Julian Cranwell sets out to find Zerzura and winds up dead.'

'I didn't swallow Kolpos's story. I sensed he was hiding something and he seemed a real money-grubber. His plea that he wouldn't break the law here in Egypt didn't ring true at all.'

'I wouldn't trust that man as far as I could throw him. What about Elena?'

'Different. Nice. Beautiful, just like you said. She didn't say much, just threatened to put a bullet in me.'

'Really. Sounds as if she liked you.'

'Hardly my type. You know I've always been madly in love with you.'

'Pull the other one, Jamie. Oh, by the way, I remembered something that might help. Some time ago, here in Cairo, I came across Professor Aurel Karlman . . .'

'What, *the* Aurel Karlman? The hieroglyphics expert – used to be professor of Egyptology at Harvard?'

'The very same.'

'I thought he'd kicked the bucket aeons ago.'

'Not a bit of it. He's no spring chicken, of course – must be ninety – but he lives in Cairo. Address in Imbaba. Now, Karlman actually *knew* Howard Carter in the 1930s. If anyone can throw light on what went on between Carter and Carnarvon and how Carnarvon really died, it's him.'

'I just hope Karlman doesn't keep a meat cleaver behind his desk, or a sexy girl with a revolver in his closet.'

'I doubt it, darling. From what I hear, the Professor has no truck with sexy girls. There was some kind of scandal years back – before your time maybe – concerning Karlman and boys from his digs. Something to do with pornography. But it was all hushed up. Anyway, the last time I saw him he was being minded by the ugliest-looking customer you ever saw. But I've got his phone number, and I'll let him know you're coming, so this time there won't be any nasty shocks.'

But nasty shocks were still in store for me that day. The first was when we called in at Shepheard's Hotel for me to settle up and check out. Doc pulled up on a side-street opposite the entrance, and together we walked through the metal-detector, nodded to the smartly dressed doormen, and approached the reception. A tall, slick young man in an impeccable black suit enquired in English if he could help. 'I'd like to check out,' I said, replying in English – it invariably commanded more respect than Arabic in an Egyptian hotel.

'What room is it, Sir?'

'Three–one–six.'

The clerk tensed suddenly, and sent me a troubled glance. 'Er . . . Mr Ross?' he said.

'Yes.'

He paused. 'I'm afraid there's been an accident.'

'What kind of accident?'

'Excuse me, Sir. I'd better get the front desk manager.'

A few moments later the manager emerged from the office, a swarthy, blue-chinned man, comfortingly plump, with a polished public-relations smile. 'Ah, Mr Ross,' he said, shaking hands with us both, 'it's nothing to worry about – it's just that there was a fire in your room last night.'

'What time was this?'

'About 3 a.m., Sir. The room-service waiter saw smoke and sounded the alarm, but it was already burning like mad. They managed to stop it spreading, but we had to evacuate all the higher floors. Then I noticed your key wasn't at reception. No one remembered you going out, so we thought you'd been trapped in the room. It was only when the fire'd burnt out and they found no er . . . remains, that we realised you must have been somewhere else.'

'I stayed at a friend's last night.'

'Very lucky, praise God.'

'Any idea how the fire started?' Doc enquired.

'Might have been an electrical fault, they can't say just yet.'

'What about my things?' I asked. 'All my traveller's cheques were in my case.'

'I'm sorry to say most of your things went up. I'm afraid you'll have to reapply to the issuing agency to replace your cheques, but the hotel will be happy to pay you the cost of your luggage.'

I settled up and filled in an Insurance Claim. As we tramped back to the car, Doc said:

'Now *there's* an interesting coincidence, Jamie.'

'Why?' I asked. 'You think it was deliberate?'

She smiled a little wistfully. 'Either that, darling,' she said, 'or else an electrical fault.'

13

At Imbaba the traffic was slowed by a herd of camels, six hundred strong, that had just been offloaded from the fleet of trucks that had shifted them from Daraw in Upper Egypt for sale here at Imbaba, the largest camel-market in the world. Before Daraw, they had been brought a thousand miles across the desert from the Sudan, along the ancient caravan-route called 'The Forty-Days Road'.

I watched them flowing past with liquid strides, their great necks stretched out swan-like, and wedge-shaped heads raised high. Some of their brands were familiar, and I felt a surge of nostalgia for the desert life. To my Hawazim cousins camels are everything, even in this age of motor travel. The very word 'camel' in Arabic is connected with the word for 'beauty', and I've only ever been able to see them through the eyes of the Arabs, not the joke animals of the British – 'a horse designed by a committee' – but as the epitome of power, endurance and grace. The Hawazim is one of the last Bedouin groups in Egypt still to travel by camel. They could have bought motor-cars – many modern Bedouin groups have done – but for them the motor vehicle is an intrusion. The camel is the real thing. I remember my mother saying, 'You can milk a camel, ride it, eat it, use it to carry your tent, yoke it to a plough, use its hair, use its skin; you can even drink its vomit if you're dying of thirst. It multiplies naturally, its food is free, and it will keep on going until it dies. Cars might be good, Omar, but only the camel is great.'

I watched the herd until it disappeared into a cloud of dust, driven by muscular, big-bellied market stewards in dirty *galla-biyyas* and headscarves carrying hippo-hide whips bought from Sudanese pedlars. The taxi nosed through a warren of half-deserted alleys, and stopped in an unmetalled street behind the camel-market. The strong sunlight of midday had faded, screened by dark cloud through which fugitive sunbeams strobed like starfish tentacles. The taxi bounced on the mud surface, a hard-caked track between craters made by the winter rains, their edges still black with stagnant sludge. I was surprised that the distinguished Aurel Karlman should have chosen a slum like this in which to spend his old age, but I remembered what Doc had said about a scandal attached to Karlman's name. Perhaps the street was the outward reflection of Karlman's inner nature. There were the rusting hulks of wrecked trucks dumped tyreless and motorless in the gutter, or shored up on bricks. Waves of empty milk cartons and super-market bags blew along the pavements. Someone had been burning rubbish, and the street was full of acrid smoke, whose stench mingled with the rich odours of camels from the nearby stalls. The street was dark, full of shadows, the tenements standing close together, teetering against one another, seeming to leer down on the car like giants. These were old houses, part of an older Cairo, much of which had been knocked down to make way for the art nouveau wintering resort which had grown up with the opening of the Suez Canal in 1869. Their facades were hidden behind baroque systems of balconies, walkways and grilled *mashrubat* windows, with arched doorways and double doors of solid cedar, studded with iron rivets and monstrous gargoyle doorknockers. As I stepped out of the taxi I glimpsed eyes peering at me from balconies and from behind the *mashrubat* screens. I walked through an open doorway, up stone flags to a deeply shadowed landing where an unnameable iron device of weights, chains and pulleys stood like a massive spider on thin iron legs. There were doors here, warped out of shape and shedding dry paint, some of them festooned with cobwebs. The walls were mouldering under trickles of green slime. I found the number I was looking for and knocked. The door opened at once and a tall Nubian in a bullet-grey *gallabiyya* stood there, regarding me malevolently with red-shot eyes. The man was huge, I realised – taller even than Hammoudi – barrel-chested, shaven-headed and hook-nosed, black as ebony, with swollen jowls for cheeks and great dewlaps of fat around the neck. He filled the whole aperture of the door, and had to bow his head slightly to fit beneath the frame.

'What?' he snapped.

'Professor Karlman?' I said. 'Does he live here?'

Suddenly a high-pitched, effete, cultured, English voice piped up from inside the dark apartment: 'Is it Ross? Let him in at once, Mas'ud.'

I stepped inside. Aurel Karlman was sitting hunched in a wheel-chair in the shadows, a small, thin, spiky man with close-cropped silver hair, his face a smudge of lines that obscured any regular shape. He wore a dark suit with a bow-tie, but like his features, his clothes had departed from their original shape under the pres-sure of successive generations of tatters and restitching. Karlman extended a fragile hand covered in liver spots: 'Forgive my not rising to greet a guest,' he said. 'It's the prerogative of age, not frailty. I am not confined to this wheelchair, but it saves effort when I'm in the flat.' The voice was curiously eldritch – New England, cold, precise as a scalpel.

The interior of the flat was large and opulent in a fusty, antique sort of way, but almost as dark as the outside, and it smelt of dust and old books – a library smell. Streaks of light from the *mashrubiyya* fell across heavy bookcases which lined the walls. I saw at once that they were full of classic volumes on Egyptology and hieroglyphics, many of them bound in vellum. 'Aren't you afraid to keep these valuable books in a place like this?' I asked.

'No. I have Mas'ud, after all, and if you look around you'll see that the flat is pretty well fortified. The floor has been reinforced to take the weight of the books; there are two sets of bars on the windows; the front door is inch-and-a-half thick cedar. I have internal locks on all the doors, radio alarms which bring a busload of armed thugs within three minutes, and I have my own four-wheel drive vehicle, well locked up at the back in a garage approached by a private staircase. I am connected by cell-phone, fax and e-mail. Evelyn Barrington let me know you were coming. I expected you.'

He snapped his fingers: 'Mas'ud. Tea,' he said testily.

'Mas'ud is such a dear,' he went on, lowering his voice confidentially. 'Unfortunately for him he has rather a problem – heroin, you know. I give him just enough money to buy it every week: I draw the exact amount out of the bank on "pay day": he knows that if anything happens to me his supply dries up at once.'

'What about the books? Aren't you afraid of him stealing them?'

'They are all listed and the list has been placed with the bank. The moment anyone tries to sell one of them, Mas'ud will be arrested automatically. He is Sudanese, and he's here without a permit: the Egyptian authorities don't take kindly to that. I've shown him the list and he understands the implications. As long as he's a good boy he will get fed and housed and his needs catered for.'

Mas'ud brought two glasses of red tea on a tray and placed them with surprising delicacy on the carved Arab table in front of Karlman. The professor motioned me to sit in an ancient leather armchair next to him. 'I serve tea Arab style,' he said. 'Does that suit you Mr *Omar* Ross?'

'Have we met?'

'No, but I know all about you, Mr Ross. You were expelled from the Antiquities Service two years ago. Abbas Rifad was the hatchet-man – a damned pen-pusher if ever there was one. Not a day's field experience in his career. The Antiquities Service ceased to be an effective force the day it was taken over by the Gyppos.'

'I'm half Gyppo.'

'I am perfectly aware of that, Mr Ross. You might be surprised to know I have Egyptian blood in my ancestry too. I'm certain you'll excuse the sentiment, though.'

'Let's say I understand what you mean.'

'Precisely. I know your work, Mr Ross, just as you certainly know mine. You have an unconventional er . . . theory . . . about the origins of ancient Egyptian civilisation, do you not? You believe that such sophistication as the first Dynastic Egyptians possessed could not have sprung into being overnight, so to speak. If the ancient inhabitants of the Nile Valley knew mathematics, astronomy, medicine, geometry, music, advanced engineering, as we know they did, where did this knowledge come from? Knowledge cannot come out of a vacuum: it must have a point of origin. *Your* answer is that this advanced knowledge was brought to Egyptian shores by refugees from an earlier, more advanced civilisation – let us call it "Atlantis" for the sake of argument. You say that the god Thoth, one of the earliest gods in the pantheon, is cited in ancient Egyptian legend as a stranger from a distant land who arrived in Egypt during the zodiacal age of Cancer, bringing with him the arts and sciences. You believe that legend to hold a kernel of truth: Thoth paved the way for more refugees from "Atlantis" – the Osiris family, who came later, strongly influenced the course of the country's history. According to you, Osiris, Isis and the others were as real as Jesus Christ or the Prophet Mohammad and only passed into myth after their deaths. You hold that the great monuments, such as the pyramids, were not merely tombs but repositories of esoteric knowledge subsequently lost, knowledge which had accrued from this earlier "Atlantean" civilisation. Is that a fair summary of your "theory", Mr Ross?'

'More or less, yes.'

Karlman put his teaglass down and tipped his head to one side, regarding me with a mischievous grin. A slow grating began deep down in his throat, as if a bellows were pumping out the last gasping breaths of air, which magnified by degrees into a full, humourless cackle of derision. 'You're more of a fool than I thought you were, Ross,' he spluttered. 'Your so-called theory is absolute balls. How could there possibly have been a pre-Dynastic culture more sophisticated than the Egyptians, a culture with telescopes and flying machines and lasers? If they had that kind of technology, where is the archaeological evidence? We have the ruins of ancient Egypt: the temples, the pyramids. We have paleolithic implements and fireplaces of *Homo habilis* dating back a million years, and dinosaur bones dating back hundreds of millions. But we have not a single whiff of this "Atlantean" culture with all its lasers and flying machines. Why? Where did it go?' Karlman cackled more loudly, more desperately: 'No, your idea is nonsense. No wonder Rifad kicked you out. Never fool about with what you don't understand, my boy; the scenario is too big for the likes of you.'

I put my glass down and glared. I felt a familiar knotting of anger in my stomach and prepared to say something biting to the old man. Then I took two deep breaths and let the anger drain out with the expelled air. What did it matter what Karlman thought, anyway?

'Thank you, Professor,' I said, 'but I didn't come to discuss my ideas. I came to ask about Howard Carter. How well did you know him?'

'Well enough to know he was a bloody fool,' Karlman said, still chuckling. 'He should never have opened Tutankhamen's tomb. There was a curse on it – Carter and Carnarvon knew that, but they went right on and unsealed the thing and let the furies out of Pandora's box.'

'How did they know?'

'Carter found a tablet outside the sealed door before he opened it, with an inscription reading: "Death will Slay with Swift Wings all who disturb the sleep of the King." He was afraid he'd be accused of grave-robbing, and there'd be a fearful hullabaloo, so he got rid of it. But he knew there was a curse all right. There were unseen watchmen in that tomb. They pooh-poohed it and forgot the ancient Egyptians were masters of occult powers for at least five thousand years – time to develop techniques unknown to modern science. That was arrogant, and the arrogance cost Lord Carnarvon his life and almost a couple of dozen others theirs.'

'You mean there were other deaths in connection with Tutankhamen's tomb?'

'My God, yes. My, you have been keeping your head in the sand, my dear Mr Ross. First off, Carnarvon's brother Aubrey, a former British intelligence officer, who was with Carnarvon when he opened the sarcophagus, dropped dead while in a state of "temporary insanity". His sister, Lady Elizabeth Carnarvon, who was also there, died of another mysterious "mosquito bite" – not malaria, note. George Jay Gould, an American millionaire friend of Carnarvon, was struck dead by an "unidentified illness" while in the Valley of the Kings. Woolf Joel, another rich socialite friend of Carnarvon's, was drowned in the Nile when he tumbled off his yacht at Luxor. Walter Morrison, the Reuters correspondent who'd secretly inveigled himself into the tomb, was found dead in his London club for no obvious reason. The same year, a distinguished British radiologist, Sir Archibald Reid, succumbed to another "unidentified illness" while preparing to X-ray Tutankhamen's mummy. The same year the professor of Egyptology at the University of Leeds, England, H. G. Evelyn-White, who had worked in the Valley of the Kings, committed suicide, leaving a note stating that there was a curse on him. Two years later, Georges Benedite and Michel Cassanova, two prominent French Egyptologists who had excavated in the Valley of the Kings, dropped dead suddenly. Professor Laffleur, a friend of Howard Carter's, died the day after entering the tomb. Two of Carter's assistants, Mace and Carver, died shortly afterwards, and an Egyptian Prince, Ali Fahmi Bey, was shot outside the tomb. In 1929, Richard Bethell, Carter's personal secretary, was found dead in a flat in London, and his father, Lord Westbury, promptly leapt to his death from a seven-storey building, leaving a note which read: "I really cannot stand any more horrors." And that's only a few of them. In all, twenty-two people directly connected with Tutankhamen's tomb were dead within six years, and almost all of them died under inexplicable circumstances. Statistically, the odds against that are phenomenal. Look at Carnarvon – the first one of the series – he supposedly died of a "mosquito bite". Now, even in an era without antibiotics, that wasn't common; everyone who visits the tropics is bitten by mosquitoes at some time. Yet we find his sister dying of the same thing.'

'What about Carter himself, though?' I asked. 'He remained spectacularly alive, yet he was the one who'd actually unsealed the tomb.'

'I knew Carter towards the end of his life. He claimed he'd

never believed the curse story, but he was a most unhappy man. Miserable as sin. He wished to God he'd never found the tomb. Actually, he and Carnarvon quarrelled bitterly even before they'd opened the last sarcophagus, and weren't on speaking terms when Carnarvon was taken ill. Carter lived until 1939, but he died a friendless loner. While he was still working in the Valley of the Kings he complained frequently of paralysing attacks of dizziness, physical debilitation, hallucinations and blinding headaches. As soon as he had completed his work on the tomb he became seriously ill and never properly recovered. In the end, Tutankhamen killed him too.'

'Why did he fall out with Carnarvon?'

'The official story was that they disagreed over press coverage and over the ultimate destiny of the treasures. Carnarvon wanted to give the whole story to the London *Times*. Carter wanted to keep it hush-hush. Carnarvon wanted to take the lion's share of the treasure home to England but Carter thought it should remain in Egypt.' I remembered the expressions of mutual distrust on the faces of Carter and Carnarvon in the newspaper photograph Julian had left me.

'Which of them won?' I enquired.

'Carter did. After Carnarvon died, of course, opposition crumbled. The press was bridled and fed only titbits. And of course the Tutankhamen collection remains in Egypt to this day.'

'Tell me, Professor, did you ever happen to come across a character called Orde Wingate – a young army officer, stationed in Khartoum in the 1930s?'

For a second, Karlman's eyes narrowed. He paused as if making an effort to remember. Then he smiled and the atlas of lines on his face reformed into an alternative configuration. 'We're talking sixty years ago, Mr Ross. Long before you were even born. It's awfully hard . . . Wingate . . . yes, I think I did run into him. One of those damned Zerzura Club people who tooled about the desert looking for lost cities, with their light aircraft and Model-T Fords. Never had much to do with them myself.'

'Did Wingate ever meet Howard Carter?'

'I wouldn't know. Carter met a lot of people. He was the hero of the time. Didn't do him much good, though. He lived his last six years in agony.'

'And you explain all this by a curse?'

'However you define it, yes. The ancient Egyptians themselves regarded the tombs with awe because they believed the astral bodies of the dead lived within them. We in the West dismiss such beliefs because they run contrary to our so-called scientific-rationalist-humanist tradition. That tradition is only five hundred years old, and it is only another set of schemata, Mr Ross, only another set of subjective beliefs. Scientific objectivity is a fallacy. You know Heisenberg's principle – in an observed system the observer interacts? That spells the end of science, Mr Ross: it pricks the bubble of the whole rationalist myth. Uncertainty. If the observer is always part of the equation, then the observer manipulates the fabric of reality. And if the observer manipulates reality, then what we see out there is really in here.' He tapped his head with a spiny finger. 'So we come back full circle to the unconscious mind – the irrational mind. Science pretends that human behaviour can be governed by reason: any glimpse of history will show you what a nonsense that is. In the human unconscious there are occult forces, forces of unbelievable power, capable of swatting aside whole races and populations as if they were flies. Look at the great genocides of this century: Hitler's Germany, Pol Pot's Cambodia, the Chinese in Tibet. Do you really think that the death and torture of millions of innocent people could be the product of rationality, Mr Ross? The Egyptians did not subscribe to our rationalist myth, yet they were advanced technologically and highly sophisticated. They had thousands of years to develop powers of which we know nothing. I am utterly convinced that they knew how to concentrate round a mummy certain dynamic forces which are beyond our comprehension. Have you ever heard of Hermes Trismegistus, Mr Ross? The ancient Egyptians were a nation of magicians and sorcerers.'

Karlman leaned forward. A beam of light caught his eyes, and they gleamed yellow for a moment, like the eyes of a cat. 'And you know what, my boy?' he whispered. 'It's all starting up again. It's already started with your friend Dr Cranwell, the mad desert explorer. That's why you're really here, isn't it, Mr Ross. You already suspect there's a link between Cranwell's death and Tutankhamen. You mark my words: Cranwell's death won't be the last. Oh yes, it's all starting up again.'

I looked at Karlman. The old man's face was contorted into a horrific mask and there was no mistaking the emotion written there: it was glee.

I got up. 'Thanks, Professor,' I said. 'I'd better go.'

'So soon. Oh, I'm so sorry. And we were getting along just dandy, weren't we.' He darted out a hand and grasped me by the fingers. 'Don't be offended by what I said about your ideas, Mr Ross,' he said. 'You were head and shoulders above the rest of the sheep. You weren't there but you were getting warm. What did that rat Rifad give as his excuse for sacking you? Some trifling article or something I expect. That was a pretext, Ross. You found something at Madinat Habu, remember? The Siriun Stela? That's the real reason they gave you the bullet, not for any third-rate article you wrote.'

I was appalled by Karlman's demented expression, by the alarming undercurrents in his talk. I tried to pull away, but his clutch was unexpectedly strong. Karlman leaned over until he was speaking almost directly into my ear. 'One last word for you before you go, my boy,' he whispered. 'Look out for the Eye of Ra.'

His repellent low chuckling followed me to the door.

I pushed through crowds of Fellahin and flocks of fat sheep outside Imbaba market, and found a public telephone. I dialled Doc Barrington's number and almost at once the phone was picked up: 'Who?' I heard Doc's voice demand.

'It's Jamie,' I said, 'I found Aurel Karlman. The guy's a fruitcake –'

'Jamie?' Doc cut in, gasping, 'Jamie, is that you? Where are you?'

'Imbaba. Is anything wrong?'

'Get here at once, Jamie,' she said, 'I've just had a call from Julian Cranwell.'

14

IN A WAY, RESURRECTION IS THE key to all the great religions. Christ rose from the dead after three days to show that there's eternal life in God, the Buddhists and Hindus believe that the dead soul is reborn into another life. The ancient Egyptians saw the cosmos as all of one piece and that in each human being there's part that's mortal and part that's an eternal aspect of the whole. It's the mortal, conscious aspect of you that makes you 'you' – Fred, Dick or Sarah – as opposed to anybody else. It's also that part that dies, while the other part, the immortal aspect, lives on for ever through the web of life. That aspect isn't 'you' as an individual, but an unconscious entity that dwells in darkness, in primeval waters, unaware and unindividuated – a collective, non-sentient force. If you like, the unconscious, immortal you is a tree that grows for ever, while the conscious, mortal you is the leaf. Only individual human consciousness can break out of the darkness by its awareness of being, a quality symbolised in Egyptian myth by the Eye of Ra. Since I reached manhood, I've never believed in the survival of personality after death, only survival of the eternal, unconscious aspect of human life. We'd scoffed at the idea of Julian's resurrection, but now, it seemed, he'd risen from the dead after three days, and the Eye of Ra was open.

The peephole twinkled, and Doc opened the door cautiously. She was distraught and pale, her eyes shot with red. She closed the door and held me tightly. 'It was him,' she sobbed. 'I swear it was Julian's voice on the phone.'

'OK. OK, Doc. Let's sit down and talk about this.'

I put my arm around her and led her to the balcony. She sat down heavily, sniffed, and dried her eyes with a tissue. I went to the fridge and poured us both a glass of iced water from the carafe. Doc took the drink gratefully.

'How do you know it was Julian?'

'One, because it sounded like Julian. You know, that kind of nasal intonation Julian had – came from blocked sinuses. And that touch of Yorkshire.'

'Cumbria.'

'Whatever. It was unmistakable. Two, he said he was Julian. "Doc," he said, "its me, Julian. Don't be scared. There's been a mistake. I've got to talk to Ross. Is he there?" – you know how he always called you "Ross", the formal English way, as if you were always his apprentice. He asked if you were there. I said "No" and he said "Tell him to meet me tonight at the Great Pyramid: he knows the place. Just past moonrise, seven thirty, and I'll explain everything. Tell him there's been a mistake. I'll explain everything tonight. Sorry Doc, got to go. Bye," and that was it. Jamie, I swear it was him.'

'OK, but if it was, who was that I saw at the pyramids?'

'Someone who looked like Julian –'

'– And who had Julian's passport. If it wasn't Julian, someone was trying to make damned sure I believed that Julian was dead, and was ready to go as far as bumping off a Julian look-alike.'

'Perhaps you weren't the object of the exercise. Perhaps whoever it was wanted to persuade the world that Julian was dead, and if you were convinced, then everyone else would be.'

'Who would have a motive for doing that?'

'Julian would. He was in trouble. He was afraid for his life. He had something others wanted, maybe the Kolpos translation of the directions to Zerzura, maybe the *ushabtis*. Maybe he staged his own death in order to escape whoever or whatever was after him.'

'And whacked an innocent man who happened to look like him? Hardly Julian!'

'We don't know the victim was murdered. The police said it was a heart attack. What if Julian just came across a heart-attack victim who happened to look like him and substituted him.'

'Doc, that implies so many coincidences, it's crazy, but it's not the craziest thing I've heard today. Karlman told me quite seriously that Carter and Carnarvon unleashed powerful psychic forces when they unlocked Tutankhamen's tomb – forces responsible for the death of Carnarvon and twenty odd others. He said it was all starting up again and implied these same dark forces had killed Julian.'

'*Ahriman,*' Doc said.

'What?'

'Dark forces – *Ahriman* – the Enemy of Light. It's a term from the Avesta, the Holy Text of the Zoroastrians dating back to about 600 BC. Steiner borrowed it in the early decades of this century. He was a clairvoyant who maintained that there was a secret battle going on between these unseen demonic forces – *Ahriman* – and the "Cohorts of Michael": the Forces of Light. He wrote that the objective of *Ahriman* was to take over the stream of human evolution and to merge with it, developing a whole new species which would be devoid of all the features we value most.'

'You mean like lying, murdering and cheating?'

'Cynicism doesn't become you, darling. All hocus-pocus aside, it looks as though Julian could still be alive and kicking.'

'Perhaps we'll find out tonight.'

'If you're going to meet him, I'm coming with you.'

'No, Doc. It might be dangerous. I don't want you getting involved.'

'Listen to the Great White Knight. I was doing surveillance jobs before you were out of nappies. It's about time I got off my fat backside and got into the field again. There's been too much sitting around since Ronnie died – and anyway, you need back-up on this.'

*   *   *

It was almost sunset when Doc motored me towards Giza in her old Peugeot 504 station-wagon. As we crawled at a snail's pace up the long boulevard of the Shari' al-Ahram, heavy with shadows, I watched the massed crowds on the pavements, the sea of cars almost bumper to bumper, the faceless apartment blocks and hotels, and remembered why the Hawazim hate the city. They call it 'the place where trails run out'. In the desert you can read everything on the surface, just like reading a book. In the city it's all noise and smells and perversions, and the trails get confused. When I was a boy I knew Hawazim who'd never been in a city in their lives. Some had been once, and never wanted to go back. Some of them had never even been in a motor-car. I've often wondered what it would have been like to stay with the Hawazim, to really have been one of them. When my mother disappeared, my father was so cut up he just wanted to get out of the country. He took me off to England and I became a proper little English public schoolboy. Of course, I was never really accepted, and in a way I couldn't blame the other boys. I had strange habits. It took me years to get completely used to living inside all the time, for instance, and once or twice they caught me kipping on the school playing-fields. It was always an effort for me to remember not to eat with my hands. The irony was that I wanted nothing more than to be like them – I wanted to be Mister-Middle-England, with an Oxford drawl, blue eyes and golden hair, instead of this dark-haired, coffee-coloured stranger with a pierced upper ear. I wanted to be the kid who won the *Victor Ludorum* shield for athletics and played rugger for the First XV, not 'that wog' or 'that bloody Gyppo'. Children are more bigoted than their parents, or perhaps they're just less hypocritical. At first I got pushed around. I just took it, up to a certain level, and then one day, after the form bully locked me in the cricket shed, I exploded. I got hold of a cricket bat, smashed a window, jumped out and went straight for him. He was a big fellow, a rugger player and all that, but he wasn't expecting the fury – or the cricket bat. I bashed him with it until his arm was broken. 'I was absolutely astonished,' the headmaster told my father when he explained to him why I was to be expelled. 'James always seemed such a quiet boy.' It was lucky the other boy's parents weren't pressing charges, he said, otherwise I might have ended up in borstal. The experience had such a devastating effect on me that as an undergraduate I took up the out-of-fashion sport of boxing, to sublimate what a psychiatrist called my 'latent anger', and it was for the same reason I learned deep-breathing techniques at a yoga class. For all that, though, I'd found out something valuable about conflict – that it's not how big you are that counts.

The pyramids loomed massively out of the dusk. At the Mena House Oberoi the lights were already up and there was a flurry of activity as cars and lamplit gharries came and went at the gates. We drove past the hotel up to the gates of the Necropolis, where a knot of Bedouin camel-men were gathered, waiting for the sunset prayer. Doc pulled up just as the last embers of the sun dissolved into a whorl of cloud across the desert, and I stepped out of the car to watch the Arabs line up behind their imam for the prayer. Each man had simply laid his woven prayer-mat before him in the sand, and they bowed in unison, reciting the familiar formulas, kneeling and touching the earth with the forehead and the bridge of the nose. I felt an unexpected itch to join them. It wasn't that I was a fanatical Muslim – even the Hawazim were really only Muslims in name – it was more of an aesthetic thing. I knew the words by heart from childhood, and I'd always loved the tranquil simplicity of the sunset prayer. It was simply the ritual which appealed to me. The Arabs repeated the sequence, and as I watched, I realised that the imam, the prayer-leader, was Sulayman, the Hazmi tracker whom Hammoudi had assaulted. In a few moments the prayer was over. The Arabs were sitting on their mats, turning their heads right and left and shaking hands with those each side in the ritual gesture of brotherhood. I walked over to the old man and shook hands. 'Peace be on you,' I said.

'And on you be peace. I was thinking about you and your friend today, Omar.'

'Oh?'

'Yes. I was wondering whether he was a kind of shaman, an

amnir, a man who'd made a pact with the *Jinns* in return for magical powers. Did he have magical powers, Omar?'

Amnir. I tweaked an image of the word over in my mind. The Hawazim, my mother's people, were led by men who supposedly had a gift for precognition, who were adept at navigating the tribe through the deserts of time. I'd scoffed at the idea as a child, but when I thought of Julian's uncanny intuition, I had to admit that he'd possessed a similar gift.

'He saw things that other men didn't see,' I said. 'If that's magic, then yes, he did. But even so, that doesn't explain his death does it?'

'Are you sure he's dead?'

'You saw the body as well as I did.'

'*Jinns* can disguise a man's face. Are you certain it was your friend?'

I was starting to feel uneasy again. The talk of *Jinns* brought back frightening memories from childhood that I'd kept safely under lock and key for years, and Sulayman's suspicions seemed to be coming perilously close to my own. It was true that features of the corpse had been wildly distorted, and since the time I'd seen Julian dead, he'd been spotted alive by a hunchback and had actually spoken to Doc on the phone. His body wasn't in the morgue, and as far as I could tell, it never had been.

'Look, Uncle,' I said, 'I want to get on to the plateau.'

'But it's night. The place is closed and it's full of guards.'

'But you know a way round the guards, don't you?'

'I do.'

'Then show me.'

'If we get stopped you know what it will mean?'

'Prison?'

'Naah.' The old man began to bleat with laughter. 'It will mean coughing up at least fifty pounds. I hope you've got money. These Tourist Police don't come cheap.'

Doc wanted to see the action. She insisted on coming with me, and it took me a long time to persuade her to stay in the car – we might need a fast getaway, I said. Finally she agreed to remain parked at the entrance, while I went off with Sulayman. We made our way along a narrow track passing under the embankment on the northern periphery of the plateau, and eventually the security lights at the gate were far behind, leaving us in darkness. The old man paced on rapidly with the raking stride of one brought up in the desert. I scurried after him, surveying the sky, noting the constellations: the Plough, Draco, Orion – and there was Sirius burning brightly, aligned with the three-star cluster of Orion's belt. Behind us lay the surreal blaze of Cairo, and in front a softer glow of gold creeping along the edge of the desert. I knew that moonrise was only seconds away. Suddenly, the huge, bloated ball of the moon shot up from beneath the horizon, flooding the world with light. It rose rapidly as I watched, deflating and growing whiter as it climbed. The old man turned and clambered up the embankment. I followed him. From the top I saw the great arrowheads of the pyramids etched in darkly by the flux of moonlight. Sulayman caught my arm. 'This is as far as I go,' he said in a whisper.

'Why?'

'This is a place of the Dead. It's full of spirits. Stay away from it, Omar, that's my advice.'

'I can't. I told you why.'

'All right. Just follow the track. It'll take you straight to the Great Pyramid. But be careful. Go in the safekeeping of the Divine Spirit.'

I clasped his thin, hard hand, then set off up the track without looking back. Somehow his talk of *Jinns* had affected me. I'd been working in tombs and burial grounds half my adult life and hadn't thought anything of it, but now, almost for the first time since childhood, I began to sense dark and inexplicable forces moving around me. There were, I knew, aspects of my early years in the desert that lay cloaked and hidden inside, and tonight I had an unnameable sense of something glimpsed long ago in a dream but not quite seen, a feeling lurking on the very precipice of terror. The silence was eerie. The crunch of my own feet, then, surely, someone else's footfalls following my own. I halted and listened. Nothing. I continued. There were the footfalls again. I stopped once more. There was an ominous low whistling – the wind, perhaps. Then I distinctly heard voices. Suddenly, I realised I was in the place where I'd seen Julian's dead body. There was a fragment of white tape, fluttering from a stick. I glanced at my watch: seven twenty-eight. The alleged Julian Cranwell had told Doc I'd know the place. This had to be it. I stood still and listened. I caught footfalls again, and whispering voices. Deep in the shadows, far away, I glimpsed the momentary play of flashlights – Tourist Police guards, I thought, doing their rounds. For a few moments there was utter silence, then a voice, very near, whispered 'Ross . . .'

Even though I'd been expecting Julian, I jumped violently, shocked by the familiarity of the voice. Nasal syllables. A touch of north country. Behind me, twenty metres away, a tall, bulky figure, the size and shape of Julian Cranwell, had emerged from the shadows. 'Julian?' I said.

'You should have come alone, Ross.'

'I did.'

'No.' He pointed. I glanced back to see two flashlight beams coming directly towards us. There was a scuff of feet and I looked back again to see the bulky figure leaping off into the shadows. 'Julian,' I called, desperately, 'Julian, come back, for God's sake.' I began to run. Julian was making for the maze of small tombs on the western side of the pyramid, running wildly, faster than I'd ever seen him run in his previous life. In a moment he was lost among the tombs. 'Julian. Julian,' I called. Suddenly I heard rapid footsteps behind me. The beam of a powerful torch hit me full in the face. 'Stop or I'll shoot,' a voice bellowed in Arabic. Three uniformed men carrying shotguns emerged from the night in front of me. Blinded, I cast about for a way of escape, but almost at once a thick arm from behind seized me around the neck so violently that my glasses were flung off. I was dragged roughly to my knees. A pulse of sheer indignation swept through me. I turned my head instinctively to the crook of the elbow, pulled on it until it gave, then snapped back and threw one of the most vicious punches I'd thrown since I boxed at university. My fist connected with soft tissue and there was a shiver of bone and an anguished scream of '*Allah!*' Other arms were on me now, and as I struggled, a cold hard object was forced against the side of my head. 'Don't move,' someone growled, 'or I'll blow your fucking brains out.' I was forced down into the sand until my eyes, nostrils and mouth were full of it, and I choked for breath. My arms were pinioned behind me and handcuffs clamped clumsily on my wrists. A hand wrenched my hair, jerking my head backwards out of the sand and I half turned to look into the face of Captain Hammoudi, holding the muzzle of his .44 Magnum Ruger revolver flush against my temple. There is something very sobering about having a loaded gun pressed to your head and knowing that only the slightest wiggle of a forefinger divides you from oblivion. 'Well, look at what fell from the stars,' Hammoudi said, grinning. 'Mr Omar James Ross. I think it's time for those questions, now, don't you?'

15

THE POLICE STATION THEY TOOK ME to stood on the banks of the Nile at Bulaq, a crumbling place of gypsum and cinderblock with warped double-doors opening into a courtyard. The yard was full of sloppily dressed black-jackets who grinned at me truculently as I was hustled in. They hurried me down corridors with dark Rorschach smears on the walls that might have been dried blood, past nameless offices with half-opened doors where men smoked and babbled aimlessly. A door opened and I was shoved into a windowless room with an uneven floor and walls that were visibly disintegrating. An old table and three upright chairs stood under a single low-watt light-bulb. They sat me down hard on one of the chairs, unlocked my cuffs and then cuffed me to it. The door slammed and I was alone. I looked around the room as the bulb swung slowly, sending a cradle of light rocking from side to side. It was airless and desolate and smelt of urine. I noticed what looked like claw-marks on the wall opposite me as if some fear-crazed, hopeless soul had tried to scrape his way through the stone. For a moment there was silence, and then someone in the next room screamed. It was a naked cry of such pain and anguish that I shuddered. There was another scream, even more intense than the first, and then a broken voice sobbing and begging for mercy. There is nothing like hearing another human scream to set the pulse racing. I guess it must be something in the collective unconscious acquired over millions of years of huddling in dark places hoping the predator would go for your neighbour and not yourself. When the door opened and Captain Hammoudi marched in minutes later, I have to admit I was well and truly terrified.

Hammoudi was accompanied by a younger plain-clothes man, a broad-shouldered, heavy-jowled peasant with a look of generic aggressiveness, whose nose was covered with a clumsily taped bandage, seeping blood. His eyes held mine glassily for a moment, and I realised it was the officer whose nose I'd punched. As they sat down, Hammoudi slapped a blue folder on the table. He lit a cigarette. The sobbing from the other room came again, and Hammoudi listened attentively. The bandaged officer smiled with apparent enjoyment. 'They've got a terrorist in there,' Hammoudi said, 'a Muslim Brother. Attached to the electrodes. Swore he wouldn't give away the names of his cell . . . now he's begging to be allowed to. Nothing like pain to break down loyalties. Sergeant Mustafa here wanted to give you the same treatment. I said no, we're not savages after all, and Mr Ross is only too happy to help us. I hope I'm right, Ross, because Sergeant Mustafa is very persuasive.'

'Why am I being held?' I demanded.

Hammoudi rocked back on his chair and blew smoke at me. 'I don't think you quite understand the situation, Ross,' he said. 'You are under arrest. I ask the questions, and you answer politely and to the point. If I decide to let you go, you walk, if I decide to hold you, you rot, and if I decide to hand you over to Sergeant Mustafa here, you'll join our friend next door.'

Mustafa fixed his glassy eyes on me as if willing me to say something provocative.

'Sergeant Mustafa is an expert at making people talk,' Hammoudi went on. 'He enjoys it. Sees it like a contest. Or an art. He's been known to cut thumbs and fingers off with a razor, one at a time. Even if they talk he continues to cut – always likes to complete a job once he's started.'

'I'm a British citizen,' I said, 'and I have a right to a lawyer and the presence of the British Consul.'

Hammoudi chortled nastily. Mustafa grinned. 'Very convenient to pick and choose your passport, isn't it?' he smiled. Then the smile faded abruptly. 'Just where the hell do you think you are? Rights are a luxury of the West. You have no rights here.'

'Could you at least unlock the handcuffs. I'm not likely to run away.'

Hammoudi considered the request for a moment, then nodded to Mustafa. The sergeant sauntered over to me resentfully and unlocked the cuffs. The steel had left painful red weals on my wrists which I rubbed slowly.

'All right,' I said. 'I've got nothing to hide.'

Hammoudi opened the file and began to read. 'So,' he said, 'you are Omar James Ross, born in a tent near Kharja, Egypt, 1960, son of Dr Calvin Ross, eminent British anthropologist, and Maryam bint Salim of the Hawazim. Must have been an odd match, that – the English scholar and the illiterate Bedouin woman. I'm astonished your father ever got permission to roam around the Western Desert during the Nasserite period, so soon after the English dropped paratroops on the Suez Canal.'

'My father made it clear to President Nasser that he sympathised in principle with Arab Nationalism,' I said. 'He thought the whole Suez fiasco a blunder and a national disgrace for the British.'

'How noble,' Hammoudi sneered. 'But then he was a rich man, wasn't he. He could afford to believe what he wanted. Inherited money from your grandfather, who was a . . . soapmaker . . . am I right?'

'Starlight Soap,' I said.

'Aha, washes the world clean. Washes away the sins of the dirty colonialists who made money out of people like me and mine. That business still in the family?'

'No. My grandfather sold it years ago, before I was born. My father never had an interest in making soap. He had a feel for the desert and its people. He loved the Hawazim because they were the tribe most marginalised, and downtrodden.'

'So there he was doing research on the Bedouin in the Western Desert when he met and fell passionately in love with the beautiful Maryam. Converted to Islam – damned fool. Only a year later you popped into the world. You spent your first seven years with them, and then your father sent you to the International School in Cairo. You spent your holidays with your people at Kharja. When you were nine, your father went back to England, taking you with him. He never returned to Egypt, despite his sympathy with Arab Nationalism. What happened?'

'My mother disappeared.'

'You mean the beautiful Maryam ran off with someone else? Got fed up with the stiff *Afrangi*?'

'Never. Maryam disappeared on a journey in the desert in 1969. They said she'd been caught in a sandstorm, but her body was never found.'

'It certainly wasn't reported to the *Mukhabaraat* at Kharja.'

'Is that surprising? The Hawazim don't trust the *Mukhabaraat*. They never report anything.'

'The Hawazim are a bunch of savages who can't stand hard work. If I had my way I'd have them rounded up and set to drudge away in the fields, like my father and my father's father had to. That would soon change their attitude.'

'It's been tried.'

'Not hard enough. Anyway, you went to school in England. Four schools in five years . . . sounds like you couldn't settle . . .'

I was going to ask where on earth they had dug up all this information on me, but I stopped myself. Hammoudi was asking the questions. Whatever the case, they'd gone to some effort to get the stuff, an ominous indication that their interest in me was more than superficial.

'You were expelled from one school for beating another boy with a cricket bat,' Hammoudi went on, chuckling as if his theory had been proved correct, 'so, as we say in Asyut, *farkh al-batt 'awwam* – "the duck's offspring floats". Your father died of cancer in 1990. You went to St Antony's College, Oxford, to study Archaeology and Anthropology, but you left after your first year. Why? Did you beat up your professors with a cricket bat?'

'I had some disagreements.'

'Ha ha! Disagreements. You transferred to the School of Oriental and African Studies, London, where you did Ancient History and Archaeology. Good academic record, marred by subversive activities. You got into student politics. You have a police record – disorderly behaviour at a peace march; ooh and what's this, oh dear, Mr Ross – caught smoking cannabis in a public place. Tut-tut. Disgraceful. You were fined both times, and the university nearly threw you out. You were saved by your sporting record. You were in the university shooting team – crack shot with both a pistol and a rifle – surprising for a four-eyes like you.'

'My eyesight didn't deteriorate until I was in my twenties. Actually, I first learned to handle a rifle when I was five.'

'You also boxed for the University of London, very successfully it says here – hence Sergeant Mustafa's broken nose, no doubt.'

'It was a reflex action. I haven't hit anyone since I boxed in my student days.'

'I think you should apologise to Sergeant Mustafa for ruining his good looks. Sergeant Mustafa is very fond of the girls.'

I glanced at Mustafa, and almost had to stifle a laugh. He was red in the face and his eyes were moist. The bandage had been applied so haphazardly that it was on the point of falling to pieces, and blood was still dripping from his nose. 'I'm sorry,' I said. Mustafa nodded, but his eyes never lost their malevolent glaze.

'That's all right, then,' Hammoudi went on. 'Let's see. You graduated in 1982, nothing spectacular, and in 1983 you were first employed by the Egyptian Antiquities Service here as an Egyptologist, initially as assistant to Dr Julian Cranwell. Digs at Luxor, Karnak, Bahriyya oasis and other places. In 1987 you went back to Britain to take your Ph.D., but you gave it up and were back with the Service within the year. You began working as director of your own small digs at Amarna, Aswan, Madinat Habu, etcetera ... but your promotion was always blocked because of rows with the directorate.' He looked up and fixed me with an inquisitive stare, the kind of stare I'd had to endure too many times. 'Tell me, Ross,' he said, 'what are you? Are you one of us or one of them?'

'People have been trying to categorise me all my life,' I said. 'The kids at school, my colleagues, now you. I came to the conclusion a long time ago that there's no *them* – there's only *us*.'

'Yes, that liberal "we're-all-brothers-together" shit sounds so sweet from the high-horse of inherited money, doesn't it. There's always *them*, even in Egypt: you're rich, you're poor, you're a stupid *Sa'idi*, you're a dumb Fellah, you're a *kaffir* Copt, you're a treacherous Bedui – even a dirty Hazmi. Your problem, Ross, is that you've never belonged to anything. I've got your record from the Antiquities Service. You were a misfit there too. You were with Cranwell at Karnak and later at Bahriyya, where you helped him excavate the Temple of Ptah. Cranwell was the only one you would work with, but you fell out with even him in the end. You had your own programme, it says here, which you followed to the exclusion of everything else. Excellent field Egyptologist, it says, superb analyst, incisive mind, acute observer, photographic memory. Inclined to be individualistic. Not a good team-player. Difficult with colleagues and superiors, follows own initiative even if contrary to official policy. That's why you were never given a major dig, only minor ones. The directorate had you down as untrustworthy. They suspected that you massaged the evidence so that it supported your own theories – theories, it says here, that were often wildly improbable. Says you claimed to have found an 18th-Dynasty stela at Madinat Habu, which you were suspected of having forged. Is that why you were dismissed from the Service?'

I felt the blood rushing to my head. This was pure libel. I was tempted to open my mouth and deliver a vicious refutation, but it suddenly occurred to me that Hammoudi might be baiting me. I removed my glasses and rubbed them slowly on my shirt-cuff, forcing myself to breathe deeply three times. 'That's absolute nonsense,' I said.

'All right, then why were you dismissed?'

'My views were unacceptable.'

'And what are your views?'

'That ancient Egyptian civilisation is not indigenous, that it came to the Nile Valley from an older civilisation.'

Hammoudi snorted. 'You mean, like Atlantis?'

'If you want to call it that, yes.'

'I've heard that kind of rot from Westerners before. They can't stand to believe that our ancestors – *my* ancestors – developed a civilisation thousands of years ago when they were still cavemen. But then you're not really a Westerner, are you, Ross?'

'I'm not interested in political ideology, if that's what you mean. I work with facts.'

Hammoudi smiled grimly. 'Oh, really,' he said, 'then perhaps you can explain a fact to me. Why does it say here in your official record that you were dismissed for trafficking in stolen antiquities?'

For a moment I just stared at him dumbly. The idea of selling vital historical artefacts was as repugnant to me as to any serious archaeologist. I had always been absolutely scrupulous in recording my finds: unlike many, I didn't even keep small items out of nostalgia. 'That's preposterous,' I stammered. 'I never heard anything so ridiculous!'

'Then you deny that you were arrested at Cairo International Airport in 1992 carrying a statuette of the god Thoth in your luggage?'

I was about to deny it. Then I remembered. It was true, I had been stopped by Customs police on my way out of the country in '92 for carrying a Thoth statuette. It was the genuine article, dating back to Old Kingdom times, and quite valuable, but I'd explained that I was removing it only for academic purposes – actually for a lecture I was doing in London – and would be bringing it back.

'I wasn't arrested, only stopped at Customs,' I told him. 'It was a matter of not having the right form. Anyway, once I'd done the paperwork they let me take it, *and* I brought it back. It's now in the Egyptian Museum.'

'Says "arrested" in your record. No mention of you being allowed to take it, or bringing it back. Sounds to me as though you paid somebody a big *bakhshish*.'

'Listen, that piece is in the Egyptian Museum. Ask Abbas Rifad, the Director of the Antiquities Service. He catalogued it himself. Ask him, he'll support me.'

'I don't think so, Ross. You see, Rifad says he's the one who sacked you for illegal trafficking. See for yourself: his signature is on the report.'

'He's lying.'

'Really. What would be the point in that? Rifad tells me that he had grave suspicions of your friend Julian Cranwell, too. He couldn't prove anything, but Cranwell had some crooked friends, like Nikolai Kolpos, the Antiquities Dealer. We've been watching him for years.'

'What do you want, Captain Hammoudi?'

'What I *want*,' he said, standing up and walking around the desk with slow and insinuating menace, 'is for you to remember who is asking the questions here.'

He flicked another Cleopatra out of the packet and lit it, sucking the smoke in deeply, and blowing it towards my face in a long bluish jet.

'Why were you running around the Giza plateau at night?'

'I thought I might find some clues to Cranwell's death.'

'In the dark? Without even a torch. I might be a stupid *Sa'idi*, mister, but even I don't swallow that one.'

'All right. I thought I might find him alive.'

Hammoudi and Mustafa exchanged a glance. Then the Captain leaned over and fixed me with a hard stare. 'Cranwell is dead, Ross,' he said. 'He died of a heart attack at the pyramids.'

'His body isn't in the morgue.'

'Ah. I heard you'd been poking your nose in there. Dr Amin may look an idiot, but he's not. Did you really think he didn't see you running for the broom cupboard? Cranwell isn't in the morgue because his relatives requested the body immediately back in Britain.'

'What relatives?'

Hammoudi advanced towards me, eyes blazing. For a moment I thought he was actually going to hit me. 'There you are, asking damned questions again,' he said. 'Cranwell's body was shipped home by the British Consulate at the request of relatives. The case is closed.'

He picked up a yellow form from the file and held it before my eyes. It was an official request for the transfer of a body to the authority of the British Consulate. Julian Cranwell's name was clearly written on the form, which was stamped by the Consulate and signed personally by the British Consul, Melvin Renner. On the base of the form was an Arabic stamp and the words 'Transferred 1/4/95'.

I tried to maintain a nonchalant expression, but Hammoudi knew I was crushed.

'We don't like people launching private investigations here,' he said, slapping the form down on the table so hard that I jumped. 'Cranwell is dead. Died of a heart attack. His body has already been shipped home. The case is closed. Got it?'

'Yes, Captain.'

'Now get out and go home. Go back to England, where you belong. If you belong anywhere. Let me get one sniff of your meddling again, and you'll be where that poor sod is next door. Got it? Good – piss off!'

Sergeant Mustafa dragged me to my feet. As we paused for Hammoudi to open the door, he said: 'Actually I feel sorry for you, Ross. The truth is that you're neither one of us nor one of them. You're nothing. You'll always be nothing.'

Mustafa marched me to the exit, back down the corridors smeared with dark stains. Just before we reached the main door he suddenly swung me into a dark entrance. He forced me up against the wood and before I could react, delivered two stinging punches into my stomach. The breath gushed out of me, and as I staggered, he caught me by the hair, wrenched my head down and kicked me viciously in the ribs, once with each foot. Then he jerked me up again. 'So you're sorry!' he grunted, 'I'll make you sorrier, *Afrangi* bastard. That's for ruining my nose!' He gave me another two kicks in the groin, and four rabbit-punches in the kidneys before he threw me out into the street.

16

Doc's 504 was parked inconspicuously in the shadows when I reeled out of the police station into the night. Mustafa's kicks had been delivered with expert force and, I suspected, long practice. I wondered if a rib was broken. I'd clocked Doc's car even before she opened the door, and I slumped into the front seat painfully. 'You look terrible,' she said. 'What did they do to you, Jamie?'

'Bastards!' I said. 'Don't ask. Just drive.'

The lights of the Corniche went past in a dream. Doc drove in silence, with continual side-glances at my red and swollen wrists – glances I ignored. My ribs stung like hell every time I took a deep breath. My balls ached. But it wasn't the physical pain that hurt me so much: I was enough of a Bedui to accept Mustafa's right to revenge. What really hurt was Hammoudi's last sledge-hammer remark: 'You're nothing, Ross. You'll always be nothing.'

My self-esteem must have rested on a very slim foundation. All my life I'd been struggling to convince myself that I was something, but I'd never really succeeded, never really felt that I belonged. I *was* as exotic to my Hawazim cousins as I'd been to the other kids at school. With the instinct of the torturer Hammoudi had winkled out my weakness with hardly any effort. He was right. I'd never quite found out who was 'us' and who 'them'. I knew deep down that the decision to take up Egyptology had been a quest to combine the two parts of me, to find out who I really was, as if you could examine your past, your antecedents with the sort of supposedly 'objective' view I was taught at school and university. There I'd been, peeling away at the layers of the past, always finding another layer beneath, always thinking that one day I'd come to the point where I could say, 'This is it, this is where I began.' I suppose I'd realised long ago that no such point existed. A sense of belonging couldn't be proved by scientific objectivity: it had to be felt, it had to be believed. Right now I believed that I was nothing and no one, and tonight not even my usual ability to focus on hard data could turn my thoughts away from a despairing sense of self-contempt.

At Doc's flat I wouldn't let her touch my wrists or look at my ribs. I locked myself in my small room and threw myself on the bed. A migraine was coming on, but I didn't call Doc for help. I decided to let it ride out, to remind me that I was nothing and not worth treating. I lay there for hours, staring at the ceiling and moaning quietly to myself, while the nauseating visual effects gave way to searing pain. Once or twice I heard Doc rapping softly on the door, saying, 'Jamie, are you all right?' But I ignored her. Even Doc was the enemy. Why the hell had I come? For a moment Julian's problem had shown me a way out of myself, out of the sloughs of depression I'd fallen into in Britain. For a moment it had restored to me a sense of purpose. Now that purpose had gone. I no longer knew whether Julian was alive or dead, and part of me no longer cared. Just as I no longer cared about my unconventional views on the origins of Egyptian civilisation. 'I deal with facts,' I'd told Hammoudi, but in my heart I had known it was a lie. Hadn't I actually developed those views to undermine the apparent certainty of an establishment I'd never felt myself part of? I wanted so much to belong, but only on my terms, only by being me.

I drifted into a kind of sleep, dreaming of the day Ahmad wald Mukhtar, my cousin, and I had ridden out on camels to Burj at-Tuyur, the 'Tower of Birds', a lone knoll of limestone in the desert where flocks of quail roosted on their arduous journey south. The Hawazim sometimes set up nets to catch the small birds, which they considered a great delicacy; by the time they reached this latitude, anyway, they were exhausted and almost tumbled into the nets. I had no interest in catching quail, but I was interested to see the lanner falcons that occasionally flew this way to hunt them, and more especially in the addax which were sometimes seen around these parts. Even in my childhood the addax were scarce. The Hawazim would shoot an addax on sight for its meat, and a thirsty traveller would drink the gastric juices from its stomach. The desert was littered with their horns, stuck upright in the sand to announce the hunter's small conquest. You couldn't tell if the horns had been there for years or generations.

That day we had seen no addax or lanners, nor even a quail, but we had camped near the hill, under a sky electric with stars. Ahmad had watched them, no less entranced than myself until I, anxious to show off my school-bred knowledge, asked him, 'What are the stars?'

My cousin had looked at me in surprise. He was a squat youth, enormously powerful but immensely good natured. I'm sure he guessed that I was showing off, but anyway he laughed. 'The stars are the stars,' he said. 'They are lights in the sky. The Divine Spirit made them. That's all there is to know about stars.'

For a moment I'd really been tempted to demonstrate my superior grasp of modern physics, to show him what a bumpkin he was, but his humility stopped me. I knew suddenly that, in his way, Ahmad was right. The stars were lights in the sky, made by God, and that was all you needed to know. The Hawazim had no need for physics. They knew why everything was there without being told. Everything around them was God's work. Their universe was a manifestation of the Divine Spirit. It struck me then how wonderful it must be to live in a world of certainties. The Hawazim knew who they were. They knew why they were here. By other standards they were ignorant, yet they had a sense of meaning, a sense of purpose, a sense of belonging to the earth which reduced my intellectual knowledge to a mere shadow.

The Hawazim had no doubts. They rarely questioned. But like it or not my schooling had condemned me to endless uncertainty. Just before dawn I awoke suddenly with a pair of questions demanding resolution. First, how had Hammoudi known I would be at the pyramids last night, when no one was aware of my rendezvous but Doc and the alleged Julian Cranwell? Second, and even more important to me, why had Abbas Rifad lied about the reason for my dismissal from the Antiquities Service? The more I thought about Rifad's behaviour the more furious I became. I have a memory like a tape-recorder, especially for conversations, and I can recall the exact words people used years afterwards as if they had been carved in my head with a knife. I remembered my last meeting with Rifad and felt the same bitter taste in my mouth that I always felt when I thought about that interview. Rifad had called me in from my dig at Heliopolis and I'd arrived at his office in the National Museum in Tahrir Square actually believing – poor fool that I was – that I must at last be due for promotion. To tell the truth, I'd never liked Rifad, and he knew it. Karlman had put his finger on it when he'd called him a pen-pusher. He was a small, plump, balding man with a big ego and a pompous style. It wasn't quite true that he'd never got his hands dirty on a dig, but his field-work had certainly been minimal, and always where there were bright lights and TV cameras and celebrity guests. Everyone in the Service knew he was more interested in politics than Egyptology.

When he called me into his office, he was holding a recent issue of *The Antiquarian Digest* between thumb and forefinger as if it was a fragment of rotten fish. 'Mr Ross,' he said, '*Ahlan wa sahlan*. There is a piece in this magazine entitled: "Was Egyptian Civilisation Created by Refugees from Atlantis?" It has your name on it.'

'It should do, it's my piece.'

'So you don't deny writing it?'

'Why should I?'

'Well, ahem, let's say – and I am being tactful here, you understand – that the piece is not worthy of you, and not worthy of the Antiquities Service.'

'Why not?' I said. 'For a start it bears a question mark, and secondly it's a perfectly valid view. Egyptian legend is packed with references to strangers who came from afar bearing gifts of knowledge. Take Thoth, for instance. He's said to have invented the measurement of time. Accurate measurement of time is one of the main building-blocks of civilisation, and in the legends, Thoth is said to have brought this skill from overseas. If the legend is based on fact – as many legends are – it suggests that superior knowledge came to the Nile Valley from a sophisticated civilisation which *preceded* ancient Egypt, but which is now lost to history.'

'You mean like Atlantis?'

'Look, Atlantis is just a story. I don't mean the "lost continent" which was said to exist beyond the Pillars of Hercules, but I'm using it as a generic title, a symbol for an ancient, unknown civilisation. If you'd read the piece properly you'd know that.'

'I really don't want to argue with you about this. I've warned you enough about your wacky theories. Don't you realise they're giving the Antiquities Service a bad name? You're making us a laughing-stock.'

'What about free intellectual exchange?' I protested. 'My theory is unconventional, but it's still a reasonable interpretation of the facts as we know them.'

'A laughing-stock,' Rifad insisted, ignoring me. 'This is a prestigious academic body and we can't put up with ridicule. You must retract this article publicly and at once!'

'I can't do that, Dr Rifad. I've been working on this theory for ten years.'

'Then I must have your immediate resignation, Mr Ross.'

And despite my arguments and Julian Cranwell's intervention, that had been that. Now that shit was telling the police that I was involved in illegal trafficking of antiquities. To be labelled 'lunatic' was bad enough, but for a self-respecting Egyptologist to be accused of stealing antiquities like some fifth-rate treasure-hunter was too much. By the time streaks of morning light were shooting in through gaps in the Persian blinds, my depression had given way to unadulterated anger. To my Hawazim ancestors reputation was a sacred thing, to be preserved by blood-letting. That's why I'd never begrudged Mustafa his kicks in the ribs. I knew I wasn't about to put a bullet through Rifad's skull, but at the very least

I would confront him with his lies. When Doc knocked at the door a few minutes later I flung it open to find her looking at me with deep concern etched on her face. How stupid it had been of me to think of her as 'the enemy'. Doc was the only friend I'd got.

'Sorry, Doc,' I said. 'For a while I just lost it.'

'That's all right, Jamie,' she said. 'I know the feeling, believe me. Let's have a look at those wrists.'

They were bulbous and painful, and when I removed my shirt Doc gasped at the reddish-purple bruise on my ribs. 'You ought to report this,' she said. 'I don't think there's anything broken, but those were really vicious kicks.'

'Delivered with a precision that came of long practice, I suspect,' I said. 'But no, Hammoudi and Mustafa would just deny it. The *Mukhabaraat* can get away with anything.'

While she washed my wounds and sprayed them with antiseptic, I described my encounter with Julian, and how the police had been waiting. I told her what Hammoudi had said about the transfer of the body to the British Consulate.

'That shit Melvin,' she said. '*Was* it Julian you saw?'

'It was Julian's voice and Julian's build, but I could not really swear it was him. I just wasn't near enough, and by God when he spotted the police he made off at a rate of knots. I never saw Jules move like that before. The Julian I knew only had two gears: "take it easy" and "stop".'

'Only the three of us – me, you and the man who rang me, whether or not it was Julian – knew about the meeting. I never breathed a word, darling, so that means you were set up.'

'I know. And if it *was* Julian, he deliberately set me up. Why?'

'I don't know what to believe any more.'

'Tell me, did you ever hear any rumours about why I was sacked from the Service?'

Doc stopped spraying and looked at me slightly embarrassed.

'Come on,' I said.

'Julian told me that Rifad sacked you over a difference of opinion,' she said, 'but there were stories flying about that you'd been caught trafficking in antiquities. Believe me, I never swallowed a word of it, darling.'

'It's a lie, Doc. It's a bloody fantasy from beginning to end. Christ, I'm going up to Rifad's office right now to throttle the bastard!'

'Do you think it's wise with Hammoudi breathing down your neck?'

'I don't give a toss about Hammoudi. This is my reputation. This is me.'

17

NINE ROADS INTERSECT IN MEDAN TAHRIR, 'Freedom Square', the very heart of Cairo city. In my youth, pedestrians had to dice with death to cross the multiple lanes of traffic, but now there are the Metro subways under pavements of concrete slabs and flower-gardens. Taxis came and went at the steps of the Nile Hilton, where tall security men in blue blazers stood by the frame of a metal-detector – a permanent fixture in Cairo hotels since the day a mad gunman opened up on a bunch of tourists breakfasting in the Semiramis Intercontinental on the Corniche just round the corner. In colonial times Tahrir was known as Ismaeliyya, and the notoriously flea-ridden Ismaeliyya Barracks, home of the British Garrison, once stood where the Nile Hilton is now. The National Museum, built in 1902 by Auguste Mariette, Rifad's predecessor as EAS Director, still stands on the northern corner of the square, almost opposite the soaring blade of the Ramses Hilton, and Doc dropped me outside among luxury coaches and lines of tourists.

The thick-set guard at the staff entrance wouldn't let me in, so I queued up with the tourists and bought myself a ticket. This was almost a pilgrimage for me. I'd first seen the museum as a small boy, and no matter how many times I'd been there since, it had never lost its magic. The Old Kingdom sculpture of a lion in blue basalt was still there outside the main door, and as the queue diminished I found myself staring at it. I could still feel that shiver of strangeness I'd experienced when I'd first seen it. It was clearly a lion, yet there was something about it, some uncanny hint of otherworldliness which transformed it from being an ordinary, everyday lion, to a lion from the wildest shores of delirium.

The guards were hustling the tourists for their cameras, but I scurried past them, on through the dark galleries and up the colonnaded stairs. In spite of my hurry to see Rifad, I couldn't resist stopping off at the 18th-Dynasty rooms. I bypassed the Tutankhamen exhibition, where lines were already forming, and dipped into the less popular Amarna exhibition. Almost at once the sandstone colossus of Akhnaton – almost thirteen feet high – halted me in my tracks. I knew then that it was this statue that had drawn me here. I looked again at the oddly distorted features of the 'mystery pharaoh', the long flattened skull, the elongated neck, the jutting chin, the uncanny leering expression, the slanted, slit-like, chilling eyes. There was something frighteningly inhuman about Akhnaton – and it was not only the strange face. His body had broad hips, swelling breasts and plump thighs, almost as if he was actually a woman masquerading as a man. Yet some of the distortions of his physique belonged neither to normal men nor to normal women. I wondered if Julian Cranwell had really found evidence that the tomb of the 'lost pharaoh' had been discovered. As I stared at the odd features I couldn't resist the feeling that Akhnaton was somehow laughing at me.

I found my way to the staff quarters through a little-used side door I'd known about for years. Rifad's office was on the top floor. A blowsy secretary – a middle-aged battleaxe with dyed blond hair – sat smoking at an ancient typewriter in the anteroom outside. 'Can I help you, Your Presence?' she enquired, exhaling smoke. Her vinegar expression clashed uncomfortably with the politeness of the phrase.

'Yes,' I said. 'Dr Rifad. Is he in?'

'He's in, Your Presence, but he's very busy. Do you have an appointment?'

'No.'

'Then can I suggest you make one?'

'You can suggest what you like,' I said, 'but I'm seeing him right now.'

I pushed abruptly past her and barged through the glass-panelled door bearing the legend 'Director General', ignoring her yell of 'You can't go in there!'

The office was large and luxurious with shelves of files and documents, a courtesy suite of leather chairs and a huge wooden desk laden with in and out trays, blotter, stationery and telephones. Rifad was standing behind the desk, his small, fat torso covered with a tailored blue pinstripe suit. He froze in the act of picking up the telephone and his moon-face, as smooth and pink as a baby's, registered alarm. The secretary was banging determinedly on the door behind me, but I forced it closed and snapped the latch. Rifad's tiny black eyes followed my movements, measuring my distance from him. 'What are you doing here, Ross?' he said at last.

I walked up to the desk. Rifad turned to face me and I saw that streams of perspiration were running down his jowls. His face was white and his whole body was quaking. He looked as if he'd seen a ghoul.

'I want to know why you told the police I was sacked for trafficking in stolen antiquities,' I said. 'You know bloody well why I was dismissed – for expressing views you didn't happen to agree with.'

Rifad began to wipe his forehead with a snow-white handkerchief. 'I don't know what you're talking about,' he said.

'You're a liar! I've heard the rumours and the shit about forging the Siriun Stela. It was genuine – you yourself assigned a team of 18th-Dynasty experts to investigate it.'

'You must be mad, Ross. You come here, barge your way into my office without so much as an excuse me, and assault me with this farrago of nonsense. What is it you want?'

'I want to know why you've clouded my reputation when you know bloody well I never helped myself to a piece in my entire career!'

'What about the statuette of Thoth they found on you at the airport in '92?'

'Christ, I can't believe this! I took that piece for a lecture in London. You catalogued it yourself when I brought it back.'

'The piece you brought back was a forgery. So was the Siriun Stela. You're untrustworthy, Ross. You were awkward from the start. You never got on with anybody but Julian Cranwell, about whom I had my doubts anyway. You've got a chip on your shoulder a mile high, and you came to the Service with your own agenda. You were determined to prove you were right at any cost, even manipulating the evidence to suit you. Anyone else would have thrown you out from the beginning but I took pity on you because you're half-Egyptian and were so keen on finding a place for yourself. In the end I just couldn't put up with your crazy aberrations any longer.'

'You're lying, Rifad. The Thoth piece was no forgery, neither was the Siriun Stela.'

'I don't want to discuss it further. I advise you to get out before the *Mukhabaraat* pick you up. You're no longer welcome in Egypt!'

That remark really touched a raw nerve. 'Just who the hell do you think you are?' I demanded, stepping towards him, feeling the fury rising to the surface – the same heedless fury which had led me to batter the living daylights out of another boy with a cricket bat at school. 'I have Egyptian nationality as well as British,' I said. 'My ancestors lived here for millennia. You have no right to tell me if I'm welcome or not.'

Rifad shrank away from me – he must have seen the look in my eyes. I don't know what I might have done to him if at that moment the door hadn't burst open and four uniformed museum guards clattered in. I froze. The guards surrounded me expectantly – all of them had night-sticks, I noticed. Rifad began to wipe his bald head assiduously with his handkerchief. 'Escort this man to the main entrance,' he ordered in a shaky voice. As the guards marched me out into the anteroom I took a last look at him. He was ghostly white and trembling visibly. From the moment I'd entered he had been scared of something. Really scared. And I was certain it was more than any physical threat I might have supplied.

18

I LEANED WEARILY AGAINST THE BAR at the Club Casaubon and ordered a Stella from the barman, a broad Nubian dressed in a button-up white shirt. He filled a glass from the green bottle and slid glass and bottle across the counter to me. I drank some of the beer. It was ice cold, and streams of condensation formed on the glass almost immediately. It was good – very good. I swallowed more and let its coldness bite in my mouth and throat. Then I looked round the cavernous cellar. It was only lunch-time and broad daylight outside, but the club was lit with ultra-violet strips, full of shadows and shrouds of cigarette smoke, inhabited by nests of dark cameos around little tables: Egyptian good-time girls in tight skirts, beautiful blond-haired Russian prostitutes, Saudi youths in designer jeans and expensive leather jackets, pimps, drunken *Afrangis*, business-men, pushers. It wasn't the kind of place I'd have chosen to meet, but Doc had some kind of romantic attachment to it. I guessed it was where she used to meet Ronnie. A band was playing on stage – a brilliantly lit cube in the gloom – with a busty female singer whose ethereal voice seemed not to suit her buxom dimensions. It wasn't traditional Arab music, I realised, but a sensuous blend of old and new, a sinuous, narcotic sway of tablas and pipes.

I spotted Doc, sitting at a table over a beer, smoking and trying to watch the band, while a young Egyptian hustler with greased hair, muscles, a square jaw and a gold pendant dangling from his open shirt, attempted to chat her up. I wanted to warn him he was courting danger, that I'd once seen Doc put two would-be muggers twice her size through a plate glass window. I elbowed my way over to them carrying the bottle and the glass, and sat down unceremoniously opposite Doc. Today she was dressed for action in brushed denim slacks and Levi shirt, with a scarlet neckerchief.

'Ah, here's my friend!' Doc said, turning to me. 'You came just in time for the *Ghawazis*, darling. The *Ghawazis* are on next.'

'Good,' I said, 'I've always liked the *Ghawazis*.'

The young hustler glared at me and sidled off.

'Doc,' I said, 'I can't leave you alone for a minute.'

'Actually he was rather nice,' she said, gazing after him a little wistfully. She puffed smoke out and turned to me. 'So, tell me, Jamie, did you and Rifad kiss and make up?'

'The shit denied everything and set the dogs on me.'

'*Non illegitimis carburundum*, as the Romans used to say,' she said, lifting her glass in salute, then drinking her beer. 'Don't let the bastards grind you down!'

'Amen,' I said.

For a second we drank in silence and watched the band. The singer was superb. The warbling melody seemed to ambush your emotions somewhere unexpectedly and send a shiver of pleasure down your spine.

'Bloody good, aren't they!' Doc said.

'The only good thing about this place. Why on earth did you pick this dump, Doc? Is this where you used to do your canoodling?'

'Me and Ronnie? No way. Here, it was strictly business. This is where I used to meet my snouts – informants for the uninitiated. Three martinis and the services of the odd hooker and they were in my pocket.'

She looked at me again, her eyes probing my face intently, 'So how *was* Rifad, Jamie?'

'Scared shitless.'

'Probably thought you were going to pulp his brains.'

'No. I mean, he was shitting frogs from the moment he saw me. I sensed it.'

'Sensed it! Jamie, you're getting more like Julian every day. Thought you laughed in the face of intuition.'

'I do. But there it was. You could have cut it with a knife. And it was more than my physical presence – more than any difference of opinion between us on the origin of Egyptian civilisation. It was like he thought I *knew* something about him.'

Doc stubbed her Rothmans out with professional efficiency. 'Ever hear of Ibrahim Izzadin?' she asked.

'Izzadin? Sure. He was Rifad's predecessor as Director General of the EAS.'

'Did you know he was zapped by a hit-and-run car leaving the museum one day in '79?'

'I knew he was killed in a motor accident.'

'Car was never traced. Izzadin had just decided to launch an investigation into the Tutankhamen finds.'

'Hang on, I *do* remember this. They said there'd been some hanky-panky at the original examination of Tut's tomb – artefacts had gone missing or weren't recorded. They said Carter'd broken into the tomb and dipped into the treasure before Carnarvon arrived. They reckoned that explained the mess they found inside later. All malicious claptrap, of course – I mean can you imagine him ransacking a tomb or failing to report a find – *Howard Carter*?'

Doc smiled enigmatically. 'Didn't Karlman say that he'd got rid of a tablet that pronounced a curse on those who disturbed Tut's sleep?'

'Carter denied it.'

'He would, wouldn't he.'

'Anyway, the decision to open the investigation got the heave-ho.'

'After Izzadin snuffed it, yes. Rifad took over and put the kibosh on it. End of story.'

'You're not suggesting Rifad was responsible for Izzadin's death?'

'You reckoned he was scared shitless. Wouldn't that give him something to be scared shitless about?'

'Doc, this is libel! Where do you dig this stuff up?'

'In Julian's computer files. And it's not all I found out. There are two more things; well, three actually.' She grinned with satisfaction, and I suddenly realised that she was excited. She'd been dying to tell me something since the moment I'd arrived, and was deliberately holding it back, playing for effect. Doc never had been much good at suppressing her emotions. We finished our beers and I ordered more from a passing waiter. The band had stopped playing, and the female singer was leaving the stage amid a flutter of applause. 'Now the *Ghawazis*,' Doc said.

Two beautiful young women came on stage, dressed in shiny black cloaks. They looked like gypsies, with cascades of jet-black curls and dark skin, their eyes heavily shadowed in kohl, their faces decorated with gold nose-rings that looked like antiques. They were strikingly similar.

'Twins!' Doc said excitedly. 'Oh, boy. This should be good! You know the *Ghawazis* are a tribe? They reckon they're descended from the *Baramika*, a family of entertainers in the time of Hirun ar-Rashid.'

I snorted. For once Doc was wrong. There were pictures of dancing-girls performing dances like those of the *Ghawazis* on the walls of Old Kingdom tombs – three thousand years before the Khalif Hirun ar-Rashid of the *Thousand and One Nights*. The *Ghawazis* were one of the oldest institutions on the Nile.

The music began with a boom of percussion, a clack of castanets, a ponderous beat of tablas. The cloaked figures began to sway almost imperceptibly, their movements perfectly synchronised, the steps seeming slightly mechanical at first but with every stroke of the beat becoming looser and less controlled, until suddenly the stringed instruments and pipes exploded like a tidal wave – a sheer wall of sound. The girls stepped and twisted, flicking off their cloaks to reveal sleek, dark, muscular bodies in red velvet bikinis beneath the transparent coverings of *tobs* and *sirwal*. Both wore rubies in their navels and heavy jewelled bracelets at their ankles and wrists. There was a pant of emotion from the audience. The music was intoxicating, and the girls seemed utterly possessed by it, their flesh undulating, thrusting, jerking spontaneously without conscious design. It was breathtakingly erotic.

'Bravo!' Doc said. 'By God, they're good.'

The crowd began to clap in time with the music. The rhythm was so powerful that the melody seemed almost entrapped in it, straining to escape from its confines into sublime rapture. The tempo increased and the girls' movements became more intense. They turned deftly with the grace of panthers, muscles working, faces ecstatic. They moved voluptuously in perfect synchrony, in perfect time with the music. The percussion built up into a thrilling surge and the *Ghawazis* abandoned themselves to it, jumping and pivoting like acrobats. Some of the men in the audience stood up and shouted. Others held them back. The girls moved still more wildly, hurling themselves sideways, doubling over backwards in a blur of movement. I gasped. The music throbbed, ebbing and flowing mesmerically, drawing the audience in, uniting them into a single pulsating unit, on and on until I felt lost in it. The beat built up and up, climbing to new levels of excitement until suddenly it reached a shuddering climax. The girls collapsed like rag dolls into perfect splits, their upper bodies folded forwards in positions of supplication. The cavern shook with applause.

'That was great!' Doc said, clapping.

The waiter brought two more beers and laid them on the table. I paid and we drank as the applause died down.

'Say what you like,' Doc said, 'you don't see dancers as good as that every day. They're trained to it from being little kids.'

'It was great,' I admitted, sipping my beer, watching her expression as she smoked. That small, wistful smile still hovered around her lips – a kind of smugness, I thought, as if she was waiting for me to pump her.

'Out with it, Doc,' I said at last. 'What else did you find?'

'There's stuff on an Eye of Ra Society,' she said.

I turned my attention on her like a headlight beam. 'As in "Look out for the Eye of Ra", Professor Spooky Karlman's famous parting words?'

'Bang on. Of course, it might be nothing. At first glance it looks like a bunch of loony-toons who believe they're descended from the ancient pharaohs. Address in central Cairo. Run by a lady called "Montuhotep XV" who styles herself "High Priestess of the Horus Throne of the Great House''. She claims to rule in direct line of descent from the goddess Isis – or *Austet* – who sat on the same throne something like ten thousand years ago.'

'Interesting,' I said. 'At least it coincides with my theory that Isis was a real person.'

'You're as cranky as she is, darling.'

'Doc, I'm not the first to come up with the idea. You ever heard of W. B. Emery? Or Flinders Petrie, the Father of Modern Egyptology?'

'Jamie, am I a complete cretin?'

'Well, both of them reckoned that the Osiris myths were much older than was generally thought, and based on real events. Their theory was that in very early times Egypt was invaded by a warrior race, the Patu, who used the falcon as their totem, and who set themselves up as an aristocracy ruled by Divine Kings – the Dynastic Pharaohs. They thought the myths describing the conflict between the Osiris–Isis–Horus family, and their enemy Set, were garbled accounts of the real struggle between the Patu and the indigenes, for whom Set was the totem.'

'Set: the god of evil.'

'Yes, he was depicted with the head of some unidentifiable beast, and was said to stalk the Western Desert, brewing up sand-storms and typhoons. That's one of the reasons the ancient Egyptians were shit-scared of the desert. But Emery and Petrie thought Set's evil persona was a later development. After the invaders had established the supremacy of the Osiris cult, Set was demonised and pushed out into no-man's land. Did Julian's notes explain the Society's beliefs?'

'No, only that it claims to be dedicated to all the Egyptians who fled from their country during the Muslim invasions in AD 640 and who preserved the ancient traditions in various parts of Africa.'

'Like the Dogon in Mali.'

'Like the Dogon, yes, but also the Bambara of Central Africa, the Beja of the Sudan, the Tutsi of Burundi, the Wolof in Senegal, and a whole stack of others. No mention of where the society gets its funding from, but not from the government or any Islamic Fundamentalist powers, that's for sure.'

'Why would Julian be interested in such a bunch of screwballs, anyway?'

'Your guess is as good as mine. Actually there's masses of fascinating stuff in those files. The only problem is that I can't see any underlying theme. It's as if Julian was just squirrelling material on any topic that happened to take his fancy at the time.'

'What was the second thing?'

'The Zerzura Club. Didn't Karlman say something about that too?'

'Yes, he said Wingate was "one of those damned Zerzura Club people".'

'The odd thing is that Wingate's name isn't on the membership list in Julian's file. The Zerzura Club was founded in 1930 by a Major Bagnold who wrote a deadly tedious book on sand-dunes that nobody ever read. Members were mostly well-to-do peacetime army officers – all stiff upper lip and state-of-the-art technology. There's people with names like Battenberg and Carruthers, a Hungarian adventurer-playboy called Count Ladislaus de Almasy, but no Orde Wingate. From the start the club was shrouded in secrecy, almost as if it had some sort of religious purpose. They trolled about the desert for most of the thirties looking for Zerzura.'

'Any members still alive?'

'There is one ex-member still holed up in Cairo, name of Dansey-Smith – Colonel Dansey-Smith. Lives on Roda island. Now, it might be worth having a talk with him about Orde Wingate. Ought to talk to Mrs Montuhotep, too.'

'Rather you than me, Doc. I had a bellyful with Karlman and Kolpos.'

We finished our drinks. 'Want another?' I asked Doc.

'No,' she said, 'That's enough, Jamie. Let's go home.'

We walked along the alleys behind 26th July Street to where Doc had parked the car, past the windows of cube-shaped shops offering glimpses into a score of tiny worlds – an ancient barber in spectacles leering over his lathered customer with a cut-throat razor, two boys sitting cross-legged at sewing-machines, running up trousers, a butcher slicing cuts from a hank of hanging meat, a fat baker in an apron drawing brown loaves from an oven on a long spatula. I put my arm round Doc. 'That's nice,' she said, smirking. 'Ought to do it more often.'

'Doc,' I said, 'you're hiding something. What is it?'

'I've got a present for you,' she said.

We found the 504 parked in a side-street, and Doc unlocked the doors. We got in, and Doc started the engine, nursing the car into the maelstrom of traffic on 26th July Street.

'All right,' I said, 'what's the present?'

She beamed. 'That photocopy you wanted enlarging,' she said, 'the one of Carter and Carnarvon in the Valley of the Kings in 1923. I got it scanned. There's a brown envelope on the seat behind you. Have a look. I think you'll find it interesting.'

I bent over the seat gingerly, with a hand on my aching ribs, picked up the envelope, and extracted a digitalised 18×12 computer-printout.

The scanner had certainly done a brilliant job. Carter and Carnarvon had been enlarged out of the picture and the newspaper Carnarvon was pointing to now filled the frame. It was the *United American Press*, dated February 16th, 1923 – the day Tutankhamen's burial-chamber had been opened. The headline was blurred but readable. It ran: 'Treasures of Tut: Important papyrus and map also discovered.' And in smaller type beneath, 'An account of Akhnaton, the mystery pharaoh – secrets of his tomb revealed'.

'Doc, you're a pleasure to work with,' I said.

'I think one champagne dinner at the Marriott is in order!' she replied, grinning with satisfaction. 'The next question is, where did that newspaper get its information? According to the official records, no such papyrus or map was ever found.'

19

It was almost sunset. From Doc's balcony, I could just make out the dark angles of the police station where Hammoudi had interrogated me, on the waterfront at Bulaq. It gave me a sudden pang of uneasiness to think that I was still in sight of the *Mukhabaraat*. I smoked my pipe and watched fly-boats being made fast to their moorings upriver amid flocks of seagulls spiralling along the wharfs. Suddenly, from nowhere it seemed, the dark shape of a falcon plunged among them like a black stone, banking and circling with magnificent grace. The seagulls flickered and flapped away frantically, the falcon pursuing now one, now another, weaving across the red and purple city sky until the whole wheeling circus was out of sight. It reminded me that to the ancient Egyptians the falcon was an embodiment of the sun-god Ra, whom they depicted as a falcon or a man with a falcon's head, wearing the sacred sun-disc. Wherever you looked in ancient Egyptian mysteries, Ra was always there lurking in the shadows. I thought of the magnificent facade of the Ramses II temple at Abu Simbel, the one that UNESCO had lifted out of the bed of Lake Nasser and rebuilt higher up the bank. Four seated colossi of Ramses II, carved out of red sandstone, grace the eastern face, two on each side of the entrance. But behind them in a niche, directly over the door, stands the image of Ra, half man, half hawk, carrying the sacred sun-disc on his head. The sinister eminence of Ra behind the pharaoh was captured perfectly by David Roberts in his painting of 1886. Ra worship was the most powerful of ancient Egyptian cults, and in Old Kingdom times pharaohs were known as 'The Sons of Ra'. The Ra priesthood was traditionally the dominant element in the Egyptian state, and there is more than a hint that it was the priesthood which influenced the king rather than vice-versa. Since Ra had created himself out of the primeval darkness, his Eye was considered all-seeing, omniscient, and thus the symbol of both knowledge and fertility. In his guise as the sun, Ra crossed the heavens in his majestic sky-barque each day, passing into the underworld at sunset, where he spent the shadow hours of the night in battle with dark forces – Doc's *Ahriman* – emerging victorious each day at sunrise. In one version of the myths, Ra's Eye was the sun itself – a burning, fiery Eye, capable of wreaking terrible revenge.

Doc came out of the shower shaking a towel, and plonked herself down on a chair opposite. She nodded in approval as I poured her a Scotch. 'Ah, my reward,' she said, holding it up to the last of the light.

'And well you deserve it,' I said. 'But let's face it, Doc. That newspaper report could be hokey. We know Carnarvon gave the story to *The Times* – maybe the others just made it up. There was a lot of hoax journalism in those days. Still is.'

'You're right. But say it wasn't. Say the story was leaked and then someone sat on it.'

'Like who?'

'Like Howard Carter.' She picked up both the enlargement and Julian's photocopy from the table and waved it in front of me. 'Look at the faces. Carnarvon seems happy about the headline, Carter truly pissed off. Perhaps Carnarvon leaked the story against Carter's wishes, and Carter later denied it, just like he denied finding the curse tablet. Two months later Carnarvon snuffs it, and there's no one to contradict Carter any more.'

'That's right, he always made a point of denying there were any papyri in the tomb, and a lot of Egyptologists found it surprising. People make a big hoo-hah over epigraphy, but the Egyptians actually wrote ninety per cent of their stuff on papyrus with pen and ink. It seems astonishing they left no historical records in a pharaoh's grave.'

Doc put the photocopy down under the outside lamp, and as my eyes fell on it I suddenly made out the features of the third figure, who I now realised was actually holding the newspaper Carter and Carnarvon had been looking at. 'Who's that?' I said, pointing.

Doc put her glass down and bent over the picture. 'Ah,' she said, 'I'd forgotten our Third Man.'

She slipped her magnifying glass out of her pocket and examined the figure closely. 'Interesting,' she said, 'want to have a look?'

The body of the 'Third Man' was obscured by the newspaper he was holding, and the face was slightly out of focus, but visible. It was hard to say with such poor definition, but it looked like the face of an old man between sixty-five and seventy-five, a rather bland, expressionless face – clean-shaven, which was unusual in that era – with close-cropped hair and rather penetrating eyes. At least that's what I read into it – perhaps half of it was merely suggested by the shadows. 'Well, who is it?' I asked Doc again.

She made an exaggerated Latin shrug. 'Maybe a minion, Mace or Carver? Weren't those the names of Carter's assistants?'

I thought about it for a minute. 'I'm sure Mace and Carver were youngish men,' I said. 'Carnarvon was in his late fifties when he died, a few weeks after this photo was taken, and Carter must have been . . . what? About fifty? But to me this guy looks older than both of them. Of course it might be just the light . . .'

Suddenly the telephone trilled.

'Let it ring,' Doc said.

I shifted uneasily. 'Might be important,' I said.

'Might be Hammoudi.'

'Surely he couldn't have traced me that fast!'

The phone trilled insistently again. 'Oh, my giddy aunts!' Doc said. She straightened her dressing-gown with crisp movements, and stalked into the sitting-room. In a second she was back. 'For you,' she said, 'Nikolai Kolpos.'

Kolpos's voice sounded strained: 'Is that you, Ross?' he said.

'Yes, it's me.'

'Look, you remember our little conversation the other day?'

'Of course.'

'Well, I've thought it over. Perhaps I wasn't quite straight with you. Come over tonight – alone, you understand – at ten, and I'll ... I'll show you what you wanted to see. You know what I mean?'

'I think so, but isn't it a bit late for a meeting? Won't tomorrow do?'

'I'm sorry, Ross,' his voice sounded gravelly now. 'It's tonight or nothing. Ten o'clock on the dot. Will you be there?'

'I'll be there,' I said.

'Alone, Ross. You know what I mean?'

'Yes, I know what you mean.'

Abruptly, Kolpos rang off.

20

I HAD A BAD FEELING ABOUT it from the beginning. I hadn't liked the strain in Kolpos's voice or the late hour of the meeting. I think that's why I wouldn't let Doc persuade me to take her with me that night, why nothing she said would shift my determination to do it by myself. After all, Kolpos had stressed that I should come alone, and I didn't want to betray that fragile trust. Second, though, I thought Doc had pushed the boat out enough on my behalf and I didn't want her getting any further into it than she already was.

We'd ordered a taxi to come to the house and when I climbed in next to the driver, for some reason I was thinking about ancient Egyptian tombs. For the ancient Egyptians, the tomb was a sort of gateway into another universe, a physical and symbolic portrayal of the spiritual journey made by the dead soul. No two tombs are identical, but all are built on a similar model. During the 18th Dynasty, the period of Tutankhamen and Akhnaton, each tomb consisted of an entrance staircase carved into the rock, and a long tunnel cut through to an entrance antechamber. From here a second stairwell led into a hall of pillars in which the sarcophagus was contained. Around the sarcophagus were store-rooms containing artefacts and priceless treasures. The tombs had a twofold purpose – first to defeat the tomb-robbers who preyed on them, and second to symbolise the voyage of the soul towards the bright illumination of Ra with which it must merge. The walls of the burial chamber were painted with brilliant scenes taken from the *Book of the Dead* which portrayed Ra's nightly journey through the Underworld and his battles with the evil demons which lurked there. The dead soul would be guided on his journey by angels and spiritual guides such as the jackal-headed Anubis, Lord of Embalming, who was also referred to as 'Guardian of the Secret' and 'Opener of the Ways'. It would congregate with other freshly liberated souls in the West, at the gateway of the sunset, to hitch a ride on Ra's barque through the corridors of the night, where it would battle demons and evil spirits until it finally arrived at the door of the Judgement Hall, domain of the god Osiris. Here, a list of forty-two mortal sins would be read out, and the dead soul was required to answer guilty or not guilty to each sin. If it answered not guilty to all, Anubis weighed its heart against a feather – the Feather of Truth. If it were found wanting, a terrifying beast, part crocodile, part lion, part hippopotamus, would emerge from the shadows and tear the soul limb from limb, thus ending for ever its chances of immortal life. If equilibrium were attained, the god Osiris would gravely motion the soul on to the next stage of transformation into a being of light. The *Book of the Dead* – actually a kind of navigation-chart for the soul's voyage through the Afterworld – is more correctly called *The Book of Coming Forth By Day*.

This train of thought dogged me all the way across the 26th July Bridge, past the squares and oblongs of light from shops and hotels along 26th July Street, through Opera Square and the ragged remains of Ezbekiyya Gardens, where my father's old Shepheard's used to stand before it was burned down in riots in the 1950s. As we halted at the traffic lights, I turned back for a glimpse of the tottering wreck of the Continental, once the grandest hotel in Cairo, where Lord Carnarvon had died of an infected mosquito bite on 5th April 1923. The first inkling that something was amiss came to me when the taxi stopped suddenly in a street near Al-Ahzar. The lighting was poor, the street a play of shadows, the buildings massive eyeless blocks whose dimensions were lost in the darkness. There seemed to be no one about. 'Why have you stopped?' I asked the driver, a long-chinned, silent man in a grey *gallabiyya*, whose front teeth protruded prominently like a rat's. He looked at me gravely. 'I have stopped for the Dead,' he said. It was only then that I saw the procession of hooded figures emerging out of the thick shadows: men in dirty white robes, pacing noiselessly in ragged file as if to the beat of a silent drum. After them came a wheeled carriage, a baroque contraption painted with black flowers and scrolls, whose canopy stood on four ornate wooden pillars and whose wheels creaked painfully. The carriage was being pulled by several of the men, I saw, and was lit dimly by flickering oil lamps in gimbals. As it passed by I realised that the dark object lying beneath the canopy was a coffin, and only then did it dawn on me that I was watching a funeral. '*Allah yarhamu*: God have mercy on him,' my driver muttered, as we watched the carriage creaking back into the darkness. 'How do you know it's a him?' I asked. The driver glanced at me sneeringly: 'The coffin was too big for a woman,' he said.

We drove on towards Khan al-Khalili, yet the eerie procession had sparked off an uneasiness I couldn't get rid of. There it was again, the feeling I'd had at the pyramids the night Hammoudi had jumped me, a sense of something glimpsed once long ago, lurking just beyond my consciousness. As we turned into the Khan, the feeling seemed to grow more and more intense, and I looked around instinctively for a way of escape. The alleys were an impenetrable warren around me, trapping me, and the glow from the street-lamps illuminated my driver's eyes with a square of light. I saw deep, leering, malevolent eyes, like the eyes of Akhnaton on the museum statue. The car halted at a crossroad, and I looked out to see the door of a shop, dimly lit by a lamp. On the door was painted a full-sized effigy of the jackal-headed god Anubis, Lord of the Dead, and the words, 'Welcome To The Underworld – The Anubis Bazaar'.

Now adrenalin began to flow through my body, unleashing all the symptoms of panic. Sweat trickled down my forehead: my palms were damp. I felt a tickling sensation at the back of my neck and realised with shock that my hair was standing on end. By the time we pulled into Kolpos's street, I couldn't stand it any longer. 'Stop!' I told the driver. 'Let me out here.' I slapped down the money we'd agreed on and, leaving the car door open, I ran down the alley towards 'The Osiris Arcade'. There was no one else in the street. My steps seemed to ring hollow on the flagstones like the footfalls of a giant. The shop door was slightly ajar and I charged in, straight through the woven hanging covering the connecting door behind the counter. The sitting-room was empty, dark and silent. Panting heavily, I paused and looked around. The luminous hands of the clock on the wall read exactly ten, and suddenly it began to chime with low, tuneless notes. I jumped and waited until the ten chimes had rung, then I pushed open the door of Kolpos's study. Kolpos was sitting behind his writing desk. His face, transfixed by a beam of light, stared directly at me with eyes that bulged obscenely from their sockets. His head was tilted to one side at an awkward angle, its flesh scarlet and bloated as a balloon, his mouth hanging open in a grimace of agony. His hands rested on the desk before him in pools of blood, and as I came near, I saw that half a dozen three- or four-inch nails had been hammered right through the palms. Quaking now, I examined his neck. A slim leather band had been tied beneath the chin and ears, and tightened expertly. Just then, my eyes moved to the full-length mirror on the opposite wall. There on the glass, in Kolpos's own blood, probably, was drawn a clumsy image of the Eye of Ra and under it, in hieroglyphics:

> Let the Eye of Ra descend
> That it may slay the evil conspirators

I didn't get the chance to take a closer look. Suddenly there was the unmistakable click of footsteps outside the room, and I stiffened. I dashed out just in time to see a tall, bulky figure lurching through the woven curtain. It was at that moment that I had the vision. Something seemed to clutch at my brain, squeezing it with vice-like pressure, convulsing my body with pain. It only lasted a fraction of a second, but in that moment I heard a door bang in my mind and saw in my head a metallic object rolling across the floor. When the connecting door really slammed, I *knew* what was going to happen. Even before the Mills grenade slid across the floor I'd taken two steps, and dived straight through the sash window that looked into the street. I didn't even hear the glass shatter or feel its slivers cutting into my flesh. My life spun by me in a frantic reel of half-glimpsed images like a video-film on super-fast rewind – my infancy in the desert, my mother's face, my unhappiness as a boy in England, Julian Cranwell's ecstatic jig at Bahriyya, my father waving goodbye for the last time at the door of his private hospital room, racked with cancer. I was flying down a dark tunnel with brilliant light at the end, when suddenly there was a deafening clap as the grenade exploded, and I felt the singeing waft of the shock-wave that followed, shredding debris around me. I had a sudden vision of myself as a huge black vulture with vast soft wings flapping noiselessly in space. I hung there for a timeless moment, poised between heaven and earth, life and death, filled with the immaculate knowledge that whatever was going to happen was now totally beyond my control. Then I slapped into the earth with a bump and found myself snapping frantically like a snake on the floor of the alley, bowling over and over, bashing my skull against the stone flags. When I sat up, tongues of fire were lashing out of the broken window, followed by billows of smoke. There were shouts in the bazaar. Shutters opened, lights went on, windows began to go up, heads poked out. Doors opened and half-clothed figures rushed by, yelling: 'Fire! Fire!' I stood up unsteadily and groped for my glasses. I found them easily enough, but to my dismay, one of the lenses was cracked. I put them on and for an instant I stood there, completely dazed. At my feet lay pieces of a clock, broken bric-à-brac, and the shattered photo of Kolpos's wife.

I've only a hazy idea of what happened after that, pieced together from fragments later. I must have passed into a dream. I recall staggering away from the light and the noise down a long dark tunnel with blood streaming from my head, face and hands. I have the impression that I stalked on blindly, passing no one, until I paused outside a shop, feeling that I couldn't go on. It seemed to be the same shop my taxi had stopped at on the way in, with the life-size image of the jackal-headed god Anubis and the words 'Welcome to the Underworld' written above it. Only this time the door was open. I was about to enter, when I thought I heard a voice calling from behind, saying, 'Omar! Don't go in!'

I recognised my mother's voice, and I looked back and saw this dark female figure shrouded in black Bedouin dress, standing behind me. I couldn't see the face, for she was wearing the full *burqa* mask with only slits for eyes, but I was certain it was Maryam. 'Mother!' I called in Arabic, my eyes filling with tears. 'Where have you been?'

'Run away, Omar!' Maryam's voice came back, 'I'm with you.'

I began to hurry along the dark tunnel, faster and faster, but no matter how fast I went I felt my mother's presence always behind me, urging me forward. She seemed to remain there behind me for hour after hour as the walls of the tunnel passed by. At last, though, I realised that a terrible thirst was burning in my throat and I came across a *zir*, a pitcher of cold water Arabs leave outside their houses as an offering to thirsty passers-by. I remember stopping to drink greedily, like an animal, from the enamel cup attached by a chain to the pot, slopping the water over my bloody face and hands. Then I recall lurching towards a nearby doorway, and vomiting all over the street. Mother stood at my shoulder, watching me. I turned to look at her and this time she was no longer wearing the *burqa*. She was smiling at me, the same beautiful face, the same wild hair I recalled vividly from my childhood. 'Mother, you won't leave me again, will you?' I said.

'I'll never leave you, Omar,' she said, 'I'll always be here.'

At that moment I heard harsh shrieks of laughter from along the alleyway, and I looked up to see a group of hooded figures in dirty off-white robes, gathered around a baroque-looking cart, lit by lamps on gimbals. I couldn't see their faces, because they were standing with their backs to me, facing what appeared to be a glowing brazier of charcoal. I looked around and realised suddenly that Maryam was gone. I must have been attracted by the light of the lamps and brazier, because I recall drifting towards the figures weightlessly like a diver. As I got near, I saw that a coffin lay on the back of the cart, just like the one that had passed the taxi earlier, but this time the coffin lid yawned wide open, and I could just make out the dark form of the cadaver which lay within. I floated down the alley through giant hunched shadows thrown by the hooded figures against the flames of the brazier, calling to them to help me. Fragments of coarse laughter drifted back. It wasn't until I could almost touch them that they turned, pulling back the hoods that shadowed their faces and I saw with a shock that they were faces I knew: Hammoudi, Rifad, Mustafa, Margoulis, Julian's fat *ghaffir*, my rat-toothed taxi-driver, even the red-haired hunchback I'd seen outside Julian's appartment. And there was another figure, hooded like the rest, but hanging back in the shadows, whose face I couldn't see at first until he moved towards me. As the light fell on him, I realised with a shock that it was Melvin Renner. They were crowing at me through red mouths full of sharp teeth, and sneering with eyes that glowed yellow in the darkness, like the eyes of a cat. I sought out Renner's features, and found his yellow eyes boring into me with an angry intensity. 'What's this all about?' I asked.

'I should have known you were one of the *illuminati*,' he said, his mouth gaping blackly. 'Now you'll never be one of us.'

'What are you talking about?' I said, backing away, to roars of flaying derision from the crowd. The brazier burnt brightly for a moment, lighting up the cadaver that lay in the coffin on the back of the cart. It was only for an instant, but enough to convince me that the man in the coffin was myself.

21

IT WAS A PARTY AT THE British Embassy, all scintillating chandeliers and tables covered with white cloths, silver dishes and magnums of champagne. I couldn't remember how I'd got there. The place was full of men in dinner-suits and Dicky-bows, and women in haute-couture dresses with expensive hair-dos and sparkling jewellery. There was a band of British Guardsmen playing jazz softly, and a buzz of animated conversation filled the room. I was dressed in a white tuxedo, standing alone, nervously quaffing bumper after bumper of champagne that a dismembered hand kept filling up for me. When I looked to see whom the hand belonged to, I noticed with a start that it was joined to the hunchback I'd seen outside Julian's, now dressed in the bottle-green jacket and red cummerbund of a waiter. As I stared, the man winked at me suggestively: 'Sweet potato!' he said. 'Very fresh! Very nice!' As I reeled away in terror Doc emerged from the crowd and took me by the arm. She was wearing a voluminous evening gown of black silk. 'Doc, do you know who that was?' I said, pointing after the hunchback who had already lost himself among the guests. 'It was no one,' she said. 'Come on, Jamie. I want you to meet the Consul, Melvin Renner.'

'But I've already met him!' I said.

She ignored me and dragged me in front of a group of immaculately dressed Englishmen, who were looking around suavely, grasping their champagne bumpers delicately between finger and thumb. I recognised Renner, whose unkempt mop of blond hair was tonight neatly slicked back. 'Ah, Mr Ross,' he said, with a touch of patronage, glancing momentarily at my earring, 'I see we're in full regalia tonight.' There was a flutter of rude laughter. 'How's the research going?' he added.

I was going to enquire what he meant by 'the research', but instead I asked, 'Didn't I see you the other night in Khan al-Khalili, wearing a dirty-white robe – you know, with the hearse?' The laughter stopped abruptly and there was a stiff silence. Renner looked at me strangely. Everyone was looking at me strangely, including Doc. I realised that the words had come out in a slur, and that I was swaying slightly on my feet. I was suddenly aware of a splitting headache, and the strong desire to throw up.

'I don't think so, Mr Ross,' Renner said, placidly. 'Are you sure you're all right?'

'I don't feel well,' I said.

'Probably too much champers.' He turned to Doc and for a second I had an impression that something passed between them, some fleeting hint of understanding.

'Evelyn, why don't you take Mr Ross to the guest-room,' Renner said.

Next thing I remember is that Doc had laid me down on crisp white sheets in a room that smelt of lilac and had a photo of the Queen on the wall. She was stroking my hair, making soothing sounds. 'You see, Doc,' I was saying, 'I never really *was* one of them.'

'I know, Jamie,' Doc said. 'Don't worry. It'll all be all right. You never have been one of them, you've always been an *illuminatus*. . . It's just that nobody realised it until now.'

I tried to open my eyes in surprise, but they were stuck fast. 'No, Doc!' I tried to say, but my vocal chords weren't functioning and no sound came out. I felt myself sinking deeper and deeper into a morass of darkness. I tried desperately to claw myself out of it, to climb back to the surface, but the darkness was sucking me down. In a moment I lost my grip and black wings folded over me, blocking out the light.

*　　*　　*

When I woke up I was no longer in the guest-room at the British Embassy, but in my old room at Doc's, with sunbeams probing the blinds and leaving mottled patterns of light across the walls. I was wearing an old pair of cotton *sirwal* as pyjamas and there was some sort of hat or helmet clamped tightly on my head like a vice. The skin of my face felt as if it had been scraped with emery-paper. I pulled myself to my feet and almost collapsed. I was weak, very weak. Then I touched my head and realised suddenly that what I'd thought was a hat was actually a massive headache. I thrust myself over to the mirror and saw a haggard, pale face that I hardly recognised. It was covered in lacerations, and my eyes were almost lost in the puffy purple mass of my swollen cheeks.

I heard the click of a keyboard from the sitting room, and threw open the door to find Doc working on her computer. When I staggered into the room she stopped abruptly. 'Jamie, you'd better sit down,' she said, jumping up and helping me over to an armchair, 'you've had a terrible bang on the head!'

'I thought it was a hat at first,' I said, giggling. 'What time is it, Doc?'

'It's three twenty in the afternoon.'

'Christ, I must have drunk a lot of champers.'

'What are you talking about, darling?'

'The party. By the way, Doc, what did you mean that I'd always been an *illuminatus*?'

'What party, Jamie? I don't know what the hell you're talking about.'

I giggled again. 'Are you telling me there was no party at the British Embassy last night?'

'Jamie, you arrived at my doorstep at three o'clock in the morning in the back of a three-wheeled baker's van. My *ghaffir* rang to tell me there was a *raagil ta'aban* – a "tired gentleman" – waiting for me. I went down and there you were, lying in the back rambling dementedly about Kolpos. You said he'd been murdered and that his shop had gone up in flames. You looked awful, your face swollen and covered in blood, your white suit torn to shreds and your glasses cracked. The baker's boy said you'd paid him fifty Egyptian pounds to bring you to this address all the way from Khan al-Khalili. I gave him another fifty and told him to keep his mouth shut. He said he didn't know what had happened to you, but said you'd told him a Bedouin woman had guided you to him.'

'A Bedouin woman?'

'Yes, he said he got a bit spooked at first, but he looked around and there was no one there but you.'

'Maryam,' I said.

'What?'

'No, nothing. I had a dream about my mother, that's all. And then this party at the Embassy. But for the life of me I can't remember any baker's boy or three-wheel truck.'

Doc went off to the kitchen while I sat and tried to remember. I couldn't. There were snatches of myself running through a long dark tunnel, vomiting in the street, Maryam's face, the demonic features of the men with the hearse, the hunchback dressed as a waiter, the word *illuminati*. No baker's boy. I tried some deep breathing exercises, but it only made the pain worse. My head felt as if it was undergoing continental drift in several places. I felt mentally shattered, singed, cut and bruised, numbed by the memory of the disgusting things they'd done to Kolpos. I tried to stop myself thinking about it, but my mind wouldn't cease cranking away, sifting through all the data, the half-seen images. I felt as if I'd just dug up fragments of ancient Egyptian ruins in the sand, aware that they fitted together in some immense design, but I was unable to see the shape of that design hidden in the sand. And beneath that there was another layer of feeling – that I really *did* know more than my mind would admit, that the design was all there in the murk of my subconscious, waiting for me to gain access to it.

I stood up, groaning. Holding my head with one hand, I limped over to one of Doc's bookcases and pulled out the *Concise Oxford Dictionary*. I dropped it on her desk and flipped through the pages with a trembling hand. At last I found it: *illuminati*, it read, 'persons claiming to possess special knowledge or enlightenment'.

I closed the book, puzzled. What special knowledge or enlightenment did I claim? Only my knowledge of the origins of ancient Egyptian civilisation, which almost everyone mocked. Suddenly snatches of a poem rumbled through my head, and I murmured them to myself:

> Let the Eye of Ra descend
> That it may slay the evil conspirators.

' "Hymn to Ra",' Doc said, bustling in with one of her seaweed-like concoctions in a glass.

'What?'

'That poem you were reciting. Isn't it the "Hymn To Ra", the one they found inscribed in Tutankhamen's tomb? Jamie, sit down, please. Here, drink this. It's a herbal infusion for pain and shock. Drink it all.'

I retched and pushed it away ungratefully. 'Christ, Doc,' I said, 'can't I get a bloody Aspirin round this place?'

She smiled pityingly and took the green mess away, returning after a few minutes with a salad of pills and a glass of water: 'Here you are,' she said, 'Paracetamol for pain and antibiotics in case of infection.'

'Great!' I said, swallowing the pills and drinking the water.

'What was that "Hymn to Ra" stuff all about?' Doc enquired.

'There was some kind of conspiracy among human beings against the god Ra, who was getting on in years. Ra sent his Eye, which in another guise was the goddess Hathor, to earth to slay all human beings, but relented and spared a few of them.'

'I know that, Jamie. What I mean is, what has it got to *do* with anything?'

'If my memory isn't playing me tricks, it was written in hieroglyphs on Kolpos's mirror – in what appeared to be blood. Christ, Doc, what *did* happen last night? I mean, I remember all sorts of things, but I can't say which of them were real.'

'Kolpos's shop burned down, that's real enough,' she said. 'I went up there to have a dekko this morning while you were out like a light. I gave the *ghaffir* the keys and asked him to look in on you. Told him you'd been in a car accident. I tell you, Jamie, there was nothing left of the place but a shell. The fire people and police were rummaging around in the ashes and then they carried out this revolting bag of oily, blackened bones on a stretcher and said it was Kolpos. I very nearly threw up. They told me they'd only identified him by his wedding ring. No other bodies in the place, they were certain. I knew you were out of it, but I thought about Elena. One of the onlookers told me that if it hadn't been for the bazaar people the whole street might have gone up. I was snooping around quite successfully, I thought, when an unmarked police car pulls up and out jumps this big bull of a man – built like a weight-lifter – domed forehead, clipped moustache. Very nasty-looking piece of work.'

'Hammoudi!'

'I recognised him from your description. "Here's trouble!" I thought, and beat a hasty retreat.'

'Did he spot you?'

'I thought not. After all, what would Hammoudi know about me? But then I remembered the fire in your room at Shepheard's. The front desk manager saw me and saw you leave with me. Hammoudi knew you'd been staying at Shepheard's, and he'd have been able to get a description of me there. So I drove back here looking over my shoulder. Quite exciting really – brought back the seventies when we were still playing Cold War games – hide and seek round the city. After I pulled out of the bazaar, I saw a black Mercedes behind me. I did a couple of circles and backtracks – not enough to let on I knew it was there – and it still clung to me. Followed me all the way to Tahrir, where I managed to lose it in the confusion. When I got back here, I parked up in the basement and looked into the street for eyes. There were a couple of youngish men in down-at-heel shoes and acrylic shirts hanging about under the *gamez* tree on the corner, smoking. They looked like off-duty servants, but who knows? From now on we can't trust anyone.'

'Kolpos's call last night was a set-up, Doc, just like the Giza thing but more deadly. Someone was there, forcing him to make the call, which is why his voice sounded so strained. They throttled

Kolpos and waited for me with the sole intention of whacking me.'

'What *did* happen to Kolpos, Jamie?'

'Strangled with some kind of garotte. Looked as though he'd died in agony. His hands were nailed to the desk.'

'Jesus wept!'

'Yes. Next thing I heard a noise, saw this figure dashing out and before I know it a grenade's rolling across the floor. It was just like when Kolpos tried to turn me into steak; I had this momentary flash of what was about to happen and I didn't even think, I just dived straight for the window. Blast hit me in mid-air.'

'That's weird, Jamie.'

'I know. But one thing's for certain, Doc. Whatever mumbo-jumbo was written on that mirror, it wasn't *Ahriman*, unseen guardians or demonic forces, that murdered Kolpos and tried to murder me. That is, not unless demonic forces come in the form of Julian Cranwell.'

22

I FELT A LOT BETTER BY the next morning. The ugly swelling on my face had gone down and though my head and ribs still ached, I felt some semblance of normality. I showered, shaved, dressed in old jeans and a clean white shirt I'd found in Doc's wardrobe, and put on the spare pair of glasses Doc had kept for me – outmoded circular John Lennon frames. I also opened an old shoe-box at the bottom of the wardrobe and found, carefully wrapped in cotton rags, my old Hazmi blade – my *khanjar*. Unlike most Arab daggers, it wasn't heavy or broad, but a slim, straight, stiletto with an edge on both sides and a long handle of carved ebony. It came in an ornamented sheath and was usually worn handle downwards on the left forearm. Like the earring, it was presented to a boy at circumcision, a symbol of the passage from childhood to manhood, and as I unwrapped it, I remembered the pain and pride of that day. They'd sat me on a camel-saddle, and the *amnir* – the tribal shaman – had tied my foreskin with a piece of leather until it had gone numb and then sheared it off with a razor-sharp stone. My father had been proud that I hadn't made a fuss, but after the ceremony of singing and dancing, he'd secretly treated the cut with antibiotic powder to prevent infection. 'Don't tell the *amnir*,' he said. 'He'd be livid if he knew.' I slipped the blade from its sheath and ran my thumb along the edges. They were still sharp. I remembered telling Doc I'd never need it again. Now I wasn't so sure.

154

I joined Doc for breakfast of fresh bread, marmalade, orange juice and coffee in the dining room. The Persian blinds were down. No more sitting on the balcony, she said; we didn't want to make things too easy for 'the enemy', whoever that was. I was just on my second cup of coffee, when there came a knock at the door. Both of us froze. 'Dammit!' Doc said, 'The *ghaffir* should have warned me!'

The knock came again. 'Well we've got two choices,' I said. 'We can either pretend we're not here, or answer it.'

Doc's face hardened. 'Can't be fugitives for ever,' she said. 'If this is it, we'll face it!'

We both got up and approached the door. Doc peered through the spyhole, and gave a little gasp. 'Oh lookee!' she said, 'Look what the cat dragged in! Miss Elena Anasis, in person.'

'Jesus! What the hell is she doing here?'

'Shall I let her in?'

'In for a penny.'

She grappled with locks and chains and flung the door wide to reveal Elena, looking very pale and exceptionally pretty. Doc sniffed suspiciously and her gaze darted along the corridor. 'Who sent you?' she demanded.

'Nobody,' Elena said, 'I came alone.'

'Why?'

'Because I was scared. Nikolai . . . died last night. There was a fire at the shop.' Her lips were trembling and she looked as if she was about to burst into tears. Doc motioned her inside and closed the door, relocking it up again with business-like movements.

'I knew about Nikolai,' I said, 'because I was there.'

Elena's eyes opened wide with disbelief. 'Nikolai was already dead when I arrived,' I went on. 'Strangled. I wish I could have done something, but it was too late. Then someone tried to kill me. I'd like to know who it was.'

She put her knuckles in her mouth and bit on them hard. She blinked and I could see she was struggling to control her emotions. If it was an act, I thought, it was a damned good one. Suddenly, tears welled silently down her cheeks. 'But the fire?' she sobbed.

'A grenade. Somebody threw it while I was still in there. I managed to get out just in time.'

She looked at me curiously and seemed to see my scarred face for the first time. 'Jesus Christ,' she said, 'you're lucky to be alive.'

'That's what I keep saying to myself. Not surprisingly, perhaps, I want to stay that way.'

She wiped the tears away with her hand and pulled her shoulders back, making an obvious effort at self-control. She stood straight, fixed me in the eye and gritted her teeth. 'I'll tell you one thing,' she said. 'Whoever killed Nikolai is going to pay. I'll never leave it alone until I've sliced their balls off with a razor.'

'Oh, the great avenger,' Doc cut in. 'How do we know you're not in on it? Very convenient for you that you were out, wasn't it? Where the hell were you?'

Elena's red-rimmed eyes remained fixed on my face. 'I've been at Robert Rabjohn's since Sunday,' she said. 'Nikolai sensed something was going to happen and he sent me round there for safety. I hardly know Robert, but Nikolai said he wouldn't refuse. I wanted Nikolai to come too, but he wouldn't. He was going to talk to you, Mr Ross. He was going to tell you the full story and show you one of the Akhnaton *ushabtis*. Don't you see? It has to be the *ushabtis* they were after. Nikolai was the only one who knew where they were. I know he wasn't always straight, Mr Ross. You have to be fly in the antiquities business. But he was always absolutely fair and honest with me. He never told me a lie, never tried to exploit me, never touched me – you know, like that. Treated me like a father – or rather like a father should treat a daughter – my father never did. Nikolai wasn't cultured or even really clever, but he was kind and understanding. I could always rely on him to help me when I needed help, without asking anything in return.'

I was thinking of how I'd narrowly escaped being sliced like a carrot at his hands only a couple of days before, and how he'd shrugged it off with some quip about there being casualties in any war. It was hard to reconcile the two Nikolais. Elena must have guessed what I was thinking, because she said: 'I'm sorry for the way he received you, Jamie. The truth is that from the day Julian Cranwell was found dead, Nikolai was petrified – not only for himself, but for me as well. Fear like that makes you do odd things.'

'He wasn't honest with me, either.'

'No he wasn't. But he had his reasons. I'm sure he really was going to tell you the truth when he was . . . he died.'

'What was the truth?'

She looked down at her hands. 'All right,' she said glancing up, 'the story of the Ramessid mine was a lie. There was no diamond mine. It was all about Zerzura. Nikolai knew that Julian wouldn't help him find the Lost Oasis if he thought some of the artefacts were going to be sold to private collectors. He invented the Ramessid mine story to fool Julian.'

I found myself watching her with renewed distaste, and I saw that Doc's expression had intensified, too.

'Please understand me,' Elena said. 'Nikolai wasn't a crook in his own mind. He used to say that during colonial times the British and the French had ransacked Egypt for treasure, just because they had the power: "licensed larceny" he used to call it. He hated the hypocrisy. If the British really cared about selling artefacts, he said, why doesn't the British Museum give back all the things they helped themselves to, beginning with the Rosetta Stone? He said the Antiquities Service was just the same; they didn't really care about their heritage, but what really turned them on was the money they would make out of tourists – fat-cat salaries for the boys. Nikolai said everyone was pretending to be holier than thou, but in fact they were all on the make in one way or another.'

'Except Julian?'

'Yes, Julian was incorruptible. Nikolai thought he was naive, because all the others were lining their pockets. He didn't think it mattered whether the treasures went to private collectors or the Antiquities Service, as long as everything was properly recorded and the historical significance known. The way he saw it, it was either money for fat cats like Abbas Rifad, or survival for us. He felt he couldn't tell Julian that, but I thought he should have. He said that Julian would have the freedom to examine and date everything, all the historical data would have been his alone. Nikolai thought it was a perfectly fair exchange, since he both financed the expedition and provided the directions.'

'And the *ushabtis* – did he intend to sell them too?'

She looked as if she might burst into tears again, but fought them back gallantly. 'I don't know,' she said, 'I just don't know. I don't think so. I told him it was all wrong. I told him he should never have tried to cheat Julian. He said it wasn't cheating. Julian would get what he wanted – the Lost Oasis – and all the glory would be his forever. I didn't want anything to do with it. But he was always good to me, Jamie. He was all I had. He never lied to me.'

'What about the translation from the manuscript, the location of Zerzura, did he still have that?'

'No, I swear he didn't!' The effort at self-control broke down suddenly and she collapsed into a paroxysm of sobs. I looked at Doc, not knowing what to say. I put my hand on Elena's shoulder, and she lifted her soft brown eyes gratefully. A spark of deep recognition passed between us, and I suddenly knew for certain that she was telling the truth: like me, she'd just lost someone special to her, and like me she was half Egyptian – an inhabitant of that no-man's land that only half-castes really know about.

'How did you know where Jamie was?' Doc snapped.

'He gave the phone number to Nikolai. Nikolai traced it to you through enquiries.'

'Did anyone see you arrive?'

'I don't know. But it's possible. Jamie isn't safe here, Dr Barrington, and neither are you. They killed Nikolai and they tried to kill Jamie. These people won't give up. They'll stop at nothing.'

'Nowhere's safe,' Doc said, looking at me inquiringly.

I knew a silent question was being asked: were we to trust Elena or not? 'Sit down,' I said, forcing Elena gently into an armchair, looking at Doc to make sure she realised I'd just answered her enquiry.

'I bet you'd like some water,' she said. Elena nodded, and Doc hurried off towards the kitchen.

'There was something weird at the shop,' I said. 'They'd painted an Eye of Ra on Nikolai's mirror in blood.'

'What was that about?' she asked unsteadily.

I shook my head. 'I just don't know. A guy called Aurel Karlman warned me to look out for the Eye of Ra, but he's a spook. It could be just a coincidence.'

'Or maybe Karlman's behind it,' Doc said, bringing water, ice-cold from the fridge, and handing it to Elena. She drank it in a few gulps.

'Robert told me to tell you that you're both welcome at his place,' she said. 'Robert has money and influence. He's got his own guards and a well-protected house. He can hold things off for a few days at least. Why don't you come?'

Doc and I exchanged glances. 'Do you know this Rabjohn?' I asked.

'Only by reputation,' Doc said. 'Professional amateur. There aren't many left, but he's one of them. Pots and pots of money. Houses in Manhattan, London and Rome. Father was a US railway magnate, and Rabjohn was brought up to dally with whatever the hell he wanted. Pally with all the nobs, a friend of President Mubarak's, and knows Sheikh Zayid of the Emirates and the Sultan of Brunei. There's a formidable mind there, though I hear he's never been near a university in his life. All self-taught. Julian said he knew more about Egyptology than any college professor. Has his own theories, too.'

'Robert's very sweet,' Elena said, 'and straight. He was the only one Julian trusted enough to show the Akhnaton *ushabtis*. It was Robert who pronounced them genuine. Nikolai trusted him too, that's why he sent me round there. Robert has donated a lot of money to government projects at one time or another, and they owe him. He said he might be able to smuggle us out of the country, but I said no way am I'm going to run until I've found out who killed Nikolai, then I'll get them, no matter how long it takes.'

I had to grin: she looked like a bad-tempered, fierce little child. 'You know what the Hawazim say?' I asked her. 'It took forty years, but the Hazmi got his revenge.'

'I'm not a Hazmiyya,' she said, 'but that's just how I feel right now. Nikolai was all I had, and they took him away. Now they'll get what they deserve, no matter what.'

Doc was studying her features with a touch of admiration. 'That's what I should have said when they got Ronnie,' she sighed. 'I've been a fighter all my life, but when it came to the crunch I just let it go. No more Mister Nice Guy though. It's still not too late to start.'

'I know it's going to look bad with the police,' I said, 'but I am a Hazmi – at least I'm half of one – and I'm going nowhere till I get to the bottom of this.'

'But you must get out of this place,' Elena said. 'Sooner or later they'll find you here.'

'I think she's right,' Doc said suddenly, as if she'd made a decision. 'We ought to move now.'

I filled an old knapsack with washing and shaving things, my passports, and my Hazmi dagger, and met Doc and Elena at the door. Doc opened it cautiously. We hurried down the stairs to the basement and Doc went over the car carefully for tampering, feeling round the wheels, looking under the bonnet and underneath the chassis. 'It's kosher,' she said.

In the street, Doc's two smokers had long gone, but soon after we crossed 26th July Bridge, a black Mercedes suddenly swung into place behind us.

'It's only a black Merc,' I said. 'There's a million in this city.'

Doc glanced in the mirror. 'It's the same bugger, I swear,' she said. 'Hang on to your hats, boys and girls.'

She swerved into a side-street and put her foot down solidly on the accelerator, just dodging a line of fruit-stalls, whose proprietors and customers leapt desperately out of our path. They shook their fists and cursed, and someone threw a tomato, which splattered across the back window. 'Sorry, chaps!' Doc muttered, turning sharply down a narrow alley. Miraculously there was no one in it, and Doc revved up to sixty, working smoothly up and down through the gears as she turned again and again. There was no sight of the Mercedes now through the tomato pulp running down the back window. Doc changed down and turned into Gala Street, a multi-lane boulevard beneath the 6th October flyover, which took you up to Ramses Square. She put her foot down and steamed into the traffic, weaving a way through the cars. 'Good motors, these 504s,' she declared, 'powerful. Ronnie used to love them – only two-wheel drive, but they win the Paris–Dakar hands down every year!'

'Do you think it was *them*?' Elena asked.

'Bet your bottom dollar.'

'But who is *them*?'

'Looked like a government car to me. Did you clock the numberplate, Jamie? Pound to a pinch of shit it was *Mukhabaraat*.'

'Why not just arrest us?'

'Maybe they think one of us knows something.'

We drove into Heliopolis on tenterhooks, looking about wildly in every direction. Rabjohn's house was easy enough to find. It was an impressive white stucco, moresco-style villa, set behind high walls in a garden bursting with date-palms, pink and white oleanders and purple bougainvilleas. There were black-uniformed guards at the gate wearing peaked crash-helmets and the blazons of a private security firm, who stopped us and asked our names. One of them held us up while Elena got out and spoke on the telephone in the tiny kiosk.

'I won't go in,' Doc said suddenly, watching Elena and the guard through the windscreen. 'I've got other business.'

'Oh,' I said. 'What business?'

'I've got to *do* something, Jamie – anything. I knew that when I saw what was left of Kolpos yesterday morning. I'm not going to get sucked into the old slough of despond like I did when Ronnie died. Couldn't even summon the energy to investigate his death, even though I didn't believe a word of the official report. That's not going to happen a second time. Elena's got the right attitude: hound the bastards till you get them. She's a remarkable lady that one; see how she bore up? Should have been like that myself, but when the chips were really down, tough-as-nails old Doc Barrington cracked right up. Time to start over.'

'But what are you going to do?'

'There's Karlman's remark about the Eye of Ra, and then the Eye of Ra you saw on Kolpos's mirror. We have a lead, the Eye of Ra Society, and I'm damned well going to talk to that Madam Montuhotep XV. Might be bunk, but it's a start. I used to be good at this sort of thing – bit rusty now of course, but I've lived in this city for twenty years and I know how to look after myself.'

She flipped down the lid of the glove compartment. Inside was a well-oiled Walther 9mm Police Pistol with three or four clips of ammunition. 'I've broken it out,' she said. 'Used to be a marksman, you know.'

'Doc, don't do this,' I said. 'If that Merc was the enemy, they know where you live and what your car looks like. This isn't the Wild West. You can't shoot your way out, no matter how good you are.'

'I'm not going to hang about playing gooseberry,' she snapped.

So that was it. Doc was starting to feel out of place. She'd jumped to conclusions that hadn't even occurred to me yet. Maybe there was a touch of premonition about Doc, after all.

'Doc, don't,' I said. 'That's rubbish.'

'Jamie,' she said, more kindly. 'What do I do afterwards? Run away? I've lived here nearly half my life. I'm not going anywhere except in a coffin, and if that's how it's got to be, amen.'

'Doc –'

'It's no good, Jamie. My mind's made up. Time to sort out a few things I should have sorted out years ago.'

I could see that wild horses wouldn't persuade her. 'You be careful, Doc,' I said.

'Always am.' She bent over and kissed me on the cheek.

'And thanks.'

'It's been good, Jamie. Feel like my old self again.'

I stood and watched her drive away. As she turned the corner, out of my life, I had a last glimpse of Doc's pale face, set hard as if intent on some terrible purpose.

23

I TURNED TO ELENA AND WE walked through the gate the guard was now holding open for us, through a green chasm of shrubs, past a fountain where light played across the path in circling prisms. Under the arched portico of the front door, an oldish man waited for us. He was tall, fit-looking, slightly bowed, his silver hair shaven, his face deeply lined, brown as old calfskin. Despite his pale blue eyes, there was an almost Oriental air of inscrutability about him: he had the face of a Tibetan High Lama, a face that concealed many secrets, watchful, mindful, wary. He was perhaps sixty-five, perhaps seventy, dressed immaculately in light cotton trousers, loose buff-coloured blazer, blue-and-white striped shirt, navy blue tie and soft leather moccasins. As we shook hands I had the sudden, unmistakable feeling that I'd seen his face before. I racked my brains to remember where, and suddenly it came: it was the face of the man in the picture of Carter and Carnarvon Julian had left me – the 'Third Man' who'd been holding the newspaper. Then I realised it couldn't be. The picture had been taken in 1923. No, it had to be somewhere else. I normally have an excellent memory, but for the life of me I couldn't recall where.

'Mr Ross?' he said with an almost imperceptible bow. 'Welcome to my house. It's sad that it took a tragedy – two tragedies, in fact – to bring us together.' The hand was small but its grip dry and strong. The voice was cultured with hardly a trace of accent.

'Thanks for inviting me,' I said. 'And it's Jamie.'

'Jamie. And Dr Barrington? She didn't accompany you?'

'She's got other things to do.'

'I'm sorry. Anyhow, I'm very glad Elena found you.' He smiled sadly at Elena. 'I admit I'm not much of a hand at comforting bereaved young ladies.'

He drew us into a large sitting room with French windows opening into garden verandahs on two sides. The verandahs themselves were so full of potted palms and rubber-trees, mingling with the fronds of wild figs and wild peppers drooping in from the lawn, that you had the impression of walking into a forest glade. The furniture was sparse: antique wicker lounging chairs and settees with richly embroidered Turkish cushions, low divan seats, octagonal Arab tables with intricate filigree inlays, a brass-bound *shisha* with a coiled pipe, handmade Egyptian rugs, shelves of books, cabinets of ornaments and artefacts. Half of one wall was almost entirely taken up with a collection of Egyptian musical instruments, another with a collection of coins, a third with a collection of faience and glass-ware, including *ushabtis*, busts, figurines, a beautiful rococo oil-flask in the shape of a Nile fish – blue glass with multi-coloured glass threads dragged over it to give the effect of scales and fins. It was New Kingdom, and obviously priceless. On a pedestal nearby stood a near life-sized head of Sesostris III, slightly scored and misshapen, but with the distinctive brooding features of the pharaoh whom the Nubians had worshipped as a god. In a special cabinet, given pride of place above the mantelpiece, were statuettes of Set – a man with the head of a nameless animal half-way between an aardvark and a rat – Anubis, in the form of a spectral black desert jackal with human eyes, and, most monstrous of all, the golden hippopotamus-god, Tueris, with open mouth and sharp teeth. There were other fragments of sculptures and stelae, most of which clearly belonged in museums. It said much for Rabjohn's influence and power that he was able not only to own them, but also to display them so openly.

Rabjohn gestured to the wicker lounging chairs, facing the garden. 'I think we'll be comfortable here,' he said. 'Coffee?'

I nodded thanks, and Rabjohn clapped his hands once like a pasha. A moment later a Sudanese *sufragi* in an old-fashioned smock and cummerbund, wearing a fez, brought in a tray of coffee and set it on the table by Rabjohn. It was served Sudanese style, from a red earthenware bulb with a long spout, set on a ring, and poured into handle-less cups like tiny dishes. Elena refused, and Rabjohn turned to me, poured my three statutory cups, balancing the hot bulb by its handle between thumb and long forefinger. He poured in silence, concentrating with oriental absorption. The coffee was powerful, flavoured with ginger and cardamom. By Arab tradition it was polite to drink no more and no less than three cups; each cup had a different consistency, and each had a distinct name in Arabic. After my third cup I twisted the vessel in my hand to show I was satisfied – a Bedouin custom rather than Egyptian. Rabjohn grasped its significance perfectly, though, and proceeded to serve himself.

'I must say, Jamie,' he began, sipping the coffee pensively, 'that you don't much resemble the Omar James Ross I met on the last occasion.'

I looked at him in surprise. 'I *knew* I'd seen you before,' I said.

He set down his cup and searched my face keenly. 'You were about five at the time if I recall correctly. It was 1965. I was visiting the oases of the Western Desert – Nasser renamed the place ''The New Valley'', over-optimistically, I thought – and I ran into Dr Calvin Ross, the anthropologist who was living with the Hawazim, your father. He had a small boy with him, rather snotty-nosed and dirty-mouthed as are all five-year olds, and I assume that was you, Jamie. I have to say you've certainly changed for the better.'

'That's astonishing. I'd no idea you knew my father.'

'Not well, you understand. But I met him more than once. He was a very stubborn chap, and very erudite. Loved the desert, loved the Bedouin. It was his whole life. Some people, the stupid ones, used to laugh at him. The more intelligent envied him. Underneath, everyone wished they could do what Calvin did, but few of them had the commitment. Going back to nature was a big thing in the sixties – the hippies and all that. It was an intensely romantic era.'

His eyes fell on my earring. 'Ah, the famous Hawazim *fidwa*,' he said, 'an extraordinary custom – quite unique, I think. Your father wore one too.'

'He wasn't really entitled to it. It's only given to Hazmi boys at circumcision. My father was too old to undergo the ceremony.'

'I suppose it was part of his romanticism. Your father was a romantic at heart, but unlike the hippies he had the strength of will to live out the fantasy. Of course, he had the money too. It was a rich man's dream, perhaps, but I never begrudged Calvin his romanticism. He accepted all the responsibilities that entailed. We got on because I myself am a traditionalist – and perhaps a romantic – too.'

'You've been in Egypt since the early sixties?'

'Yes, but not consistently. I have other houses, other countries, other interests. That's the luxury of not being a specialist. I am very glad I never studied Egyptology. With all due respect, Jamie, academic study these days has become so specialised that academics rarely step outside their own cloistered worlds. Instead of making them broad-minded – which I always understood was the purpose of education – they have become more narrow-minded. There they are, fighting their pathetic little wars behind closed doors. When I think of it I am always reminded of Swift's Lilliputians. I suppose, in the end, it is all the fault of the ancient Greeks.'

'Why do you say that?' Elena asked.

'Ah, sorry, I'd almost forgotten they were your ancestors. Yet I have to say it: it was the Greeks who first decided that the universe ought to be analysed, cut up, divided into parts and each part named separately. The naming of parts, that was almost entirely the sum of their so-called philosophy. Our modern science adopted the idea, hence all our modern problems. Now, the ancient Egyptians thought differently. They knew that nature was more than simply the sum of its parts. They knew that God could not be discovered by slicing up the building-blocks of life. God was self-evidently extant. It was Ra, the sun, crossing the sky each morning on his royal barque. While their godhead was fragmented into dozens of deities, they knew that all these gods were only separate aspects of the One.'

'You were never tempted to become an academic?'

'Fortunately I never needed to. My father owned a railway and I was born very rich. Had I been poorer I might have nursed the ambition to collect degrees and qualifications, but as it was I had the freedom to pick up and discard just as I liked. I worked my way backwards through modern art to medieval art, to Roman architecture, to ancient Greek art and philosphy, back to the Hittites, the Etruscans, the Babylonians, the Assyrians, the Sumerians – even the Incas, the Mayas, the Aztecs. I even dallied at one time with native American culture. But none of them fascinated me like the ancient Egyptians. It was powerful. Absorbing. I found that I could not discard ancient Egypt as I discarded the others. I read everything I could find, visited every site, and I'm still learning.'

'Kolpos told me you were an expert on ancient Egyptian artefacts.'

'Poor Nikolai. Yes, I've had the opportunity, the money, the time to see and learn from almost every artefact ever found in ancient Egypt. I have visited every collection, public and private. There have been almost no doors barred to me.'

'Is that what these deaths are about? Ancient Egyptian artefacts? Akhnaton *ushabtis*?'

Rabjohn went silent for a moment. 'Whoever did this to Julian and Nikolai,' he said, 'wants to keep people's mouths shut. The question is – what about? If it's really about the Akhnaton *ushabtis*, then we could all be in trouble. You see, of the two *ushabtis* Julian brought to Cairo, one is right here.'

He walked casually over to a library shelf and pulled a handle. A section of the shelves rolled out silently on a hinge and I saw that it was concealing a small wall-safe. Rabjohn twisted the combination lock, opened the safe and brought out a figurine. He carried it over to me carefully, with an air of reverence. 'Jamie,' he said, 'I give you Akhnaton.'

I gasped. The figure was no more than eight inches high, yet it was the perfect miniature of the statue of Akhnaton in the Egyptian Museum.

'May I?' I said, taking the statuette. It was heavy faience, beautifully crafted, and the features of Akhnaton were unmistakable – the narrow face, unnaturally thin neck, slanting eyes, the grotesquely distorted features: bulbous, dolichocephalic skull, pronounced breasts, swollen belly, thighs and buttocks. The hands were crossed over the chest in mummiform fashion, holding a crook in the left and a flail in the right.

'I suppose there's no question about its authenticity?' I asked Rabjohn.

'None whatever, in my opinion. In some periods *ushabtis* were crudely made, but under the late 18th Dynasty they were finely crafted and commonly done in faience, as this one is. Note the accuracy of the posture. The crossed arms holding crook and flail – *heq* and *nekhakha* – denote death. The crook gathers in, the flail symbolises the three aspects of being.'

'Where did you get it?' I asked.

Rabjohn and Elena exchanged glances. 'I brought it,' Elena said. 'Nikolai had them hidden – buried in a disused brick-kiln at Abu Rawash industrial estate. Even I didn't know the exact place. He was petrified that someone would find them by chance. Two days ago he decided to move them. He brought them back to his shop, gave one to me and told me to bring it to Robert and stay here. Robert knew about the *ushabtis* and had already offered to look after them. Nikolai thought this one would be safer with him.'

'So who does it actually belong to now?'

'Please don't misunderstand, Jamie,' Rabjohn said. 'I've no intention of purloining the piece. Rightfully it belongs to the government. It's just that it is one of the rarest pieces ever found and I think we have a duty to preserve it. We also have a duty to preserve ourselves, of course, and since Julian was killed in the process of revealing it to the Antiquities Service, that move seems to be contra-indicated right at present.'

'OK,' I said. I hadn't let either Elena or Rabjohn into my doubts about Julian's death, and I decided that nothing would be served by telling them now. 'What about the other one?'

'Nikolai had it with him in the shop,' Elena said. 'He was going to show it to you. Either the murderer took it, or it went up in the flames.'

'Did anyone else know he had the *ushabtis*, or that he'd moved them two days ago?'

'Apart from me and Robert, no one. At least I don't think so. But somebody could have followed him to Abu Rawash.' She took the *ushabti* out of my hands and looked at it in disgust. 'Akhnaton killed Nikolai,' she said, fixing the figurine with such hatred that for a moment I thought she was going to dash it to pieces against the floor. For a fraction of a second Rabjohn's face lost its benevolent look. Then, with the grace and speed of a ballet-dancer he moved in and took the statuette from her.

'Three and a half thousand years on,' he muttered, 'the Great Heretic is still inciting such hatred!' He carried the *ushabti* back to the wall-safe as attentively as if it were a baby and returned to the chairs looking relieved. 'That's the way it always was,' he said. 'No one can look at Akhnaton without some kind of passion. Personally, I believe the world would have been a better place without him. But then I'm a traditionalist, as I said.'

'Why so much trouble over this one pharaoh?' Elena asked.

'It's a long story,' Rabjohn said, 'and one better told over lunch. I've asked Madani to serve it on the verandah.'

As Rabjohn led us out, I paused to look at a painting hanging by the door. It was vaguely familiar. It showed three figures: a bearded man in long robes, a magician of some kind, displaying engraved tablets to another man in eastern dress, while a woman looked on – a grey eminence in the background. He saw me looking: 'Ah, the Pinturiccio,' he said. 'Not a very famous painting, but interesting.'

'Who is the magician?' I asked.

'Hermes Trismegistus. The other figures are Moses and Isis.' As I examined the painting it suddenly occurred to me that Karlman had talked about Hermes Trismegistus.

'Are you familiar with the name Trismegistus, Jamie?' Rabjohn asked.

'No,' I said. 'It's just that Professor Karlman mentioned him.'

He stiffened visibly with surprise. 'Oh, you've been talking to the Professor, have you?' he said.

'I've met him, yes. Wait a minute, I've seen this picture before. Isn't the original in the Vatican?'

Rabjohn showed his teeth in a wan smile. 'Is it?' he said. 'Nowadays it's often difficult to say which is the original and which a copy, don't you agree?'

I wondered if he was being deliberately obtuse. Surely a man as rich as Rabjohn didn't have to be vain enough to pretend all his *objets d'art* were originals. 'Come to lunch,' he said gently.

The table was an oasis of glass, silver, white cloth and ceramics, standing out against the bare red tiles of the verandah. Three places had been set impeccably with heavy silver cutlery and cut-glass. Rabjohn held the chair politely for Elena, then seated himself at the head of the table. He lifted a crystal carafe. 'Wine?' he asked, raising an inquisitive eyebrow. 'It's imported burgundy. I think you'll find it satisfactory. I only drink French wine. Occasionally you find a good bottle of Chianti, even Californian, but most others are pale imitations.' He poured me a glass and I tasted it. He was right; it was almost maddeningly good. Elena waved the carafe away, but Rabjohn insisted. 'It's excellent for the digestion,' he said. 'A glass of good wine is just what you need right now.'

'I don't feel like eating or drinking anything,' she said.

But I noticed she let herself be persuaded.

The *sufragi* brought us borscht, served with cream. Elena toyed with her spoon, Rabjohn ate elegantly. As I savoured the smoothness of the soup, I looked out at the garden. There must have been at least an acre of lawns, trees and flowerbeds. Another fountain dealt whorls of pastel colours across the grass, and I noticed that the fountain itself was a miniature copy of the colossus of Ramses II in Ramses Square, depicting the pharaoh striding powerfully, with balled fists at his side. An image of power. A matched pair of sacred ibises suddenly landed on the lawn and began trawling for food with their long, sabre-like beaks, strutting with casual grace while the sunlight shone brilliantly on their white feathers. There was something of Rabjohn in their unruffled dignity, I thought. He watched them with pleasure for a moment. 'They always return,' he said. 'Ibises are territorial creatures. They evidently believe my little patch is their territory.'

He took a sip of wine, patted his lips with a crisp, almost preternaturally white napkin and cleared his throat. 'Now, you enquired about Akhnaton,' he said to Elena as if addressing a freshman student at a tutorial. 'A most fascinating subject for enthusiasts. Less so, perhaps, for laymen. However, I shall endeavour to compress as much as possible. Let us begin by saying that very little was known about Akhnaton until recently. That was the result of a deliberate policy by the pharaoh's successors to erase his very name, and those of his family, from history. If it were not for the persistence of Western Egyptologists, they might very well have succeeded. In the King Lists of ancient Egypt, the names of Akhnaton and his sons, Smenkhare and Tutankhamen, do not appear, because it was considered afterwards that they had not lived subject to the approval of *Ma'at*. Are you familiar with the concept of *Ma'at*, Elena?'

'I've heard of it. Isn't it the ideal of justice and truth?'

'Yes, to the ancient Egyptians, *Ma'at* was the personification of divine harmony – a harmony they later believed Akhnaton had violated. You see, Elena, despite the sophistication of their society, in many ways the ancient Egyptians lived very simple lives. They were farmers and stock-breeders, symbolised respectively by the flail and the crook, and their lives were regulated by the sun, the seasons, and above all by the river Nile and its annual inundation. When you remember that only about eleven per cent of Egypt is cultivable land, almost all of it on the river banks, you begin to see that it is actually a kind of long oasis, a thin ribbon of brilliant green in the midst of the most arid deserts on earth. Everything in ancient Egyptian life depended on the Nile and the arts and sciences the Egyptians had were developed almost exclusively to help them control, predict, maintain and understand the passage of the sun, the sequence of the seasons, and the rise and fall of the waters. That was what *Ma'at* really meant, and anything which interfered with that was a betrayal of *Ma'at*.'

'And Akhnaton interfered with it?'

'Devastatingly. When Akhnaton arrived on the scene, about 1350 BC, the most powerful god in the Egyptian pantheon was Ra, or Amun-Ra, the sun god, served by a corps of priests that had already been in existence for thousands of years. Akhnaton was originally called Amenophis, and he had not been raised to become pharaoh. The heir apparent to the throne was Thutmose, son of Amenophis III. Thutmose died mysteriously, allowing Amenophis to take his place eventually as Pharaoh Amenophis IV. He married a beautiful woman called Nefertiti, and in the fifth year of his reign, he changed his name to Akhnaton, publicly renouncing any further association with Ra. He declared that only one god would be worshipped henceforth, the Aton or Sun-Globe, which, with its cascading rays, represented the life-force of the cosmos. All other gods were banned. The ancient priesthoods of Ra and others were disbanded, images of the gods thrown down, their names expunged from monuments, their temples closed, their funds sequestered and diverted to other projects. He also moved his capital from the traditional site at Thebes downriver to Amarna, near Asyut, where he built a sacred city dedicated to the Aton, known as Akhetaton – "The Horizon of the Aton". He lived a secretive life, apart from Nefertiti and apart from his courtiers, only meeting with them on ritual occasions. Yet despite this secretiveness, a great many new ideas seem to have emanated from him. Under his rule the ancient Egyptians developed dazzling new art forms, new ways of thought which can only be described as scientific, and began to make preparations for a new universal culture which would eventually take over the entire world, uniting east and west. Some scholars regard Akhnaton as the "first individual in history", a thinker millennia before his time, the precursor of monotheistic religions including Judaism, Christianity and Islam. Some consider him a religious mystic, others a bigoted tyrant and egotist. Much that's written about him is pure speculation – actually, we still know very little about him. We don't know why his features appear so distorted, or why he is shown as a hermaphrodite in statues, and we don't know where his ideas came from. We don't even know for certain who he was, whether a prince of the royal family or a stranger from outside.'

The *sufragi* cleared away the soup-dishes and laid plates. He served us helpings of *mahshi* – vine leaves stuffed with minced mutton and rice. 'I thought a light dish was in order,' Rabjohn said. 'Please eat something, Elena.'

She picked at the food with her fork moodily. 'I'm sorry,' she said, 'I'm just not hungry.'

She sampled her wine and fixed her eyes on Rabjohn. 'What happened to Akhnaton?' she asked.

'That's the greatest mystery of all,' he said, laying his fork down and taking a sip of wine. 'You see, after ruling Egypt for seventeen years, he simply vanished without trace. Neither his mummy nor that of his wife Nefertiti have ever been found. The official tombs built for them at Amarna were never occupied. We have no idea how he died, or even *if* he died in his seventeenth regnal year.'

'What about the Davis find?' I asked. 'Pete Margoulis told me it was the largest human cranium ever found.'

'You're referring to Tomb 55 in the Valley of the Kings, excavated by Davis in 1907? Yes, it's true that at first it was thought to contain the mummy of Akhnaton. The tomb was unfinished and had been hastily prepared, and there was speculation that the king's body had been brought back to Thebes after the failure of his revolution. The skull was oddly shaped, just as Akhnaton's is shown to be in stelae and statues. But the latest studies of genetics and cranio-morphology suggest that the mummy in Tomb 55 is actually that of Smenkhare, who was probably Akhnaton's son and Tutankhamen's brother.'

'Why *did* Akhnaton fail?' Elena asked.

'Again we don't know. There was certainly tremendous opposition to his rule, especially among the disbanded priesthood of Ra. There may even have been some open rebellion. The opposition was almost certainly masterminded by people very close to the king, including Ay, a high priest, and Horemheb, a general, who outwardly supported Akhnaton during his reign, but who quickly reasserted the old values as soon as he was gone. Akhnaton's official successor was Smenkhare, his son, who died within a year under mysterious circumstances, and then Tutankhamen, who was only nine when he came to the throne and thus well under the thumb of Ay and Horemheb. Tutankhamen died aged nineteen, probably murdered, and was succeeded by Ay, who now openly took the reins of power he'd actually been wielding secretly for so long. He only lasted four years, then he too died suddenly and inexplicably, and was replaced by Horemheb. The reaction against Atonism was already beginning in Tut's time – which is why he was forced to change his birth name from Tutankh*aton* to Tutankh*amen* – and to move the capital back to Thebes. The priesthood of Ra was restored, the old temples reopened, the revenues flowed again. Under Horemheb it reached frenzy level. The Aton temples at Thebes were smashed, the names of Akhnaton, Smenkhare and Tutankhamen excised from every monument and statue, the Great Temple of Aton at Amarna taken apart stone by stone, tombs of nobles who'd served the kings were desecrated, and anyone found continuing the worship of Aton was liable to have his nose amputated and be sent into exile. Horemheb had gangs of workers sent to the city of Akhetaton, which had been uninhabited now for years, with orders to raze it to the ground. Not a single stone of the place was left standing. The ruins were buried under drifting sand and lost until they were discovered by chance after thousands of years.'

The *sufragi* had by now cleared away the remnants of the main course. Rabjohn offered us ice-cream or fruit, but neither of us felt like eating more. He drew us over to the lounging chairs, which the *sufragi* had pushed out on to the verandah. 'Shall we rest over there,' he said; 'can I offer you a liqueur? No – then perhaps more coffee.'

'Coffee would be fine.'

We sat down in the chairs and I lit my pipe slowly. The *sufragi* brought the coffee – this time Turkish coffee in miniature handled cups. We sat in silence for a few moments. The sacred ibises gave up their trawling and took wing. I watched them as they climbed higher and higher into the silk and azure sky. I took off my John Lennon glasses, rubbed them vigorously on my shirt cuff, then replaced them. 'Tell me, Robert,' I said, 'I mean, Horemheb's attempt to eradicate the names of Akhnaton and Tut from history strikes me as almost paranoid – out of all proportion to the threat. What on earth was he so frightened of?'

'He was absolutely determined that nothing like Akhnaton and the danger he presented to *Ma'at* – to the world order – should ever raise its ugly head again for the rest of eternity. But it wasn't only Horemheb. He came to power with the help of the Ra priesthood. It was the brotherhood who were behind all these strokes.'

'Were they behind Tutankhamen's murder, too?' Elena asked.

'Almost certainly. They were hand in glove with the courtiers, of course. As a boy, Tutankhamen would have been easy for them to manipulate, but he might have become more assertive with age. The brotherhood had got its power back and wasn't about to lose it again. Ever.'

'But there's a strange anomaly here,' I said. 'Why, when Horemheb went to such fantastic lengths to expunge the names of his predecessors from all records, and even desecrated the tombs of nobles who'd served them, did he leave Tutankhamen's tomb intact?'

'That's a good question,' Rabjohn said, 'and one that's never been satisfactorily answered. The simple solution would be that he was afraid of something inside the tomb.'

'But the tomb was broken into twice shortly after Tut's death. The thieves were caught and executed by Horemheb's guards. If Horemheb hated Tut so much, why execute them instead of letting them get on with it?'

'To keep their mouths shut?'

'If that's the case, then Horemheb was not only afraid of whatever was in Tut's tomb, but also didn't want anyone to know about it. Maybe the thieves threatened to blab, and had to be taken out.'

'But no one touched the tomb for nearly three and a half thousand years,' Elena said.

'Precisely,' I said. 'That means that Carter and Carnarvon must have found the secret when they opened the tomb in 1923.'

'But everything they found has been recorded.'

'Has it?' I said, bringing the *United American Press* printout from my rucksack and unfolding it in front of them. 'Then what about this?'

24

I TRIED TO PHONE DOC BEFORE I went to bed, but there was no answer. That worried me. I knew she could look after herself, but I'd have been far happier if she'd stayed here with us. Rabjohn showed me to a spacious bedroom on the first floor, with en suite bathroom and its own small balcony overlooking the garden. 'I call this the ''Arab room'',' he told me. 'I thought it might amuse you, Jamie. It is the only room in the house totally devoid of anything ancient Egyptian.'

Actually it was furnished and decorated with exquisite taste. The bed-head, the wardrobe and the writing desk were superbly carved hardwood antiques – abstract Islamic work probably from Zanzibar or Yemen – and there were a couple of excellent oil paintings on the wall, heavily framed in gilt. One showed Arabs mounted on camels – I recognised it as *Pèlerins Allant à La Mecque* by the French artist Auguste Belly – and the other Arab horsemen sweeping past in frantic action. 'Delacroix,' Rabjohn said as I peered at it. 'A most complex person, a romantic like your father, Jamie. He toured North Africa in the 1830s and was utterly entranced by the brilliant colours and pristine images he found.' I gasped inwardly as I took in the information. A Belly and a Delacroix! These two paintings alone were worth hundreds of thousands of dollars.

There was a rug of shimmering colours spread in front of the open fireplace, which Rabjohn seemed very proud of. 'Handmade by the Qashgai nomads of Iran,' he said, 'and quite unique. Not strictly Arab of course – the Qashgai are of Turkish extraction – but appropriate all the same, I think.' He went out for a moment, and I put my knapsack down and stepped on to the balcony. From here you could see the ceaseless play of lights along Al-Urubba street – cars and buses heading to and from the airport. Above me lay the night sky with its luminous chains of stars. Rabjohn followed me a couple of minutes later with a bottle of Cognac and two small glasses. 'Care for a nightcap?' he asked.

'All right,' I said.

He placed glasses on the wrought-iron balcony table, poured the Cognac, and handed me a glass.

'Please – sit down,' he said and we seated ourselves in the two old-fashioned lounging chairs standing one each side of the table.

'Cheers!' I said, raising my glass.

'*Sahhatak!*' he answered in Arabic, 'your health!'

'You speak Arabic?' I asked.

He shrugged, '*Shwayya*,' he said. That could have meant 'little' or 'a little': honesty or modesty.

'Tell me, did Julian mention where he got the *ushabtis*?'

'No. I admit I was curious, but I agreed it was better not to know. In a business like this you can't be sure of anyone.'

'How did you come to meet Julian? I mean, I knew him pretty well up till two years ago, and I never remember him talking about you.'

'No, we met after your time. Of course, I know all about your trouble with the Antiquities Service. Julian was launching the Zerzura Project, and he came to me for sponsorship. I was able to give him some little help, of course, but not as much as I would have liked.'

'I thought the Antiquities Service funded the Zerzura Project.'

'Yes, but you know how it is these days. Unless it's something big and brassy that will attract the tourists, no one's enthusiastic. They gave him only a pittance. I have to say that I don't always get on well with Egyptologists. Good Lord, they're so precious now that they bark at you if you call them ''archaeologists'', as if

Egyptology and archaeology were completely separate disciplines. But more than that, it's their *approach* that bothers me. They are, generally speaking, exclusively utilitarian. That is, they're interested almost entirely in what one might call *ephemera*.'

'I object!' I said, grinning. 'That argument coming from a collector like yourself is certainly the pot calling the kettle black!'

He laughed. 'Touché!' he said. 'It's true I'm a collector – I love to own beautiful things and to have them around me.'

'Your collection is impressive.'

'Oh, you've only seen the surface skimmings. Beneath this house is a very extensive basement, containing what one might call my private collection. I shall show it to you one day. No, I'm proud of my collection, but don't be misled into believing that artefacts are my only or even my main concern. Many Egyptologists are so obsessed with the form of things that they miss the symbolic and esoteric elements in ancient Egyptian culture. One cannot ascertain the meaning of such elements by reason alone – one must use both reason and insight.'

'You begin to sound like Julian.'

'Now you understand why Julian and I got on so well. Yes, I admired him because he was one of the few Egyptologists able to step out of the narrow confines of the discipline and enter the ancient Egyptian *mind*.'

'According to Karlman the ancient Egyptian mind was full of occult secrets.'

'Ah, yes. The Professor. Tell me, how did you get along with him?'

'I didn't. He ridiculed my theory about the origins of Egyptian civilisation, then told me half an hour later that I was ''head and shoulders'' above the rest. The man's completely off his chump!'

'That's true enough. But with all due respect, he might have had a point. Why do you hold such a difficult view?'

I paused, searching among an array of possible truths. 'I don't know,' I said at last, 'I mean on one hand it's not such a remarkable theory. It's clear from the archaeological record that some time in the Predynastic period a race of outsiders arrived in Egypt, bringing with them advanced knowledge. Hieroglyphic writing, monumental architecture, art, sciences, these things all seem to have sprung to life in ancient Egypt without any evidence of slow development from earlier forms. They can only have been introduced fully-fledged from somewhere else. No one has yet been able to pinpoint an actual place of origin for this advanced race. I like to call it "Atlantis", but I'm speaking only conjecturally. "Atlantis" is a symbol of some unknown, undiscovered civilisation.'

'Fine. That much is at least one reasonable interpretation of the data. But a civilisation with lasers and telescopes? Advanced technology that was later lost? Where's the evidence?'

'Well, look at the pyramids. No one has yet explained satisfactorily how they were built or even when. After the invasion of Egypt in the seventh century, the Arabs discovered a manuscript revealing that there were at least thirty caches of "treasure" concealed inside the Great Pyramid. This "treasure" wasn't gold or silver, but ancient artefacts – detailed maps of the earth and the sky on a glass-like material which was indestructible, powerful weapons that fired beams of light, instruments which allowed one to see pictures from far away, and others which could send messages to the stars.'

'Simple fantasies, perhaps?'

'Perhaps. But this text was written in the seventh century, an era in which people still fought with swords and spears and believed the earth was flat. Fantasies are based on current knowledge and suffer its limitations. A man who knows a horse might fantasise about a flying horse, and one who knows a boat might imagine a celestial boat, but a man who believes the stars are tiny lights in the sky is not likely to fantasise about space-travel. How could men of the early Christian era even imagine about lasers, plastics, radio and TV – technology inconceivable before the development of modern physics?'

'But the artefacts were never found, of course.'

'They've never come to light, no. Whether or not they were found is a different question. In the ninth century al-Mamun, the Governor of Egypt, succeeded in breaking into the pyramid. He appears to have kept very quiet about what he discovered there, if anything. Of course it's possible he found nothing – either that there wasn't and never had been anything to find, or that somebody had got there before him. But when you think that Carter and Carnarvon may have kept quiet about something *they* found in Tutankhamen's tomb, it seems at least possible that the same thing happened when al-Mamun unsealed the Great Pyramid, a thousand years earlier.'

'Perhaps. But in both cases, I'd say the evidence was inconclusive. Is your theory of ancient Egyptian origins based simply on these unsubstantiated facts?'

I paused again. Rabjohn's manner was subtly penetrating, almost hypnotic. It made you want to tell the precise truth. 'Not really,' I said. 'I suppose I already had this feeling before I started – that there was something about the conventional theories that just *wasn't right*.'

'Aha! Intuition! I thought so!'

'I've always rejected the idea of intuition, if you mean any more than an ability to add up facts and see where they lead.'

'Really? Are you certain, Jamie? Why was it, then, that you were attracted to someone like Julian, a naturally intuitive man? Isn't it possible that you have spent your life trying to conceal something from yourself?'

'I don't think so.'

'I see,' Rabjohn said. 'Yet years ago your father told me a most interesting story. He said that he'd been carrying you across the desert on his camel, when in a certain place you began to yell and screech, hysterical with fear. "Don't go, Daddy! Bad! Bad! *Jinns! Jinns!*" you shouted. Calvin said that you'd been so terrified that he'd turned back and made a long detour just to calm you down. A week later, when a stray camel passed the same spot, its leg was blown off by an unexploded World War II mine!'

'I don't remember,' I said, but I knew it was a lie. This and other childhood memories were things I'd deliberately shut out of my life as a civilised Englishman, things I'd bottled up and imprisoned in the dark side of my psyche. A cold shiver suddenly ran down my spine. Rabjohn was watching me intently, and I had the sudden frightening hallucination that he knew more about me than I knew myself. 'I was just a child,' I added lamely.

'Nevertheless,' he went on, unrelenting, 'Elena tells me you had a "feeling" about Nikolai's death, only two days ago.'

How had he known that, I wondered? Then I remembered mentioning it to Elena on the way here. Earlier, she and Rabjohn had talked alone for half an hour or so when he'd escorted her to her room. I took off my glasses and rubbed them on my cuff, looking at him in silence, unable and unwilling to make myself foolish by denying any more. I drew a deep breath and replaced my glasses. 'What exactly are you driving at, Robert?' I asked.

He put his Cognac glass down and looked back at me mildly. His eyes had lost their piercing quality. 'Nothing,' he said. 'I didn't mean to be impertinent. It's just that I think you may be hiding your light under a bushel.'

With that, he wished me good night, went out, and closed the door.

25

After he'd gone, I showered, lathering and scrubbing myself, trying to scour away the sudden bitter-sweet memories of my childhood he'd induced so vividly. What the hell had he meant with that parting shot, 'hiding my light under a bushel?' Deep down, though, I suppose I knew, and didn't want to admit it. I *had* had a feeling about Nikolai all right, and I'd sensed what was going to happen a couple of seconds before it had occurred. I couldn't kid myself; those two seconds had saved my life. And this wasn't the first time. The same thing had happened when Kolpos had tried to carve me up: I'd had a clear image of the blade a split second before he'd whipped it out. I had lied to Rabjohn, of course. I knew the story he had told about me and my father was true – it was still talked of in hushed voices by the Hawazim today. If I was absolutely honest with myself, I'd admit that things like this had been happening to me since I was a kid, only I'd always tried to pretend to myself there was a logical explanation.

I forced myself to stop thinking about it. Like Doc had said, you could go wacko playing these mind-games. I towelled myself as energetically as I dared, carefully dabbing at the bruises on my body and the lacerations on my cheeks, which were still painful but beginning to heal. Then I went to examine some bookshelves I'd spotted in the corner of the room. Almost all of the books were on Bedouin life, I noticed. Some were classics: Doughty's

Arabia Deserta, the first folio edition, and Burckhardt's two-volume *Notes on Bedouins & Wahhabys*, dated 1830. There was Tregenza's *Red Sea Hills*, Murray's *Sons of Ishmael*, and even my father's book, *Ghosts of the Desert – The Hawazim of Egypt*. I flipped open the title page, and read in Dad's crabbed handwriting 'To Robert, The Eternal Amateur, Kharja 1968'. It brought an unexpected lump to my throat, this reminiscence of my father, on top of Rabjohn's stories. As a boy I remember him as vibrant, full of life, with his big black beard and sparkling blue eyes. His nickname, *Abu Sibaahi* – the 'Father of the Desert Rat' – was a great tribute. The Hawazim revered the Desert Rat – *Jaculus orientalis* – which never drank water for its entire life, and whose ability to survive in the most hostile of conditions was proverbial. My father was a survivor, but I suppose there'd always been a black hole at the centre of his being, a black hole that Maryam filled. Anyway, his will to survive had certainly faded away after she went. It was as if the colours had all been washed out of him – turned him almost literally grey. He became nearly a stranger to me in England. He simply eked out the rest of his existence waiting – waiting for her to return, I think, because he would never use the word 'dead' in relation to Maryam, only 'disappeared'.

I climbed in bed and switched out the light. I couldn't sleep. My ribs and my head were still aching, and I thought about taking a painkiller, then rejected the idea. The blinds were drawn back, and bars of yellow light penetrated the darkness from the security-lamps outside. I lay there for an hour before the ache began to subside. I was just drifting downhill into slumber, when there was a soft knock at the door. I leapt out of bed and opened it cautiously. It was Elena. She was wearing plain but loosely cut pyjamas, and her hair, caught in a jet of light from the outside lamps, made a sheeny cascade down her back. Her eyes and mouth were little thickets of shadow against the soft lamplit ochre of her face. For a moment I was stunned by the vision, unable to summon the will to move.

'Sorry,' she said, almost in a whisper, 'were you asleep?'

The words broke the spell and I opened the door wide. 'No,' I said, 'I couldn't sleep.'

'Neither could I.'

I had a sudden impulse to take her head in both hands, run my fingers through that beautiful hair, and kiss her passionately. 'Come in,' I said. As she entered her hair brushed my shoulder. I caught the faint scent of sandalwood. 'Would you like to sit on the balcony?' I asked.

'No, let's sit inside,' she said.

We sat down side by side on the bed and when I switched on the side-light, I noticed she was holding a book in her lap, a dog-eared notebook with a black all-weather cover. 'I'm sorry for intruding, Jamie,' she said, 'but I had to give you this.' She handed me the book.

'What is it?'

'It's Julian's journal for the last three months. He gave it to Nikolai for safekeeping when he thought he was in danger. Nikolai couldn't read it because it's written in cipher.'

I took the notebook and flicked through it. The title page read 'Dr Julian Cranwell, Diary Beginning 1st January'.

'So Nikolai did *try* to read it then?' I asked, more harshly than I'd meant to.

'Look, Jamie, you've got Nikolai wrong. He wasn't such a bad guy really. It wasn't the origin of the *ushabtis* that concerned him so much as what had happened to Julian. He thought the diary might shed some light on that.'

'OK, I'll take your word for it. Why have you brought it to me – why didn't you give it to Rabjohn?'

'Nikolai's instructions were very clear. If anything happened to him, the *ushabti* was for Robert and the diary was for you. I wasn't even to tell Robert about it until you'd seen it.'

'Are you going to tell him?' I asked.

'Nikolai trusted him. Julian did too. Nikolai didn't say that I wasn't to reveal the existence of the diary, only that you must have it first. Robert's the only real friend we've got, Jamie. He's been very good to me since I've been here. Of course, he's very intense – absorbed – but I think that comes from being alone for so many years. He's very cerebral, always got something ticking away in his mind, always got his head in the clouds. But I feel he's a good guy, don't you?'

I shrugged, and held Julian's diary under the pale light from the bedside lamp. 'When did Julian first appear with the *ushabtis*?' I asked.

'It was, let's see . . . around the beginning of February.'

'OK, so let's start about 20th January.'

'Can you read Julian's cipher?'

'Yes, he taught me years ago, so I could read the nasty things he wrote about me when he was in a bad mood, he said. Said it was a very salutary lesson to be able to see ourselves as others see us. It's a long time ago, of course, but I think I can do it – if I remember rightly, it wasn't exactly the Rosetta Stone.'

I turned to the page for 20th January and examined the rows of figures in Julian's erratic copperplate. The cipher would have presented no problem to a specialist. Julian's zeros represented 'e's and the sequence continued from there, with 1 for 'f', 2 for 'g' and so on. It seemed an incredibly painstaking way of writing, and hardly worth the bother for the few things Julian had to hide. Or so I'd thought before.

I took my own notebook and a pencil from the bedside table, and began to work through the ciphers while Elena watched, sitting on the pillow at the bed-head, her long legs drawn up to her chin, her small feet protruding from under the cuffs of her pyjamas. It took twenty minutes to decipher the entry for 20th January:

20th January
Kharja villages. Main centre geographically for Zerzura legends.
    Suwayri wald 'Ali, headman Dimashq village tells me legend that 5 miles due west of Buwayr necropolis is limestone saddle with small chapel buried in sand. Under floor of chapel is buried a box containing book and looking-glass. Book describes route to Zerzura, and glass shows what place looks like. Asked Suwayri if he'd ever dug for it. Said yes, but nothing found. Night on Suwayri's floor – fleas terrible.

'Nothing much there,' I told Elena, holding out the deciphered page for her to read, 'except that he'd identified the Kharja area as a possible starting point for the Zerzura quest. Shall I go on?'

'It looks hard work.'

'No, but it's tedious and long. If you have the patience to wait, I'll continue.'

'All right,' she said. 'I'd rather be here than on my own, anyway.'

Now I'd got in the swing of it, the second page went more smoothly. I finished it in fifteen minutes:

21st January

AM mention W to Suwayr. Goes silent. Then says Ws headman in '33, Hilmi wald Falih is still alive – old man, loony. Was shut away for a time but let out some years ago. Living in Kwayt village. I drove there arrived PM. Found Hilmi after some trouble. Crazy all right. Hardly articulate. Nothing about W but told me to ask at al-Maqs village, Mukhtar wald Salim.

I read the entry through with mounting excitement. 'W' was Orde Wingate, I was certain. Against all odds, Julian had run to ground Wingate's headman on the 1933 expedition, and now we had a name for him: Hilmi wald Falih, almost certainly a Hazmi, I thought. All Wingate's men would have been Hawazim; no other Bedouin knew the desert like them. And then Mukhtar wald Salim. An unbelievable coincidence that I certainly hadn't anticipated. Julian had really been on the trail of something here, and he knew it. I felt a sudden resurgence of admiration for him. I handed the paper to Elena. 'Who's W?' she asked.

'Orde Wingate,' I said.

She looked at me inquisitively.

'Wingate led an expedition into the Western Desert in 1933 in search of Zerzura,' I explained, 'and of the fifteen Bedouin with him, only this Hilmi ever came back, and he'd gone completely off his chump. No one ever discovered what happened out there.'

'Zerzura seems to be poison,' she said, but I'd already started on the next entry. This time I worked through it in less than five minutes, my pencil flashing across the page with excitement. The entry was extremely short:

22nd January
Al-Maqs village A M. Headman Mukhtar wald Salim.

Bought 2 x *ushabtis*. Authenticity uncertain.

Missing Journal. Account of *anachronae*.

'Eureka!' I said. 'That's it! That's where Julian found the *ushabtis*. Al-Maqs village in Kharja oasis!'

Elena read the deciphered entry quickly. 'But what's this?' she asked, '"Missing journal" and "*anachronae*". What on earth does that mean?'

'I really don't know,' I said, 'but Mukhtar wald Salim might.'

26

I AWOKE ON THE FLOOR TO find Elena sleeping peacefully in my bed. She lay curled up protectively with her head in the crook of her elbow, and her raven hair thrown wildly across the pillow. We'd talked till it was almost light and I'd finally agreed to tell Rabjohn about Julian's diary. She'd simply fallen asleep, exhausted, leaving me to doss down on Rabjohn's priceless Qash-gai carpet. I left her sleeping and went downstairs to the kitchen where I found Rabjohn already up, drinking coffee and feeding a golden canary in an antique-looking cage. 'Morning,' he said.

'Morning,' I said, 'I didn't know you had a canary.'

'Yes. I call him ''Carter'' after Howard.'

'You never knew him?'

'No. Before my time. You know the story of his canary don't you? He brought it back with him from England on his last season. You know they were actually going to give up looking for Tutankhamen; this was to be the final effort. Anyway, he found Tut's tomb that season and the men said the canary had brought him luck. That's why they named it the Tomb of the Bird. Then, the day they opened the tomb, a cobra sneaked into the bird's cage and killed it. Then they said it was revenge for having disturbed the peace of the king.'

'I've heard the story.'

'The significance, of course, is that the cobra was an emblem of kingship in pharaonic Egypt, representing both the fecundity of the sun as well as its destructive aspect. Actually, the cobra was a manifestation of the Eye of Ra.'

'*Lux in tenebris*,' I said suddenly, 'light in the darkness. Wasn't that what the Eye of Ra was supposed to represent?'

'In one of its aspects, yes.'

Rabjohn sat down at the pine table and I joined him. He poured coffee – this morning ground coffee in large cups – and served boiled eggs, cheese, butter, jam and fresh bread. A real Egyptian breakfast, I thought.

As I rolled and peeled an egg, I noticed that my computer-enlarged photocopy of Carter and Carnarvon at the Valley of the Kings in 1923 was spread out on the breakfast table next to the original photocopy Julian had left me. Rabjohn had been looking at them. 'Interesting, eh?' I said.

'Yes,' he said, 'comparing their expressions.'

'You know, when I first saw you I thought for a minute you were the third guy visible in the enlargement, the one holding the newspaper.'

Rabjohn squinted at the picture and laughed. 'I might be ancient, Jamie,' he said, 'but I'm not Methuselah.'

'Of course – it was just a passing impression. I must have retained a subliminal memory of you from the time I saw you in the oases.'

'I tell you who this picture does look like.'

'Who?'

'A slightly younger Aurel Karlman.'

Now it was my turn to scrutinise the picture. He was right, there was something of Karlman in the austere features. 'It does look a bit like him,' I said, 'but it couldn't be, could it? This is clearly an old man, and in 1923 Karlman would have been a teenager.'

He was about to answer when the door opened and Elena entered looking misty-eyed, dishevelled and beautiful. She sat down and Rabjohn poured her coffee.

'Sorry if I disturbed you last night, Jamie,' she said.

Rabjohn looked up in surprise but refrained politely from asking what she meant. We ate and drank in silence for a while, then he said, 'I think we have to decide on the next step. We must assume the police suspect Nikolai was murdered. They'll also find out you visited him the same night, Jamie. They're certainly going to want to talk to Elena too.'

'Isn't it better just to talk to them?' Elena said. 'I mean, we haven't actually *done* anything. Running away will make it look worse.'

'You know how the *Mukhabaraat* are,' Rabjohn said. 'They maim and torture first and ask questions later.'

I thought of Mustafa's electrodes. I had to admit he was right.

'I think we must be very careful,' he went on. 'Sooner or later they're going to find their way here. My high-level contacts in the government may hold the dogs off for a while, but I'm still a foreigner and I can't protect you for ever. After all, people have been murdered. What I suggest is that you both get out of the country. I have access to a private jet and I could certainly ensure a passage to Israel or Cyprus, and a safe place to hide out once you're there.'

'No,' I said. 'I'm not leaving. I'm not a criminal, and I'm not running away till I find out what's behind it.'

'Neither am I,' Elena said, 'especially as we now know where Julian got the *ushabtis*.'

For a split second Rabjohn's self-possession slid, and he looked at her with undisguised astonishment. 'Oh?' he said. 'How?'

'Julian's diary,' she said. 'I'm sorry, Robert. Nikolai gave strict instructions that it was to go to Jamie.'

'No. That's quite all right. I'm just amazed that I never thought about a diary. May I see it please?'

'Yes,' I said, bringing the diary out of my knapsack. Rabjohn leafed through it, studying the ciphered figures carefully. 'How curious,' he said, 'that Julian should go to all the trouble of using a cipher.'

'I know.'

'May I keep this, Jamie?'

'I'm sorry,' I said. 'This is going with me to al-Maqs, where Julian found the *ushabtis*. I'm planning to talk to the headman Mukhtar wald Salim.'

'I'm going with you,' Elena said.

'No,' I said, 'there might be trouble.'

'Yes, there might,' Rabjohn agreed. 'There's no telling where the villagers got those statuettes and the penalty for dealing in antiquities is a stiff prison sentence. It's not going to be easy to get there, either – Kharja is about six hundred kilometres south of Cairo, and there are at least a dozen police checkpoints on the way. In a taxi you'll never make it and if you try to take a bus or a plane they'll pick you up.'

'Once we get into the Western Desert I'm in Hawazim country,' I said. 'That's where I was brought up.'

'Then perhaps you can tell us how the Hawazim evade police checks,' Rabjohn said.

'Simple. They don't stop at them, they just go round. Of course, they travel by camel.' Rabjohn's face brightened suddenly.

'I don't have a camel, Jamie,' he said, 'but if you insist on going, I *can* offer you the next best thing.'

The garage was the size of a small hangar – it took up the whole of one side of the house, and inside there was a fair-sized workshop with workbench, welding equipment, and block and tackle. Crates, packets of spare parts, quarts of Castrol GTX, empty jerrycans, and old bicycles had been teased into nooks and crannies. There were three cars – a gleaming white Mercedes limousine, a dusty Porsche, and a state-of-the art Toyota Land Cruiser. I wondered if it was the Land Cruiser Rabjohn had meant, but he hustled us behind the cars to where a brand new 500cc Honda dirt-bike stood, wrapped in polythene sheeting. He pulled the polythene away, and the bike was revealed in its full glory, like some enormous, rare, beautiful, brooding insect – red-and-black livery, double seat, panniers, knobbly tyres, high handlebars, swept up exhaust, and a non-standard fuel tank so large that it probably tripled the fuel capacity of the machine.

'Yes!' I said.

'You're familiar with motor-cycles, Jamie?'

'I'm what you might call an enthusiast.'

'How interesting. I bought this thing for some expeditions I intended to do in the desert. The idea was to use it for site trips in places where four-wheel drive cars couldn't penetrate. I never got round to the expeditions, of course. Things came up. I offered it to Julian and he almost collapsed laughing. Not a motor-bike man at all.'

'Is it run in?'

'Yes, it's all fully serviced and ready to go. I can give you a full tank of fuel and even a couple of extra jerrycans, more than enough to get to Kharja.'

'You mean you want us to go to Kharja on that monster?' Elena asked incredulously. 'I mean I'm happy to go and everything, but on *that*!'

It was late afternoon by the time we were ready. We'd agreed that it was better to travel by night anyway. The big problem would be getting out of the city unnoticed, for once out of Cairo we'd hit the dirt-trails, invisible to the valley-people whose world centred on the Nile, but known to my mother's folk, the Hawazim, for countless generations. Once he saw we really meant to do it, Rabjohn didn't talk about us leaving the country any more, but applied his organising ability to assessing and acquiring everything we needed for the journey – a pair of down sleeping-bags, blankets, a ten-litre collapsible water carrier, miniature gas-stove and cooking apparatus, food, binoculars, maps and compass. He even added a couple of old waxed Barbour jackets, helmets and *shamaghs* – Arab headcloths – he found in his store-room.

Finally, I started the bike up and tested the engine, letting it into gear and crawling round the yard. It sounded rich and pearly. When I returned to the kitchen, Rabjohn placed a thick wad of Egyptian pound notes in my hand. 'Elena tells me you lost your money in the Shepheard's fire,' he said. 'It's all I've got in the house. It's only about $1000 but it will keep you going.'

'I couldn't,' I said. 'You've been really kind, Robert. Too kind. But I can't accept cash.'

'I suggest you take it, and if everything works out you can pay me back. Unfortunately I can't accompany you – there isn't room for three on a motor-bike, and anyway I have some work to finish. But I could meet you there in a few days.'

'OK,' I said, taking the money reluctantly, 'and thanks.'

27

THERE WAS A FIERY SUNSET. Rabjohn and I stood in the yard by the motor-bike, watching stripes of magenta, murex purple, sky blue and flame-gold tilting at angles across the western sky, their ragged edges boiling slowly until the mass of colours coagulated into an irruption of whorling magma. Somewhere nearby a muezzin started up – a voice as pure as crystal, ringing the changes through the Call to Prayers. I stopped for a moment to listen. In no other city I've ever been in are the muezzins so perfect as in Cairo.

The muezzin's voice faded. 'We'll give it a few minutes,' I told Rabjohn, 'till it's really dark.'

At that moment the telephone rang in the kitchen. Rabjohn hurried off to answer it and was back in a second. 'Dr Barrington,' he said. 'For you.'

'Doc?' I said as soon as I picked up the receiver. 'Is that you?'

'Yes, it's me, Jamie. Listen –'

'Doc, I've been worried sick. You didn't answer the phone last night.'

'I'm sorry, Jamie. I wasn't in any state to.'

It was only then that I noticed how taut her voice sounded. A warning bell rang in my head. I remembered the strain in Kolpos's voice on the phone the night he'd been killed. '*Ma sei da sola?*' I asked in Italian – a back-up language we had in common, and which we'd always used in the past when we didn't want Arabs or English-speakers to understand us – '*Puoi parlare? Can you talk?*'

'It's all right, Jamie,' she said. 'This isn't a set-up. I'm alone. It's just that I've found out something I didn't really want to know – I'm glad I *do* know, of course, but then I bloody well *knew*. The bastards!'

There was a muffled sound from the other end, almost like sobbing.

'Doc, what is it? You're not making sense.'

'OK. Sorry. Give me a sec, darling. Will you?' A series of sniffs. 'OK. Sorry. Must pull yourself together, old girl! Jamie? Are you there? Let me start at the beginning. Now. When I left you the first thing I did was ring Madam Montuhotep XV – you know – the Eye of Ra Society. This very smooth-talking guy answered the phone. I told him I was a journalist named "Smith" and I wanted to do a piece on the Society. Told him I'd got the address and data from the Internet. I knew there was stuff on the net, because I'd already surfed for it. It was all sweetness and light – I made an appointment for next week, and he confirmed the address in Qasr an-Nil Street in the city centre. So that was all set up.'

'Yes.'

'My next assignment was Colonel Dansey-Smith on Roda Island, last survivor of the Zerzura Club. Wasn't difficult to find, lives in a run-down apartment that was once posh – fortunes diminished by the look of it. Stiff old boy about eighty, very British, too British in fact. Felt as if he was putting on what he thought a real English gentleman should be like. Accent a little bit too Etonian, you know – "acrorse" instead of "across" and "het" instead of "hat" – that kind of thing. Anyway, I told him I was a journalist doing a piece on the Zerzura Club and he was very guarded at first. Icy. In the end, though, he asked me in and offered me Earl Grey tea and mouldy biscuits. Had the feeling he hadn't had any visitors in a long time. Furniture once good but all holes. Photos of World War II aircraft – Spitfires and Messerschmitts – and armoured vehicles on the walls – Boy's Own Scrapbook sort of thing. Anyway, I started with simple questions

– when was the Zerzura Club formed and all that, and he was very wary. "Formed in 1930," he says, "by Major Ralph Bagnold, Royal Signals, in a bar in Wadi Halfa."

'He went on, very dry, and didn't tell me anything I didn't know. "What was the inspiration behind the formation of the Club?" I asked.

' "The quest for the Lost Oasis of Zerzura," he said.

' "Yes, but were its members privy to any special information about the nature of the Lost Oasis and where it might lie?"

' "I'm not at liberty to discuss *thet*," he said, as if it's a big-deal secret. ' "The members of the Club were sworn to utter silence on the matter. I've never discussed it with anyone and I never will."

'I'm just about thinking I'm flogging a dead horse, when suddenly the old boy's looking at me with these beady eyes, quite frightening. "Wait a minute!" he said, and his tone suddenly changed, "Wait a minute, I know what you are! Yes, I do, you're one of those bloody MI6 snoopers! I've seen your like before!"

' "Oh. When?" I said.

' "Oho, I've seen you lot all right, doing your dirty business."

' "Look, I'm out of the Office, now," I said.

' "That's what they all say," he said. Then suddenly the tone changes again, and he's almost pleading. "Can't you leave an old man alone?" he said. "Pestered and plagued us right from the beginning you Six people!"

' "You mean MI6 were there from the start?" I asked.

' "You ought to know!" he said. "Haven't you seen the file? The Zerzura Club was Six's baby. Bagnold was MI6. Then there was that bloody Yank bible-puncher – 'The Monk', we used to call him."

' "The Monk?"

' "Yes, Yank with a German name – Karlberg . . . Karlsbad or something. Expert on hieroglyphs."

' "Do you mean Aurel Karlman?" I asked.

' "That's him," he said. 'Very odd fellow. Sinister. Used to wear the togs of a monk – Benedictine or something – but he wasn't like any bible-basher I've ever met. Always sneaking about going into secret conflab with Bagnold. You could see Bagnold was in awe of him. Bagnold was the desert expert – he did the planning – but it was 'The Monk' who really pulled the strings.''

' ''Who did Karlman work for?''

' ''Nobody told us. We were just the work-horses, you see. I was Royal Engineers; transport was my speciality – keen as mustard when it came to engines.''

' ''What about Orde Wingate? Did you know him?''

'The old man guffawed. ''Wingate fooled the lot of them. There we were tinkering with light cars and aircraft, and Wingate arrived and did it on camels. Off he toddled with his Bedouin in '33 and came out of the desert making out he'd lost his memory. We knew he was faking; Six must have known it too. But Wingate had high clearance and they let him get away with it.''

' ''Let him get away with what?'' I asked.

' ''If you don't know, look at the file!'' he said.

' ''Look, Colonel,'' I said, ''I swear I'm not working for the Office, and I swear that when I did, I didn't come across any such file.''

'He seemed a bit pacified. Must have been my charm. ''Well, the file exists,'' he said, ''I know, because I had a friend who saw it. I don't even know if he told me his real name, but he was MI6 all right, and at first he came here asking questions, snooping just like you. I didn't trust him to start with, but in the end I realised he was a good fellow and we had interests in common: he was a motoring enthusiast and he liked aeroplanes – had an amateur's pilot's licence. He told me he had come across a file in the MI6 office here in Cairo that went back to the formation of the Zerzura Club in the 1930s. For some reason, he said, it went under the title 'Operation Eye of Ra'. Damn' odd name, of course. All bloody hooey! Can't think why they called it that!''

'As you can imagine, darling, I'm suddenly sitting up. ''What else was in the file?'' I asked.

' ''I don't know,'' he said. ''My friend didn't tell me much. Only hinted that he'd checked out my story and found it accurate. Then one day he came to visit me, very worried, and told me that the file had been removed. When he asked the clerk about it, the man said it'd been 'transferred to MJ-12' – that was all he knew.''

' ''What's MJ-12?'' I asked.

' ''Some kind of Yank set-up, I think. Anyway, I never saw him again. The next day he was dead, killed in a motor accident, here in Cairo. Speeding, or so I heard. Hard to believe. Damn' good driver – used to drive the Monte Carlo.''

' ''When was this?'' I asked.

' ''About six years ago – 1989, that's it. I remember the date he died distinctly because it was April Fool's Day.''

'By this time I'm wired up, Jamie. Tears are streaming down my face, and the Colonel's looking at me as if I'm a complete loony-toon. I suppose the stuff about being a motoring enthusiast and an amateur pilot had already told me. And the Monte Carlo. Then the date of the accident confirmed it. You see, 1st April 1989 was the date Ronnie was killed in a supposed motor accident in Cairo. Dansey-Smith's ''friend'' – the last person to have access to the Operation Eye of Ra file – was my husband, Ronnie Barrington.'

28

WHEN I PUT THE PHONE DOWN Rabjohn was eyeing me inquisitively. 'Anything wrong?' he enquired.

'Not really,' I said.

'You should have insisted that Dr Barrington came here with you. She's as much at risk as us. More, in a way.'

'I know. You try insisting with Doc. She's a black belt. Do you know her personally?'

'Only by reputation. I once met her husband, Ronnie. He was a good man, one of those unassuming Englishmen who keeps on plodding along till he finds out what he wants to find. Killed in a motor accident, I believe. Tragic.'

Together we walked back out into the yard, where Elena was putting on her Barbour jacket, using her red speckled *shamagh* as a scarf.

'Tell me something, Robert,' I said. 'Have you ever heard of an American organisation called MJ-12. I mean, is it part of the CIA or FBI or something?'

Rabjohn paused and stared at me, his eyes sparkling. Then he let rip a peal of laughter. 'MJ-12,' he said, 'yes, I've heard of it. Code named "Majesty". An ultra top-secret committee made up of twelve members – key people from the CIA, FBI, US forces and so on. At one time it was supposedly answerable to the President, and has included figures like Allen Dulles, Henry Kissinger and Zbigniew Brzezinski. MJ-12 is said to have been set up by US President Harry Truman in 1947, in the wake of the so-called Roswell Incident in New Mexico, but it was formed out of an older organisation, The Jason Scholars, which goes back at least to the twenties, maybe earlier.'

'What was the Roswell Incident?'

Rabjohn stopped laughing and stared at me hard as if wondering whether I was serious. Then he grinned again. 'Roswell is a secret USAF test-site in the New Mexico desert. A lot of state-of-the-art aircraft were tested there. In 1947, it was rumoured that an alien spacecraft had crashed there while trying to make contact with human beings. They set up MJ-12 as a result, to investigate contacts with extra-terrestrials – a sort of watchdog against UFOs.'

He must have seen my jaw fall slack, because he laughed again, even louder this time. 'Forgive me, Jamie, I don't mean to pry, but did this question originate with Dr Barrington?'

'In a sense, yes, why?'

'Well, forgive me for saying this, but she has a reputation for far-fetched conspiracy theories. I heard that her husband's death really shook her up badly. They tell me she had a nervous breakdown – the full works – and started seeing reds under the beds and little green men in the closet – conspiracies everywhere. It seems that she still hasn't recovered. No, I shouldn't laugh, but the fact is that MJ-12 is just a myth – a story cooked up by cranks. There is no MJ-12 and there never has been. It simply doesn't exist.'

It was full dark by now, and already cool. Rabjohn watched as Elena and I put on our helmets.

'Go carefully with the natives of al-Maqs, Jamie,' he said. 'We don't know how they came by the *ushabtis*. Don't expect hospitality from them. Smuggling antiquities is illegal. I don't think they'll want to talk about it.'

It was my turn to laugh. 'OK,' I said. 'Thanks for everything.'

'I'll get down there as soon as I can. Just as soon as I've finished off one or two jobs.'

'See you there.'

I straddled the bike and pressed the starter. Power rumbled through her. I twisted the throttle slightly. Elena swung herself on to the back of the seat and put her arms round me. I clicked the bike into gear and taxied towards the front gate, which Rabjohn's guard held open for us. As we rolled down the drive I found myself chuckling out loud. Elena gave me a squeeze. 'What on earth are you giggling about?' she demanded.

'Sorry,' I said. 'It was Robert's last comment about the "natives of al-Maqs".'

'What's so funny about that?'

'Well, the "natives of al-Maqs" are my relatives. That's where my mother was from. In fact, this Mukhtar wald Salim is my uncle!'

We rumbled slowly into the street, past parked cars and the gates of well-lit villas. I throttled up quickly – this bike could accelerate from zero to thirty in only five seconds. By the time we reached the road junction we were fairly tripping along. Just at the end of the road, a tall, dark figure stood smoking a cigarette, silhouetted by a street lamp. He was built like a weight-lifter, and as we approached his domed forehead and clipped moustache came into focus, just for a split second, as he threw away his cigarette, and turned casually out of the light.

29

I KNOW NOW, OF COURSE, THAT it was Hammoudi. The following were among police documents stolen from his briefcase some time afterwards:

Memorandum – Confidential
For the Eyes of the Officer Commanding SID Only

To: Col. Sultan al-Faid, OC *Mukhabaraat* SID Division.
From: Capt. Boutros Hammoudi, i/c *Operation Ushabti*

Subject: Source Jibril (COPY)

Sir,
The subjects Ross and Anasis left Rabjohn's house at about 2010 riding a motor-cycle. The bike took me by surprise, and I didn't recognise them until they were almost past me. I was able to ascertain the make and registration number of the vehicle in question, which has been traced to Robert Rabjohn, an American citizen, the owner of the house under surveillance. At the end of the street, the subjects turned right down al-Urubba, towards the Abbasiyya flyover.

The house had been under surveillance by my SID team since the previous afternoon, following a tip-off from Source Jibril that subjects Ross and Anasis were hiding out there. I had ordered the team to move in and arrest them at 1200 hours, but at 1100 I got a message from Major Rasim Bakr – Source Jibril's contact in SID – to cancel the arrest operation and continue surveillance until further notice. As the commander of the operation on the ground I questioned Major Rasim's orders, as I suspected they came straight from Jibril. I am not aware of Jibril's identity, but I do know it is not standard operational procedure in SID to let informers run investigations. Maj. Rasim then pulled rank on me and said to me that he would be reporting my attitude to you personally. I had to accept his orders, but as the operation should rightly have been under my command, I'm writing this report to you to let you know my side of it.

I believe that Source Jibril has had too much influence on this op. It was Jibril who first reported Cranwell's body on the Giza plateau, and Jibril who informed Maj. Rasim Bakr that the victim might have been killed by drugs. It was for this reason that I ordered Cranwell's flat to be searched the same day, and discovered documents showing a link between Cranwell and Nikolai Kolpos, a known trafficker in illegal antiquities, whom we have had under surveillance for some time.

My hypothesis was that Cranwell was supplying valuable antiquities to Kolpos, who was smuggling them out of Egypt to private collectors. He had many contacts especially in the Arab Gulf States. Cranwell recently obtained two rare 18th-Dynasty *ushabtis*, which Kolpos was getting ready to sell. We have not yet been able to ascertain where these antiquities came from. Cranwell was found dead at Giza, and my own view is that, due to the great value of the objects, Kolpos and Cranwell disagreed, and Kolpos paid two killers to murder Cranwell, and disguise it as a natural death. Cranwell's *ghaffir* informed me that he was last seen leaving his flat in Khan al-Khalili with two oddly-dressed men after a row. I ordered a post-mortem on Cranwell's body, but before it could be completed the corpse was transferred to the British Consulate on the authority of Maj. Rasim Bakr. When I asked him for an explanation Maj. Rasim warned me not to interfere. In my opinion, the transfer of the body was carried out on the request of Source Jibril.

Next, Jibril drew Maj. Rasim's attention to Omar James Ross, a known associate of Cranwell's with a background of trafficking in antiquities. Ross was expelled from the EAS two years ago for the offence. He is also suspected of forging antiquities. I thought at first that we might have uncovered a smuggling ring which might be responsible for some of the major operations of the last ten years. Source Jibril told Maj. Rasim that Ross would be meeting a contact on the Giza Plateau. I was lying in wait and arrested Ross on that occasion, but was unable to trace his contact. I was ordered by Maj. Rasim to let him off with a warning, and without even trying to ascertain who this contact was. In my opinion it was the girl Elena Anasis, who Ross was trying to subvert.

The result of this premature action, I believe, was the murder of Nikolai Kolpos, carried out by Omar James Ross, either in revenge for the Cranwell killing, or more probably to get back the *ushabtis* that Kolpos was hiding. I also think Anasis was an accessory to the murder, because she moved out of Kolpos's flat two days before. Eyewitness accounts tell us that a man answering Ross's description was seen fighting with Kolpos in his shop two days prior to the incident. The same evening Ross's room at Shepheard's was burnt out – this may have been a bid by Kolpos to eliminate Ross, who was in fact, out of the hotel at the time. It is possible he was tipped off by the Anasis girl. A man wearing an earring on his upper right ear, as Ross does, was seen by eyewitnesses near Kolpos's shop when it was blown up.

On the morning after the fire, I identified Dr Evelyn Barrington, a known associate of both Ross and Cranwell, at the scene. I put a tail on her, which she managed to throw off in Tahrir Square. That reminded me that Barrington is or was an operative of the British Secret Intelligence Service, MI6. She is reputed to have left the Service years ago, but this may be deep cover. I am certain that she has been involved in operations against this country in the past, and her arrival changed the current investigation. When I informed Maj. Rasim Bakr this, he told me I should confine my investigations to antiquities smuggling and murder. Technically this was beyond his authority, as such decisions are properly the business of the operation commander – in this case, myself. I believe this order also came from Source Jibril. It seems to me that the informant Jibril is running Maj. Rasim Bakr, rather than the other way round, which is not standard procedure. Anyway, I now know that Barrington is involved in the Kolpos affair at least as an accessory. Through a secret informant I picked up a baker's assistant called Mohammad Ghali, who broke under interrogation and informed us that he had taken an injured man answering Ross's description to an address in Zamalek in the middle of the night. There, he was met and paid off by a foreign woman speaking fluent Arabic – Barrington – who took the injured man to her place. Unfortunately, Ghali had a heart attack under deep interrogation and was unable to reveal more. We put a watch-team on Barrington's block, and the following day, her flat was visited by the girl Anasis. They all set out together in Barrington's car, but again she was wary and threw off our tail. The next thing we knew Source Jibril was informing us that the subjects were at Rabjohn's house in Heliopolis.

It seems odd to me, Sir, that while Source Jibril's information initiated this operation, he has constantly obliged us to change tack. First, he informed us that Cranwell had been poisoned, then he asked Maj. Rasim to stop the post-mortem operation that might have proved it. He let us know that Ross would be meeting a contact at Giza, but asked us not to hold him or even find out who the contact was. As a result of this, Kolpos – who might have told us a great deal under deep interrogation – was murdered. Last, Jibril informed us that the subjects were hiding at a house in Heliopolis, then made sure we didn't arrest them. I cannot help suspecting, Sir, that Source Jibril might be using this operation to his own purposes, whatever they might be. The presence of Barrington, and now Rabjohn suggests to me that foreign powers might be involved. As you well know, Sir, I am first and foremost a patriot and a defender of the integrity of Egypt, which was the world's first civilisation and the world's leading power when the ancestors of these foreigners were still naked savages living in caves. It seems to me that a threat to our integrity must be dealt with by action. Many times in the past foreign intelligence organisations have tried to infiltrate us and make fools of us. I fear that there could be a lot more to Operation Ushabti than smuggling artefacts – Source Jibril could be a foreign agent, and SID could be just a pawn in a game played out between foreign powers. Can I suggest that we investigate the identity of Source Jibril before continuing with the operation?

Memorandum – Confidential

From: Col. Sultan al-Faid, OC *Mukhabaraat* SID Division.
To: Capt. Boutros Hammoudi, i/c *Operation Ushabti*

Subject: Source Jibril

Capt. Hammoudi,
Thank you for your report. Your points are noted, and your allegations will be investigated as soon as possible. In the meantime, you are to move your surveillance team, with a support group of the Special Operations Section, to Kharja oasis in the Western Desert. You are to be at Baris, in Kharja, by sunrise tomorrow without fail. You will await further instructions there. You will be i/c operation on the ground, subject to the orders of Maj. Rasim Bakr.

PART II

THE WESTERN DESERT OF EGYPT 1995

30

WE SIGHTED OUR FIRST POLICE CHECKPOINT beyond the pyramids, where al-Ahram Street merges with the desert road. There was a pale moon and little traffic, and I cut the lights and nursed the motor-cycle off to the west, putting a good two miles between us and the asphalt strip. The desert was gravelly here, but uniformly flat without holes or banks and the Honda's chunky tyres could easily deal with the small stones. My eyes soon adjusted to the darkness. The stars were already out in their full royal majesty, and I kept the Great Bear and the Pole Star directly behind my shoulder. I didn't need a compass to travel in the desert – from my Hawazim forebears I'd inherited a compass in the head. Soon, Giza was an archipelago of light far behind us and I pushed even farther west, leaving six, ten miles between us and the road. Giza was swallowed up by the darkness, and there was nothing but ourselves and the sound of the engine in the vastness of the night. Beyond the wall of darkness, I knew, the Sahara stretched on and on like an ocean. We could have turned west and driven in a straight line and never crossed another asphalt road, nor a river, nor come across another big city in three and a half thousand miles. That was the distance between here and the Atlantic coast.

It was almost midnight when we halted. The night was cool and still, and when I scanned the stars I saw that they were opaquely visible through a screen of dust. That told me the *ghibli* might be on its way. Elena stretched, swinging her arms to get the circulation going. 'I never dreamed I'd be sleeping in the desert tonight,' she said. 'You sure no one will find us?'

'Nobody knows we're here,' I said. 'That's the beauty of the desert. If you have the confidence you can just fade into it. The Egyptians of the Nile are terrified of it, even now. For them it's like another world, so big they can't imagine it. They just try to pretend it's not there.'

We began to turn our arbitrary stopping place into a home for the night, laying out our blanket and sleeping-bags. I lit the gas cooker and Elena cooked rice and sardines. Afterwards we drank tea from big plastic army mugs sitting by a fire I'd kindled from a few shreds of wood I'd picked up in Rabjohn's garden. The flames flickered wildly in the stones. I lit my pipe. There was no sound but the low soughing of the wind, increasing gradually in volume. I listened carefully and glanced up to see an even thicker nebula of dust scouring across the stars. Pieces of grit struck my face suddenly. From the west there came a steady, tympanic boom as if some giant creature was stamping across the desert floor. Elena shivered. 'That's Raul,' I said.

'Who's Raul?'

'In Hawazim legend he's the demon drummer.'

She shivered. 'I can see why the Egyptians were so scared of the desert,' she said. 'It's like the sea – you feel overwhelmed by its bigness. You feel its power can break you.'

'That was the lesson my mother's people learned – flexibility. You don't try to stay the same, don't try to make a stand against nature. If anything does that it's bound to fail in the end. You roll and move with the landscape. The Hawazim did it and they've survived for thousands of years.'

'Your mother was really one of the Ghosts of the Desert?'

'Yes, she was.'

'What happened to her?'

'Nobody really knows. They say the desert took her. I was nine years old.'

Elena shivered again. 'Doesn't that make you afraid?'

'No, because I grew up in the desert. It has its hazards – but so does the city. My mother's people are looked down on by the so-called "noble" clans of the desert fringes who live more comfortable lives. The Hawazim have been persecuted by governments since they came out of the ark – the Mamluks and the Turks hounded them and forced them out into the farthest and most arid tracts of desert, where they learned to survive. They can find their way in the desert literally blindfold, by feeling the texture of the sand and by the direction of the wind. They can remember the tracks of every camel and every person they've ever seen. They can locate sip-wells in absolute desert where there are no known water-reserves and drink the water using a hollow reed. They can smell open water miles away. They will drink the gastric juices of oryx and gazelles and even the vomit of their camels to survive. They can live on locusts and desert rats for days. Those were the lessons they learned from the desert. A Hazmi in the town or the village is despised as a dirty Hazmi, but in the desert nobody despises him.'

'And you can do all those things?'

'Not as well as them – after all, I'm only half Hazmi. But as the Hawazim say, "a thing learned when young is a thing carved in rock" – I learned desert skills as a boy – to track, find my way, live on plants and animals, to handle camels, to shoot a rifle, to set game-traps, to throw a knife. A lot of it I learned from my mother. She was as competent as any man.'

'Yet the desert killed her?'

'She was very independent. She sometimes insisted on going off with the salt-caravans into the Sudan – a fifty-day trek. It was a man's job really, but she did it. It was pride, I think. She didn't want it thought she was being kept as a charity by some well-heeled *Afrangi* – that she'd forgotten how to live in the desert. I know she never wanted me to go away to school in Cairo. I think she thought it was a reflection on her – that she couldn't look after me properly or something. But my father insisted. So while I was away she'd occasionally go off with the caravans to prove what she was worth. The desert got her in the end.'

'How did she die?'

'That year there'd been some terrible storms – the *ghibli*

brought with it clouds of dust the colour of blood. That's why they referred to it as ''The Year of the Great Red Dust'' – their years are names not numbers. Anyway, the *ghibli* can be so powerful that it strips the paint off cars.'

'It was the *ghibli* that got your mother?'

'The story went that she was travelling with a salt-caravan, when some camels broke their hobbles and got lost. Maryam went to track them down and never came back. A *ghibli* blew up and covered her tracks completely. They never discovered her remains. My father was completely shattered by it. He never referred to her as being dead – always said she'd ''disappeared''. I got into the same habit, I suppose.'

'That's awful.'

'It was 1969 – a long time ago now.'

'And the Hawazim don't live in the desert any longer?'

'A lot of them are half-settled in villages on the edges of the oases. But don't be fooled by that – it's just for the sake of appearances. They can pack up and head off into the sands any time they please.'

'What about your uncle – Mukhtar wald Salim? You think he'll welcome us fugitives?'

'Has to. It's the desert law. A guest is always welcome – even a stranger or an enemy. Blood ties are utterly sacred to them. Mukhtar's my mother's elder brother – the *amnir* of my section of the tribe.'

'What's an *amnir*?'

'It literally means a guide, but actually he's a kind of shaman. Mukhtar was chosen early, and had the responsibility of heading the clan since he was quite young, because my grandfather also died prematurely. He's an old man now, probably in his midseventies – hard to say exactly, because the Hawazim have no idea of birth-dates.'

'A shaman? I thought the Hawazim were Muslims.'

'They are, but only in name. For them Islam is a veneer over a much more ancient religion – a belief in the spirits of the earth and the cosmos.'

'How long *have* they been around?'

'According to them, for ever. They say they're the Arabised descendants of a people they call the Anaq, who lived in The First Time – when divine beings visited the earth. There's traces of ancient Egyptian belief there, too. They have traditions about some of the Pharaohs – even Akhnaton, whom they regard as the embodiment of evil – they call him "The Fallen One".'

'What was your uncle's attitude to your mother marrying an *Afrangi*?'

'At first he was against it. To the Hawazim any townsman is a wimp. To live with them means living by their standards and believe me, they're no pushover. The up side of it is that you won't find any more hospitable, generous, courageous or loyal people anywhere. They live by their own code, and have this fetish about reputation that's absolute. I mean, if you fall short – even if you're a stranger – you're damned for ever. On the other hand – the down side you might say – you won't find any cripples among them. Anyone who can't keep up with the caravan when they move is left to die.'

'That's disgusting!'

'To an outsider, yes. But they've learned over the centuries that the strength of the tribe is what counts.'

'And your father was made of the right stuff?'

'I suppose he was, or he'd never have been given a Hazmiyya. In Hawazim tradition, a girl's first cousin has the right to marry her, and Maryam's cousin stuck to his right. Then my father invoked an ancient custom – *nifaas* – a sort of duel to see who could survive the longest in the desert without food and water. Mukhtar agreed that it was his right by desert law. The cousin came back after a week. My father staggered in half dead three days later. That's why they called him *Abu Sibaahi* – "The Father of the Desert Rat". There was no opposition from Mukhtar after that.'

'He sounds like a fair man.'

'I think he is. But how he's involved in this business of the *ushabtis*, I just can't say.' I paused and listened. The fire had gone out, but the booming of the wind had begun to die away. I looked up to see the stars twinkling more clearly. 'I thought so,' I said.

'It was a false alarm. The storm's passed over. Maybe it'll hit tomorrow or the day after.'

We crawled into our sleeping-bags and lay back, our heads close together, staring at the stars.

'Must be wonderful to belong somewhere,' she said.

'I wouldn't know. Hammoudi was right when he said I wasn't one of them or one of us. I'm an in-betweener. What about you?'

'My mother was Egyptian, like yours.'

'Was?'

'Yes, she died when I was young too. I had two elder sisters. My father is Greek – a drunken bully. He had a good business selling imported furniture, but he let it all go and we almost starved. He'd take his frustration out on us – used to beat us with his belt. But that was only part of it. He first raped me when I was twelve. He'd already been doing it to my sisters for years. We daren't tell anyone, we were so ashamed. We even thought that it was *our* fault for being what we were. We lived in this filthy flat in Alexandria. We had to cook for him, and if he didn't like what we'd cooked, he would use it as an excuse to thrash us with his belt. After he'd beaten us all, he'd usually drag one of us into his room and rape her.'

'Jesus!'

'Believe me, the times when we were all together were the best. My sisters both got out of the house and attached themselves to men. For me, the abuse went on for four years. Four years of living purgatory – nobody helped, nobody cared. I could have been a good student at school, but I couldn't concentrate, knowing what I had to go back to every night. I covered up the bruises by wearing a *burqa* – a face veil – some of the girls thought it was odd, because they knew I wasn't a Muslim. I was always very neat and clean about my dress, so that no one would guess what was really going on. Anyway, I knew it couldn't continue like that. I was going out of my mind – literally going mad. By this time he was getting drunk out of his head almost every night – and in a way that was good because when he was really drunk he just fell asleep in his chair without doing anything to me.

Anyway, one night I thought he'd fallen asleep in the chair and I was sneaking off to bed, thinking I'd managed to avoid it for another night when he suddenly opened his eyes and caught me by the wrist. He laughed – actually *laughed*. ''Thought you'd got away with it did you, little bitch!'' I realised he'd done it on purpose – pretended to be asleep to torture me! Bastard! I think it was that – the deliberate cruelty – that sent me over the top. There was a heavy old shovel standing by the fireplace – I don't know how it got there. Anyway, when he laughed with his stinking *araq* breath, I saw red. I picked it up and bashed his head with it over and over and over. Even when he'd fallen down and was lying on the floor, I bashed him again and again, until he was lying in a pool of blood. I thought I'd killed him – I hadn't but I wish I had. I just took the little money I'd saved, and whatever he had in his pockets, and got the bus to Cairo.'

'Jesus Christ!' I said. 'How could any man do that to his own daughter?'

'My uncle took me in – he was a good man, a tailor in Khan al-Khalili. It was him who introduced me to Nikolai, who was looking for an assistant. At first I thought Nikolai might be the same way as my father, but I soon discovered he had no bad intentions. He educated me – sent me to Ain Shams University to study art, literature, languages: I can speak English and French as well as Arabic and Greek. Nikolai taught me everything. Perhaps he wasn't the most honest man alive, but he was a real father to me.'

'What will you do now?'

'I don't know. But I learned one lesson from my real father – that whatever happens I can handle myself. I'll never let anyone abuse me again.'

She looked so defiant that I couldn't help putting my arm around her. Despite her tense muscles, she didn't resist. I was half-expecting a rebuff, but suddenly I felt her body relax. For a moment we looked at each other, and I saw starlight reflected in her eyes. I bent my head, pulled her close, and kissed her softly. She responded, pressing her lips against mine. The kiss seemed to last for ever, and we were lost in it, lost to the desert, the stars and the universe, present only in that single endless moment of conjunction – until Elena pulled away and brought us sharply back to real time once again.

31

SOMEONE WAS CALLING ME URGENTLY BACK from the dark fathoms of sleep, and I awoke with a start to find Elena shaking me. 'Jamie,' she hissed, 'there's someone out there.' I rolled out of my sleeping-bag and scanned the desert night. Somewhere north of us, not far off it seemed, was a bubble of light. At first glance it looked stationary – low intensity light, like the beam of a torch. We lay on our stomachs, watching. Minutes ticked by and the light remained in the same position, motionless. 'It's a man with a flashlight,' Elena said, 'standing still.'

Then, as we watched, the light leapt forward and underwent binary fission, splitting into two, then four, then – after more minutes – into six, eight and finally twelve. Twelve dots of light streaming towards us out of the darkness. Suddenly the dots themselves were each cleft into two. 'They're headlights,' I said. 'Twelve cars.'

'The police,' Elena gasped. 'They're coming straight at us.'

'It's impossible,' I said. 'It's a trick of the light. They're still miles away. Listen – you can't even hear the engines yet.'

It was a good ten minutes before we heard the growl of motors and the grating of gears, and then the vehicles roared out of the darkness like a squadron of dragons with fiery eyes. For a moment the headbeams blinded us, and we hugged the desert surface, convinced that they were about to run straight over us. When I looked up I realised that this was another illusion. In fact, they were slipping past us in file perhaps four hundred yards to our right, the engine-sounds changing tone, dopplering as they moved away. For a long time we watched their tail-lights fading and coalescing in the darkness. 'Christ,' Elena said at last. 'Do you think they were looking for us?'

'The *Mukhabaraat* can't be that stupid. It'd be like looking for a grain of sand on a beach. The only people who use this route are smugglers – running hashish from the borders of Sudan.'

'But Jamie, those vehicles were heading south – *towards* the Sudanese border.'

'Yes, you're right.'

Neither of us felt like sleep after that. The appearance of the cars had shattered the comforting feeling that no one knew where we were hidden – safe in the folds of the night. Elena began to shiver and I realised suddenly how cold it was. The air had a raw sting to it, the sharpness of a knife. We wrapped ourselves in our sleeping-bags and I lit the stove for coffee with freezing fingers. 'It's six hours to sunrise,' I said, 'I reckon we're already near Farafra. In ten hours we could make Kharja oasis.'

'But can we do it in the dark? I wouldn't want to plunge over a cliff.'

'The desert is dead flat as far as Kharja – no sand, no big stones. I came this way plenty of times when I was a boy. You never forget. If we start now you'll see Kharja by midday.'

'What's it like?'

'Well, it's not two palms and a pond – that's how most people think of an oasis. It's fifty miles long with scores of villages, millions of palms, lakes, thousands of feddans of farmland, scrubland and acacia forest. It's like a big green island in a sea of nothingness.'

'Beautiful?'

'Yes. But not as beautiful as the desert.'

The Honda hummed hypnotically away as the night and stars passed by. Orion came up, with Sirius sparkling brightly beside. Slowly the cloak of darkness buckled and warped and a crimson fireglow spread along the eastern horizon. Moment by moment the blackness was shorn off by a kaleidoscope of colours – deep rose pink burning out to volcanic yellow, tangerine, ultramarine, turquoise, royal blue, streaked with a rippling blanket of cloud the colour and texture of sand-dunes. As the sun drew higher its top half was obliterated by wreaths of dust, giving it the appearance of a golden boat in a child's drawing. For a moment you could almost believe that it was the barque of the mighty Ra, emerging victorious once again from his nocturnal battle. My arms were aching and my body shaking with cold after six hours' driving, and I stopped the bike for a few minutes to get the blood moving and to admire the sunrise, while Elena broke out the stove and laid out the coffee things. I watched as she tossed her luxuriant black hair out of her eyes, occasionally stopping just to stare at the vastness of the desert – the infinity of powder-blue and black stone that lay beyond our streaks of shadow, stretching to every horizon, unbroken but for ghostly crags of hills in the far distance. In all that expanse we were the only living, moving objects, lost in the bigness of it like microdots. 'It's like we suddenly landed on another planet,' she said. 'Where's the rest of the human race?'

'This is the emptiest place on earth,' I said. 'No one lives here but the Hawazim – and there aren't many of them. I once travelled here for a month and never saw a single soul – that's how empty it is.'

She set a mess-tin of water on the stove and stood straight, her eyes following me as I stamped my feet and slapped my arms across my body, trying to warm myself up. 'You look . . . somehow . . . bigger,' she said after a while. 'As if you'd grown into a giant in the night.'

I chortled. 'That's what the desert does to you. It's so huge that you feel like an ant in it, but its emptiness makes every object look as if you're seeing it through a magnifying glass.'

'A paradox.'

'Paradoxes. Illusions. This place invented them.'

By the time we'd drunk our coffee the sun was a tight firebrand leached of its soft goldness, and the horizons were already shimmering with heat-haze. I scanned the landscape with Rabjohn's binoculars until I made out two cairns of black stones close together, about two miles away – the only sign of human existence in the void. When we pulled up near them on the bike minutes later, I found what I had been looking for – a serpent of grooves oscillating away into the distance – a roadway cut into the desert floor by the feet of millions of camels over hundreds of years. 'It's the camel-road,' I told Elena. 'The Hawazim used to bring camels this way for sale in Cairo, before others started shipping them from Daraw by truck. This is the way caravans used to come up from the Sudan, or across the Sahara from as far away as Morocco. The caravaneers piled rocks into cairns to mark the way – when you get two cairns together at the side of the grooves like this, we call them ''Gateways'' . . .'

'Gateways into what?'

'Gateways into nowhere – on one level it's a kind of Hawazim joke. On another the gates are entrances into another universe, a different space–time dimension. That's not how a Hazmi would describe it, of course, but that's the way he thinks of the desert. To him every rock and dune is alive – not alive quite in the way animals and plants are alive, perhaps – but alive in the sense that they're part of a whole, constantly evolving, cosmos. It runs parallel with ancient Egyptian beliefs – they saw their tombs as gateways too – the Book of the Dead is full of references to gates the dead soul had to pass through, each guarded by a fierce deity.'

'How come these tracks have remained visible so long?'

'That's because of the surface – in stony desert like this your passage lives after you for ever. You can still find Roman chariot-tracks in places.'

'Really? Is the camel-road still used?'

'Rarely now. But it'll take us just where we want to go.'

For the whole morning we followed the camel-grooves across a volcanic black wasteland so flat and featureless it seemed that we were not moving at all but simply staying in the same place while the sun described a slow parabola above us. Apart from the camel-grooves with their occasional cairns and nests of ancient sun-bleached bones, there was no sign of life. The blue sky was without blemish. Apart from ourselves, the only thing moving was the heat-haze, and the occasional flicker of reflected light out of the desert, winking at us provocatively like a demonic eye. Occasionally we crossed playas – ovals of earth where water had lain in the past – which glistened with the liquid light of snow-white salt crystals. Every kilometre seemed to take us farther and farther into a wilderness beyond the bounds of the known world. At ten, we sighted the wind-moulded buttress of Guss Abu Sa'id mountain, a giant's fortress lurking in the haze, and I steered the bike to the west, leaving the camel-grooves and skirting the side of the mountain. Abu Sai'd passed behind us, melting back into the shimmer and we joined the camel-road again as it swept round east towards Kharja. By late afternoon we sighted the smoky line of palm-groves spreading through the desert. It was past noon when we came in among the sand-belt that surrounded the oasis like a defensive wall, and there, in the hollow of a crescent dune lay the stone rim of a well. I recognised it at once from my childhood as Bir Abu l-Hissein – the Well of the Fox – an appropriate name, for the sand around it was littered with the burrows of fennec foxes. I stopped the bike near the well and we stepped off it and stretched our legs. High above us, on the dune-crest, sand-devils were at work in a series of smoking vortices. The crests were constantly on the move, while the parent-plinths – which made up the bulk of the dune – remained stationary for centuries. In fact these dunes were exactly as I remembered them from childhood. At the base of the slip-face – the side of the dune away from the prevailing wind – there was a colony of plants, hardy colocynth melons whose dry husks rattled in the breeze. An old leather well-bucket and rope had been stashed nearby under an overhanging rock, and I picked it up. 'Let's see if the water still tastes the same,' I said.

I stood on the lip of the well and began to swing the bucket. Suddenly Elena screeched, 'Jamie!' and I turned to see a tribesman poised not more than ten feet away pointing an old service-rifle in our direction, peering at us intently. He was a bit older than me, dressed in a russet-coloured *jibba*, gathered in at the waist by a cartridge belt heavy with bullets, and he was as lean as a pikestaff – his body looked as if it had been honed down by *ghibli* winds into an irreducible core. His feet were hard as horn from a lifetime of walking on sand, and his sleeve was rumpled by the shape of the *khanjar* which lay concealed beneath it. The man wore a silver earring on his right ear, but no headcloth, and his hair was an unkempt mop, his bearded face a series of grooves and dark angles like blades of carven stone. It was the eyes that gave him away, though. One fixed us fiercely over the rifle-sights, the other lolled waywardly to the side, giving the impression it was looking at something neither of us could see. 'Who are you?' he demanded. 'Don't you know this well belongs to the Hawazim?'

'Yes, I know,' I said. 'You may be Water-Bailiff of the tribe, Mansur, but since when do you deny water to thirsty travellers?'

He looked at me as if I'd punched him, his loose eye blinking wildly. 'How d'you know my name?' he demanded.

I unbuckled my motor-cycle helmet and took it off. 'Is this how you greet your cousin?' I said. Mansur let his rifle drop and his one good eye gaped. 'Omar!' he cried, 'Omar is it you? You've been away too long.' He ran and threw his arms around me, giving me the triple nose-kiss of the Bedouin. He slapped my shoulder violently, shaking my hand: 'Omar! Omar!' he roared. 'Welcome back. Thank God for your safe return. God be praised! Upon you be no evil! May the Divine Spirit grant you long life.'

'No evil! May the Divine Spirit grant long life to you and yours.'

'Mukhtar said you'd come.'

'How is my uncle?'

'He's well, God be praised – you'd hardly guess he's an old man. He can still shoot and ride and walk like a youngster. But there's been a tragedy in the family this year and it's weighed him down. Aziz, my nephew – Bakri's son – died of some terrible illness, may the mercy of God be upon him. It hit Mukhtar very hard.'

He turned to greet Elena who had also removed her helmet, shaking hands with her more formally. 'Peace be on you,' he said.

'And on you. Do you always sneak up on people so silently?'

Mansur grinned, letting his face relax and his blank eye

roll until his features assumed their most humorous aspect. His good eye twinkled. 'God knows there are strange folk about,' he said, 'and the strangest ones of all turn out to be your own cousins!'

'Mansur's the Water-Bailiff,' I explained. 'He's responsible for all the water used by his tribe.'

Mansur smiled again with pleasure, 'I've got a new son now, Omar – Zayid – born last summer – the thanks be to the Divine Spirit.'

'Praise be to God. I hope he grows into a fighter like his father.'

'With God's will, less a fighter, more a Shiner,' Mansur said, laughing. 'We've got plenty brawn, it's brains like yours we need.'

I grinned at the compliment.

'Come! Come to the village,' he said. 'Mukhtar's longing to see you. We've missed you, by God. You get on that contraption and I'll lead you down.'

Within minutes al-Maqs village lay below us, a gaggle of dilapidated mud-houses tucked in among sharp crescent dunes and unkempt clusters of date-palms. The peaks of black tents showed above the fractured mud-walled yards, and other tents were pitched in the streets outside, where dozens of camels mooched about chewing the cud amid the debris of clover-stalks. Clusters of small black goats prowled the alleys and there were sleek *saluqis* resting in slats of shade. Mansur slithered down the dune ahead, while Elena and I manhandled the bike through the sand. 'I hope they're not all going to greet us at the point of a gun,' she said, 'or we won't last very long.'

'Hey,' I said, 'look who's talking.'

'That was different.'

'Not from where I stood.'

'I thought you said they were hospitable?'

'They are, but they're not stupid. People have been raiding them for centuries and they like to know whose side you're on before they welcome you. From their point of view we snook up on them from the back.'

The bike stuck in the sand for a moment, and we halted to

catch our breath. Below us Mansur stopped and looked up. 'Need any help?' he shouted.

'No, that's all right,' I said.

'Who is that guy, anyway?' Elena asked.

'He's Mukhtar's eldest son – they call him the One-Eyed War-rior. Used to work the salt-caravans into the Sudan – a very tough guy. He's been doing it since he was a kid – it's a fifty-day journey in absolute emptiness, so it's not a jaunt for the faint-hearted. Anyway, the very first time he went they loaded up with salt and set off back. I suppose Mansur was about ten, and there was only him and his cousin Zaki, who must have been twenty-five or so. No sooner had night fallen than they got jumped by a big gang of Gor'an – black nomads from Chad – who shot them up. Zaki took a bullet in the guts, and Mansur was hit in the eye by a sharp rock from a ricochet. The Gor'an took all the salt and most of the camels, but Mansur managed to get away on one camel with Zaki slung over the saddle. He travelled day and night with Zaki delirious, but by the time he reached Salima Oasis, Zaki'd pegged out. Mansur buried him there, and made it home alone.'

'That's an incredible feat for a ten-year-old.'

'Yeah, but not only that. When he was about fifteen, Mansur went off back to the salt-place with his half-brother Ahmad, tracked down the Gor'an who'd killed Zaki and wasted them one by one. I told you: "Forty years later the Hazmi got his revenge." They're not people who forget things easily.'

We heaved the Honda out of the sand and wheeled it down to where Mansur was standing. He led us through the camel-herd, and I noticed that the animals bore the distinctive 'lizard' brand of my mother's family. He halted us in the square between the houses, and at once six or seven small boys came screeching out of the shadows, with a pack of *saluqis* barking at their heels. The boys were dusty, barefooted and half-naked with shocks of curly black hair, and their sudden appearance brought a lump to my throat. Once, I thought, I'd been just like them, and as happy as a sandgrouse. Inquisitive faces appeared at door and windows, and as Elena and I stepped off the bike, tribesmen flowed out.

Wedge-like faces peered into mine – there were loud exclamations of 'Omar! Omar!', and the men pressed around me, slapping my shoulders, clasping and releasing my hand. There were shrieks and ululations as a swarm of women in woad-blue shawls and loose trousers came gushing out, patting Elena's shoulders and even touching her long hair. Some of these women were strikingly beautiful, their faces traced with blue tattoos, their oiled hair hanging in tight braids. In their own camps, Hawazim women never wore the face-mask or *burqa* – and had no shame about showing their hair. They were as tough and resourceful as their menfolk – they could shoot and fight, and each carried a *khanjar*. Suddenly there was a hush among the crowd. They stopped shaking hands and someone whispered 'The *amnir*'. I looked up to see a sinewy brown figure coming towards me. His face was a net of lines, his body as knotted as a rope, so lean that you could have delineated each muscle. His hair was pure silver and hung in eldritch locks about his shoulders. He was barefooted, dressed only in a pair of *sirwal*, with a rosary-set around his neck, and an old *khanjar* strapped on his forearm. His face was wispily bearded and looked as if it was carved out of granite, his nose like the beak of an old eagle, his eyes slate-grey and penetrating, smouldering with suppressed fire. He held a six-shot rifle in the crook of his elbow, walking with an electric, springy stride which seemed to belong to a much younger man, and with a pride and dignity which were almost palpable. It was Mukhtar wald Salim, my uncle.

For a second he stared at me in silence. Then, in a low, strong voice, he said, 'Omar, *inta wahashtana, wallahi*. By God, you have left us in the wilderness.'

I presented my hands, palms towards me, fingertips upwards, in the traditional gesture of supplication to God for the spirit of the recently departed. Mukhtar made the same gesture, and everyone else present followed him. 'Al-Fatih,' I said, and the Hawazim began to recite the first verse of the Quran in low voices. 'Man's life is short,' Mukhtar said finally, 'but the Divine Spirit endures for ever. Welcome back, Omar.' He advanced on me and embraced me, giving me the triple nose-kiss, his eyes filling with tears of obvious delight. 'Upon you be no evil,' he chanted. 'May the Divine Spirit grant you long life.'

'No evil. May the Divine Spirit grant long life to you and yours.'

He placed both hands on my shoulders and stared into my eyes steadily. 'It is said,' he quoted, 'that he who strips himself naked will one day get cold.'

I stared back, slightly embarrassed. I took his meaning at once: those who turned their backs on their family would suffer for it. It might be an admonition for my long absence, but I knew it could also be a warning.

Mukhtar led us away from the crowd, beyond the square to where a large goat's and camel's hair tent had been pitched on the side of a dune, and from where you could see the dune-crests aboil with sandsmoke, and taste the spice-scent of the desert wind. The tent enclosed a cool oblong of shade. It was open on one side, decorated with richly woven carpets, leather pads, hard cushions, hand-made camel-saddles, saddle-bags and camel hangings stitched with cowrie shells. As we entered a very pretty young girl rose to meet us. She was clad in vivid black and red *sirwal*, with a coarse blue cotton shawl covering her midriff and breasts, but exposing patches of copper-coloured skin. Her eyes were out-lined in kohl, and she wore a single silver stud on her nose, her braided hair falling half-way down her back. 'You remember Aysha?' Mukhtar growled at me, proudly. 'My latest wife – my tenth. Of course, she's young – but that's what keeps you on your toes, I always say.' I squinted at Aysha and she smiled with full, coconut-white teeth. 'Aysha,' I said, 'the little girl who used to sit on my knee. You've certainly grown up.'

'Thanks to God for your safe return, Omar,' she said. 'Mukhtar said you would come.'

'You saw me in the Shining?' I asked my uncle.

He shrugged. 'I have no power in the Shining. Best of a bad bunch. The Hawazim haven't had a good *amnir* in seven gener-ations, the last was al-Ghami, back in Turkish times.'

'That's modesty, Uncle.'

'No, I'm not modest. The tribe is not what it used to be. It used to be strong, united against the outside. Now it's fragmenting. People are even going to the cities, by God. We've actually had men joining the army of their own free will. That has all come about because we've had no strong *amnir* to guide us.' He examined my face reproachfully. 'There's but one Hazmi alive blessed with the power in the Shining, worthy of *amnirs* of the past, and he has always turned his back on it.'

I felt myself blushing. I knew Mukhtar was talking about me. In my childhood, he'd claimed that he'd recognised special abilities in me. He'd encouraged me to train as *amnir*, and even shown me his pharmacopoeia of dried plants, including the *tuffah al-jinn* used to induce the trance state the Hawazim called the Shining. But I'd never had much interest. I'd been more intent on school and conventional studies. I'd wanted to be a 'civilised' man so much that I'd dismissed it all as primitive hocus-pocus.

'When you were an infant,' he went on, 'I never felt the power in anyone so strongly.'

'I never even predicted my mother's . . . disappearance.'

'You deliberately suppressed the power as you got older. A gift must be used. As a tiny child you were richly gifted.'

'A few coincidences,' I said. 'Luck, chance. If I had it, I would know, Uncle.'

He looked at me through narrowed eyes. 'Perhaps,' he said, slowly, 'perhaps not.'

We sat down on a rich carpet, and watched while Mukhtar kindled the fire in a pit in the centre of the floor, his calloused hands working deftly with spills of wood. 'Aysha. Bring the coffee-set,' he shouted, and almost at once his young wife appeared with a brass tray on which stood a large hornbill-spouted coffee-pot, and three thimble-shaped cups. Coffee making was a ritual to the Hawazim and not a thing to be rushed. My uncle sank to his haunches, and we looked on as he teased coffee-beans out of an embroidered bag on to a long iron spatula and began to roast them, shaking the instrument sharply as he held it over the flames of the fire. The delicious scent of roast coffee permeated the air. When the beans were ready he scraped them into a brass mortar and began to crush them powerfully with a pestle, making dring-drang notes that rang out as clearly as a bell. The ring of the coffee mortar was an open invitation, and each Hawazim family had its own signature-rhythm, so that everyone would know at once who was making coffee and head for their tent.

By the time Mukhtar was pouring out the first cinnamon-spiced cupfuls for myself and Elena, tribesmen had begun to enter. They came in one by one, moving with an almost feline grace – thickly bearded men whose wild hair was bleached with camel-urine and greased with animal-fat, and whose faces seemed to shine with a kind of joyous, elven life. They were almost uniformly small and spare, bodies whittled down by hunger, thirst and fatigue, with gymnasts' broad shoulders and slim waists. Most were barefooted, clad only in *sirwal*, cartridge-belts and woollen shawls – their necks decorated with strings of rosary-beads, their ears with the familiar earring. Each wore a *khanjar* on his lower arm, and each carried a rifle as lightly as if it were an extension of himself. They seated themselves crosslegged and straight-backed around our rug, their rifles over their knees, while the women pressed in behind them, all of them firing direct questions at us without restraint: Why hadn't I been to see them for five years? Where had I been? What had I been doing? Why was I here? How long was I staying? Where was I going? Was Elena my wife? They wanted to know everything I'd seen, done and even thought since I'd last seen them; no detail was too trivial to be mentioned, no fact too unimportant to be left out. Like all illiterate peoples the Hawazim had acute memories. Whenever two parties met in the desert it was the custom to sit down and spend time exchanging what they called *saqanab* – information, news, experience – and nothing was omitted. They knew that even the most insignificant trifle might mean life or death. I saw their faces closely intent on us, their eyes full of genuine interest, real concern. No people, I thought, could ever be more welcoming than this.

When the coffee had done its rounds, the food was brought in on three great brass trays. My cousin Mansur had slipped out to slaughter a couple of goats while we'd been talking, and the freshly grilled meat was piled on beds of rice drenched in fat.

'Come, eat,' Mukhtar ordered Elena and myself. 'We have a special delicacy for you.' He took a steaming earthware pot the size of a football from Aysha, and removed its woven raffia lid. Inside were some revolting-looking soft eggs set on rice. I saw Elena's nostrils flare slightly. 'You don't recognise it, Omar?' Mukhtar enquired. 'By God, you *have* been away a long time. It's boiled monitor-lizard eggs. A real rarity. Come on. Eat.'

The eyes of the whole company were on us now. I took an egg and a handful of rice with my right hand. Elena was hanging back, and I guessed she was fighting to prevent herself from gagging. 'Eat,' I whispered to her rapidly in English. 'They'll be mortally offended if you don't.' I ate my lizard-egg with every show of enjoyment, and as I watched out of the corner of my eye, I saw Elena steeling herself, almost visibly to do the same. She put an egg in her mouth, chewed slowly and gulped it down, then forced herself to take another one. She even ate a third, then smiled and said: 'That's good.' The Hawazim cheered. I felt a flush of warmth at Elena's determination. 'Come on. Come on,' Mukhtar shouted. 'What about the goat? It's getting cold.' The tribesmen and women crouched round the trays with gusto, and began to devour the rice and meat.

After everyone had eaten their fill we cleaned our hands in soft sand outside the tent. Here, not a single drop of water could be obtained without effort, so not a drop was wasted for washing. By sunset the crowd had thinned out. One of my cousins made sweet, red tea while the others took out their carved and ornamented pipes. I broke out my own pipe and passed my tobacco pouch around.

'Good tobacco,' Mukhtar said, letting out a long jet of smoke. 'We don't get *Afrangi* tobacco any more.'

'You don't send caravans to Daraw?'

'It's difficult now, Omar. The government are always on the watch for us. When we go into town now we have to cover our earrings and put on peasant garb.'

'Why are the government out to get you?'

'It's always been the same, Omar. They hate us because we

don't pay taxes or submit to military service. They try to find any excuse to throw us in jail. They know that no Hazmi can stand being confined, so it's a punishment worse than death for us.'

'How are your relations with the tribes?'

He scoffed. 'Still trouble. Always trouble. Last year some "noble" Harba went out into the fringe pastures in their noisy motor-trucks and found two little Hawazim girls guarding twenty head of camels. They thought they'd have the camels for wealth and the girls for fun. Hawazim girls are beautiful but deadly – they should have known. As soon as the Harba laid their hands on them, out came the *khanjars*. One of the Harba won't be siring any more sons, by God, and another will have to shoot left-handed for the rest of his days, that's if he can hold a rifle at all. The other Harba got their clubs out and would have finished the girls, but just then their little brother – a boy about knee high, comes over the dune with a rifle, kneels down cool as a lizard, and pots them all – one, two, three, four, five. Five shots, five hits. The wounded Harba dragged the dead back to their trucks and off they went. Of course, they had to inform the police, carefully leaving out their own intentions, no doubt, and the police came down here to arrest us.'

'And did they succeed?' Elena asked, fascinated.

Mukhtar blew out a ring of smoke and grinned at her half mockingly. 'All they found was an empty village. We know the police. Our people never had anything from them but persecution. That's why our ancestors moved farther and farther out into the desert where no one else would live. I knew they were coming almost before they knew themselves, and we moved into al-Ghul. No one can track us there. Out there we don't need anyone. Our camels live on the secret pastures only we know about, and we live on their milk, and on insects, rats, lizards, anything we can find. We can stay out there for years if need be. Omar knows that. He knows the life of the Hawazim.'

'Yes, I know. So did my mother. Didn't do her any good, though.'

'Maryam – may God's mercy be upon her – was taken by the Divine Spirit, Omar. Everything that happens is His will: everything that happens is for the best. We are all in His hands, Omar. We all die when it is time for us to die.'

'Amen.'

In the hour before sunset, Mukhtar and Mansur took us around the village and showed us the deep well, where tribesmen and women, naked but for *sirwal*, were drawing huge buckets of water on a sweep-arm – a timber balanced on a pedestal, counter-weighted by a basket full of heavy stones. The water was poured into an intricate system of feeder canals that brought it to the gardens and palmeries.

'Everyone takes it in turn to draw water,' Mansur told Elena. 'Only women near their time are exempt.'

'How do you regulate the supply?' Elena asked.

'It's turned on and off by a system of stones. Each family is assigned so many periods of flow, according to their needs and according to the time each has spent working at the well. The periods are judged by the movement of the sun. As Water-Bailiff it's my job to work out just how long each family gets. Every single drop of water has to be accounted for.'

Two big bull camels were standing nearby gulping water from a catch-basin, their great crane-like necks bowed, their neck muscles working like water-pumps. As they drank, they staled backwards, and a man squatted under their tails catching the pungent urine in a wooden bowl.

'Ugh,' Elena gasped. 'He's not going to drink that is he?'

Mansur chuckled. 'We don't drink camel-piss,' he said, 'but it's very useful as bleach or for washing wounds.'

'The camel is God's gift,' Mukhtar said. 'We use every part of it, even its urine, and its manure for lighting fires.'

Elena seemed intrigued by everything she saw. She asked end-less questions and my uncle and cousin never tired of answering her. We walked past the well and into the palm-groves, where we were halted by the sudden crack of a whip, a grunt of pain and a burst of applause. A few paces further on we saw a group of young men and women – some of them only children – gathered around a muscular young boy lying almost naked, face down, in the sand, with a bloody streak from the base of his neck down to the small of his back, a diagonal groove where the flesh had been deeply ruptured. Another boy, about the same age, clad only in *sirwal*, was standing over him with a vicious-looking hippo-hide whip, poised to strike, while the other youngsters pressed around fascinated. 'You want more?' the boy with the whip was saying. The youth on the ground grunted again and the whip snaked down, slicing into the broken flesh. The boy stiffened as if electrified. Every muscle tensed as he arched momentarily out of the sand, his mouth rounded with shock. 'Aaaaaaargh!' he screamed. Fresh blood pumped wetly from the new wound. The audience cheered, clapped and ululated, and Elena looked at me, pale with shock. 'Stop it, Jamie, please!' she winced.

'I couldn't,' I said.

Mansur's blank eye bobbed at her. 'It's the custom,' he said, 'when two young men want the same girl, they hold a contest to see how many lashes of the whip they can take before calling a halt. The one who takes the most is the victor. Win or lose they carry the scars for the rest of their lives as a sign of manhood.'

'Horrible!' Elena said in English.

'Yes,' I said. 'Primitive, I suppose, but their lives are incredibly hard, and the quality they admire most is endurance, the ability to deal with pain in one form or another, heat, cold, thirst, hunger, exhaustion. This looks brutal but you can see it as a sort of microcosm of their whole existence.'

As the sun sank, Aysha spread a carpet for us on the dunes, and we sat quietly, enjoying the evening cool, watching tight knots of camels and goats being brought in from the rough fringe pastures of the oasis by young boys chanting ancient herding songs as they went. Occasionally riders passed us and shouted a greeting, sloping into the village on tall camels fully decked out with woven saddle-bags and tassels that swung majestically as the animals walked. The sun was a gold sovereign hovering on the western skyline, its power burned out, and within minutes it was gone. As the darkness seeped in to take its place and the stars came up, Mukhtar lit a coffee-fire outside and a few dark shadows moved in to join us.

Mukhtar set the coffee-pot on the fire, brushed the sand off his hands and said, 'Omar, the Divine Spirit has sent you and you are welcome. Now it is time to tell us why you have come.'

It was a direct approach and it deserved a direct answer.

'It's about dealing in *antikas*, Uncle,' I said.

I regretted the shot as soon as I'd said it. Mukhtar was my uncle and my host, and had just welcomed us into his home with unqualified warmth. He took a deep breath and turned his hawk-like eyes on me. There was disappointment in them. 'The Hawa-zim don't deal in *antikas*,' he said quietly. 'You come to your own family as a representative of the government?'

'This is not about the government. I ceased to work for the government two years ago. You had a visitor last winter, someone who wanted to buy *antikas*.'

'A visitor? We have few visitors here.'

'His name was Julian Cranwell, one of my father's people, an Englishman.'

Mukhtar was looking at Mansur with a mystified expression. 'Did we have any visitor, Mansur?' he asked. My cousin turned his blind eye on me and blinked.

'I don't think so, Father.'

'He came here to buy something from you, Uncle,' I said.

Mukhtar put his pipe down and frowned. 'And what is he supposed to have bought?'

'Akhnaton *ushabtis*.'

'What?'

'Small statues, figurines of the Pharaoh Akhnaton, "The Fallen One".'

Mukhtar's face dropped. 'The Fallen One,' he said, flicking up two fingers – the Bedouin gesture of defence against the Evil Eye – 'God protect us from the Stoned Devil.'

Mansur's blank eye blinked again, and he made a half-hearted effort to copy his father's gesture.

'Cranwell said he bought two statuettes from you, Uncle.'

'He told you that himself?'

'No. It was written.'

'Where is he now?'

'He's dead.'

Mukhtar looked at me gravely. 'What is your connection with this Englishman?' he enquired.

'He was my good friend, a blood friend. I know you understand that, Uncle. Actually, I'm not sure if he's really dead. But either way, he's been destroyed, and whatever destroyed him is in some way connected with the *ushabtis* he bought from you.'

The whole company had gone silent now. The air of celebration that had attended our arrival had evaporated. Mukhtar hadn't insisted in his denial, I noticed. It was obvious that he was holding something back.

I stood up and Elena followed. 'Uncle,' I said, 'at least two people have died for the sake of those *ushabtis*. If we don't sort this out, I've got a feeling that others will die too.'

I thanked Mukhtar for his hospitality, and Elena and I made our way to a sleeping space the women had prepared for us nearby.

32

I AWOKE WITH A START TO find Mukhtar jogging my arm roughly, the second time in two days I'd been woken up suddenly. 'Quiet, Omar,' he told me gruffly, putting a finger to his lips. 'Just wake the girl.' I woke Elena as gently as I could. She gasped when she saw the dark figure standing over us. 'What's this about?' she demanded.

'Shsh!' Mukhtar growled, 'no questions. I have something to show you. Here, put these on.'

He handed me two clean sets of *jibbas* and *sirwal* – the knee-length Hawazim shirt and baggy trousers, dyed a russet colour to blend in with the desert – and two pairs of hand-crafted Hawazim sandals, a large and a small pair. We put the clothes on quickly, and I was glad to get into Bedouin dress again; it's more comfortable and more suitable to a life in public view than anything Westerners have designed. When we'd dressed, I buckled my *khanjar* under my sleeve, just in case. We pulled on our sandals, grabbed our *shamaghs*, and followed my uncle outside. There was a chill in the air, and on the eastern skyline a fissure of blood-red light split the darkness. Venus shone vividly, hanging low over the edge of the night. Near the tent three camels were couched, all of them fully saddled and caparisoned with cushions, woven saddle-bags and waterskins. They were small, fit beasts of the Hawazim's own breed, specially raised and trained to cover long distances on the minimum food and water, each one marked on its shoulder with my family's lizard brand. Mukhtar slung his rifle from the saddle-horns, picked up a hooked camel-stick, and gestured to us to mount up. Elena looked at me nervously and I remembered that she'd never ridden a camel before. I chose the most patient-looking of the three, removed its knee-hobble, and stood on its foreleg to prevent it from rising suddenly. Elena giggled softly as I helped her into the saddle. 'Hang on tight!' I whispered. I stepped off the camel's leg and poked it in the shoulder with my toes. It groaned once and began to stand, tilting forwards, backwards, then forwards again as its multi-hinged joints unlimbered. I was about to tie its headrope to the horn of my own camel, when Elena hissed, 'No! Give it to me! I'm not going to be a passenger. I'll drive it myself.'

'It's not a car!' I said, admiringly, handing her the headrope and the camel-stick I'd found on the ground. 'Tug left for left, right for right, and pull back for stop,' I told her, 'Kick gently on the shoulders and shout "*Hut! Hut!*" to make him go.'

She nodded. I unhobbled my own camel, picked up the stick leaning against its flank, and mounted, crooking my knee around the forward saddle-horn. As the animal rose, snorting, Mukhtar leapt into the saddle of his own beast as nimbly as a youth. He beckoned to us silently, and we moved off through a tunnel of smells – slumbering woodfires, damp camels' wool, cured leather – then through the palm-groves and out into the fresh, chalky scent of the desert.

The streak of blood across the sky widened almost imperceptibly, like a torrent gathering strength until it burst its banks, shattering the greyness into ragged fragments which gradually fell away like sloughed skin to reveal an inferno of orange fire beneath. The camels padded on placidly and the morning was still and soundless but for the solid crunch of their feet on the sand, and the occasional clink as one of them struck a stone. I was dying to ask where we were going, but Mukhtar had said 'No questions,' and I guessed he would tell us in his own time. We crossed the dune-belt, where water-seams had favoured the growth of tiny ecosystems, tufts of coarse esparto grass whose roots provided moisture for beetles and solifugid spiders. The sand was criss-crossed with the stitch-marks of their tracks. We left the dunes and rode out into the plains, on and on until almost every vestige of vegetation was left far behind us. The dune-belt already lay an hour at our backs when Mukhtar reined in slightly to let us come abreast. We rode in silence for a few more minutes, then suddenly he said, 'Did your mother ever mention your grandfather, Salim wald Salman, Omar?'

'He was lost in al-Ghul wasn't he?'

'Yes, long before you were born. I was only a boy at the time myself. Not long after he went, I took responsibility for the clan. I had to decide everything; it isn't an easy job deciding for others.'

'I guess not.'

'Did Maryam say what happened to our father?'

'Only that he was lost.'

'It was the Year of the Englishman.'

'You mean my father?'

'No, another Englishman. He came looking for fifteen men to take him out into al-Ghul. Your grandfather was one of them. The Englishman said he was looking for Zerzura – the Lost Oasis. His name was Orde Wingate.'

'Wingate!' I gasped. For a moment I looked at him, half stupefied, wondering if I'd heard right. 'No God but God! My grandfather was with *Wingate*?'

'You know him?'

'I've heard of him. When was this?'

'You know we don't understand foreign reckoning. We call it "The Year of the Englishman", that's all.'

My head reeled. I'd guessed that Wingate had used Hawazim guides and camel men, but I'd never dreamed my own family history was involved. Questions crowded into my mind in a whirl of confusion. I removed my glasses, wiped them on my cuff and took three deep breaths. Then I replaced them with as much calm as I could muster.

'What happened?' I asked.

'Well, this Wingate hired fifteen Hawazim from various clans and off they went. They'd been away, oh, perhaps twenty days when, one morning, the Englishman and the headman of the expedition, Hilmi wald Falih, came staggering out of the dune-belt dragging half-dead camels, and ranting to themselves. We knew at once they were possessed by *Jinns*. I was only young but I remember it as if it was yesterday. Their faces were shocking. Hilmi looked as if he'd come face to face with the Devil himself, eyes bulging out of his head, quaking, teeth chattering. The Englishman was calmer, but he kept repeating that he couldn't remember what'd happened, and just sat staring into space. Hilmi never said another sane word in his life. Later, other English came in a motor-car and took them both away. Neither my father nor any of the others ever came back. We heard later the English had put Hilmi in some kind of place for those possessed. They had no right. His family were furious. What happened to Wingate in the end I don't know.'

We rode quietly. Elena and I stared at each other. The crunch-crunch of the camels' feet seemed as loud as a snare-drum.

'Everyone warned Salim not to go with Wingate,' Mukhtar went on. 'We all knew about Zerzura. Not one of us had ever been there, but we heard about it from our fathers and our fathers' fathers. It was a place of evil – a haunt of *Jinns* and demons. They say that there were palm-groves there with the best dates you ever tasted, and grapevines with fat grapes, pools of sweet water and buried store-rooms packed with treasure. But you could never find the Lost Oasis twice, no matter how hard you looked, and if you took fruit and water it would turn to dust by the time you got home. It was magic – black magic. It only "opened" at certain times, but there were shamans who knew how to open it by sacrificing human beings. Some said Wingate was an evil shaman who'd sacrificed the Hawazim to open the oasis.'

'Do you really believe that, Uncle?' I asked.

'Me? I don't know. Only God knows. But I'd like to find out what happened to my father.'

'Where are you taking us?' Elena said softly.

He pointed with his camel-stick. It was fully light now, and in the distance I made out a long wall of crescent dunes, a ripple of amber sand on the plain, like a sea-serpent.

'Uruq al-Anaq,' my uncle said. 'Remember it, Omar? It's a sand-sea of crescent dunes rising in a horseshoe from a gravel beach. Within the horseshoe there's a ruin from *Zep-Tepi*, the First Time; we call it Khan al-Anaq, "The Inn of the Ancient Ones". You've been there before, Omar.'

There was a sudden flash of memory, of playing among ancient ruins with my father, and the name, Khan al-Anaq – Anaq, the name the Hawazim gave to their legendary ancestors.

The camels strode on, and within half an hour we'd come face to face with the dunes. We worked around their base along the gravel beach, and as we passed the arm of the horseshoe I saw a cluster of ruins, half buried in the sand. Closer up I saw great toppled pillars, blocks of masonry, broken obelisks, even two ram-headed sphinxes peering out of a drift of sand. It was the sphinxes that clinched it for me. Now I remembered. This was the first ancient Egyptian temple I'd ever visited as a small child. I recalled being awed by it even then; the sphinxes with their inscrutable expressions, the hieroglyphs, the strange stelae showing falcon-headed men and lion-headed women had fascinated me right from the beginning. Mukhtar couched his camel by a massive stone wall and went to help Elena. 'No!' she protested. 'Let me do it! I've got to learn!'

'Just let the headrope go limp,' I told her, 'tap him on the head with your stick and make this noise: *khkhkhyyaa! khkhkhyyaa!*'

She tapped and rasped and after a few moans of protest the camel knelt gracefully in the sand. We hobbled the animals, while Mukhtar took a thick coil of rope from his saddle-bag and looped it round his shoulder. 'What's that for?' I asked.

His eyes twinkled at me. 'Wait and see,' he said. He slung his rifle over his spare shoulder. 'There's an electric torch in the saddle-bag,' he said. 'We'll need it. Better bring a couple of canteens of water, too.'

There was a sudden powerful squall of wind across the open sands, and Mukhtar's expression changed abruptly. 'There's a *ghibli* coming,' he said. 'It'll hit us before the day's out if I'm not mistaken. Come on – we'd better get moving!'

We followed his small, quick figure – astonishingly quick for an old man – into the shadows of the ruin, passing through broken archways and clambering over shattered columns. I stopped to look at a relief of the god Set, with his half-rat, half-aardvark head. It must have been one of the first reliefs I'd ever seen, yet it was still as alien as anything I'd encountered in ancient Egyptian culture.

'You remember?' Mukhtar repeated.

'Yes, I think so.'

'Come and look at this, then.'

He halted in the middle of a portion of wall which was engraved with numerous stelae. They were Old Kingdom, I noticed, and were thick with references to the old gods of the ancient Egyptian pantheon: Thoth, Osiris, Isis, Horus, Nepthys and Set.

'Now,' Mukhtar said, 'you're an expert on *antikas*, Omar. How old is this place? I mean, does it go as far back as *Zep-Tepi*?'

'What's *Zep-Tepi*?' Elena asked.

'It means the First Time – the Time of Creation, when the gods lived on earth. I'd say this place is at least five thousand years old, maybe as much as twelve thousand. That certainly makes it as old as *Zep-Tepi*, yes.'

'Right,' he said, pointing at a nearby stela with a calloused finger. 'Now, look at this.' I examined the stela carefully. It showed a sky full of what appeared to be winged disks, trailing fire and smoke, with, beneath it, an ibis-headed figure – obviously Thoth – handing what looked like a basket of fruit to a human figure. 'Look closely,' Mukhtar said. I peered at the human figure. It had to be the same age as the other figures in the tableau, and yet it was strikingly familiar. It was a man with a mop of wild, curly hair, and unlike the usual images of ancient Egyptian men, wore a beard. He carried a spear and a shield and had a slim, stiletto-like blade attached, handle downwards, to his forearm. On the right lobe of his upper ear, he wore a carefully drawn earring. 'A Hazmi!' I said.

'An Anaqi,' Mukhtar corrected me, 'one of our forefathers. You see, Omar, we were here at *Zep-Tepi*, when the Ancient Ones walked the earth.'

I felt an unmistakable pulse of excitement swelling through me. Was this the elusive image I'd been searching for all these years – the point at which I could say: 'That's where I began?'

'I've never seen this anywhere else!' I said. But now I wondered: had I actually seen this image before, right here in Khan al-Anaq? I strained my memory, concentrating hard for a moment, trying to remember, but it was impossible to crank up images over so many years – I couldn't have been more than four or five the last time I'd been here. But, was it possible, I wondered, that the image of Thoth handing a gift to one of my remote ancestors could have lain dormant in my subconscious for all that time? Could it have been this that subliminally sparked off my interest in the ancient Egyptians, and the origin of their civilisation?

Mukhtar pointed to the basket of fruit Thoth was handing to the Anaqi. 'See these bulbs,' he said, 'they are *tuffah al-jinn* – Demon's Apples.'

I examined them carefully and caught my breath. These I had seen before.

'What are Demon's Apples?' Elena enquired.

'Mandrake,' I said, '*Mandragora officinarum*. Dried specimens of it were found in Tutankhamen's tomb. It's believed that the ancient Egyptians used it for some religious ritual. In the right quantities it has psychedelic properties. It's still in use today.'

'By whom?'

I glanced at my uncle, embarrassed. 'By the Hawazim,' I said. 'It's used as a hallucinogenic to induce trance state, what they call The Shining.'

'Yes,' Mukhtar said, not thrown in the slightest, his eyes sparkling now. 'You see, Omar, the Demon's Apple was brought to our people by the Ancient Ones at *Zep-Tepi*. Now, look at this . . .'

He pointed to a second stela beneath, which showed the same Anaqi figure, this time without his weapons and in a relaxed sitting position. The same winged sun-discs filled the sky, but the curious thing here was that rays of sunlight seemed to be emanating not from them, but from the man's head, upwards.'

'See!' Mukhtar said, 'the Shining. The power of the Shining was given to us by the Ancient Ones, but over the generations it has almost disappeared. You may be the last one with the power, Omar!'

I sighed. 'Is this what you brought us to see, Uncle?' I asked.

'No – that's only part of it. Come on.'

We came to the centre of the sprawling ruin, a labyrinth of broken masonry and crumbling walls, where six enormous columns, as thick as old oak-trees, sprouted from an expanse of deep sand. Mukhtar leant his rifle against one of them, put down the rope, and began to brush away the sand. 'Here's something you won't remember, Omar,' he said, 'only a few of us know about it. Come on, help me clear the sand. Uggh! Should have brought a shovel, too.'

Elena watched him incredulously, as if convinced she was in the presence of a lunatic. 'What on earth is he doing?' she said in English. 'Has he brought us all the way out here to make sand-castles?'

'Just trust him,' I said.

We began to scrape away the sand with our hands; by now the sun was hot, and clearing the sand was unexpectedly hard work. Soon we came to a hard surface, and within half an hour we had uncovered a thick, flat stone, perfectly disc-shaped, about four feet in diameter, capping what looked like a round plinth. In the very centre of the disk an Eye of Ra was sculpted in relief. There were some hieroglyphs carved into the stone beside it, and I leaned over them, brushing the last grains of sand aside. What I read sent a shiver down my spine, and for an instant it came back: Kolpos's face, distorted with death-agony. The sound of the Mills grenade rolling across the floor.

'What does it say?' Elena asked.

'It's from the Hymn to Ra,' I said. 'It reads:

> Let the Eye of Ra descend
> That it may slay the evil conspirators.'

Elena blanched. 'Isn't that what was written on Nikolai's mirror the day he was killed?'

'It's a common enough hymn in ancient Egypt,' I said offhandedly, turning to Mukhtar and changing the subject. 'This stone must weigh a ton,' I said, 'I hope you don't intend to lift it with that rope, Uncle.'

Mukhtar smiled mysteriously. 'Here's the real secret,' he said. He crouched over the capstone and touched the pupil in the Eye of Ra relief with the palm of his hand. Instantly there was a clunk and four cracks appeared in the disc, dividing it into quarter segments. There was another clunk and the segments opened inwards, revealing a deep, dark, humid-smelling aperture. Elena stared into it with wide eyes.

'Good God!' I said, dropping down to examine the segments, 'I've never seen anything like it! How does it work?'

'Don't ask me,' Mukhtar said, 'they were clever people, the Ancient Ones.'

'Must be some kind of weight and balance system,' I said, 'but to stay in working order for so long!'

'What *is* it?' Elena asked.

Mukhtar picked up a pebble and dropped it into the hole. 'Listen!' he said. A few seconds later there was the distinctive 'plink' of the pebble hitting water.

'A well!' Elena said.

'Yes, a secret well. But more than that, a kind of hiding-place too.' He picked up the rope and began to feed it through a stone bracket which had lain hidden under the sand on the rim of the well.

'What now?' I enquired.

'Now we go down the well,' he said. 'I hope you can both use a rope. First you, Omar, then the girl, then me.'

'Jesus!' Elena said. 'Are you serious? What's this about?'

'Trust me,' Mukhtar said, 'you'll find out.'

Elena looked at me appealingly. 'We might be walking into a trap,' she said in English. 'Once we're in there, who knows what will happen.'

I gulped. 'I trust him,' I said, 'he's my uncle.'

She drew in a deep breath, 'OK,' she said, 'then I go first.'

'You'd make a good Hazmiyya!' Mukhtar said, with obvious admiration. 'But no, let Omar go. You need only descend a man's height, on the rope, then you'll find a shelf and a ladder. The ladder takes you down to the height of six men, where there's another stone shelf.'

'What does he mean, six men?' Elena enquired.

'It's the way the Hawazim measure depth,' I explained. 'They don't have metres or yards, so they use the height of a man with his arm fully extended over his head. You can say one man is about three metres, so six men is eighteen metres – roughly fifty feet.'

'Come on!' Mukhtar urged me, 'Yallah!'

I took the rope, tied the end around my waist and poised myself backwards on the lip of the well. Mukhtar handed me the torch and a canteen of water. He took up the strain on the rope, and I paused for a moment, looking at him straight in the eyes. Then I flung myself into the darkness. For a few moments I experienced a pang of sheer terror which ended when my feet came into contact with hard stone – the first ledge, about six feet down. I untied the rope and shouted to my uncle to pull it up. The well smelt fetid, and as I groped around the ledge for the ladder I hoped it was not inhabited by snakes. I soon found the ladder – like everything here, it was stone, not steel, and perfectly made. 'OK!' I shouted up, 'I've found the ladder!'

'Coming down!' Elena said, and her slim body swung suddenly above me. I caught her and helped to steady her as she shed the rope. A few minutes later, Mukhtar was standing beside us. 'That's the first bit done,' he said. 'Now the ladder. You first, Omar.'

I felt for the steps uncertainly and began to climb down. 'Steady does it,' my uncle said, 'take your time.' I squinted down through my feet to see the palest of reflection of light on water far below. Or perhaps I imagined it. Once or twice I stopped to get the torch out of my pocket and examine the wall. This was certainly no Arab well. It was constructed of huge masonry slabs which had been shaped and fitted with perfect precision. The ladder too, cut out of solid stone, was a magnificent piece of engineering. It took me only ten minutes to arrive at the next ledge, some thirty feet down, and I shone the torch upwards to see that Elena and Mukhtar were both on their way. I flashed it around the walls again, and saw at once that there was a small archway opening off the shelf into a dark tunnel beyond. A few minutes later, Elena and Mukhtar had landed next to me on the shelf. 'I hope someone doesn't come along while we're down here and shut us in!' I said. 'I wouldn't like to be stuck here for the rest of my life.'

'God is generous!' Mukhtar said, feeling his way towards the tunnel. 'Watch out here, there are sometimes scorpions.' He took the torch from me and led the way into the tunnel, which appeared to have been bored through solid rock. Within twenty feet, though, it opened into a much larger chamber. Almost as soon as we entered, the torch went out, and for a second we stood in utter darkness. The second seemed to last a lifetime, and in that moment, I must admit, a flash of doubt about Mukhtar did cross my mind. Then there was the sound of a match being struck and the cave was full of light again. I saw my uncle crouching over an oil lamp, carefully lighting the wick. The chamber was not as big as I'd first thought, no more than ten feet by ten and the same in height. In the light of the lamp I saw that its walls were decorated with the effigies of ancient Egyptian gods – Anubis, Osiris, Horus, Thoth – with scores of hieroglyphs and cartouches. But I wasn't looking at the wall-paintings. Over in the corner of the cave, standing upright like model soldiers, were no less than ten perfect Akhnaton *ushabtis* – each different in detail, but each as exquisitely made as the one I had seen at Rabjohn's. Next to them stood a small wooden chest, green with age. Mukhtar took a key from his pocket and opened the chest. From inside he brought out a tattered book, which he held out to me, lifting the lantern so that I could read it properly. It was a standard British Army Field Memorandum. I flipped open the cardboard cover. On the first page, in pencil, was written, 'The Journal of Lt. Orde Wingate, R.A. Western Desert, Egypt, 1933'.

'What is it?' Elena asked.

'I think we've found the Missing Journal,' I replied.

33

ELENA EXAMINED THE *USHABTIS* BY THE light of the torch. 'These are exactly the same quality as the ones Julian brought back,' she said. 'You realise what they'd be worth!'

Mukhtar eyed me uneasily. 'So Cranwell *was* here, Uncle,' I said. 'I thought your sign against the evil eye was a bit anaemic; Mansur's was even more feeble.'

He hunkered down and uncapped a water-bottle, offering it first to me and then to Elena. Finally, he took a gulp, screwed on the cap, and fixed his steady eyes on my face. Lamplight flickered, bringing the wall-figures to life. 'Yes, your friend was here. God forgive me, Omar, but I didn't know why you'd come back. I thought you might be connected with the government. I know you used to work for them, and dealing in antiquities is illegal. They can lock you away for that. A Hazmi can't be locked away.'

I felt a surge of resentment against my uncle, who could seriously consider I might be here on behalf of the government. It was a clear statement of what I'd always suspected: despite my blood, and despite their enthusiastic welcome, the Hawazim had never really considered me one of them.

'Uncle,' I protested, 'I'm enough of a Hazmi never to betray my own blood.'

Mukhtar looked down at his feet. 'Of course,' he said. 'God forgive me. It was an unworthy thought. Last night Mansur told me so frankly; he said that he'd known you since you were a baby and you could never betray us. He reminded me you'd said others could die, and advised me to show you this.'

'What *is* this place?'

'All I know is that it was built by the Ancient Ones in the First Time, ages ago, and probably as a hiding-place. Our people – some of them – have known about it for a long time. The secret has been handed down. I learned about it from my father when I was very small.'

I took the torch from Elena and began to scrutinise the hiero-glyphs. They were definitely New Kingdom and probably late 18th Dynasty, indicating that the chamber was much more recent than the ruins above. It was the size and shape of a tomb, yet it wasn't a tomb. The ancient Egyptians hadn't built tombs in wells. There were no texts from the *Book of the Dead*, no Anubis or Osiris symbolism, no scenes from the life of the departed. In fact, the only thing I'd ever seen like it was the chamber at Madinat Habu where I'd found the Siriun Stela. That had also looked superficially like a tomb, yet had turned out to be some kind of secret store-room.

'Was there ever a door to this place?' I asked Mukhtar.

'They say there was, long ago. You'd probably find it in the water if you looked. They say that it was decorated with a flying disc and a Wedjet Eye, like the one on the stone above.'

I peered at the hieroglyphs again and noticed for the first time that there were a number of cartouches referring to Horemheb as Pharaoh. So it *was* late 18th Dynasty. Why had Horemheb built such a secret chamber out here in the desert? Had he built a similar one at Madinat Habu to hide the Siriun Stela? Why?

'Have these *ushabtis* always been here?' I asked Mukhtar.

'Good God, no! You haven't worked it out yet? Wingate brought them out of the desert.'

'Wingate!'

'Yes. When Wingate and Hilmi came out of al-Ghul half demented, in that year long ago, they brought these things with them in their saddle-bags – a dozen of them. Hilmi just blubbered, and the Englishman wasn't much different. We thought he might die, but after three days the light came back into his eyes and he seemed a bit better. We begged to know what had happened to our relatives, but he said he'd lost his memory. I tried The Shining to help him.'

'What did you see?'

'Men screaming. Guns firing. Camels floundering in drumsand. That was all. No place, no details. Strange thing was, Wingate had power in The Shining too.'

'You mean he was an *amnir*?'

'His power was weak, like mine, but it was certainly there. Couldn't bring back his memory though. He said that he thought something really dreadful had happened, and that we were all in danger. We had to get rid of the *ushabtis*, he told us. Some of the elders were for destroying them, but most were against it because The Fallen One is pure evil – the Devil – and if we smashed his statuettes, there's no telling what misfortune might befall us. Now I wish to God we *had* destroyed them.'

'So you hid them away here?'

'It was the perfect hiding-place. Wingate said he didn't want to know where they were hidden. He gave us this box with the book inside, together with the key and made us promise never to touch them or reveal where they were. One day, many years in the future, he said, they might be of use.'

'So they lay here in the well for sixty years.'

'Yes.'

'Until Cranwell came along, and you sold him two.'

'That's right.'

'It's not like you to break a promise, Uncle. Or did you think the time had come when they would be of use? What happened?'

Mukhtar's gaze wavered, then held mine again. 'I have been responsible for this family ever since my father was lost,' he said. 'Of course, my uncles gave me advice for a time, but they passed away one by one. This year, I had to make a decision concerning one of the family, Aziz, my son Bakri's boy.'

'The one who died earlier in the year?'

'Yes, may God's mercy be upon him. He was dying from some terrible sickness that eats away your heart. He was in terrible pain, and Bakri was frantic. Of course, it was the will of the Divine Spirit, we all knew that, but my son begged me to help. He said he'd heard of a place in Cairo where they could cure it. I was tempted, Omar, tempted to think I could save him. May God forgive me. This place cost money, of course, and I had none, but just at that moment your friend Cranwell arrived, asking about Wingate and Zerzura and it seemed like a sign from God. I thought about the *ushabtis* for the first time in years. It was true that we'd all promised never to touch them, but there were so many, I thought two wouldn't matter, if they went for a good cause. I showed them to Cranwell. I didn't bring him here, of course, or reveal how many there were. He said they might be fakes, but he was willing to buy them, anyway, for a good price. Then he asked if I had any souvenirs of Wingate, and I showed him this book; it was the only thing Wingate left behind. When he read it he got very excited. I thought I could sell him the book, too, but he said no, put it back where you've been hiding it, it's safer there. That was the first sign I'd let a Demon out of a bottle. Anyway, off he went with the *ushabtis* and the very next day, Aziz died. I burned the money: it was dirty. I knew I'd done wrong. That's two mistakes I've made this year, Omar: doubting the will of the Divine Spirit and doubting the loyalty of one of the family, yourself. No Hazmi betrays another. Even if your father was a stranger, he was accepted by the tribe, and you're one of us. God forgive me for questioning your intentions. Like I say, I am only *amnir* because I was the best of a bad bunch. My grandson's illness was the will of the Divine Spirit. I should have accepted that rather than dipping my hands in evil. Now I've brought this great catastrophe down on us all.'

Mukhtar spoke the last words in deep anguish and I realised how difficult this confession had been for him. All his life he'd had utter and complete faith in the benevolence of the cosmos. Only once had that belief wavered, and it had brought tragedy. For a moment he looked a very old, exhausted man. 'You know what the Hawazim say?' he commented sadly, ' "*Ghaltat ad-dalil bi 'alf ghalta*" – the guide's mistake is a thousand mistakes.'

'You know what the Alexandrians say, Mukhtar!' Elena interjected suddenly, ' "*Illi faat maat*" – the past is dead, let's face the future.'

I saw him blink in surprise. In his entire life no one had spoken to him like that, probably – certainly not a woman. His mouth groped fish-like for something to say, but he thought better of it.

'Jamie,' Elena said, 'let's have a look at the diary while we've still got light.' She held the torch for me, as I opened the first page and read aloud from Wingate's pencilled scrawl:

Zerzura, the oasis of fluttering birds, is the only one of a number of oases referred to in old manuscripts and travellers' tales that has not been identified. Following the finding of the *anachronae* by Carter and Carnarvon in Tut's tomb, we have every reason to believe that a mystery of earth-shattering importance will be solved by the discovery of the Lost Oasis – not to mention incredible riches. The Zerzura Club have been scouring the desert with their planes and Model-T Fords for two years, with no result as far as I can ascertain. I feel I can beat them to it, using the traditional methods – camels, and an escort of the Ghosts of the Desert. We do not know what Zerzura looks like – perhaps it is entirely hidden. Nor do we know exactly where it lies, except that it is meant to be in the Sand Sea somewhere to the north of Jilf Kibir – the Zerzura Club have played their cards very close to their chests. However, I feel confident that even without their data, I can locate the Lost Oasis. Zerzura is more likely to be found by a man who travels slowly by camel and on foot than by the man in a motor-car whose contacts with the surface he is investigating occur at 20-mile intervals . . .

I stopped. In places the writing was entirely illegible and in others devolved into brief notes so cryptic that it was impossible to understand. 'Go on, Jamie,' Elena said.

'It's difficult,' I said. I read on, silently now, picking up bits here and there. The fragments sketched in the story of an incredible journey through al-Ghul, battling sandstorms, heat, thirst, hunger and fatigue. Though the account was episodic, I became utterly absorbed by it. I turned the pages avidly. Many were missing and it looked as though they'd been deliberately torn out. Yet I was completely absorbed. It wasn't until Elena nudged me almost an hour later and pointed to the guttering wick of the lamp, that I remembered where I was, closed the book and let out a long sigh. A deep sense of excitement was stirring inside me. I had the strong feeling that something had guided me here, that I was meant to be here all along. It was hot in the chamber and sweat had soaked my *jibba*. Mukhtar offered me water, and I drank it down in long gulps. 'Time is like a sword, Omar,' he growled. 'If you don't cut it, it cuts you. We've got to get out before the *ghibli* strikes.'

'I know, I know,' I said. 'Tell me, Uncle. Did Cranwell or anyone else tear any pages from the book?'

'No, it's just as it was when Wingate left it.'

Elena jabbed me on the arm impatiently. 'For Christ's sake, Jamie,' she said, 'what does it say?'

I grinned at her, trying to keep the excitement from showing. 'Well, Wingate found Zerzura all right,' I said, 'but for some reason he was dissuaded from revealing to the world what he'd found. There's no description, no map coordinates, no navigational data of any kind; it looks as though all the geophysical stuff has been torn out.'

'What about the *ushabtis*? Where did they come from?'

'They came from Zerzura. They were going to be Wingate's proof that he'd found it, only something went badly wrong.'

'But how come the *ushabtis* were lying around at a desert oasis?'

'Because the Lost Oasis of Zerzura wasn't just an oasis,' I said, 'Zerzura was actually Akhnaton's tomb.'

34

IT WAS ALMOST NOON WHEN WE climbed back to the surface and the sun was directly above us, grilling the sand and reducing the shade to purple patches among the ruins. As soon as we'd pulled the rope up after us, Mukhtar touched the Eye of Ra device on the capstone and the segments closed with a sharp thud. He stood upright suddenly and sniffed the air. 'Do you smell it, Omar?' he asked.

I inhaled deeply and tasted the faintest flavour of fire-ash on the wind. 'The *ghibli*,' I said, 'it's on its way.'

'Yes,' he said, 'but more than that. Oil – engine oil. Motor fumes.'

'What is it?' Elena asked.

I sniffed again, this time with deeper concentration. Suddenly I felt as if a hand was clutching at my brain, squeezing it, and a voice I hardly recognised as my own said: 'The ones looking for us are already here.'

Mukhtar stared at me in shock. Elena turned pale. 'Come on,' she said, 'we'd better get this covered up before someone else finds it!'

It took us only minutes to shovel the hot sand back over the capstone with our hands, level it off and smooth its surface with *shamaghs*, so that no one would guess there'd been activity there. When it was done, Mukhtar hid the coiled rope carefully in a crevice behind a fallen pillar, and picked up his rifle. He cocked it quietly, and set the safety catch. 'Ready?' he asked. We nodded. 'Let's go.'

We followed his jerky, spring-like step through the ruins, until we came to the last square of shade. The camels were happily regurgitating and masticating cud, exactly where we'd hobbled them, about a hundred yards away. One had rolled over in the sand, and now sat up with its saddle worn at a ridiculously squinted angle. Mukhtar stood very still, his head forward and slightly raised, silver dreadlocks fluttering, scanning the desert with eyes as keen as a predator's. To the east lay the range of interlocking, amber-coloured dunes, their crests alive with smoking sand-devils. There was no other movement in all the landscape, but for the tiny black dot of a single kite, circling higher and higher into the methylene-blue sky. Mukhtar looked at me closely. As our eyes locked there was a sudden inward flash, and I felt the same vice-like grip clutching at my brain, the same alien voice whispering, 'They're here. Behind those dunes.'

'We might make it to the camels if we run,' Mukhtar said.

'No, Uncle! We won't!'

'It's the only chance we've got,' he snapped. 'Come on!'

He launched himself into the open, sprinting with amazing speed, with myself and Elena dashing frantically behind. We'd covered almost three-quarters of the distance between ourselves and the camels, when the engines roared. For an instant we froze in our tracks and I looked up to see two, then three, four and five olive-coloured Jeeps bulleting towards us through the soft sand, each carrying a huddle of black-clad police troopers in steel helmets. On the first Jeep a blue light was flashing. I saw Mukhtar look about desperately for a way of escape. He raised his rifle for an instant then let it drop. 'Too many to fight,' he said, 'and they've got us cold.' The first Jeep ploughed around us in an arc with exquisite slowness, and an unusually tall man with a domed forehead sprang out of the front passenger's seat, waving an enormous Ruger .44 Magnum in our direction. It was Hammoudi. Sergeant Mustafa, his nose now tacked up with a dirty Band-aid, jumped out of the back brandishing what looked like a baseball bat. 'Ah, Ross!' Hammoudi said mockingly, 'I told you, didn't I!

Don't imagine you're going to get off lightly this time with a warning and a kick in the ribs. Oh, no indeed.' He was pointing his Ruger at Mukhtar. 'Drop that weapon, grandad,' he snapped, 'or I'll leave your old bones for the kites!' Mukhtar sneered as he laid his precious rifle in the sand. Two black-jackets seized his arms and forced him down.

'Curse your fathers!' Mukhtar grunted.

'Careful,' Mustafa said, 'these monkeys have tricks up their sleeves.' He tore off Mukhtar's stiletto, and handed it to a burly corporal then delivered a flying kick to my uncle's belly. Mukhtar let out an 'Ooof!' and lurched sideways. I struggled to get to him against the dozen or so police troopers who were swarming around us now. The same corporal ripped off my *khanjar* and its sheath, and they forced us to our knees, pinning our hands behind us, handcuffing us roughly. 'Take your hands off me, you filth!' Elena squealed. There was a slapping sound as a trooper hit her across the face with an open-handed blow. I couldn't see her any longer, but I heard her panting. 'Bastards!' I shouted, and the corporal whacked my head with the butt of his Kalashnikov, while someone else booted me in the spine, making me double over in pain.

'That's enough!' Hammoudi snapped. 'I'm sure they're ready to cooperate,' he added in his Call-Me-Mr-Reasonable voice. 'Just tell us where the rest of the *ushabtis* are and everything will be all right.'

All three of us stared back in defiance.

'Oho!' Hammoudi said. 'The Bedouin Law of Silence is it? I advise you to reconsider. Now, where are they?'

Mukhtar spat into the sand. Mustafa stepped forwards and dealt him a vicious blow across the ear with his baseball bat. There was a crack of bone and my uncle slumped into the sand. Two policemen hauled him up again, and I saw to my relief that he was still breathing, though his eyes were closed tightly and blood was trickling out of his ear.

'Search the ruins!' Hammoudi snarled, and Mustafa detailed a squad of troopers to go with him. Elena and I exchanged silent looks. Her cheek was bright red where the trooper had slapped her, and there were pinpoints of tears in her eyes. Hammoudi holstered his Ruger in his waistband, removed his dark jacket and threw it into the Jeep. Then he lit a Cleopatra and puffed at it pensively.

'What's this all about, Hammoudi?' I blurted out. The heavy corporal made a move to boot me again but Hammoudi motioned him away.

'You tell *me*, Ross,' he said. 'Is it about smuggling antiquities? Your pal Cranwell dug them up, Kolpos found the buyer and Miss Feisty Anasis here was the mule?'

'A mule I wouldn't mind riding!' the corporal grunted, leering at Elena.

'Shut up!' Hammoudi barked. 'What happened, Ross? Did Kolpos and Cranwell have a thieves' fall-out? Kolpos wasted your crony, so you blitzed his shop with a firebomb, was that it?'

Elena lifted her eyes and gave me a painful glance.

'It's not true,' I said.

'You were there. We know you were there. Bungled it, though, didn't you? What happened? Set the timing wrong and got your hair singed? Then you paid a poor baker's boy named Mohammad Ghali to haul you to Dr Barrington's flat in Zamalek. Oh, we know all about Dr Barrington. Yes, poor Mohammad Ghali – nice boy. Squealed like a pig. No longer with us, I'm afraid. I told Sergeant Mustafa it was going a bit far to stick the electrodes on his balls like that; there's so much paperwork when somone croaks under interrogation. Next time you kill one, I said, you can damn' well fill in the forms yourself!'

'You fucking bastard!'

'You better believe it. What happened, Ross? You get even with Kolpos for wasting your pal? You get Miss Sweetlips here to set him up?'

'Shit!' Elena spat.

'Ooh, talks too! A fall-out among thieves, is that it? Or is it something else. Something to do with Source Jibril?'

'I don't know what you're talking about!'

'I think you do. I've got a feeling in my bones. This is more than antiquities. I know how many times you foreign bastards have tried to penetrate our service. What about '67? They found a whole team of Israeli spies actually posing as Egyptian army officers in key posts. They'd been through officer selection and training – everything – even spoke with Cairo accents. Now that's what you call deep penetration!'

'I don't know anything about deep penetration.'

'May be. May be not . . . ah, here's our friend Sergeant Mustafa again.'

Mustafa appeared with a squad of his black-jackets, carrying Mukhtar's coil of rope on his shoulder.

'That all you got?' Hammoudi demanded.

'The place is clean,' Mustafa said.

Hammoudi took the rope and examined it. 'Well-rope,' he said, 'palm fibre, handmade Bedouin stuff. You find a well in the ruins?'

'No.'

'Then what were they doing with a well-rope? You . . . Sheikh of all Araby . . .' He prodded Mukhtar with his toe-cap, 'What's this rope for?'

Mukhtar opened his eyes and pulled himself up painfully. 'For stringing up a cop,' he grunted, 'shooting's too good for dogs!'

Almost before he'd finished, Mustafa had dived in with his baseball bat and given him two stinging blows across the shoulders. Mukhtar slumped and lay still.

'So!' said Hammoudi, grinning brightly. 'No *ushabtis* in the ruins. So where are they?'

Elena and I stared dumbly at the ground. Hammoudi sighed. 'All right,' he said, 'I think you *will* talk to my persuader. Mustafa, the girl first!'

Mustafa smiled and gestured with his club. Four police troopers grabbed Elena. 'Get your bloody hands off me!' she shrieked, squirming away from them, 'I'll kill you!' The corporal hovered near me with his rifle at the ready. I bit my lip and watched Mustafa, still smiling hideously, as he opened the bonnet of the nearest Jeep. A faint haze shimmered up from the engine. 'Bring the wires!' he ordered, and a trooper hurried up with a mess of orange flex attached to four crocodile-clips, the type of connection used for jump-starting cars. The four troopers were holding down Elena's wriggling, screeching figure on the sand. Mustafa attached the clips to the Jeep's battery and ran the wires to the struggling group. 'Tits or crotch?' he mused out loud with evident relish, as if inviting suggestions. 'Tits to start with, I think,' he said, winking at the troopers. 'Leave the crotch for you boys afterwards.' A trooper tore open Elena's *jibba*, with excited hands, exposing tanned breasts. The cloth snagged, and he pulled out a bayonet, slitting it up to the neck and pulling it wide. Another policeman gagged her with a hand over the mouth. 'You bloody bastards!' I shouted, and the corporal's rifle-butt slammed into me again, sending me spinning. I pulled myself up to see that the troopers had bound Elena's arms and legs with thick cord, and watched helplessly as Mustafa sauntered to the Jeep with glassy eyes and a small sliver of spittle at the corner of his mouth. He climbed into the driver's seat, ready to start the ignition which would send a massive shock through Elena's body. I saw him hold the keys up ceremoniously, and Elena screamed again, her wild eyes started at me frantically from their sockets.

'OK, let's fry the bitch!' Mustafa said, planting the key in the ignition. At precisely that moment one half of his head dissolved into a mess of bloody fragments, as a single gunshot cracked out of the desert's silence.

35

For a fraction of a second the police troopers stared at the bloody remains of Mustafa. Then a light machine-gun opened up with a crisp rat-at-tat from the crest of a dune five hundred yards away, and they scrambled madly in every direction, yelling and loosing shots into the air. Hammoudi, his face distorted with rage and shock, was waving his Ruger, searching for a target, and snapping out useless orders. Suddenly there was an eerie whistle as a mortar-shell fell out of the sky like a stone, smack on to the first Jeep, which erupted into an orange fireball. The explosion made the ground shake. Hammoudi and the troopers near by were bowled over like skittles in the shock-wave. I saw Elena rolling frantically away from the blast, knocking the electrodes off as she did so. A dense dust-cloud mushroomed up and covered the entire column for a few moments, and when it cleared a host of dark, elvish figures seemed to pop up out of the ground only fifty yards away. They came weaving and leaping towards us, screaming war-cries – barefoot brown men with wild mops of hair, naked but for baggy *sirwal* and cartridge-belts, firing at the run. As the troopers backed desperately into the cover of the Jeeps, the hidden machine-gun began traversing the vehicles with deadly accurate tracer, ripping up the light alloy, smashing windscreens, puncturing tyres and igniting fuel-tanks. Two or three of them burst into flames. The truculent corporal who had used my head as a cricket-ball slapped a bayonet on his AK-47 and stepped towards me. 'You'll die for this!' he growled. He drew the weapon back for a powerful thrust and as I rolled frantically away I glimpsed the face of my cousin Mansur standing behind him with his *khanjar* in one hand, a grim smile on his lips and his blank eye gleaming horrifically. The razor-like stiletto flashed once with lightning speed and the corporal dropped into the sand clutching at his windpipe. A streak of blood splashed across the sand. 'The keys!' I bawled to Mansur, 'that one has the keys and our blades!' I watched as my cousin grabbed the handcuff keys from the dead man's pocket and then found our *khanjars* in his belt. He knelt beside me, unlocked the cuffs and offered me my stiletto blade. 'You need this?' he asked.

'I'd be undressed without it!' I said.

Mukhtar was already on his knees near by. 'What kept you, son?' he smirked.

'Sorry, Father,' Mansur answered seriously, 'but you never told us where you were going!' He unlocked his father's cuffs, handed him his *khanjar*, and examined his bleeding ear with concern. 'You all right, Father?' he enquired.

'Can't hear properly,' Mukhtar said, 'but I'll survive. Set the girl loose, and let's get out of here!'

I picked Elena up and Mansur cut her free with his dagger. 'You OK?' I asked.

'Yes. I'll kill those pigs!' she said, grabbing at Mansur's rifle, but he moved it out of her reach deftly, laughing.

'A real Hazmiyya!' he said. 'It'd be yours with pleasure, but we don't have time for revenge now. We've got to get out of here!'

Together, Elena and I ran to unhobble the camels, which were straining against their ropes and bleating in fright. The Hawazim – now lying flat on their stomachs – were pouring fire at the troopers among the burning skeletons of their vehicles. Hammoudi's giant figure, his face streaked with dirt and blood, could be seen through the smoke, firing off his pistol and cursing. Just then a second mortar-shell whizzed out of the heavens and fell in their midst with a deafening crump. As another tidal wave of smoke and debris washed outwards, the Hawazim popped up again and we raced back towards the shelter of the dunes. The smoke and dust were already clearing and the troopers behind the cars had rallied and were firing salvoes towards us. One of our tribesmen was hit and I saw Mansur halt to pick him up in a fireman's lift. Even at this distance I could hear Hammoudi's strident voice bellowing orders, massing the troopers for a counter-attack. Just as he yelled 'Get them!' the machine-gun clattered out again from its secret position, tearing what remained of the Jeeps to shreds. The troopers ducked and fell flat and the attack broke up abruptly.

'That'll keep their heads down!' Mansur snarled. A moment later we plunged into the shelter of the dunes, where we found the rest of the Hawazim camels – at least fifty of them – knee-hobbled in ranks in the sand. They were fully equipped for travelling, I noticed, with bulging waterbags, blanket-rolls, and saddle-bags packed. Mansur put down the injured man and raced up to the crest of the dune to sweep the desert with a small brass telescope he pulled out of his *jibba*. He ski'd down, kicking up spouts of sand. 'Here come the reinforcements,' he shouted, 'another seven Jeeps coming across the horizon. Better get moving, fast!'

There was a wild scramble as the tribesmen unhobbled their camels, slung their rifles, and leapt into the saddle. The camels squalled and rumbled with excitement. I couched Elena's animal for her. 'But they're going to catch us!' she said. 'We don't stand a chance in the open with those vehicles after us!'

'They'll never catch us,' Mukhtar said, barracking his own camel. 'Not today. Look!' He pointed at the sky with his camel-stick. An hour ago it had been pure azure: now it was grey and brown, blurred with tracings of dust. 'The *ghibli*'s almost on us,' he said. 'In a few minutes those cops won't even be able to see their own feet!'

Soon we were all in the saddle, following Mukhtar down off the dunes into the open plains at a slow trot. The tribesmen, who always fought bare-chested, were struggling to don the long white *jibbas*, cloaks, hoods and headcloths they wore on long desert journeys. Already the western horizon was dark with columns of dust moving with the rapidity of a forest fire. Within minutes a troop of fast riders came wheeling towards us, seven or eight Hawazim with their rifles slung across their backs and their camels heavily laden. 'It's 'Ali, my half-brother,' Mansur told me. 'It was him and his men who covered our retreat with the machine-gun and the mortar.'

The newcomers rode straight up to the head of the column. I remembered 'Ali as a gangly boy, thin as a rake – the son of one of Mukhtar's wives who'd died in childbirth. Even as a child, I recalled, he'd had a fascination for weapons, constantly taking rifles and pistols to pieces and reassembling them. He looked like a younger version of Mukhtar himself, wiry even by Hawazim standards, with a long, narrow face and a trim goatee beard. 'Peace be on you!' he called.

'And on you!' I replied. 'Who shot the plain-clothes man?'

'I did!' 'Ali said proudly, holding up a sniper's rifle with a telescopic sight. 'I call this weapon Hawk's Eye.'

' "The master's stroke is worth a thousand",' I said, quoting a Hazmi proverb. 'A split-second later and Elena might be dead. Where on earth did you get those weapons from anyway?'

'We stole them in Libya, and a Hazmi who'd been in the army taught us how to use them. We're crack shots now!'

'Thank you!' I said. 'You saved our lives!'

'The thanks is to God. One day, perhaps – God willing – you will save ours!'

The troop rode off and joined the column farther down. Mansur spurred his camel and caught up with us. 'Aren't we going back to the village?' Elena asked him.

'No. It's the first place they'd look,' he said. 'Even if the men weren't there, they'd hold the women and children hostage. Thank God they didn't already. They came into the village not long after sunrise this morning in a convoy of twelve vehicles.'

'The convoy that passed us in the night!' Elena said.

'I don't know, but they were looking for you, and somehow they knew you might be with us. We swore we hadn't seen you, but they searched the village and found your motor-cycle. Things looked bad, and I thought they might try to take some of us hostage, so I offered to show them where you were.'

'Thanks.'

'It was the only way to be sure we knew where *they* were. Anyway, they sent seven cars off somewhere else and five after you. I guessed from my talk with father last night you were heading for Khan al-Anaq and sure enough, I located your tracks. I'd already primed our best trackers to follow. While the police were lying up behind the dune, waiting for you to come back, our men silenced the sentries and brought the camels up quietly. Then I slipped away from the police, sent 'Ali and his guns up to a high position to cover us, and we crawled through the desert until we were near the ruins.'

'Praise be to God.'

'The Blessings of the Divine Spirit be upon us. We'll need it where we're going.'

'Where *are* we going?' Elena asked.

'To the Jilf.'

'What's the Jilf?'

'It's a Hawazim place.'

'It's a natural fortress in the middle of al-Ghul,' I explained, 'a huge mountain massif as big as Corsica, riddled with cave complexes so vast you can get lost in them, and criss-crossed by wadis with walls thousands of feet high. The Jilf's like a whole country in itself, and it has everything the Hawazim need: water, grazing for the animals, shelter. There are only two entrances: one through a cleft called the Siq, and another underground through a series of caves – so they can't be sneaked up on.'

'How far is it?'

'It's three days' ride across al-Ghul – a hard journey at the best of times, but in a *ghibli* . . .'

'Sssh!' Mansur hissed. 'Look at this!'

He pointed with his camel-stick. For a moment I held my camel back and listened. There it was, that eerie boooooommm! boooooommm! of Raul's drum that set your teeth on edge, and icy fingers clawing your spine. The columns of dust had mushroomed into giant whirling vortices hundreds of feet high. 'Get out your ropes,' Mukhtar bawled. Every man snatched from his saddle-bag a length of rope ten or twelve feet long, looped at both ends, and fitted one loop around his front saddle-horn and flung the other to the rider in front, who fitted it over his rear horn. 'This is the only way we can keep together in a *ghibli*,' Mansur shouted. 'Once it strikes, it's like the darkest night.'

Elena and I rummaged in our saddle-bags, found our ropes and fitted them, only just in time. Suddenly Raul's drum was a deafening roar – the engines of a B52 bomber fed through a million amplifiers. I saw Elena cover her ears. The very earth seemed to shake. The Hawazim pulled down their hoods, knotted their *shamaghs* across their faces and bent low over their saddle-horns. 'Here it comes!' Mansur growled, as the air convulsed and the wall of dust punched into us with incredible speed, almost knocking us out of our saddles. The camels tried to swing around away from the onslaught. The power of the wind was shocking. I never remembered having been through any storm as raw and terrifying as this. The whole desert seemed alive with some malicious, primeval force. I felt a wave of fear breaking inside me; it was the storm rumbling back across the generations, an instinctive terror out of the collective memory of the tribe. The sky was so dark that I could scarcely make out the riders in front of me, and the sand-devils screamed around my head like banshees, chattering, rasping, cackling in my ears. I leaned across the saddle-horn like the others and held tight as my camel pounded on grimly, snuffling as the sand gathered around its sealed nostrils, turning its head out of the storm. Seams of damp red sand began to form along the folds of my *jibba*. There were crashes like peals of thunder overhead, and beneath the camels' feet the ground seemed to bank and yaw. The dust clouds coiled around us like enormous serpents, wailing and spitting. Suddenly I saw the shadows of more camels – dozens of them – standing, half-hidden in the furls of the dust. These were big bull-camels, heavily laden with litters of tiny cloth tents that billowed like sails, and hung with rolled tents, rugs, blankets, saddle-bags, chests, pots and utensils. They carried the women, children, old people, and the entire possessions of the tribe. The Hawazim women had quickly and efficiently loaded everything they owned on to their camels and simply faded into the desert as they had been doing for generations. They had nothing that couldn't be carried on a camel; their belongings were pared down to the bare minimum. As we drew nearer, Aysha's child-like face peeked at us cheekily out of her litter, and I saw that she was now dressed in a full-length dark shirt, her hair covered with a tightly-bound headcloth. 'Peace be on you!' she screeched through the storm. 'Thank God for your safe arrival!'

As we passed, a brown arm emerged from the litter, swinging a length of rope with a loop on the end. 'Join on the last camel!' Mukhtar shouted at her. The caravan halted for a moment while the women's camels were hitched up. Mukhtar ordered 'Ali and his men to take a Hawazim tabla and bring up the rear.

'What's that for?' Elena yelled to me. Her voice was so tightly muffled by the *shamagh* across her face that she sounded as if she were trying to shout under water.

'It's an old Hawazim trick!' I yelled back. 'The last person in the caravan beats the drum so that the guide knows the caravan is all there. It's used for night marches. Simple but ingenious, like most Hawazim things!'

In a few minutes 'Ali's tabla boomed out from the back. Mukhtar gave the order to move, and the camels plodded into the eye of the storm. For hour after hour we marched to the beat of the drum, until we were half mesmerised by the noise and the constant barrage of dust in our faces. Soon night fell, and we stalked on in almost total darkness, unable to do anything but cling on to our camels, each of us marooned in his or her own private world. We were heading straight into al-Ghul, the most fearsome tract of desert on earth. We could not go back, for behind us Hammoudi waited. Our lives now depended on my uncle, Mukhtar, and all the skill and knowledge he'd acquired in a lifetime of survival. Tonight there were no stars to guide him, no moon to steer by, and I prayed to the Divine Spirit I'd ceased to believe in long ago, that he knew the way. For the slightest variation from true would mean ending up in waterless, trackless desert, hundreds of miles from anywhere, completely lost.

36

IT TOOK THREE DAYS TO REACH the Jilf, and they were three of the hardest days I remember. The wind never let up completely, and we rode on blinded by dust with grit in our throats, and a constantly nagging thirst. During the occasional lulls Mukhtar would halt the caravan, and we'd drink a gourd of water each – no more, no less – and eat a strip of biltong. Sometimes we'd halt long enough to snatch a few hours' sleep under a blanket slung from the camels' backs, but very soon it would be off again into the cutting edge of the storm. When the *ghibli* finally blew itself out an hour before dawn on the fourth day, the desert seemed so unnaturally silent that my ears filled the night with imaginary seashell sounds. The sunrise brought us a new desert of many colours, washed and raked clean by the wind, and there, blocking out the horizon, lay the massive granite island of the Jilf.

It was as breathtaking as I remembered it, a baroque city from a mystic's dream, an ochre-coloured sprawl of grooves, clefts, galleries and twisted natural pillars that gave the impression in places that it was in the process of meltdown, and in others that there were strange beasts – dragons, griffons and centaurs – imprisoned in the rock straining and stretching to get out. As we neared the entrance to the Siq, almost invisible until you were upon it, Elena craned her neck to gaze up at an ancient, sand-blasted red butte that towered thousands of feet above us, shaped like a hunchbacked man crouching forward with his hands around his knees. 'They call that "The Doorkeeper",' I told her, and realised suddenly that my lips were cracked and painful. 'It guards the entrance to the Siq.'

'When did you last see this place, Jamie?' she asked hoarsely.

'Not since I was small. It's amazing what stays in your head.'

Mukhtar couched his camel near the entrance, and all around us camels blubbered and rumbled as they were barracked and unhitched. Many spread their legs and staled and the air was heavy with the smell of camel-urine. Men and women slid out of the saddle, stretched, groaned, and began to unlace waterbags for a drink. Elena and I dismounted stiffly and went to join Mukhtar, crouching by the Siq entrance. 'I wouldn't have believed it if I hadn't seen it!' I told my uncle, coughing dust. 'Three days' march across al-Ghul in a Mother storm, and you bring us right to the point you were aiming for.'

Mukhtar moistened his white lips with his tongue. '*Man shabb 'ala shi shabb 'alay*,' he said, ' "He who grows up with a thing grows old on it". It's simply a skill, like any other. The praise belongs not to me, but to the people. Not a peep of complaint even from a child. You couldn't have got a trained army to do that. And thank God it only lasted three days. It was a Mother storm all right, but I've seen worse. I remember one that lasted two whole weeks.'

'Yes, so do I,' Mansur said, his one good eye glittering wryly as he hunkered down with us and unstrung a waterbag, 'but we didn't ride through it, did we!'

He filled a gourd with water and handed it to his father.

Mukhtar took it with both hands: 'The thanks is to God,' he said. '*This* is my reward.' He drank a little, then lifted the cup. 'Here's a salute, Omar!' he said. 'To your friend Elena. She's the only one here not brought up in Hawazim ways, yet she went through the *ghibli* without a murmur. At first I thought her a mollycoddled city girl. But she's proved herself as good as any Hazmiyya.'

'Amen!' I said, knowing that Mukhtar had just doled out the highest praise anyone could ever expect from a Hazmi. Elena blushed, but looked pleased.

'If you don't marry her, you're a fool,' my uncle added. 'And do it quick, or I'll marry her myself!' Elena and I looked at each other, and burst into embarrassed laughter.

'Here,' Mansur butted in roughly, pushing a cup in my direction, 'drink water. It's the last you'll get until we reach the Makhrubat. The waterbags are all flabby as townsmen's bellies. One more day would've killed us all.'

'At least the government won't be able to follow us here,' I said. 'Our tracks are long gone.'

Mukhtar stood up, as if reminded suddenly that Hammoudi was after us. 'Aye,' he growled, 'the *ghibli* has covered our tracks all right, but the government have got aeroplanes and those whirling chopper things. They'll soon be out now the storm's down. We must get under cover. Mansur, send 'Ali and his scouts into the Siq to clear it. Get everyone else mounted.'

The Siq was a fissure in the rock, made aeons ago when the mountain above had split apart due to tectonic pressure, and was just wide enough to allow the camels to pass in single file. It twisted and turned into the heart of the massif, under overhangs and through half-caverns where the light washed along the walls in prismatic colours, along the foot of sheer, vertical chasms where the surface patina of manganese red seemed to have dripped and trickled down like toffee. It took an hour to get through it, and out into the great wadi beyond, opening like a magnificent imperial amphitheatre between stacks of sandstone so massive that an aeroplane could safely have wheeled and turned between them.

'Ali and his scouts returned to the main column a little later and reported that the way ahead was clear. 'There are no fresh tracks, Father,' 'Ali said. 'No one has been here recently, and there has been rain this year; the grazing is abundant.'

'Thanks be to God!' Mukhtar muttered. 'As long as the beasts have grazing, we shall have milk.'

The news spread like wildfire through the company and the tribesmen began to urge their camels forward. The line broke into a series of knots as the animals lifted their heads, pricked up their ears and stretched out their great necks, pressing flank against flank together. Someone began to sing a tribal chant. First one man, then another, picked up the strain, and soon voices were combining in unison as the whole tribe roared together in full-throated harmony. Elena laughed. 'What are they singing about?' she asked.

I cocked my ear to pick up the words. 'About the beauty of women,' I told her, 'about the coolness of water, and the gift of green things, a description of Hawazim paradise.'

She laughed again and my spirits soared suddenly. The dark alleys of Cairo – Julian, Nikolai – it seemed a world away. As we surged along the great wadi, the sandstone stacks seemed to grow even higher, their walls so grainy that they might have been vast pieces of ancient machinery pitted and rusted by time. In places pinnacles had separated themselves from the stacks and stood alone, planted in drifts of strawberry-pink sand, tilted over at perilous angles. Some of them were still attached to the main stacks by natural bridges, and others looked like trees or giant fungi with slender pedestals at ground level, and broad heads hundreds of feet above. Elena studied them with a round 'o' of wonder on her lips. Then, with no warning, Mukhtar swung his mount sharply into a hidden recess, an oval of rock half a mile in depth, so perfect it might have been hollowed out with a laser. Suddenly the voices fell silent. The knots of men began to fracture into single file. Some way up the facing wall, at perhaps two or three hundred feet, I saw two great arches opening in the rock. 'That's our place!' Mukhtar said, pointing upwards. 'You remember, Omar? Makhrubat al-Musawwara – The Caves of the Pictures.'

The caves were reached by a perilous, winding path, wide enough for a laden camel to pass but so steep the beasts were panting before they arrived at the entrance. We slipped down from the saddle and hauled them the last few yards, through the mouth and into the caves. The caves were even bigger than I recalled. They were vast, a system of interlocking galleries opening out of each other, deep into the belly of the rock, incorporating rock pedestals, pillars and arches, so that they actually gave you the impression they'd been designed by warped and delirious human beings. 'This is incredible!' Elena said, as we led the camels inside. We both stared at the high vaulted ceiling in awe. The cave – which would have housed a division of troops – was divided into two by a dry-stone wall which separated the humans' quarters from those of the camels. The Hawazim barracked their household camels amid a cacophony of noise, and unloaded their gear. Saddles, litters, boxes, and saddle-bags were thrown down, bedrolls and rugs quickly spread, three-stone fireplaces set up and camel-dung fires lit. Families gathered around their own hearths. The dring-drang of coffee-mortars rang out invitingly, amplified by the acoustics of the chamber. The herdsboys collected the camels and led them down the steep path to the wadi where they would graze for the day. Mukhtar despatched guards for the herds, and sent 'Ali and his scouts to set up the machine-gun in the Siq, just in case anyone should try to take us unawares.

While Aysha supervised the unloading of Mukhtar's baggage, my uncle took an oil lamp and led Elena and me into a series of tunnels at the back of the cave, through an aperture only just wide enough for us to pass, and into a cavern as large as the entrance-cave. High up in the rock ceiling a single opening let in a thick shaft of light, which was reflected back on a rippling, translucent surface. Elena sniffed at the moisture in the air, and whispered, 'Water!'

Mukhtar laughed with pleasure. 'This is the real treasure of the Jilf,' he said, shining his torch on a water-pool that extended fifty yards through the cave. Even though I'd seen the pool before, I couldn't stop my mouth falling open in astonishment. This really was a Hazmi's paradise.

'When I was a young man I once dived into the water to find out how deep it was,' Mukhtar said. 'They tried to stop me; they say a demon serpent of immense size haunts the place. Anyway I did it, and it was so deep I couldn't find the bottom. And by God it was *cold*! I didn't find any serpent, though.'

'But where does the water come from?' Elena asked.

'Listen,' I said. In the silence you could hear the 'plunk, plunk' of water droplets falling into the pool. 'It's fossil water,' I explained, 'it seeps out of the sandstone aquifers above us – from rain that fell thousands of years ago, probably.'

'But it does rain here. 'Ali said it'd rained this year.'

'Yes, the Jilf is a wind-trap – the peaks milk the rainheads of their moisture as they pass over. That's probably why al-Ghul is so arid. It's a rain-shadow area. By the time the wind gets there all its moisture is gone.'

'But it doesn't rain often,' Mukhtar added. 'One good rain in four seasons is enough to keep the wadis green.'

'Why don't other tribes use it?'

'It's a Hawazim secret. We've been coming to this place since the First Time, look . . .' He shone his torch against the walls and Elena gasped. They were covered in etchings of human figures and animals, done in naturalistic style. We peered at them closely. The humans wore earrings, drawn unnaturally large to emphasise their importance; the artist wanted to make a clear statement about the identity of these people: they were Hawazim – or Anaq. They careened across the rocks like Chinese puppets, running, sitting, herding cattle, dancing roped together in some hypnotic dance, hunting animals. And what animals they hunted – buffalo with giant horns, reticulated giraffe, rhino, elephant – even hippopotamus.

'Hippopotamus!' Elena said incredulously. 'But these can't be for real. How could such animals live in a desert?'

'It wasn't a desert when these pictures were made,' I said. 'See: there are no camels in them. The people are herding cattle. I've often thought about these pictures. Camels were first brought to Egypt by the Persians in the sixth century BC, so they have to be older than that. The geologists say this area has been desert since at least 3000 BC, which puts them back much earlier. They *must* be at least 5000 years old, and they *could* be as much as 10,000.'

'Jesus!'

'Now look at these,' Mukhtar said, holding up the lamp in another part of the cave. 'You saw them when you were tiny, Omar, but you may not remember.'

I didn't, and what I saw now fascinated me beyond words.

Here were a bunch of six figures with scaly, fish-like bodies and heads like featureless inflated white balloons. They were clearly differentiated from the Anaq, whose features were carefully drawn, and who surrounded these globe-headed men in deferential postures, kneeling or standing with their arms raised.

'Gods!' Elena said. 'They're worshipping the globe-heads as gods, but look here, they've become ancient Egyptians.'

She was right. In the next tableau, the six globe-heads had become transformed into the gods of ancient Egypt, crudely but clearly drawn: ibis-headed Thoth, falcon-headed Horus, aardvark-headed Set, and three human-headed figures with fish-tails which might have been Osiris, Isis and Nepthys. While the other gods seemed to be standing around watching, Thoth was handing out bulbs of mandrake-root to the surrounding humans. It was a crude version of the image at the Khan al-Anaq temple we'd seen only a few days before.

37

BY THE TIME WE GOT BACK to the entrance-cave, Aysha had arranged the saddles and boxes, laid out rugs and cushions and lit a fire of camel-dung. The cave was smoky now, full of the hum of voices from the Hawazim families around us, and the shriek of little children playing. Mansur came to join us, and Aysha poured us coffee spiced with cinnamon. 'I feel unworthy of all this,' Elena said, drinking her coffee, 'I mean, you moved your entire clan across the desert to a different home just for us.'

'For the tribe,' Aysha said. 'The tribe is sacred. We couldn't allow any one of us to be taken by the police – and that includes you, Omar's friend, our guest. It doesn't matter where we live, in a cave, in the desert, in tumble-down houses, because to us home is people, not a place. The tribe is everything, place is nothing.'

'But you know they'll never let you get away with it,' Elena said, 'you *killed* policemen . . .'

'We killed only two,' Mansur said. 'Both were about to attack you and Omar. A few may have been injured accidentally in the shooting and bombing, but it's not our custom to kill unless somebody's directly threatened. Not unless it's a blood feud.'

'Still, she's right,' I said. 'No matter what the circumstances, they won't forget it.'

Mukhtar snorted. 'The government has been trying to get rid

274

of us as long as anyone can remember,' he chuckled. 'They haven't succeeded yet. Besides, we have plenty of unsettled blood feuds with the police. And we never forget, either.'

'God is generous,' Mansur said. 'We all go to the Divine Spirit when it is time.'

'So what do we do now?' Elena asked.

'Tonight,' Mukhtar said, 'there will be a great Shining. The Divine Spirit will show us the way.'

In the pre-sunset cool, Elena and I walked down to the wadi where the camel-herds were browsing in the acacias under the watchful eyes of the herdsboys and their armed guards. We wandered past them, nodding and exchanging greetings, and sat down on a bank of soft sand. There was silence except for the occasional snatches of song from the herdsmen, the snarl of a camel, the buzz of insects in the grasses, the gentle whisper of the breeze. The *ghibli* had cleared the air, unlocking the chalk smell of the open sands, the multiple odours of grazing camels and heavy acacia-bloom. I felt my body relax completely for the first time since I'd returned to Egypt. I didn't want to think about Orde Wingate's diary, but I knew we had to face it some time. I'd been brooding on it all the way through the storm, and now I had to tell someone. To my surprise, though, Elena pre-empted me.

'We're no nearer to the bottom of this are we, Jamie?' she said.

'If you mean we still don't know who killed Nikolai and perhaps Julian, you're right.'

'Why, ''perhaps Julian''?'

I recounted my experience at Giza: the man who'd sounded like Julian but had run away too fast, the hunchback's story that he'd spotted Julian after he was meant to be dead, the alleged Julian's phone call to Doc, and the bulky Julian-like figure I'd glimpsed at Nikolai's shop. She sucked in her breath when she heard the last bit.

'You're trying to tell me Julian killed Nikolai, and tried to kill you?' she demanded.

'I didn't say that. The fact is I just don't know.'

'So that's what Hammoudi meant when he said it was a "thieves' fall-out".'

'I don't go for it. I mean, Julian and I were like two fingers for more than ten years. He sometimes threw tantrums, but I never knew him do anything he thought dishonourable. He just wasn't that kind of guy – passionate about his work to the point of obsession, yes, but never concerned over material issues. Anyway, even Hammoudi didn't seem convinced that it was really a rift between thieves; he kept rattling about "deep-penetration" and "Source Jibril".'

'That man's a psychopath.'

'Maybe, but he's not an idiot. Look: Wingate's story is that Carter and Carnarvon found something in Tut's tomb they referred to as *anachronae*.'

'What does that mean?'

'It's an archaic term used by archaeologists to denote artefacts which seem to be out of time in a dating sequence.'

'So the secret find was "out of its time".'

'That's the implication. Whatever it was, this find revealed the fact that Tut's father, Akhnaton, had been buried out in the desert somewhere. So far it makes sense. Akhnaton was a heretic. When he died his henchmen thought his mummy would be ripped up for compost and his shrouds used as toilet-paper, so they built a tomb for him and Nefertiti far out in the desert where no one would ever find them. Over the centuries the rumour of his burial-place became transformed into the Zerzura legend – a white city with a king and queen asleep on a hoard of treasure. Now I think of it, I'm a dummy not to have seen the resemblance to a pharaonic burial a mile away. So they've got this secret find and they've discovered that Akhnaton's tomb – the legendary Big One of Egyptology – is not on the Nile like all the rest, but stuck out somewhere in the boondocks.'

I paused to watch a herdsboy nearby milking a plump she-camel, standing on one leg with the other foot lodged against his knee, his hands working nimbly at the animal's udder, squirting the milk into a wooden bowl. The she-camel lifted her great grasshopper head, and groaned contentedly. When he'd finished, he put the bowl down and tied up the teats with a rope and peg, to stop the young suckling and finishing the milk. He brought the bowl over to us and offered it to me. 'Drink!' he said.

I passed the bowl to Elena, and she took it apprehensively. 'Take it with two hands,' I told her, 'and squat down when you drink. It's an offence to drink milk standing up.' She squatted on her haunches and gulped. When she passed it back to me, there was a half-moon of white froth around her mouth. I giggled and drank deeply. The milk was warm from the udder, and slightly salted. You could taste the flavour of the desert herbs in it. I wiped my mouth with the back of my hand and gave the bowl back to the boy.

'Thanks,' I said.

'The thanks is to God.'

We watched as he hurried to offer the milk to the nearest guards. 'Good stuff, camels' milk,' I told Elena, 'but watch out. If you're not used to it it gives you the Mahdi's Revenge.'

'Now, you tell me.'

'Sorry. Anyway, where were we?'

'Yes. They discovered that Akhnaton's tomb is out in the desert and that it's the legendary Lost Oasis, Zerzura.'

'Right, and what's the next thing they want to do?'

'To track it down, of course.'

'Right, but what actually happens is that Carnarvon snuffs it, followed by two dozen of his chums. How come?'

'Could they have been bumped off by someone who wanted to keep the whole thing under wraps?'

'Bang on! There was a curse on Tutankhamen's tomb all right – Karlman was correct in that – but it wasn't any hidden guardians. It was flesh and blood, some group who not only wanted to run Akhnaton's tomb to earth, but were also pretty desperate to make sure no one else rumbled it. In fact they were willing to go to any lengths to make sure.'

'But somebody did rumble it: Wingate for one, and the Zerzura Club, too.'

'Right. So we've got two little bands of interested parties. One lot – the Carnarvon Group – are wasted, the others – the Zerzura

Club – go look for the tomb, but don't strike lucky. Wingate comes along and *does* hit it, but on the way his whole party disappears – probably wasted too. Wingate is allowed to live, though.'

'So if you're right, whoever's protecting the secret of Akhnaton's tomb has already whacked thirty-seven people. That's large-scale murder!'

'And there are other possible victims, don't forget: at least four. If Julian is dead, there's him, Nikolai, Ronnie Barrington and probably Ibrahim Izzadin, the former DG of the Antiquities Service.'

'A nice fat total of forty-one.'

'Yes, and that's the problem, Elena. I can't imagine anyone knocking off forty-odd people for the sake of a pharaonic tomb. As you say, this is really big-time murder – *mafia* stuff.'

'But think of the value: if there was anything like what there was in Tut's tomb, it would be worth millions.'

'That's true, but Wingate himself wrote that whoever found Zerzura would solve a mystery of "earth-shattering" importance. OK, on its own Akhnaton's tomb would have been a major arch-aeological discovery, but would it qualify as "earth-shattering"? I don't think so. It wouldn't have altered the lives of people, nor changed the world. And if Wingate was right, *he* must have solved the mystery. It would have made him famous. Yet he never breathed a word about what he found.'

'Maybe he only found the *ushabtis*?'

'I don't believe it. I reckon Wingate was being forced to hide something – something that had immense global implications, something that some group were prepared to kill for, and keep on killing over six decades. Doc found out that the Zerzura Club was a front for British intelligence, for a start. If my hunch is right and all those people were rubbed out to stop them blabbing, it has to have been for something far more mouth-watering than just another pharaonic tomb.'

'Like what?'

'The only way we're going to find that out is by visiting Zerzura ourselves.'

38

WE CLIMBED UP THE STEEP PATH to the caves in the wake of the camel-herds being driven to their night quarters by herdsboys, chanting rhythmically and tapping their camel-sticks. The camels were magnificent creatures, not large as camels go, but strong and perfectly formed. The Hawazim referred to their camel-herd as *al-bil*, and were intensely proud of it. It had been bred from generations of prime stock and most of the animals were the unusual colour they called *aghbash* – off-white, with an undertone of cobalt blue. The sour smell of saltbush-fed camels filled our nostrils, and the animals keened, grunted and snorted as they climbed. Across the valley, the sun was slipping down into a square in the rock-wall the Hawazim called 'The Gateway of the Sunset' – another doorway into a different dimension – throwing long sequences of colours across the wadi floor, stretching out the spiny shadows of the saltbush and the flat-topped acacia scrub. A silence had descended on the Jilf, even more serene than that which had reigned by day. 'It's like being on a different planet,' Elena said softly, 'no cities, no slums, no motorcars, no engines. Wouldn't it be wonderful to live in a world like this all the time!'

The entrance-cave was in twilight now, but a large bonfire was already blazing in the centre of the great vaulted hall, and men and women were spreading their rugs and cushions around it.

Their shadows were giant cameos on the high rock walls. Mukhtar, clad only in his *sirwal*, saw us coming, and beckoned us over. His hands were stained orange and I saw that he'd been pounding some reddish substance in a stone mortar. 'Demon's Apples,' he said. 'You'll both join us in the Shining tonight?' Elena gave me a puzzled glance.

'It's a great honour to be invited,' I told her in English, 'and an insult to refuse. I've never been invited before myself.'

Elena eyed the orange mess cautiously. 'They drink that?' she asked.

'*Al-liksir*,' Mukhtar said, 'it was the gift of the Ancient Ones to our ancestors – The Divine Water that brings the Shining. Will you join?'

'Is it dangerous?' she asked.

'No more dangerous than riding across the desert in a *ghibli*,' I said.

'Will you join, Omar?' Mukhtar asked.

I thought for a moment. The Shining had its risks, I knew. There was something inside me holding me back, some fear that once into this thing I'd no longer be able to hide from my real self. But I guessed I would never get the chance again. This was a solemn gift my uncle was offering me – a chance to join communion with the Hawazim – to *be* one of them. Mukhtar and his family had risked their lives for us, simply because I was a blood relative. I knew deep down that I couldn't refuse.

'OK, I'll join,' I said.

'Good,' he said. 'And you, Elena?'

Elena looked at me hesitantly. 'What the hell,' she said, 'I've been hit, shot at and almost electrocuted. I rode for three days through a sandstorm. What have I got to lose?'

It was pitch dark in the cave now but for the roaring bonfire. Beyond the opening, the night was softly moonlit and spangled with stars. The camels lowed and chewed cud soothingly at their hobbles just beyond the dividing wall. We sat down on rugs at the front amid a murmur of voices and a rustle of robes; the firelight skipped from one profile to another, outlining each for an instant then passing on. There must have been two hundred people sitting around that fire I guessed. We had been there only minutes, when Mukhtar appeared out of the shadows, followed closely by Mansur, 'Ali and a host of other tribesmen carrying sloshing waterbags. The crowd hushed. Mukhtar took the first waterbag and held it up before the assembly, his gaunt biceps straining. The light from the flames played along his spare body, as weathered as the sandstone stacks outside. 'Behold the Divine Water!' he cried, in a voice I hardly recognised. 'We drink this in memory of the departed ones – all the souls of our family back over the generations to the First Time. We drink this that we shall join as one – living and departed – in the Divine Spirit that never dies.'

'The Divine Spirit lives!' the assembly roared back.

Aysha and other women emerged from the crowd carrying carved wooden bowls and there was a slosh as Mukhtar emptied the first waterbag into one of them. Behind him, hidden in shadows, other bowls were filled. Mukhtar held his bowl up, 'As *amnir* of the tribe I take first draft of this Water,' he said. 'May the Divine Spirit guide me in the Shining and direct me to the way.'

'The Divine Spirit lives!' the crowd roared again. Mukhtar put the bowl to his lips, took a long draught, and immediately sank to his knees, letting out a long sigh. The audience cheered and clapped. Mansur offered the bowl to each of us in turn. The other men moved silently along other rows handing their vessels around. I took the bowl from Mansur and looked at Elena. 'Drink!' my cousin said. 'May the Divine Spirit guide you!' I took a sip. The liquid tasted sour, like native beer brewed from sorghum. 'Drink!' Mansur ordered me, his one good eye sparkling excitedly in the light of the flames. I took a long swallow, then a second. Mansur passed the bowl to Elena, who drank without hesitation. Suddenly, tablas struck up with electrifying rhythm from out of the shadows, and at once hands began to clap in time. The fire crackled and sent bursts of wild light across the gathered faces. Voices began to chant, at first in waves of deep bass resonance like the sound of a great mountain-horn being blown again and again – waves forming and breaking until the bass was counterpointed by the shrill of the women's chorus. As I watched, Mukhtar stood up in the firelight, his eyes scintillating, focused on something far, far away. He waved his brown arms, throwing back his ancient, ravaged head and howling out a song. Everyone stopped to listen, then roared back a response. On and on it went, Mukhtar roaring the lead ecstatically, the audience roaring back, and I realised suddenly that the *amnir* was literally guiding his people, moulding and shaping the form of their vision. At first I was simply aware that I'd been drawn into the music and felt myself swaying to it as the others swayed. Then, suddenly I'd slipped inside it – actually *within* the music, within the mouths and the minds of the singers and the song. Abruptly, the progression of the song seemed suspended, a continuously repeated pattern with no beginning and no end, lasting for eternity in a timeless now. I was still aware of the cave and the people around me – in fact I was much more aware of them than I'd been before. Suddenly, instead of being *out there*, a mass of distinct individuals, each an island to him or herself, they were suddenly *in here*: there was no longer any barrier between 'me' and 'them'. All my life I'd desperately wanted to belong; now I saw with devastating clarity that everything was part of everything else, everything fitted like a vast cosmic jig-saw, everyone and everything belonged. There was no dualism of object and subject; existence was one. The sense of alienation I'd always felt was a self-invented obstacle. My life hadn't begun with my birth, but with the birth of all creation; my real body wasn't this corporeal envelope I wore, but the cosmos itself. I knew with equal certainty that I'd always been aware of this. I'd tried to suppress it, but in reality I'd never left the Divine Spirit. I knew suddenly that it was this sense of oneness that allowed the Hawazim to live as they did: they didn't see themselves as individuals but as a whole, in daily connection with creation, with their true body, the universe.

The drug fizzed through my blood, breaking up my awareness into a billion particles of being, shooting them along a laser-beam into the horizon. I retained my consciousness of everything around me, yet at the same time I was floating somewhere above it all, in utter silence. I heard a heart beating fast – mine – and heard heavy breathing, felt muscles tensing and relaxing, feet pounding like pads on the flat white sand of a desert, and looked down to see that I was no longer in my human body at all, but in the frame of a spectral desert jackal – Anubis – my ancestral spirit, the embodiment of all that lay in my past and my future. There were tracks behind me, tracks that led from England to Cairo, to al-Maqs and through a *ghibli* to Jilf Kibir. I'd left visions in my wake, Julian's body in the sand at Giza, Julian running away in the night at a speed that wasn't Julian's, Nikolai's agonised face, a crude Eye of Ra on his mirror in blood, the explosion at his shop, myself flapping like a kite, Karlman's fingers digging into me, Rifad's sweating forehead, Rabjohn saying 'you may be hiding your light under a bushel'. I strained into the distance to see where my tracks led to and glimpsed even more disturbing images – Doc's limp body hanging by a belt from a ceiling, an old Hazmi with a tortured face, Elena unconscious in a dark cave, a tall fair-haired boy lying dead in the sand. I peered towards the desert horizon beyond these images, but I could see only a black hole into which all paths seemed to disappear, a dark nebula beyond which I could observe nothing. Something told me that space was called Zerzura, and as I looked the blackness formed into the gigantic shape of the Eye of Ra. Suddenly, though, I was distracted by a brilliant white light that seemed to enfold me, and I looked up to see a fiery sun-disc emanating rays that ended in small hands – hands that seemed to stroke my skin coaxingly. I looked up towards the sun-disc and a deep voice startled me: 'The Chosen One,' it said. I felt myself rising out of the trance like a bubble rising through water, and suddenly, with shocking intensity, I knew many things. I knew that Mukhtar had been right. I *did* have the Shining power – had had it since I was a baby, in fact, and had tried to suppress it. I laughed at the stupidity of my self-denial. The power was still there, had always been there, smouldering powerfully in my psyche. It had saved my life several times: as a child when I'd foreseen the unexploded mine, when Kolpos had tried to slice me up, when the grenade had been rolled across the floor – and it had warned me on other occasions, like when I'd known the police were waiting for us at Khan al-Anaq. The dreams I'd had while knocked out at Doc's had been telling me that same thing – I *was* an *illuminatus* – not 'nothing' as Hammoudi had told me, but 'something' after all. And as full consciousness dawned around me, I knew that I could never, ever go back to being what I'd been before.

When I came fully to myself, I saw Elena looking at me with pupils wide as saucers. I had no idea how much time had passed. The music had ceased, the fire burned down to its last embers, and the cave was full of smoke. Many of the Hawazim had retired to their own hearths, others had fallen asleep where they were, or were rocking gently still to some internal soundtrack. Elena took my hand, and a bolt of sheer sensuous electricity shot through me. 'We belong,' she said. I felt the truth of her words. Silently, we got up and, hand in hand, walked unsteadily out of the cave and into the starlit night. The moon was bright above us, and we descended the path easily. We found the soft sand-bank where we'd sat earlier and laid out the blanket and rug we'd brought with us. The night was warm and perfectly still. When I took her in my arms and kissed her, it seemed that her lips were on fire. Wild energy flowed between us. Again and again we kissed, exploring each other's mouths with our tongues, clasping each other's bodies. The Shining drug had somehow made my senses so acute that each touch of mouth or hands sparked off a small shock of ecstasy. Elena must have felt it too, for she moaned when I kissed her neck, and gasped as I ran my fingers through her hair. In a moment we had shredded off our clothes and lay naked on the blanket, panting with desire. I stroked her breasts and her back softly and she responded, parting her lips and brushing my inner thigh with her fingertips. When I entered her I knew this wasn't lust, but true belonging, a moment of real communion with eternal life.

39

I AWOKE TO A BITING HEADACHE, and found an inquisitive early-morning camel sniffing at my hair, nibbling at me with drooling prehensile lips. A young herdsboy, a small brown figure in torn *sirwal* stood near by, laughing at me. 'You're lucky it's only a camel,' he said. 'Last time we were here, one of the men woke to find a huge hyena licking the fat out of his hair. I don't know whether he or the hyena got the bigger shock!'

I tried to grin but my head hurt. I looked round for Elena, and the boy nodded up the hillside. 'At Shallala,' he said.

Shallala was a spring half-way up the sandstone stack on the south side of the amphitheatre, easily reached in ten minutes' scramble over a boulder scree. I guessed somebody had told her that a small pool of crystal-clear water was to be found there. It was ideal for bathing, but was hardly ever used because the Hawazim had been brought up to treasure every drop of water, and had never got into the bathing habit even when water was plentiful. I climbed up over the boulders and found the pool under a rock overhang, its walls worn smooth by the passage of water over the centuries. Elena, crouching in the water up to her neck, was the only occupant. She looked relaxed and serene. 'How do you feel this morning?' I asked.

'I woke up with a terrible hangover,' she said, 'but now I feel wonderful. How do you feel?'

'A lot better now I've seen you.'

'Come on in!'

I glanced around. There were no prying eyes, so I took off my *jibba* and *sirwal* and jumped in. The water was as cold as ice, and the shock knocked the breath out of me.

'Sheeeesh!' I said.

'Forgot to tell you – it's cold. Good cure for a hangover, though.'

I put my arms around her waist under the water. 'You shouldn't bathe naked here,' I said, smiling, 'there's not much privacy.'

'Oh,' she said, parting her lips and slipping her arms up my back. 'And what about you?' I kissed her deeply and gently, then harder, and she responded passionately, caressing me. Suddenly her hands stopped moving, and I felt her fingertips tracing the ridge of scar-tissue that I knew traversed my spine diagonally from neck to the buttocks. She drew in a breath and turned me round gently. 'Good God!' she said. 'It's the Hawazim whip-mark. You were lashed when you were a kid!'

'It was all voluntary,' I said, 'but I don't advertise it. The kids at school in England used to call me a "savage". I was never allowed to forget.'

'Over a girl?'

'No, it happened soon after my mother's disappearance, when a boy said she'd run away with another man. I took the lash, stroke for stroke, against him. And I beat him. By Jiminy, that was the most painful thing I've ever taken in my life, as if you'd been struck by lightning. They say it's worse than being stabbed. My father went spare – I was only nine years old.'

'Jesus Christ, and I thought my childhood was painful!'

I kissed her again, harder this time and held her tightly. The drug had worn off, but the magic was still there. 'It wasn't just the Divine Water, then?' she said, smiling.

'No,' I said. 'We belong.'

We climbed out of the pool later, shivering, and dried ourselves with our discarded clothes. She'd been right about the water – my hangover was completely gone. The sun was already hot, and our wet clothes dried almost immediately. As we made our way down into the wadi, I noticed a new herd of camels, packed tightly shoulder to shoulder, being driven by mounted men cracking hide whips and chanting. The camels were mostly females with bulging udders – the milch-herd of the tribe. After them came a flock of goats, drifting across the valley in a sheen of dust. 'What's this?' I asked the nearest herdsboy.

'The flocks and milch-herd,' he told me. 'Ahmad wald Mukhtar has just brought them in from the fringe pastures.'

'Ahmad!' I said. 'I missed him at al-Maqs.'

'Another cousin?' Elena enquired.

'Yes, my favourite cousin,' I said. 'The one I used to go on desert forays with when we were kids. He's built like Samson – the only man I know who can lift a full-grown she-camel. He's younger than me, but he used to be a sort of minder to me when we were boys. I'll never forget the day some village youths were beating me up and calling me a "Dirty Hazmi", and Ahmad came flying round the corner like a whirlwind. A lot of the kids were bigger than him, but next thing I knew he'd floored the two biggest. Out came the old *khanjar*. "You touch my cousin again," he said, "and I'll come to your houses at night and cut your throats so silently you won't know about it till you wake up!" You should have seen the look on their faces, I mean they actually *believed* him. We had a good laugh about it afterwards.'

When we arrived in the entrance-cave, we found Ahmad sitting with Mukhtar, Mansur, and 'Ali at the coffee-hearth. They looked like Red Indians, with their weathered brown bodies, their unkempt fat-smeared hair, and their rifles nursed in the crooks of their elbows like magic wands. All of them stood up to greet us in the formal Hawazim way. 'Thanks to God for your safe arrival,' I told Ahmad. He was a short, squat man – a sort of pocket Hercules – almost neckless, with a head like a boulder, a shaggy beard, and pectorals that bulged under his *jibba*.

'Omar!' he yelled, slapping my shoulders and squeezing my arms with massive hands. 'Still a city pipsqueak, I see! Muscles like sparrow's knee-caps. You ought to get back on a diet of mutton-fat and camels' milk. Make a man of you, by God!'

'You're right,' I said, 'I need a holiday in the desert!'

He shook hands with Elena and we sat down at the hearth. 'Where were you when the real men were fighting the government?' I asked.

He beamed. 'If I'd been there it wouldn't have been a fair fight, let's face it, cousin!'

Everyone laughed. 'What kept you, anyway?' I enquired.

'When you arrived at al-Maqs I was herding the flocks and the milch-herd on the fringe pastures. Mansur sent me a messenger, so I struck camp and made my way here by a longer route. I sent scouts into Kharja town to put their ears to the ground, and they caught me up on the second day. A whole regiment of police-troops has arrived at the airport in big aeroplanes, with vehicles and even armoured cars.'

'Allah!' Mukhtar said.

'And there were helicopters and spotter aircraft there too, all with police insignia. One of our scouts dressed up like a peasant and got into the airport. He said he saw a giant of a man with a head like an egg.'

'Hammoudi,' I said.

'That's the man; our spy heard them call him Captain Hammoudi. He was greeting an officer in uniform who looked like his boss, and who'd just got off the plane with the police troops. Our man listened to their talk, and the giant called the boss Major Rasim.'

'I've heard of him,' I said. 'Rascally-looking fellow?'

'That's him. There was an old man with him who watched everything, but didn't say much. At first our spy thought he might have been a foreigner, but when he did speak, his Arabic was that of an Egyptian. Major Rasim seemed in awe of him, but the giant one looked at him suspiciously.'

'What was his name?'

'They heard him referred to as Jibril.'

'Was he a police officer?'

'Might have been. Our man couldn't tell. Said that he seemed to have authority, though. Rasim said to the giant one, "We've got to put a trace on Ross and the girl. I want them found as soon as possible, but don't lay a finger on them till I give the word. As for those damned Hawazim rebels, I want them caught!" '

There were chuckles from all sides.

'Anyway, the scouts passed through the fringe villages on the way back. The government have gutted al-Maqs. Houses burnt down, well damaged, feeder-canals ruined, palm-groves and gardens destroyed. Oh – and I'm sorry, Father – they found the secret hiding-place at Khan al-Anaq. Broke through the capstone and climbed into the well. Our scouts say the *ushabtis* and the book are gone.'

'Bastards!' I said.

'Yes, but that's not the worst of it. Omar, do you remember our old share-cropper?'

'Yes, always looked after the place when you weren't there – Swaylim wasn't it?'

'Yes. The scouts found him tied to a tree with his throat cut.'

'No!'

'Yes. Feet were burned, so it looks like they were trying to get your whereabouts out of him.'

'God have mercy on him!' Mansur said, shaking his head, his good eye blazing. 'Those pigs – Old Swaylim knew nothing but his land and his dates. Wasn't even a Hazmi, by God!'

'We'll take his price in blood when the time comes,' Mukhtar growled.

'The scouts also passed through Kwayt village. There's a rest-house for travellers close by, and someone stopped them and gave them *saqanab* – the news. The news was that there was a man staying in the rest-house, a foreigner, who'd come looking for you, Omar.'

'Must be Rabjohn,' I said, glancing at Elena. 'What was he like, an oldish man, American?'

'The scouts didn't see him, but apparently he went to al-Maqs, found it burned out, and passed on to Kwayt. Said he had an urgent message for you.'

'Might be a government spy,' Mansur said, 'a trap.'

'No, Rabjohn's a friend of ours. It must be him; he's the only one apart from Doc, another friend, who knew we were going to al-Maqs. He helped us get here.'

Everyone fell silent for a moment, weighing up the situation. It looked as if the police were determined to fight this one out. Mansur took a brass coffee-pot off the fire, and poured out the first cup for Mukhtar.

'Well, what did the Divine Spirit tell you, Uncle?' I asked him.

The old man knocked back his coffee in a single gulp and handed the cup to his son, shaking it from side to side. 'The Divine Spirit told me two things,' he said. 'One is that the source of all this trouble is Zerzura, the Lost Oasis. All the evil that has befallen us emanates from there. If we wish to know what this trouble is really about we must go there . . .'

'Yes, that's exactly . . .' I began, but Mukhtar silenced me with a raised hand.

'The Divine Spirit also reminded me that my responsibility is the strength of the tribe. We may not be safe here if the government comes after us in force. We will only be safe across the border in the Sudan. That is why I propose to take the tribe across the frontier as soon as possible.'

'Uncle, if we don't find Zerzura, we'll never know what happened to your father,' I said.

'Zerzura killed my father and so many of my relatives. The *ushabtis* Wingate found there have brought death and destruction. Nothing has come from Zerzura but corruption.'

'Uncle, I must go there.'

'But how will you find it? Zerzura is only a legend. We know the desert better than anyone, but none of us has ever seen it.'

I thought for a moment. 'Look, Wingate found it. If he could, so can I. His headman, Hilmi wald Falih, is still alive. Maybe he could tell us something.'

Mukhtar shrugged. 'Hilmi is possessed by *Jinns* – that's what he got for seeking Zerzura.'

'Look, Uncle, give us a few days – maybe a week. If we can't find Zerzura in that time, you take the tribe across the frontier.'

'But who will go with you?'

I scanned the faces of Ahmad, 'Ali, Mansur and the other

Hawazim who'd gathered around. They remained impassive and inscrutable.

'I'll go alone if I have to,' I said.

'I'll go!' Elena said, suddenly. 'I'll go with you, Jamie. I'm not afraid!' She stared round challengingly at the men, who began to shift uncomfortably.

'Surely you'd not let a woman shame you, Ahmad!' I said, unfairly.

'Damn you to hell!' Ahmad said, beaming. 'All right, Omar. I'll go.'

The broad man clapped his half-brother Mansur on the arm. 'Since when has the mighty One-Eyed Warrior been scared of *Jinns*!' he said. 'Just one glance from that dead eye of yours is enough to send them off in terror!'

'All right,' Mansur said, slowly, 'count me in.'

'And me,' said 'Ali. 'Never let it be said that my half-brothers showed me up!'

'One of you must stay,' Mukhtar said. 'Which is it to be?'

They stared back at him stoically, none of them wishing to give in now they'd committed themselves.

Mukhtar smiled. 'You are sons to be proud of,' he said, 'you put your father to shame. But one of you must stay. All right, Omar. The tribe will remain here until Zerzura is found – or not. 'Ali, you stay here. And I shall go with Omar, too.'

'You're a brave man, Uncle. No one would expect it at your age.'

'I'm not brave, Omar. It's just that I have nothing much to lose.'

'The tribe has a lot to lose,' I said.

He smiled.

'What about Hilmi?' Ahmad asked. 'God knows, he might remember something.'

'He's in Kwayt,' Mukhtar said.

'Good,' said Ahmad, 'then we can go and find him, and while we're there, Omar can talk to this foreigner who wants to see him so urgently.'

40

WE ARRIVED IN KWAYT BY NIGHT, after a two-day dash
across the desert on the finest camels the tribe owned.
Mukhtar had lent me Ghazal – a famous racer with a loping stride.
Elena had stayed at the Jilf, but with me were Mansur, Ahmad
and two other tribesmen named Nasir and Ghanim, as well as
my uncle, Mukhtar. Kwayt village was larger than al-Maqs, and
inhabited largely by Hawazim who'd intermarried with oasis
people, given up the life of the desert, and made a living from
their gardens and palm-groves. We dismounted in the dune-belt,
left Ghanim in charge of the camels, and crawled up a dune to
survey the approach. There was a fair moon, and the buildings
were nests of acute angles, some of them illuminated from within
by lamplight. A dog barked somewhere near us. 'Damn that
hound!' Mansur said. He pointed out Hilmi's house, standing a
little apart from the others. 'Where's the rest-house?' I asked.

'It's over there on the edge of the village,' he said, indicating
a brightly-lit building. 'The only place with a generator . . . listen!'
I cocked my ear and could faintly make out the lub-dub-dub sound
of a small generator across the dunes.

'Which one first?' I asked.

'Hilmi,' Mukhtar said. 'He lives alone. Everyone's wary of
him, because he's cracked. His niece, a widow-woman, comes to
cook for him every day.'

We crept down the dune cautiously, with Mansur leading, his

rifle at the ready. We had almost reached the house, when the dog barked again, this time a savage baying, very close to us. We froze. A huge wolf-dog was standing in the shadows, baring its teeth at us, about to spring. Mansur knelt down suddenly, his diverging pupils giving him an oddly puppet-like appearance in the moonlight. He began to make a high-pitched warbling in his throat, almost like birdsong, which grew steadily louder, vibrating on and on. After a moment the wolf-dog yelped, and began to back away.

The last we saw of him he was leaping off into the night.

Mukhtar crouched down next to his son and beckoned us to him. He put his finger to his lips, then raised his hands before him, thumbs and forefingers touching. It was the opening phrase of *Yidshi* – the ancient sign-language of the Hawazim, invented long ago for hunting and raiding when absolute silence was required. Mukhtar began to work his fingers and thumbs fluently, crossing them, crooking them, joining and separating them in a sequence of signs. I'd learned *Yidshi* as a child, and though I hadn't practised for years, I immediately got the gist of my uncle's message. 'I'll go in with Omar,' he was signing. 'Hilmi knows me. You – all of you – spread out in the shadows and keep watch.'

Ahmad, Mansur and Nasir all made the finger and thumb circle which meant 'I will do as you ask' and disappeared into the shadows as stealthily as if they'd been shadows themselves. Mukhtar and I approached the house, a small cube of mudbrick, with a rack of water-pots standing outside and a woven curtain across the door. Inside, it smelt of urine and vomit. We turned into a small, bare room with a bed in one corner where a dark figure lay asleep, his face transfixed by a shaft of moonlight that streamed through the window. 'Hilmi!' Mukhtar said. He stepped close to the bed, and shook the old man gently. Hilmi sat up fast, his ancient, ravaged features transformed into a mask of fear. 'Devils! Devils!' he screamed, 'God protect me!'

'Sssh,' Mukhtar said. 'Hilmi, don't you know me? It's Mukhtar.'

The old man pushed the covers away feebly, and looked round at us with wild eyes.

A large cockroach scuttled out of the blankets and shot across the floor. Hilmi grimaced at it. His face was slack and grey, the face of a man who'd long ago given up on life, and his dark eyes were vacant as if they looked permanently into another world.

'Mukhtar?' he moaned, trembling.

He stepped off the bed and groped for an oil-lamp on the floor. He took matches out of his pocket, lifted the mantle and tried to light the wick with a quaking hand. Mukhtar took the matches from him and lit the lamp with a single strike. Shadows raced across the walls, and Hilmi cowered back. 'Who are these people?' he groaned. 'Have you finally come to kill me? What do you want here?'

'There's only my nephew, Omar,' Mukhtar said, chuckling. 'No one's come to kill you. We want to know what happened in the Year of the Englishman. What happened to my father, Salim, and the rest of the Hawazim who went with Wingate.' Hilmi had pressed himself into a corner of the room, with his hands over his eyes.

'Wingate?' he whimpered, 'God deliver us from the Devil!'

'You mean Wingate was the devil?' I asked, feeling a surge of pity for the old man, whose life had been destroyed by forces beyond his control.

'Not Wingate,' he said, 'Wingate was an *amnir*.'

'Look, Hilmi,' I said softly, picking a spill of wood up off the dust floor. 'Wingate and you brought some statues back – like this . . .' I drew a hasty sketch of an Akhnaton *ushabti*, in the dust, accentuating the features – the long chin, the predatory slitted eyes. Hilmi peered at it in the lamplight and stifled a cry with his knuckles in his mouth. 'The Fallen One!' he gasped, making the two-fingered sign against the evil eye.

'Where did you get them?' I asked him. 'Where was Zerzura?'

The old man sighed and sat down heavily on the floor beside me. He made a visible effort to control himself, and for a moment I glimpsed a soul struggling to emerge from behind those wild eyes. 'Zerzura?' he said, stammering, 'Zerzura can't be found.'

'But Wingate found it?'

'It only opens at certain times. You . . . you may come across it by chance, but you can never find it twice.'

'Then did Wingate find it by chance?'

'Wingate was an *amnir*. He had the power. But not enough to save us!'

'What happened out there?' Mukhtar asked.

'I'm an old man now.'

'Can you remember any details of the route?' I asked. 'Anything at all.' Hilmi took the twig from me with arthritic fingers whose nails were knapped to the bone, and began to draw a rough circle shakily in the dust. 'The Jilf,' he said. 'You ride due north across the Desolation till you find a hill with double peaks – it's called the Wolf's Fangs. Then another sand-sheet, perfectly flat. Beware, there are quicksands in the sand-sheet and they can't be seen . . .' He broke off and began to sob, piteously. 'God deliver us from the Devil!' he said again. 'Can't you leave an old man alone?'

Mukhtar nodded. 'Just this,' he said, 'then we'll go.'

Hilmi sniffed and dragged a dirty sleeve across his nose. He drew a small circle in the dust. 'You cross the flats leaving the Wolf's Fangs behind your left shoulder until you come to a belt of low dunes, beyond which is a well called al-Muhandis. After the well you enter the Sand Sea – you leave the well behind your right shoulder and cross huge dunes for two days' ride. On the other side you see the iron tree . . .'

'The iron tree?' I said. 'What's that?'

'That marks Zerzura.'

'But what does the oasis looks like?' I asked. 'Are there palm-trees? Water?'

Hilmi had dropped the twig, and began to whimper again, 'There's nothing . . . nothing there . . .' he sobbed, 'only fear.'

His eyes had gone completely blank, and he was mumbling to himself incoherently. Mukhtar touched my arm, shaking his head sadly. 'Let's go,' he said.

41

WE LEFT HILMI'S HOUSE AND GATHERED with the others in the shadows, looking around carefully to make sure the old man's cries hadn't alerted anyone. There was no sign of movement, but an old feeling was awakening in my stomach – the feeling I'd had the day Kolpos had been hit, that something just wasn't right.

'Shall we go for the rest-house?' I asked Mukhtar.

He looked troubled, and I wondered if he felt the same as I did. 'We must now we've come all this way,' he said. 'Why?'

'Just . . . I don't like it, somehow. Too quiet.'

'Come on!' Ahmad hissed.

We worked our way around the village, keeping well out of the light, remaining amid the sand-drifts and copses of stone pines. The Hawazim moved like trained saboteurs, halting every time there was a rustle or a movement. Once, an owl hooted, and we froze as the startled creature swept past in a shoosh of wings. The rest-house stood outside the village, and as we neared it the throb of the generator stopped abruptly. Then the lights went out. 'Good!' I whispered.

'Shh!' my uncle said, holding up his hands, palms out, forefinger and thumbs touching. 'Talk *Yidshi*!' he signed.

A door slammed, and we threw ourselves down softly among the stone pines near the house. A couple of men – Hawazim by their accents – hurried towards the village down a well-worn track.

They paused to light cigarettes and for an instant we saw two strained, Arab faces in a circlet of light. We scanned the shadows opposite, about three hundred yards away, where there was a dense palm-grove. The uneasy feeling stirred itself again. There were no vehicles in the driveway, I noticed, so if it was Rabjohn where was his car? It might not be Rabjohn at all – the whole set-up might be a trap. I had to go in cautiously – the feeling that something was amiss had grown even more powerful as we approached. I signalled to the others to gather round me and poised my hands in the opening phrase of *Yidshi*. When I had their attention I began to work ponderously through the signs – it was a travesty of Mukhtar's fluency, but at least I got my meaning through: 'I'll go alone,' I signed. 'You cover me. If it's a trap, we'll all have a chance.'

'We'll do as you ask,' Mukhtar answered forming thumb and forefinger into an 'o'. Then he fanned out his fingers, meaning 'We'll spread out here.' He felt inside his robe and brought out a revolver. 'Take this,' he signed. I took it reluctantly. It was a Smith & Wesson .380 and its weight brought back memories. Before my eyesight went, I'd been a crack shot. Now, without my glasses, I couldn't have hit a barn door at twenty paces. I still had my glasses, though. 'Be careful, Omar,' Mukhtar signed, crossing forefinger and second finger. 'Go in the safe-keeping of the Divine Spirit.'

The rest-house was much larger than Hilmi's house – an ugly modern structure built hastily of cement and breeze-blocks. As I worked my way round to the back door, it seemed as silent as the grave. I pressed myself up against the wall near the door and tried the handle. It was open. I took a last glance around outside – the Hawazim were invisible in the shadows. I stepped into a spartan kitchen, beyond which another door opened into a long corridor – the bedrooms, I assumed. The corridor lay in complete darkness, but for a single slit of light under one of the doors. I crept along the corridor, cupping the revolver in my hands. I pressed the door softly with my sandal. It gave. I peered through the crack and saw a young man sitting reading a book at a table, in the light of an oil lamp. So it wasn't Rabjohn, after all. Then who the hell was it? Suddenly the door creaked. The man looked up and saw me, and in almost the same instant I kicked the wood hard and leapt into the room thrusting the muzzle of my pistol towards him with both hands. He fell backwards out of his wooden chair with a crash, picked himself up and raised trembling hands. 'It's cool. Don't shoot!' he said breathlessly. 'It's cool, man!'

He was tall and slim, about twenty-five, with a sensuous face, bright blue eyes and pursed lips. He wore his blondish hair in a pony-tail and a gold stud on his ear. His clothes were loose-fitting, cotton chinos, a white cotton shirt and an embroidered waistcoat. He wore chunky Jesus sandals and a leather pouch hung on a string round his neck. There was something distinctly familiar about him.

'Who are you?' I demanded.

'My name's David Barrington,' he said, his voice quavering.

'What?' I said, stupidly, almost dropping my weapon in surprise.

'Barrington . . .' he said again.

I realised I'd heard right, and as I struggled to take it in, I saw suddenly that the face was a younger version of Doc's. I knew I'd seen it before often – minus pony-tail and earring, and a good deal younger – in the photo at Doc's flat. I held on to the pistol, though. I had to be sure. 'Passport!' I said.

'Are you the police or something?' he asked.

'Just show me your passport.'

'OK. OK,' he said. 'It's cool.' He fumbled with the leather pouch, brought out a creased British passport and handed it to me with trembling fingers.

'All right,' I said, 'now sit down and put your hands on the table where I can see them.' He sat. I lowered the revolver and examined the passport with one hand. It seemed genuine enough. I handed it back to him. 'OK,' I said. 'Tell me where your mother was born?'

'Is all this necessary?'

'Just answer the question.'

He looked at me resignedly. 'OK. Mum was born in Kampala, Uganda.'

'And your father?'

'My father was born in London.'

'How and when did he die?'

'In a car accident in Cairo, 1989.'

I stuffed the Smith & Wesson into my belt. He looked relieved. 'Why weren't you at the funeral?' I asked.

'How do you know about that?'

'Answer the question.'

'I'd been in the States since I was eighteen, and I'd sort of, you know, like dropped out of college. The usual trip – sex, drugs – I just wasn't in a state to face Mum. I mean, Mum and Dad were always wrapped up in this like, cloak and dagger shit. It was the only thing in the world that turned them on, and I didn't want any part of it. Look, shit, it's cool and everything, but why are you giving me the Gestapo treatment?'

'I'm Omar James Ross.'

'No shit! Hey, why didn't you say so? You're the guy I've come to see. I've got a message for you from Mum.'

'Why didn't Doc come herself? Where is she?'

The young man's face seemed to collapse. Buds of tears flecked the corners of his eyes. 'You didn't know?' he said. 'Mum's dead. Suicide. Found strung up from the ceiling of her flat.'

'No!' I said, I feeling the blood rushing to my head. I staggered slightly as if I'd been dealt a massive blow. My heart began pumping iron, and I had to lean for support on the edge of the table. I whipped my glasses off, rubbed them on my sleeve, forced myself to take five very slow, retained breaths and replaced them. For a moment reality swept away from me in a whoosh and I remembered the vision I'd had at the Shining, of Doc hanging from the ceiling. I remembered the feeling of foreboding I'd experienced before coming here. I held on tight to the table, until my knuckles went white and my legs started to shake.

'Hey, you look kind of rough,' David said. 'Sit down. Have some water.'

I sat down on a broken chair opposite him. He poured me

some water from an aluminium canteen into a plastic mug. It was warm but I drank it gratefully.

'When?' I asked.

'About a week ago. I was in Seattle and the British Consulate got in touch with me – I'm like, next of kin, you know, so I flew over. It hit me real hard. I mean, Mum and I were never very close, but I saw suddenly how we could have been. See, I got my head together in the end, met a wonderful chick. I've got a kid of my own, now, and I was just starting to understand, you know, the parent–child thing. You can't bring it back, can you, man?'

'David, I'm really sorry. Doc was about my best friend in the world.'

'Yeah, I gathered that.'

'You think it was suicide?'

'Funny thing is Mum never struck me as being the kind who would do herself in. I know she had a bad time after Dad went, and hit the bottle a lot, but I never thought she was that sort.'

'Was there any sign of violence in the flat?'

'Well, the police had been in and out, like, but the thing was, when I looked round it was all too *neat*, you know what I mean?'

'Neat?'

'Yeah, like Mum wasn't a tidy person, you know. But everything was in place – no, that's not it – things were tidy, but they *weren't* in place: stereo speakers the wrong way round, floppy disks filed under the wrong headings, printer connected to the wrong socket on the computer – that kind of shit. It was, like, as if someone had tidied up in a hurry.'

'You mean as if the place had been trashed and then put right?'

'That's exactly right. Shit, there was even stuff *broken*, as if it'd been thrown on the floor then picked up again.'

'You said there was a message for me?'

'Yeah, it was weird, man. I booted the computer to see if there were any messages – I knew Mum's password. There was a message file on the disk, but all it had on it was this one thing, ''Omar James Ross, al-Maqs village, Kharja oasis'' – and the words, ''indaloo''.'

'Indaloo?'

'Yeah, it was kind of a joke way of saying "in the loo" we had when I was a kid. So I think she's telling me there's something in the John. I went in there, lifted the lid of the porcelain, and there it was, in a plastic bag strapped inside under the pipes so cleverly you'd have had to know it was there to find it. That was Mum's cloak-and-dagger training.'

'What was it?'

He fumbled in a ragged army-surplus knapsack and came out with a standard cassette tape. 'It was this. Addressed to you.'

'You listened to it?'

'Yeah, but I don't have a clue what she's talking about – Eye of Ra Society and Monterhopper fifteen or something – Mum's usual claptrap. I mean, I used to get all that up to the neck when I was a kid and it just turns me off. Then, right near the end things start to sound a bit hairy. Why don't you listen to it?'

'How?'

'*Vee hef vays ov mekkin things tok,*' he said, pulling out a black Sony Walkman. He snapped the tape in, then pushed it over to me. I attached the earphones carefully and punched 'play'.

42

J AMIE – DOC'S VOICE BEGAN SHRILLY – IF you're
listening and you've found this tape, then I'm probably in deep shit. Anyway, I had to do what I did, darling,
and I don't regret it. I owed it to Ronnie, at least. Since I
found out what happened to him and that I'd been right all
the time, I just haven't given a shit any more. Last time we
spoke on the phone I told you I'd made an appointment
with Montuhotep XV of the Eye of Ra Society. Well I kept
the appointment and I have to say from the beginning I'm
impressed: offices over a department store, all very swish
– and I get the feeling that apart from the downstairs the
Society occupies the whole place. I mean plenty of dosh,
you know. Uniformed doorman takes me up in the lift –
very smart and clean by Cairo standards – and I'm plonked
in a waiting room with potted papyrus plants and prints of
Seti I, Ramses II, and assorted 19th Dynasty pharaohs.
There's the Roberts print of the Temple at Abu Simbel
done in 1886, with the colossi of Ramses II sitting there
complacently half-buried in sand, and there's the Perriot-
Chipiez engraving of the same pharaoh seated holding the
crook on his shoulder. There was definitely a preoccupation
with the 19th Dynasty, I noticed – no 18th Dynasty, no
Tutankhamen, no Old Kingdom. And of course, everywhere
you looked there was the goddess Isis, the Ankh symbol

and the Eye of Ra. Five minutes later a man comes out, brown as a berry, shaven head – hairless, deep-lined face, about sixty-five, seventy. Looks as if he should be wearing some kind of Hare Krishna get-up but instead he's got on this very nicely cut dark suit. Doesn't look like a religious maniac. In fact, there's an air of dignity about him – still eyes, watchful, weighing up everything. I suppose that's the most dangerous kind. He's dominating somehow, as if he's used to dishing out orders. 'Mrs Smith?' he asks. Immaculate English. 'And which magazine is it you write for?'

'I work for the Gamma Agency,' I say. 'We can speak in Arabic if you want. I'm quite fluent.'

He looks at me as if I've just farted. 'Arabic is not the language of our people,' he says, 'it is the language of foreign invaders. Our language is ancient Egyptian. Do you speak ancient Egyptian, Mrs Smith?'

'Not fluently, no,' I say.

He smiles, quite charmingly as if he gets the joke. 'Then might I suggest we confine ourselves to English?' he says. It's all good humoured and civilised, but I have the feeling he's watching me closely. And I feel he's not Egyptian, not even Arab. His English is just too perfect – Yank accent, cultured. I feel like asking him to give me a burst of ancient Egyptian just to see how fluent *he* is – but I decide against. We sit down and some lackey brings coffee. Without turning a hair he introduces himself as the Scribe Sha-Tehuti, but then he sort of grins and says, 'But you can call me Jibril.' He asks how he can help. 'I did want to talk to Montuhotep XV,' I say.

'Her Grace is very busy, you understand,' he says. 'She can only see you for a few minutes. Meanwhile, perhaps I can be of assistance.'

'All right,' I say, making a show of how disappointed I am. I launch into my interview: origin and objects of the Society, and that kind of thing. 'The Society was formed around the turn of the century,' he says, 'coinciding with the intense interest in Egypt arising in the West. Its founders wanted to preserve the authentic culture of ancient Egypt, which they were afraid was being lost under Western romanticism. Has it ever struck you, Mrs Smith, how deeply the memory of ancient Egypt has infiltrated the Western psyche? Have you ever noticed, for instance, that the American dollar bill depicts both a pyramid and the Eye of Ra? Did you know that the sign doctors make on a medical prescription, ''Rx'', is derived from the Eye of Ra symbol? Are you aware that the Freemasons trace their rites back to ancient Egypt? All these are, of course, worthless simulacra, debased by centuries of foreign interference, a travesty of the true forms which may be traced back to the dawn of Egyptian civilisation. It is the aim of the Eye of Ra Society to re-establish those original forms.'

'But isn't such debasement inevitable?' I asked. 'I mean old forms always take on new meanings as societies develop.'

'The ancient Egyptians had a concept called *Ma'at*. *Ma'at* was perceived as a beautiful woman – the personification of harmony and truth. It is *Ma'at* which determines the true forms – forms which were interrupted more than once even in ancient times but which were always eventually re-established.'

'So *Ma'at* means the status-quo?'

He snickers. 'A cheap Latin phrase,' he says, 'cannot express an idea of Divine Harmony which governed a most sophisticated state for thousands of years – millennia before the Latin language even existed. No, Mrs Smith, *Ma'at* is quite definitely *not* the ''status quo''. *Ma'at* is the cosmos as it was meant to be. The Eye of Ra Society is the twentieth-century guardian of *Ma'at*.'

'Fine, but if your Society only goes back to 1900, how come Madame Montuhotep claims direct line of descent from Isis, 10,000 years ago?'

He smiles as if he's been expecting this one. 'Of course,' he says. 'The Eye of Ra Society is only the latest incarnation of an institution known by many names, that has existed since time immemorial. It flourished as a focus of resistance during the Arab invasions of the 7th century AD, for instance, but it had already been in existence for ages then. You can say that, in one form or another, the Eye of Ra Society has never ceased to exist since the *Neteru* walked the earth.'

'*Neteru?*'

'Some call them ''gods'' but the term is inaccurate. We call them the Shining Ones, or the Dwellers-in-the-Sky. In Mesopotamian myth they are called *Oannes*, in Dogon mythology *Nommos*. Isis, Osiris, Horus and the others were real flesh and blood, and were only absorbed into myth after their deaths. That is why it is more correct to refer to them as *Neteru* than gods.'

It's just getting interesting, but before I can quiz him again there's a buzz and he pulls a cell-phone from under his jacket. He excuses himself for a few minutes, then comes back saying it's time to meet 'Her Grace'. He escorts me down a corridor to a very plush-looking office suite – sound-proofed, air-conditioned, marble floors and pillars and Persian carpets. A stately, powerful-looking woman – sort of Elizabeth Taylor as Cleopatra – is sitting behind a giant desk in the middle of it all, wearing some kind of gold lamé dress and a tiara with a cobra design on it. Behind her desk there's a huge Eye of Ra painted on the wall. She stands up and gives me her hand; I wonder if I'm expected to kiss it. Her face is aristocratic – high cheekbones and sharp angles – and she's heavily made up, eyes lined with *kohl*, eyelids stained black. Rich perfume. She looks very chic, but also stern and regal – about forty-odd with dark eyes, jet-black hair done up in an elaborate coiffure, ivory white skin as if she's never been in the sun at all. We sit down in a very ornate courtesy suite and there's a bit of small talk about how difficult it is to keep up the standards of Divine Kingship after ten thousand years, and how you can't get the help these days. I ask her what's the significance of the 'Lotus Throne' and her eyes take on this faraway look.

'The world was once a boundless sea,' she says in this ethereal voice – heavy accent – 'and out of the sea rose a shining lotus bud which brought light and perfume to the earth. The lotus became the sun which breaks forth from the dark waters each morning. The lotus is the soul of Ra.'

'OK,' I say, not quite seeing the point, 'but how come you're sitting on the throne of Isis?'

'I am the incarnation of the Great Mother,' she says, 'after ten thousand years. In every generation Isis is reborn. In this generation I was chosen.'

'By whom?'

'By the Society. It is the Society that makes the King, and Isis is the Society.'

I want to point out the obvious – that she isn't a king – but then, I think, she might cite Hatchepsut, the 18th Dynasty queen who ruled as a pharaoh. I take it her answer means she's self-appointed, anyway, so I ask where the Society gets its funding. 'From the subscriptions of its faithful members,' she says, 'but the Society does not exist for profit. It exists to promote the re-establishment of the concepts of ancient Egypt in their purest form. Isis and Osiris will be resurrected!' I notice that her eyes are shining – she really believes this drivel.

Suddenly Jibril's cell-phone buzzes again and he answers it. While he's talking in monosyllables I look around and once again I notice that there are all these 19th Dynasty artefacts and images on the wall. When Jibril's finished his conversation, I ask: 'Why this preoccupation with the 19th Dynasty? Where's Tutankhamen and Khufu and the rest?'

'The 19th Dynasty restored *Ma'at* after the depredations of the Great Heretic,' he says.

'Great Heretic?' I ask. 'Do you mean Akhnaton?'

Suddenly, they're both staring at me as if I've said a four-letter word, and I see I've hit paydirt. 'Wasn't he just a religious dreamer? A sort of mystic?'

Again, it's Sha-Tehuti – 'Jibril' – who answers. 'The Great Heretic banished all the *Neteru* and replaced them with the Aton. He was a tyrannical dictator who wanted to force his beliefs on the people. He betrayed *Ma'at*. It wasn't until Seti I, Ramses II, and the 19th Dynasty that the menace was removed for ever. The Great Heretic's name should have been excised from history. It probably would have been if not for meddling foreigners.'

'Like whom?' I ask, but they're both watching me silently and I think Jibril has had enough. I decide to risk it anyway: 'Do you mean like Dr Julian Cranwell?' I ask. Montuhotep looks lost. Jibril screws up his eyes. 'Who?' he asks.

'The eminent Egyptologist. He was found dead last week at the pyramids. Did you ever meet him?'

'I've never heard of him,' he says, but there's a hesitation. I'd swear he's lying. It's too late, though. My last question has blown it. Jibril's regarding me very suspiciously.

'Just who are you, Mrs Smith?' he asks. Voice cold as a cobra.

'A journalist.'

'Funny,' he said, 'I've just phoned the Gamma Agency. They've never heard of you.'

The situation was looking very dicey. 'I'm freelance,' I said, 'I *have* worked for the Gamma Agency in the past, they probably just didn't remember my name.'

'I feel you have come here under false pretences,' Jibril said, 'and I suggest you leave at once, or else I shall call the *Mukhabaraat*.'

I beat a hasty retreat. That question about Julian was way out of line – impulsive – but then he'd blown my cover anyway. I'd parked my car down the street, but when I got there I decided I'd hang out a bit to see what kind of 'clients' went in and out of the place. Montuhotep seemed the full-flown head-banger, but I wasn't so sure about Jibril. There was a calculating manner beneath all his talk of 'The Shining Ones' and the 'Great Heretic'. I couldn't get over the obvious opulence. Where did the money come from? Not from the contributions of faithful believers alone. I wondered if there was something behind it like drugs or gun-running. Maybe they're just a couple of rich crackpots who like dressing up as Pharaohs. All good clean escapism, why not? But I had a feeling, so I sat there and lit a fag and an hour went by. Nothing. Nobody went in or out. Another hour passed, another couple of fags. Nothing. I'd forgotten how deadly boring surveillance assignments could be.

I sat there for another half-hour, and I was just about to give up and go round to the Semiramis for a snort, when a man got out of this limo outside the office. An Egyptian – small chap, pot belly, balding. Looked round furtively then marched inside. I only saw him for a second, but I knew the face at once: it was your friend Dr Abbas Rifad, Director General of the Antiquities Service. What the heck was he doing there? I'd have loved to be a fly on the wall when he met Jibril. I decided to wait and see how long he stayed, and another twenty minutes passed. It was evidently not going to be a quick meeting, so I decided I wasn't going to sit there for another three hours till he came out. I was just about to start up, when another car pulled up outside the office, and out jumped a European. I knew him too: it was Her Britannic Majesty's Consul, Melvin Renner.

That was enough for me, Jamie. I started up and headed off hotfoot. I get back, bolt the door and look out of the window. Guess what? My two smokers are back outside under the tree. Something tells me I was right first time – they're eyes. They've got a bead on me. I know you were right. I should have gone to Rabjohn's with you, but I just couldn't, Jamie. It would have killed me. So I cocked the old PP and started making this tape. I don't know what all this shit is about, but there's one thing for sure. Whatever it is the Eye of Ra Society is up to, the Antiquities Service and the British Foreign Service are in it up to their scrawny necks . . .

* * *

The sound-track crackled and went dead. I switched it off.

'Is that it?' I said.

'Yeah, that's it.'

'Look David, we haven't got much time. Are you sure nobody followed you here?'

'As sure as I can be. I mean I never wanted to be mixed up in all this secret squirrel shit. Came on the bus to Kharja, actually. Checked out al-Maqs, where you were supposed to be, and it looked like it'd been struck by lightning. Houses all burned out, and *shit*, man, there's this old guy tied to a tree with his *throat* cut. I mean for Chrissake, man, what's all this shit *about*?'

'So you checked in here?'

'Yeah, some dump, eh?'

I cast an eye over his belongings. 'Is that all you've got?' I asked.

'Yeah.'

'You'd better come . . .'

'Hey, I don't know.'

'Believe me,' I was saying, 'you'll be safer with us . . .' when an image tweaked my brain so hard I caught my breath – a momentary picture of the window shattering and the two of us rolling on the concrete floor. 'Get down!' I yelled, and a split second later gunfire stabbed out of the night with a shock that split the glass into slivers and sent the oil-lamp spinning. 'Shit!' David grunted. I listened, and heard the ruckle of sub-machine-guns, followed by the crack and thump of rifle fire. 'Somebody bumped us!' I said.

'No shit! Let's get out of here!'

We dived out into the night to find a battle in progress. Tongues of yellow flame were spouting out of the palm-groves opposite. The Hawazim, dug in behind sand-banks under the stone-pines near by, were blazing back with aimed shots. We raced for the pine-grove, reached some low dunes and threw ourselves behind them. Mukhtar moved out of the shadows as stealthily as a panther and rolled cleanly into place beside us. 'The police!' he spat, glancing suspiciously at David. 'Who's he?'

'A friend,' I said. 'He's coming with us.'

'All right,' he said. 'Listen. If we stay here we're going to be mincemeat. When I say go, we pull out skirmishing and run for it. Whatever happens, we meet at the camels.'

'You stay with me, David,' I said.

'Go!' Mukhtar yelled, and there was a whump of fire from the pines. I fired three or four rounds at the palmeries, and the sharp tang of cordite filled my nostrils. My cousins pulled out in pairs with the oiled discipline of trained soldiers, one covering, the other moving fast, rolling and firing while his partner moved. David and I just got up and dashed helter-skelter for the camels, hugging the shadows. Answering drumfire sizzled out of the palmeries and David screamed and fell, rolling into the sand. For a moment I stood rooted to the spot.

'Move, you city pipsqueak!' Ahmad bawled in front of me.

'He's hit!' I shouted, jogging back towards him, while more fire crackled out of the darkness. I didn't stop to examine his wound – there just wasn't time. I picked him up in a fireman's lift and charged after the others. Out of the corner of my eye I made out figures running from the palms, firing as they came. Ahmad turned, squared his massive chest and sank down on one knee. 'Go!' he snapped, and as I dashed past a spear of fire stabbed out of his rifle-muzzle with a deafening whap. 'Gotcha!' I heard him grunt as he clicked the bolt. We were at the camels. Ghanim had couched them expertly, ready for a quick exit. As I laid David's body down nearby I heard rounds crumping into the sand and whizzing over our heads. 'Here they come!' Ahmad yelled from behind, dropping on one knee again in the cover of a dune, and snapping off shot after shot. 'Got another of the bastards!' I heard him yell.

'Quick!' I hissed to Mansur, gesturing at David's inert body. 'Help me get him on the camel!'

Mansur's dull eye blinked at me balefully. 'Too late for that, Omar,' he said, 'God have mercy on him.'

I suppose I'd known it all along, really. I'd felt the blood soaking my *jibba*, far too much for a light wound. Carrying his body those few hundred yards had been a last tribute to my friendship with Doc. I laid David's body out, and only then did it hit me – the vision I'd had during the Shining of a tall, blond young man lying dead in the sand. A bullet – probably a dum-dum – had holed his lungs and penetrated his heart. His shirt was a pulp of blood. I closed his eyes with my finger and thumb, shaking with grief and anger – first Ronnie, then Doc, now David, I thought.

Ahmad raced past me, slamming a new clip into the breech of his .303, 'Ride, Omar, ride!' he bellowed, swinging aboard his camel. 'Leave him!'

I bent over and whispered in David's ear: 'I'll get them, Doc. I'll never rest till I find out who's behind this.' I heard shouting. Sub-machine-gun fire spattered around me, and suddenly a very tall man came over the ridge – a faceless cameo figure toting an enormous revolver. I snap-fired a shot at him without even aiming, and heard a groan as he fell out of sight. Then I leapt on to Ghazal's back, urged him up with my stick, and rode at a gallop out into the silent labyrinth of the desert night.

43

NOT LONG BEFORE SUN-UP WE COUCHED the camels on the sandy shore of a lake without water, between melting black limestone walls, where we rested our aching bodies for an hour or so. Fool's Dawn came – a slowly reddening aurora over the lip of the crags – and in the half-light the lake-bed glimmered, pure virgin white from long-deposited mineral salts. The rock gully was entirely blocked by a great transverse dune, like a dam, which would have trapped rainwater behind it, though whether fifty years ago or five thousand years was impossible to say. While Ahmad and Ghanim collected a pile of dried camel-dung for the fire, Mansur poked around in the sand, reading the surface intently with his good eye. The desert surface was history and geography to the Hawazim, and it was such attention to detail which made them brilliant trackers. Trifles which others missed might provide the balance between survival and extinction – even the track of a beetle or the spoor of a lizard told its own story. Suddenly he cried out 'No God but God!' and called us over to see some camel-tracks. 'This is the she-camel that strayed from Salih wald Balla of al-Khadim!' he announced. 'You remember, Father! She was called *Shatra*, "The Clever One", and she strayed four summers ago after her foal died. Salih tried to track her down, but she was lost in the gravel *rej* where he could no longer follow her.'

'How can you be certain it's her?' I asked.

'I know it's her. I've seen her tracks before. Just like you can read your books, Omar, I can read the desert. I can remember the tracks of every camel I've ever seen.'

Ahmad grinned. 'The One-Eyed Warrior can even tell from its tracks whether a camel was brown or white!'

'But seriously,' I said, 'how could a camel survive on its own out here?'

Mansur pointed to some clumps of sedge, like miniature shrubs, along the edge of the dry lake. '*Had*,' he said, 'good nourishment for camels. That sedge will keep growing for four or five summers after a single rain. She probably wanders between here and the oasis fringes. But these tracks look fresh; I wonder if we could track her down.'

'Forget it,' Mukhtar said. 'We've more important things to do.'

Mansur didn't mention the tracks again, but as we were packing away the coffee things, he came back with a handful of objects in his headcloth and emptied them in front of me like an offering. They were neolithic artefacts – a stone hand-axe of polished blue basalt, a couple of finely-knapped arrow-heads, a chopper, a cleaver and a long-bladed stone that looked like a primitive version of a Hawazim *khanjar*. 'See!' Mansur said. 'These are Anaq things. Our forefathers lived here in *Zep-Tepi*, when there was water in this lake all the time!'

The sun was already hot when we climbed out of the gully, and on the plateau above we sighted a great crescent of pink and apricot-coloured dunes, curving across our path. For a while Mukhtar and I rode together, letting our camels pace each other through the sand. 'They were waiting for us at Kwayt,' Mukhtar said solemnly, 'and you knew, didn't you, Omar; you sensed it. If we'd all gone into the rest-house together we'd have been dead meat now. Do you still deny you have the Power?'

I hesitated. 'I felt something in the Shining the other night,' I said.

He turned his old turtle-like eyes on me with interest. 'What?'

'I understood for the first time that we're all part of one thing.

I don't mean just us, men and women, the Hawazim, even human beings, I mean everything – the insects, the birds, the grasses, the trees, the rocks, the desert, the sun, the moon, the clouds and the stars – we all . . . *belong*. It was the first really religious experience of my life.'

Mukhtar's eyes dropped and began trawling the desert again, picking out the tiny tracks, stones, blemishes and discolorations on the surface.

'You saw the past and the future, didn't you?'

'Glimpses of it, yes. It was like reading tracks in the desert, knowing where they'd come from and where they were going.'

'I'm an old man, Omar,' Mukhtar said, without taking his eyes off the surface, 'soon – today, tomorrow, next summer, I'll be going with the Divine Spirit. That's not important. What matters is the tribe. I have four good sons and I'm proud of them all. They are good men, courageous, generous, faithful, compassionate. You can't ask more than that. But to be *amnir* you need all those things and more – call it intuition – an inkling of what lies ahead, the ability to navigate the caravan through the future. The Shining power. None of my sons has it. Only you have it, Omar.'

'Thank you, Uncle,' I said, 'but I have a life to live, a life back in civilisation.'

'Are you sure that's really civilisation, the city, crowds, madness, perversion of nature – the place where trails run out? People matter, not places: "He who strips himself naked will one day get cold."'

I was about to answer when Mansur let out a cry, pointing high up into the creaseless sky, where a tiny silver speck was floating, high up, leaving a trail of vapour. Mansur peered at it through his telescope. 'That's a spotter,' he said, 'and it's heading straight for the Jilf.'

As soon as we couched our camels under the Cave of Pictures, 'Ali, Aysha and Elena came running to greet us. 'Thanks to God for your safe return!' 'Ali panted. 'Aircraft flew low over us twice today, one at sunrise and the other just before noon. They must have been looking for us, because they circled like vultures.'

'We spotted one of them,' Mansur said.

I hugged Elena tightly. 'We were really worried about you,' she said. Suddenly she noticed my blood-soaked shirt. 'What is it, Jamie,' she asked, 'are you hurt?'

'By God's will no evil?' 'Ali said.

'We found a friend and lost one,' I said. 'It was Doc's son David,' I told Elena. 'Doc's dead. So is he, now – the government shot him.'

'Oh, my God!' Elena said, thrusting her knuckles into her mouth.

'The mercy of God be upon him,' 'Ali said.

'We will take his price,' Mukhtar growled. 'Tell me about these aeroplanes, boy. Were the herds under cover?'

'Thank God, they were. All the scouts and pickets managed to get under their camouflage-nets.'

'Camouflage-nets!' I exclaimed. 'That's new!'

' 'Ali's idea,' said Mukhtar, with a touch of pride.

'We made them ourselves,' 'Ali said. 'Our only defence against air-attack is to become invisible – we can hide the camels under them, too. By the way, Father, our scouts on the southern periphery also reported two helicopters in the distance. They didn't come near us this time, but I think they'll be back.'

'Looks like the government means business,' Mukhtar said.

'I think so, Father, yes.'

'From now on the herds graze only at night. No large parties in the wadis in daytime – only ones and twos. And double the number of scouts and lookouts.'

While the herdsboys unsaddled our camels and set them to pasture, we climbed up to the cave, and settled around the coffee hearth. Later, in the last glow of sunset, the herdsboys brought us bowls of frothy camel's milk straight from the udder. 'Drink!' Ahmad said, thrusting the bowl towards me. 'We'll make a city pipsqueak into a man yet!'

'It'll take a man to ride to Zerzura,' I said. 'Sure you're up to it, cousin?'

'Tell you what, Omar: you ride and I'll carry you and the camel!'

'Did you ever hear of anyone finding Zerzura?' Elena asked Mukhtar.

He handed her his milk-bowl. 'Drink!' he said. 'I did once meet a Hazmi who said he'd been there. He was pasturing his camels on the fringes of the Jilf here and one of his colts wandered into *al-Khuraab* – the Desolation. He followed it for days, till his water ran out. He was almost dead when he sighted this oasis full of palm-trees and grapevines, with a pool of water, and sure enough the colt was there. He said the dates were the most delicious ones he'd ever tasted. He collected dates and filled his skin with water. On the way back he ate the dates and dropped the stones every so often so as to be able to find his way back. When he got to the Jilf he got his brothers and cousins together and they set off to find the Lost Oasis. They never found it. They didn't even find a single one of the stones he'd dropped. Zerzura can only be found by chance – and it can never be found twice.'

'If it can only be found by chance, how on earth can we find it?' Elena asked.

Mukhtar shook his head slowly. 'Only the Divine Spirit knows,' he said.

We left the Siq just after sunrise next morning, a trail of termites on the endless flats of al-Ghul. There were nine of us in the party: myself, Elena, my uncle Mukhtar, Ahmad, Mansur and four volunteers from the rest of the clan, riding the best camels available. Elena had been favoured with Ahmad's champion racer, al-Jadi – 'The Pole Star', while I rode my old friend Ghazal. The day was calm, without a breath of wind, and the sky was a polished sapphire touching every horizon. On the fringes of the Jilf there was a belt of coarse yellow grasses raised by the occasional rain, and further on we found thorn trees twisted into spectral shapes by the *ghibli*. By noon, though, we'd come to a shelf overlooking a sandslope that dropped two hundred yards into a vast plain – a sterile, featureless ocean of open desert that seemed to go on for ever. As we halted to survey it, Mukhtar said, 'We call this plain the *Khuraab* – the Desolation – nothing lives down there, no insects, no snakes, not even a lizard. There isn't a single leaf or clump of grass for the camels, and not a drop of water until we reach the al-Muhandis well. If we don't get back to the Jilf within two weeks, the camels will die.'

For three days we rode towards a horizon that never seemed to get any closer. Sand alternated with alkali flats, where the surface glistened so blindingly that it made your eyes hurt. The Desolation was utterly featureless, as if we'd crossed a time-warp and entered another dimension of reality. When we halted for a gourd of water, we would huddle together and speak in hushed voices, looking over our shoulders at the emptiness as if it were watching us with bad intent. Even the camels felt it, for as we rode they would press themselves together flank to flank. The days dragged on interminably as we seemed to mark time in a trembling, diaphanous haze that smouldered on and on to the ends of the earth. I once asked my uncle where he thought we'd end up if we rode day after day in a straight line, and he considered my question carefully, as if trying to fathom whether I meant to mock him. 'We'd fall off the edge of the world, of course,' he said, 'into the Sea of Darkness from which there's no return.'

By noon on the third day we'd sighted the Wolf's Fangs through shrouds of sand-mist, and in the evening we camped at its foot in a crescent-shaped pocket of sand. We dumped our gear, hobbled the camels and fitted their nose-bags, then threw ourselves down, exhausted. There was no time to rest, though. A camel-dung fire had to be lit and a meal cooked. Ahmad made Hawazim bread – a flat loaf baked in the sand under the fire – and we ate it with sour camel's milk from our skins. Afterwards, as we sipped scalding tea and smoked our pipes, I asked my uncle if he'd ever heard of the quicksands Hilmi had told us about. 'Only in legends and stories,' he said. 'They're called Abu Simm – the Place of Poison – and they say that in old times whole herds of camels and armies disappeared into them. There's supposed to be an island in the middle of them where a hoard of treasure is buried.'

'How can you distinguish the quicksands?'

'Often they look exactly like the desert all around, but sometimes there's a giveaway pattern on the surface. There's no water under them, no mud as you'd find in the Qattara Depression salt-bogs – Abu Simm is pure drumsand.'

'What's drumsand?' Elena asked.

'There's a sort of crepitation when it subsides,' I said, 'like somebody rubbing the skin of a drum.'

'But you can guide us through them, Mukhtar?' she enquired.

'In a place like Abu Simm, only the Divine Spirit can be your guide.'

When the tea was finished and the pipes smoked out, we simply fell on our backs and stared at the stars. Here in the open desert, they crowded the sky. I saw the Great Bear, Draco, Taurus, the Pleiades, and not far above the horizon, Orion, with Sirius scintillating brightly below. 'See that, Omar,' Mukhtar said, pointing to Sirius.

'That's al-Mirzin. When it lies low on the horizon like that, you know that the hot season's coming.'

'That means we're going to need more water.'

'Exactly, and it's already low. We're going to be thirsty before we make the well.'

'Tell me, Uncle,' I said, 'did you know that al-Mirzin has a dark companion, a sister-star that we can't see?'

'If we can't see it, how can you know it's there?'

'It's been seen by machines.'

'Aach! Machines! Well, I didn't know, but I can tell you one thing about al-Mirzin, Omar: that's where the Ancient Ones came from – the ones who built the temples, and brought us the gift of the Shining.'

When we awoke next morning we found ourselves on the edge of another great sand-flat, alive with wild colours. As we rode on later, Mukhtar pointed out strange sights – firefly flashes that darted out of nowhere, giant dust-devils whirling across the landscape, steamy mirages that suggested tropical lakes. 'These are the works of *Jinns*,' he said, 'sent to spin our heads.'

'Why?'

'Who knows the ways of *Jinns*? Perhaps there's a great treasure ahead they want to stop us finding. In the legends they say Abu

Simm is inhabited by a race of human ticks, half-man half-dog, who will kill you to suck your blood. But that's just a story for scaring children.'

'It's not the *Jinns* outside you have to worry about,' Mansur said, darkly, 'it's the *Jinns* inside. *Jinns* love desolate places. They wait there for endless ages until they find a human body to take over, then they possess you. That's what happened to Hilmi, of course.'

'God protect us from the Stoned Devil!' Mukhtar said.

There were strange noises, too, inexplicable rumblings, clickings, whistlings and chatterings which Mukhtar said were the voices of the *Jinns*. 'If a *Jinn* calls your name, don't answer, Omar,' he told me. 'If you do, you'll be dead within a year!'

Once we passed through a whole forest of yardangs, giant stone pedestals carved by wind and sand into the shapes of mushrooms and artichokes. 'The Devil's graveyard!' Mukhtar called it. A hush fell over the company until the weird sculptures were long gone. The only sound was the slosh of water in the waterbags, the creak of the saddles, and the soft crunch of the camels' pads on the sand. After the yardangs the sand-flats became featureless again, and once more I had the overpowering impression we were going nowhere, marking time on the same spot. Some time after noon, though, Mukhtar halted to point out a ragged line of glittering objects which appeared to be just short of the skyline. 'Are those real or another illusion?' Elena asked. 'And if they're real, what are they?'

We padded on towards them, but it was impossible to say what they were, or even how big – these sand-flats demolished any sense of scale. They were the only blemish on the desert's surface, and could have been vast objects far away, or tiny objects near by. It wasn't until we'd come almost up to them that Mukhtar suddenly shouted, 'Bones! The bones of camels!'

At precisely that moment an invisible hand reached out and squeezed the inside of my head. I grunted in pain as a split-second image of Elena disappearing into deep sand pulsed through my mind. There was a scream of 'Jamie!' from behind me, and a dreadful creaking of silicon particles as wave upon wave of sand collapsed. I turned to see Elena's camel – al-Jadi – thrashing in liquid sand up to its hocks, squealing in terror. This was no illusion. I dropped my headrope and leapt off my camel. The others had halted, frozen to the spot, wary that their next step would take them into the sough.

'Stay where the bones are!' I bawled. 'That must be solid ground!'

They couched their camels by the bones and were about to run towards us, when Mukhtar roared, 'No! Only me and Ahmad! Otherwise someone else will be sucked in.'

'Jamie! Help!' Elena screeched. Al-Jadi was already wallowing up to his shoulders, and she was squirming, preparing to jump off his back. I steadied my feet and extended my arms to catch her. 'Stay where you are, Elena!' Mukhtar bellowed, running to help me. 'Don't jump!' It was too late. She jumped, missed my arms and plunged into the sand up to her waist. Behind her, the camel gurgled and bleated with fear, vomiting up globs of green cud. I knelt and whipped off my *shamagh*, casting one end to her. She struggled violently, lurched for it and missed. Her efforts took her further down, almost to her armpits now. I took three deep breaths to guard myself against panic and tried to recall what I knew about drumsand. On most sand surfaces the grains were compacted together, but drumsand was formed in deep basins where the grains had been built up by winds into loose layers, with tiny air-pockets between, so that any pressure immediately forced them to compact and collapse. As the layers collapsed, anyone or anything in them would be sucked down to the bottom of the pit, and some of these pits were big enough to swallow a tank.

'Jamie!' Elena wailed. 'Do something for Christ's sake!'

'Don't struggle!' I yelled. 'It only makes it worse! We'll get you out, don't worry!'

I saw her calm herself with an incredible effort of will and almost simultaneously Ahmad was at my side, tensing his great pectorals and swinging his hitching-rope. Elena caught it on the first swing. I took the end from Ahmad and flung it over the saddle-horn of my camel. 'Hold on, Elena!' I shouted, 'Now listen.

I'm going to draw my camel forward. Whatever you do, whatever happens, don't let go of that rope. Wrap it round your wrists – anything – but don't let go.'

Elena nodded desperately. 'OK,' she said.

'Ready?'

'Yes.' She tightened her hold on the rope, and I wrenched Ghazal forward. The rope tautened. There was a moment of resistance, then Elena was pulled clear with a jerk and lay panting and whimpering on the hard sand. 'Jesus Christ!' she said as I picked her up and hugged her, 'that's as near to the Sea of Darkness as I ever want to get.'

'Al-Jadi!' Ahmad cried, tears streaming down his cheeks, 'I've got to get him out!' I realised he was actually about to plunge into the sough to try and save the camel, and I gripped his great biceps. 'Don't be a fool, cousin!' I growled. 'Strong as you are, there's nothing you can do. Your muscles will only take you down faster, and once in there, you'll never get out.'

Ahmad nodded his massive boulder of a head sadly, and we stood and watched the camel's death-throes. The quicksand was already up to his withers and he made a last futile attempt to extract himself. His heavings only made him go down faster, and in a second the wildly thrashing head was all that was visible above the surface. Al-Jadi stared at us beseechingly with eyes popping out of his skull. Then he was gone. Elena burst into tears. 'Jesus wept!' she said.

Ahmad snuffled. 'Brought him up since he was a tiny colt,' he said.

I was about to say something soothing, when I was interrupted by a terrible cry from Mukhtar. My uncle had knelt down to examine a scattering of bones near by, and I suddenly realised that there were human skeletons among them – I saw at least three femurs and fragments of skulls. The piece Mukhtar was staring at, though, was definitely camelline, a massive thigh-bone attached to a wizened scrap of mummified skin. When he held up the dried skin to me, I saw that his face was distorted with shock. 'Look!' he said. On the skin was the clearly discernible lizard brand of our clan, with two chevrons added above the head. 'That's my father's personal brand!' Mukhtar said in a voice thick with emotion. 'This is the place your grandfather met his death!'

44

MANSUR GATHERED THE SCATTERED HUMAN BONES reverently, feeling for drumsand with his camel-stick. It was a pathetic collection – a few thigh-bones and bits of shattered skulls. 'I suppose the rest of the fifteen and their camels are in the drumsand with al-Jadi,' he said.

'This was my vision in the Shining all those years ago,' Mukhtar said pensively. 'Drumsand and camels sinking into it. God have mercy on them all.'

Suddenly, Ahmad startled us with a shout, and held up something small and greenish. 'Didn't you hear gunfire in your vision, Father?' he asked.

'Yes.'

'Well look at this: a spent cartridge case. And there's more of them. Scores of them in the sand.'

Within minutes we'd raked at least fifty rounds out of the desert surface within a radius of a few metres. 'Incredible!' Elena said. 'Someone must have saturated the place with fire.'

I took one of the cases and examined it. It was brass, greened by oxidation and unusually short and stubby – too thick for a modern high-velocity round. 'That held a .45 bullet,' I said, 'they aren't used much today except in pistols. Up to the end of the forties they were used in sub-machine-guns – not very efficient ones, they were too heavy. It's not the kind of weapon used by the Hawazim or any other Bedouin tribe – no good for hunting, only for attrition.'

'Who then?' Mukhtar demanded. 'The government?'

'American and British special forces had them in the 1930s and 1940s but there were also some in private hands. What happened here, Uncle, was a deliberately organised massacre. Wingate's party was mowed down, camels and all, and their bodies thrown into Abu Simm, with the carcasses of their camels after them.'

'Not all of them,' Mansur cut in. 'It was a poor job if they wanted to cover it up.'

'Seems like it was all done in a hurry,' Elena said. 'Why?'

'Wingate and Hilmi?' I suggested. 'They got away. Maybe whoever did this was so keen on catching them they botched the rest of the job.'

'How do we know Wingate didn't set it up himself?' Ahmad said.

'Whatever happened,' Mukhtar answered grimly. 'It wasn't a chance encounter. No, to bring that off out here, against the Hawazim, in their own country, it would have had to be carefully and deliberately planned.'

We committed the souls of the departed to the safekeeping of the Divine Spirit, standing with our hands raised palms inward, fingertips up, in Arab fashion, while Mukhtar recited *Al-Fatih*, the first verse of the Quran. From there on we walked in single file, pulling our camels by the halters. Mukhtar led silently, brooding, jabbing the sand angrily with his camel-stick. It was painstaking work, made the harder by the first pangs of real thirst. Our water was now almost finished – two half-full waterbags had gone down with Elena's camel – and we daren't drink more than a couple of gourd-fuls each a day. After another day's march, though, we sighted a belt of low dunes in the distance – marshmallow pink, unreal against the pitiless sky. 'There's the dunes Hilmi described,' Mukhtar said. 'We'll make for them. The drumsand should be behind us now.'

Once in the dunes we were able to ride again, but our respite didn't last for long. Now, the hot season was really on us, and the sun came out like a flashing sabre, so hot that it felt as if we were wearing greatcoats. To cap it all a khamsin wind kicked in, leaching us of moisture until our mouths were thick with mucus and we were doubled over our saddles with the terrible gut-pain of thirst. Since Elena no longer had a camel she had to sit awkwardly on the back of mine, clinging on to my saddle-horn. She perched there so silently that I sometimes had to feel for her to make sure she hadn't dropped off. That night we drank the last of our water on empty stomachs. We couldn't even spare enough to make bread. Elena and I huddled together all night, too hungry and thirsty to sleep, but just before dawn I must have dozed off, because I awoke suddenly from a dream in which I was standing before the al-Muhandis well with a fearful look on my face.

That day we were almost past caring whether we lived or died. We simply clung on to our camels and let them take us. As a boy I'd talked to plenty of tribesmen who'd almost died of thirst in the desert, and once, on a desert jaunt with Ahmad, I'd gone three days without drinking, myself. I remembered how the thirst had become more and more agonising as it gripped our bodies until we'd had to tie our headcloths tight round our stomachs just to be able to stand upright. Our mouths had gradually got so clogged with mucus that our tongues seemed welded to our palates, and our eyes seemed to sink into our skulls. It was the camels that had saved us; they'd taken us home with the certainty of arrows. When we had turned up half-dead at al-Maqs, my uncle had forbidden us to drink, saying it would kill us. Instead, he'd made us suck drops of water from a wet rag for a whole night. Mukhtar told me that he'd once found three mummified corpses in the desert, three men lying on their blankets next to the carcasses of three hobbled camels. The men had lost their way, run out of water, simply lain down to die. I shivered as I remembered that chilling story now – that must have been how mother died, I thought suddenly, in slow agony, alone in the desert. No wonder my father had never wanted to talk or even think about it. Since we had no water, there was no reason to stop at midday, and we had no strength to walk, so we let the camels drift on, hanging barely conscious on their backs. It was almost sunset when Elena shook me excitedly, and I roused myself long enough to glimpse the stone lip of a well standing not far from a barrier-wall of high dunes, so tiny we might easily have missed it. 'Al-Muhandis!' I croaked through the bleeding skin of my lips. 'Thanks be to God! We're saved.'

We couched our camels by the well, hobbled them, then sat panting in the twilight. 'Come on!' Elena said. 'Let's get water or we'll just sit here till we die.' I had to grin. Her face was red raw in the places that had been exposed to the sun, bleached white in others, her eyes sunken and bloodshot, rimmed with dust, and her fractured lips moved with the slow deliberation of a mechanical toy. 'You look a mess,' I said.

'Jeez,' she said, 'have you seen yourself?'

Mukhtar opened his ancient, turtle-like eyes and smiled. 'She's right!' he rasped, sighing. 'Let's get to it.'

We rose to our feet, rummaging for our hitching-ropes and a leather well-bucket. We worked slowly, licking our thick lips. 'God!' Mansur said, 'that water's going to taste like syrup to me whatever it's like!'

'Remember, don't drink too much!' Ahmad said, excitedly. 'Only a mouthful at once!' The ropes were joined, the well-bucket attached, and Ahmad swung it into the well. There was an empty, dry slap of leather meeting sand. We looked at each other, hardly believing our ears. Ahmad pulled up the bucket hand over hand, too easily, I saw. At last the bucket came out of the shaft, empty. 'God damn that Hilmi to hell!' Ahmad hissed, hurling the bucket into the sand at his feet. 'If we ever get out of this I'll throttle him. This well is completely dry!'

For a moment I just eyed the others wildly, my senses spinning, remembering the dream that morning, the fearful expression on my face. I removed my glasses and forced myself to breathe deeply, calming my galloping pulse. I closed my eyes and for a moment it seemed to me that I heard an almost deafening flop-flop-flop sound. I opened my eyes and saw it: a desert rat hopping frantically across a sand-ridge. I followed the rat's tracks with my eyes and had a clear vision of my father, *Abu Sibaahi*, the Father of the Desert Rat. To win the right to marry my mother, he'd had to survive in the desert for ten days without any water but what he'd found there. Suddenly I remembered how he'd done it; 'Sip-wells!' I said.

'What?' Elena asked.

'There's a colony of *as-sibaahi* – desert rats – here. They never drink, but they prefer to live where there's dampness. If we could find a seam of moisture, we could suck out the water bit by bit.'

'Come on,' Ahmad said, 'let's look for a seam!'

It took almost half an hour to find what we were looking for – a rat burrow, carefully hidden where a dune touched the desert surface. We dug it out and found a damp seam beneath. When we'd made a hole a couple of feet deep, Mukhtar brought over his precious hollow reed, inserted it into the sand and began to suck. His eyes lit up suddenly. 'By God, Omar!' he said. 'It's a bit brackish and gritty, but it's the best water I've ever tasted!'

When I drank my gourd-ful, I could actually feel the liquid seeping through me, trickling into every cell, restoring the balance, setting my body's delicate mechanism in motion. There was an almost instantaneous feeling of well-being. After we'd all drunk, Ahmad began to collect water to make bread, sucking it into his mouth and spitting it into a gourd. No one objected. By the time we'd eaten, a magical transformation had taken place. We made ourselves comfortable and smoked our pipes, while Ahmad began to regale us with a story about a Hazmi he'd once pulled out of a deep well. 'It was old Annad of the Qura Hawazim,' he said, 'he'd been following a stray camel on foot into al-Ghul and run out of water, and there he was dying of thirst by the time he came to Abu 'Ashara – the well ten men deep.'

He paused to take a drag from his pipe, and we watched him intently.

'Anyway, there he was dying of thirst, see, and the water's down there ten men below him, but he doesn't have a rope. He's being tortured by thirst and he can *see* that water just gurgling and swilling down there, but he can't get at it. So you know what he did?'

'What?'

'He *jumped* in the well, that's what! Plummets ten men down – could easy have broken his neck.'

'Or drowned.'

'Or drowned, yes, or both. But the Divine Spirit was with him, see, the water was only up to his chest. So he drinks his fill, and just stands there in the water, waiting. He waits a day and a night, but at least he's not thirsty any more. The next morning I trot along there with my herdsmen to water the herd, and one of my boys says, "Look, there's a pair of Hawazim sandals." I looked and there's this pair of sandals, left neatly like somebody's coming back for them, but there's no tracks leading away, so I say "There's somebody in the well, by God!" And there was. We pulled old Annad out; he was a bit shaky but at least he was alive. I said, "You're a very brave man to jump into a well like that!" You know what he said? He said, "It's remarkable what thirst will do."'

Later, Mukhtar ordered us to turn out all our rations. The sour camel's milk was finished, and there was no more than a bottle of liquid butter, some tea and sugar, and a few kilos of flour. It looked pitifully little spread out on the blanket in front of us.

'There's enough for us all to eat for four days,' Mukhtar announced. 'It's five days from here to the Jilf, so even if we set off back now, we'll go hungry. But the water situation's even worse. It'll take us for ever even to fill one waterbag from this seam, and that won't last a day in the heat. And what about the camels? They've already done five days without water, and there's nothing for them here at all.'

Ahmad looked at me sadly. 'We'll have to go back, Omar,' he said. 'There's no choice. If we go on we'll certainly die.'

'I'm not giving up,' I said. 'Not so close.'

'Neither am I,' Elena said.

Mukhtar shook his head. 'It's your choice,' he said, 'but even if you find Zerzura, there may be no water or food there. How will you make it back? The camels are already thirsty. If you don't find water for them, they'll die within a few days.'

'The Divine Spirit will guide us.'

Mukhtar considered it for a moment. 'Very well, Omar,' he said. 'We'll fill a waterbag for you, and give you some flour and the best camel we have for Elena. That's all we can do. We'll wait for you here for four days. If you aren't back on the fourth, we'll leave.'

'That still means you'll have a five-day ride without food!'

'No, we'll save our food and live on *as-sibaahi* while we're here. If there's rats, there may be lizards and snakes we can eat. God bless us, since you're determined to go on the least we can do is wait for you. If we make it back to the Jilf we'll give you another week before we move into the Sudan.'

'That's very reasonable of you, Uncle.'

'The Divine Spirit is generous. But how you're going to find your way across the Sand Sea just on Hilmi's instructions, only God knows.'

45

I N MY DREAMS THAT NIGHT THE dunes of the Sand Sea towered above us like frozen tidal waves, and I awoke to find that in reality they were even more massive. From our sleeping-place they looked like some vast organic growth with giant limbs and excrescences turning at almost every conceivable angle, stretching right across the skyline, with crests that must have been a thousand feet high.

'How the hell *are* we going to get across them!' Elena said, and I could hear the awe in her voice.

We collected round the fire Mukhtar had kindled in a three-stone hearth, and he passed us glasses of sweet tea. 'There's a pattern to the sands,' he explained. 'Dunes are the embodiment of the wind; they have souls, they give birth like animals. The crests are their children, which leave their parents' backs when they mature and travel across the desert alone. But the parents – the old root-dunes – are very ancient, and they always lie along the axis of the prevailing wind. Here the wind is from the north, so beyond the first barrier wall, the dune-chains should be arranged in avenues.'

'Then why is this first set so irregular?'

'Because this is a place where the winds meet.'

'I can't see how we can ever get the camels up those slip-faces,' Elena said, 'they look as if they'll slide as soon as we step on them.'

'Don't worry,' I said. 'Slip-sand assumes an angle of 33 degrees, max – more than that and it collapses. Those slip-slopes are at maximum elevation, but they're stable.'

'Anyhow, there's a way up,' Mukhtar said. 'If you traverse the slip-face in a zig-zag you'll find layers of hard sand. But be careful on the windward slopes – they seem much gentler, but you'll find drumsand there. Probably nothing like Abu Simm, but worth avoiding just the same.'

While we'd slept the others had spent hours patiently filling a waterbag for us from the sip-well. As we hefted it on to the camel's back later, though, it seemed to offer a pathetically small margin of survival. Ahmad had generously lent Elena his own mount, a famous she-camel called Dhahabiyya – 'The Golden One'.

'Please,' he said, concernedly, 'take good care of her.'

'I will, I promise,' Elena said.

We stood by our camels, and they lined up to watch us mount. There was no ceremony – the Hawazim excelled in 'hallos' but called goodbyes 'The Little Death'; they were a too-frequent part of a nomad's life, too regrettable to be lingered over.

'May the Divine Spirit protect you,' Mukhtar said. 'Go in peace.'

We mounted our camels and headed towards the dunes.

We dismounted at the base of the dune-wall, craning our necks at the boiling crests hundreds of feet above. We tied the camels together and began to slog up the slope, myself pulling from the front and Elena driving from the rear, digging our camel-sticks in as we went. Miraculously, I managed to navigate on a firm path all the way up the face. 'Jamie, how on earth do you do that?' Elena said.

'I don't know,' I said, and it was true. I'd never crossed dunes as big as this before, but suddenly I felt confident, as if something inside me just *knew*. By the time we reached the crest, though, we were drenched in perspiration and the camels were breathing hard. 'Drink?' Elena asked.

'I'd love one, but no. We've got to save water.'

We tried to forget our thirst and scanned the landscape instead. More dunes, even higher, lay before us, rippling into the distance in fold upon fold. They seemed insubstantial, like vast heaps of smouldering gold-dust, or mythical whalebacked sea-monsters run aground. 'Jamie, I see no pattern,' Elena said, 'it's just an endless tangle.'

She was right; from here the dunes appeared to be a honeycomb of interlocking cells, wave after wave of them without entrance or exit. 'The camels are going to be exhausted after a couple more climbs like that one,' she said.

'I know,' I said, 'but we have to go on.'

'Come on then.'

All morning we battled the strange physics of the dunes, heaving the camels up slip-slopes and slithering down the windward sides. Each time we thought we might be coming to the end of the labyrinth, some new vast fold reared up in front of us. As the sun climbed and dilated, the purple shadows of dawn dissolved, transforming what had appeared a complex three-dimensional sculpture into a landscape without dimension of any kind. The sand burned with a phosphorescent glare, and sometimes we would stumble into deep pits hidden in what seemed a continuous expanse of flat sand. At other times we would step carefully on to acute inclines to find that they were actually quite gentle slopes. 'It's like being in a hall of huge mirrors,' Elena said breathlessly as we skidded into yet another invisible sand-hole, 'nothing here is what it seems!'

By midday we were shattered, and the camels rumbling with fatigue. We flung ourselves into a drift of soft sand, and Elena poured us a gourd of water each from the skin. 'How the hell did these things get here, anyway?' she croaked hoarsely.

'River beds,' I panted.

'Rivers? *Here*!'

'A long time ago. There was a river system as big as the Amazon under this Sand Sea. It all dried up when the climate changed, and the wind blew the desiccated river beds away until they piled up here as dunes.'

'When was that?'

'Only a couple of million years ago!'

Reluctantly we roused the camels, and went on. We climbed another slip-face and were sashaying down the windward side when there was a sudden startling crepitation – a noise almost like chalk squeaking on a school blackboard – that set your teeth on edge. I felt Ghazal jerking back on the headrope and turned to see him struggling frantically in deep sand. 'Drumsand!' I yelled, leaning hard on the headrope. Behind him, Dhahabiyya pulled back instinctively with such force that the lead-rope snapped. Ghazal wobbled for a moment, then fell headlong down the steep slope, rolling helplessly over and over, scattering gear after him. There was a nauseating cracking of limbs, and a sudden pop as the waterbag burst like a balloon, leaving a long dark stain along the sand. Finally, the camel lay still beneath us. I slid down to him as fast as I could: he was still breathing, but his eyes were clouded and a trickle of blood ran out of his right nostril. I knew Ghazal would never walk again. The waterbag was in shreds and completely empty.

Elena brought Dhahabiyya down and hobbled her on the flat. 'Bring a bowl and the spare waterbag,' I said, drawing my blade.

'What are you going to do?' she asked.

'I'm taking his stomach-water,' I said. 'That's all we have now.'

'Do you know how to do it?'

'Of course,' I said, untruthfully, 'I saw it done often when I was a boy.'

I hobbled his four legs firmly and he stretched his neck, staring at me with big, liquid eyes. 'Sorry, old boy,' I told Ghazal, 'you don't deserve this.' When I slit open his soft belly, he squirmed, groaned once and lay still. Blood splashed across the sand, followed by a spurt of brown liquid that smelt like vomit. Elena retched as she held the bowl to catch it. She filled the bowl, and poured the vile-smelling stuff into the spare skin. For a moment we just stared at it, wondering how long we could last on only four litres of greasy brown gastric juice, even if we could ever force ourselves to drink it.

*   *   *

It's remarkable what thirst will do. At first we could hardly bear the filthy liquid near us, but by sunset we were in such pain that we were glad to drink it. About midnight, we grabbed a few hours of sleep and were on our way again before dawn, when the sands began to quiver with heat. By noon the last of the stinking juice had gone, and within a couple of hours we were walking doubled over in the agony of thirst once again. The dunes were lower, now. 'I think they're settling into a pattern,' I told Elena huskily.

'Too late,' she croaked, 'I'm already shot. So is Dhahabiyya.'

I hauled the camel on, and Elena began to lag further and further behind. I turned into a wide avenue between the dunes and realised with a shock that she was out of sight completely. I hurried back and found her spread full length in a sand-drift moaning softly to herself. I lifted her into a sitting position and she lolled against my arm. 'Jamie, I can't,' she whispered. 'It hurts. I can't go on. Just leave me here.'

I pulled her up and squeezed her to me. 'I'm not losing you now!' I said, fighting back tears. 'You're going on. We belong, and we're going to do it together.'

I couched the camel by her and lifted her into the saddle. She sprawled there only half conscious, and I looped a rope round her waist and tied her on. When I got Dhahabiyya up her legs almost faltered under the extra weight. I tied the headrope around my waist and slogged on through the sand, numb to thirst, numb to pain, soaring above it like a bird, seeing myself a mote on the dunes far below me, no longer feeling myself present in my own tortured body. Hour passed hour, and I stumbled on. A sandstorm began, seething in my face, assaulting my ears, but I was oblivious of that too. Night came, but the sand-dust was too thick to see the stars. I'd long since given up trying to navigate consciously anyway, yet somehow I knew my direction. It was as if some far-away homing-beacon was calling to me across the emptiness, guiding me to it. Often I lost touch with the surroundings all together and felt myself pounding along in the body of my Ancestral Spirit, the jackal Anubis, across a clean white desert. When I closed my eyes I could see that homing signal flashing like fire, brightly, far away in the darkness.

I was brought back to earth suddenly by a jerk on the headrope, and I turned to see Dhahabiyya sitting down in the sand. I knew instinctively she was finished. Elena was rambling deliriously in the saddle. I untied her, lifted her off and laid her down.

The storm licked and thrashed around me as I hobbled Dhahabiyya. When I slaughtered her, slashing her belly, seams of sand-dust built up along the open wound at once. I caught the gastric juice in a bowl and tipped it into the waterbag. Then I picked up Elena, slung a saddle-bag over my shoulder, and half-dragged, half-carried her across the sand. I have no idea how long the agony lasted, only that at one point I thought I heard wolves baying far off, or perhaps they were human voices howling at me through the whorls of dust. I saw yellow slits of eyes behind me in the darkness, and dark figures lingering ominously from high places – hollow black demon shapes with burning red eyes. I slithered and fell down a dune-slope, picked Elena up again and saw what looked like the mouth of a great cave looming over me. I dragged Elena inside, out of the storm, and laid her down in the shallow entrance. I put her head on the saddle-bag and covered her with a blanket. Then I poured the filthy liquid into a bowl and stood it next to her. I examined her face by torchlight. Her features looked distorted, unfamiliar – transformed into a mask of suffering. 'I didn't have the right to bring you here,' I said softly. I kissed her and her eyelids flickered. 'Jamie,' she whispered, shivering, 'Jamie, there's somebody else here!' She closed her eyes and lay still.

I looked around, chilled. She was right. By the door of the cave, just outside, a dark presence lurked. I drew my pistol and cocked the hammer. 'Come forward!' I spluttered, coughing. 'Come forward or I'll shoot!'

Suddenly, the figure called 'Omar!' and I knew it was my mother's voice. It couldn't be, I told myself. This wasn't a dream – it was real, and Maryam was dead. Long suppressed childhood fears began to uncoil like snakes in my mind. A *Jinn*, was it? What was it Mukhtar had said – 'if a *Jinn* calls your name, don't answer'?

'Omar! Omar!' – the voice drifted to me again and I looked harder at the dark figure. It was Maryam.

'Mother!' I cried. 'You said you'd never leave me.'

'Omar, where are you going?' she asked, advancing slowly into the cave.

'To Zerzura. Only I don't know where it is.'

'Come. I'll show you.'

'How do you know, mother?'

'I went to Zerzura, but failed. My power wasn't strong enough.'

'Strong enough for what?'

'You'll see. Come.'

When I stumbled out into the night after her, the storm hit me with renewed shock. It seemed even more savage than it had been earlier. Maryam was drifting across the sand before me and I struggled on after her for what seemed ages, deafened, disorientated, addled by the sheer noise and weight of the storm. For all I knew I might have been going round in circles – I probably was, but I felt only the blind, unreasoning impulse to follow Maryam. I tripped over in soft sand and fell headlong, rolling over until my body came into contact with something hard and cold. I opened my eyes wide and put out my hand. It was a metal pillar standing about a yard above the surface of the sand, perhaps a foot in diameter. I realised suddenly that I'd found Hilmi's 'iron tree'.

'*It marks Zerzura.*'

I lit my torch and examined it. On the surface of the pillar, polished shiny by wind-borne sand but still clearly discernible, was etched a sun-disc with rays emanating from it – rays which ended in tiny hands: the Aton sun-disc, symbol of the pharaoh Akhnaton.

'Touch it, Omar,' Maryam's voice said, and I looked up to see her, unveiled as she'd aways been at home, her eyes sparkling, full of vitality as I remembered her. I touched the Aton symbol gingerly and at once there was a crack, the whirr of machinery, the hiss of hydraulics. I gaped incredulously to see that a part of the desert surface nearby had lifted itself up – a circular mechanical door, some three yards in diameter had simply opened in the sand. In the dark aperture beneath the doorway, I glimpsed stairs – a stairway descending right down under the desert. I lingered there hesitantly.

'This is Zerzura,' Maryam said. 'This is what you were meant for. Go on.'

'Are you coming?'

'I'll see you there,' she said. Suddenly she was gone.

The tunnel was tube-shaped, constructed of some rough metal, its sides scrawled with abstract patterns – whorls, moons, crescents, caducei, scarabs, Aton sunbursts, five-pointed stars. As I entered the noise of the storm disappeared almost at once, as if the whole place was somehow soundproofed. The stairs seemed to go down and down until I must have been scores of feet under the desert surface. Then, abruptly I found myself facing a gnarled and rusted metal door bearing an effigy of the pharaoh Akhnaton bathed in the Aton's light. Beneath the figure there was a cobra and a vulture – the twin symbols of kingship in ancient Egypt. Suddenly a phrase from the Zerzura legend came into my head: 'On the door is the effigy of a bird. Take the key in the beak of the bird and open the door of the city . . .' I examined the vulture with my torch. There was no key in its beak, so I pressed it instead and the door creaked aside, driven by some unseen mechanism. I suddenly felt overwhelmed with excitement. I sensed rather than saw a huge cavern beyond and smelt the wetness of water-vapour, quite distinct from the moisture-starved air I'd grown used to during the last few days. I took a step through the doorway and there was a sluggish clanking of invisible machinery. Green strips of light began to blink far above me and I gazed upwards to see a ceiling as high as the sandstone stacks in the Jilf. An aircraft could easily have wheeled round inside. I looked down and took in a sight that staggered me. I was not in a cavern or a city, but in the hold of some unimaginably gigantic vehicle, on what appeared to be a walkway passing round the circumference of a circle so vast that I couldn't see the other side. The space in between was full of floating machinery – at least that's what I thought it was at first – on the other hand it might equally have been some epic sculpture. There were great complexes of ovoids and cylinders standing on end, festooned with ranks of tubes and pipes like a collection of great church organs. There were clutters of blocks, braces and mountings – all of which might have been hand-carved. None of the surfaces was smooth – each was scored with an intricate pattern of tracing, like an endlessly complicated series of micro-circuits – or was it simply that the surface was deeply pitted, like the Jilf stacks, by the ravages of time? The machinery – if that's what it was – was completely asymmetrical: no two bits were the same, and there was no matching or balancing arrangement. Though I'd have sworn it was made of metal there were no joins or connections, as though the whole thing had been fused together or moulded in one huge piece. 'Who the hell made this?' I found myself wondering. There was a sense of great antiquity about it, as though it'd been here for aeons – the same essential alienness I'd felt when, as a child, I'd first encountered ancient Egyptian artefacts. I stepped over to the edge of the walk-way, and glimpsed galaxies of lights winking and flickering down a shaft far below me. Whatever it was, this thing was bigger than the biggest cruise-ship – bigger even than a pyramid, I thought.

There was an open archway before me between squat, fluted pillars or bulkheads, and I walked through it, finding myself in another chamber in the middle of which stood two large transparent cases, both mounted on plinths. The walls were decorated with thousands, perhaps millions, of hieroglyphs and elliptical cartouches, which seemed, at first glance, to be telling a long and complicated story. As I stepped over to them, a familiar pattern caught my eye: it was the hieroglyph for Sirius, contained in a circle and orbited by an ellipse made up of dots. I realised with a rush of excitement that it was the twin of the Sirian Stela I'd found at Madinat Habu. There were other familiar images, too, human figures with beards and wild hair – the Anaq – receiving gifts from Thoth; these were the counterparts of the engravings we'd seen at Khan al-Anaq and in the water-cavern. There was so much to see and understand that I wandered from stela to stela in a sort of trance. This was a vast museum, yet it had more wonders than any museum ever built – the single most important find, I realised suddenly, in the whole history of archaeology.

The chamber was confined by galleries of pillars – all subtly different, all intricately decorated with symbols. Further on, there were raised panels showing tableaux of the pharaoh Akhnaton and his wife and daughters – all with their strange, elongated skulls, standing washed by the rays of the Aton sun-disc. The panels were full of winged discs trailing fire, ankh life-symbols, winged sphinxes or griffons and lions, lion-headed women, weird pylons, rows of cobras carrying sun-globes, and a host of other objects I couldn't even recognise, painted in brilliant colours which didn't appear to have faded. Around the transparent cases stood gilded boxes, gold-bound chests and alabaster vessels, gold-covered chairs and couches carved with the heads of lions, hippos and crocodiles. Among them were scores upon scores of beautifully-made Akhnaton *ushabtis*. On a stela above the first case was carved a giant sun-disc with its emanating rays of light. I moved as if hypnotised towards the case and peered in through the glass cover. There was no mummy inside, no wrapped shrouds or ornate gold masks, but a body preserved by some process I'd never encountered before. At first glance I could see that it was Akhnaton – the distorted features, the slitted, tigerish eyes, the hermaphrodite figure were all familiar – but a second look sent me reeling back in shock. This wasn't the body of a misshapen man, but something else, something completely different. As I steeled myself for another look, a clammy hand seemed to touch me on the shoulder. I jumped almost out of my skin, pivoted backwards and drew my pistol from my waist in a single turning movement. I would have fired if I hadn't recognised Maryam, standing over me in her dark robes, smiling. 'You're not my mother, are you?' I said.

'No, I'm just a projection of your own mind, given power by the ship.'

'Ship? So it is a ship, then?'

'Yes. A star-ship built thousands of years ago. You're a very gifted being, Omar, an *illuminatus*. You were on the right track – head and shoulders above the rest – but as Karlman told you, you weren't quite there.'

'How do you know what Karlman told me?'

'Because I'm partly a projection of you. I have access to all your memories. I know the whole thing was in your head from the beginning – it was there in your subconscious, but you tried to hide it from yourself by espousing your "Atlantis" theory. Your uncle recognised great psychic power in you as a baby. At least once your prescience saved your father's life. You could have been a great *amnir* for your people, a great seer, but you tried to shut out that part of your psyche, because you were terrified of it. That's why you never felt at ease anywhere – because you were trying to deny the real you. Now it's time to look at yourself in the mirror, Omar. Your whole life has been leading you to this moment. You were chosen. The idea that the Ancient Ones came from somewhere like Atlantis was preposterous, just as Rifad and everyone said it was. The Ancient Ones came from far, far away, but not from anywhere in your world, and they were not of your kind. Have another look at Akhnaton and see for yourself, Omar; the creature your people call the Fallen One was not a human being at all.'

46

I TOOK ANOTHER, CLOSER, LOOK AT Akhnaton's corpse. There was something terrifyingly feral in that leering mouth, the narrowed eyes, the elongated snout – something which raised your hackles instinctively. Close up, the body wasn't familiar at all, I realised. It belonged neither to a man nor to a woman, but to something that had been trying desperately to assume human shape and had never quite managed it.

'Akhnaton's race have the ability to alter their own genetic code,' Maryam said.

'*Race?* You mean there are more of these things?'

'Yes, they are numerous. They were advanced in genetic engineering thousands of years ago, before your civilisation even existed. They are what you would call shape-shifters, but as you can see, in Akhnaton's time their ability was only approximate. Akhnaton could never have passed for human at close quarters, which is why he lived an ascetic life in his own city. No one was allowed to get close to him but slaves and minions, and they were expendable. Have you ever wondered why the stelae depicting Akhnaton in nobles' houses show him with distorted features, while those among the common people idealise him? It was because he had to get those who actually saw him – albeit from a distance – accustomed to his unusual appearance.'

*   *   *

I didn't really have any doubt what lay in the second sarcophagus, anyway, I read the cartouche before I looked inside. It was the body of Akhnaton's beautiful queen, Nefertiti, preserved in the same alien way as her husband. Except that, unlike Akhnaton, Nefertiti was clearly one of us – I mean, *Homo sapiens*. So here was the Zerzura legend, I thought: 'a king and a queen asleep on a hoard of treasure' inside a 'white city'. Either someone had found the ship in ancient times, or the story of Akhnaton's burial-place had leaked out by word of mouth and come into legend in garbled form. The description Nikolai had found in al-Khalidi's *Lost Treasures* – the one Julian had worked on – was probably a garbled version of a garbled version. I wondered whether it would ever have led them here.

'Who *are* you?' I asked.

'It's better if you think of me as Maryam.'

'No, but who are you really?'

'A projection', she said, 'part of the ship's defensive mechanism – it has the power to read human minds telepathically, and use the images it finds there.'

'Defences against what?'

'When we finally rid the earth of Akhnaton millennia ago, we could have destroyed the ship or removed it. Instead we decided to leave it as a message for humankind. The message would be meaningless until humans were ready for it, of course, so we installed a defensive device. Over the centuries many Bedouin stumbled across it by accident, but once in the ship's field they were guided by projections – apparent reflections of themselves, if you like – which deflected them harmlessly and gave them selective memories. Our intention was never to harm humans unless they threatened themselves.'

'What do you mean, threatened themselves?'

'Advanced technology in primitive hands is a recipe for disaster. We wanted to avoid that at all costs.'

'Who is *we*?'

'Your friend Doc Barrington got it right when she talked about "The Cohorts of Michael".'

'You mean you're an *angel*?'

'That's about the nearest human concept to what we are, but of course we're not really that. You might call us the *Guardians*.'

Three types of beings, I thought – humans, *Jinns* and Angels. Where had I heard that before?

'Did you build this ship?' I asked.

'No, it was built by Akhnaton's people – you can call them *Nommos* or *Neteru* – a race from the star-system you call Canis Major. They have been in contact with this planet for at least twelve thousand years. They were what your people call the Ancient Ones, The Shining Ones, the Dwellers-in-the-Sky, who created Egyptian civilisation on earth . . .'

I remembered the wall-paintings in the water-cavern – six globe-headed gods who were later transformed into the gods of ancient Egypt, the *Nommos* of Dogon legend, the *Oannes* of ancient Mesopotamia.

'Come, Omar,' Maryam said, 'you're hungry and thirsty. Let me show you more of the wonders of this place.'

She led me to a kind of elevator, constructed of the same pitted metal I'd seen in the other chamber, which descended into the depths of the ship. It was cylindrical, but inside I saw no switches, buttons or flashing lights. It was as if the lift knew where we wanted to go, and it glided down soundlessly. We walked along tunnels and corridors full of strange symbols and unnameable instruments, all of them with that 'fused together' look that had characterised the floating machinery upstairs – no wires, no sockets, no plastics, no protrusions or sharp angles – everything looked as if it had been carved by hand, honed down into soft curves and then etched with a fine needle. We entered another huge chamber, where, under a domed ceiling brilliant with light-strips, was an oasis, a real oasis out of a Bedouin's dream. There were fruit trees, looking something like date-palms, but subtly different, laden with what seemed to be ripe fruit. The floor of the chamber was covered in sandy earth, and amid the trees was a deep pool of pure blue water. I threw myself down at the water's edge and prepared to drink like an animal. 'Careful!' Maryam said. 'You're dehydrated. You could damage yourself.' I stopped myself, removed my *shamagh* and dipped it in the water. Little waves rippled out from my hand, glittering richly in the light – it was like dipping my hand in a rainbow. I sucked the water little by little from the cloth, and Maryam brought me some sticky brown fruit from the trees. 'What is it?' I asked. 'Just eat,' she said. I sampled the fruit, it tasted like a combination of date, strawberry, pineapple, mango, guava and a dozen other flavours combined in one. I ate ravenously and 'Maryam' passed me more. 'This is a dream,' I told her, 'it has to be. I'm going to wake up soon. I mean, an artificial oasis, inside a *star-ship*?'

'This is the only part of the ship that most of our visitors remember,' she said, laughing.

'Of course! The Bedouin legend – lush palms, grapevines and open water.'

'It's the Bedouin concept of paradise. Their interest usually went no farther.'

'What is this place?'

'It's a cybernetic system, a hydroponics network that recirculates moisture and gases filtered out of the desert over thousands of years. A self-sustaining life support circuit for a long voyage through space. The star-system you call Sirius B is 8.6 light-years away – a long voyage by most standards.'

'How did they achieve it?'

'They developed an anti-matter drive converting almost ninety per cent of the fuel-cell's mass into pure energy. This ship can accelerate to within ten per cent of light speed, but even at that speed Sirius B takes more than fifty years.'

'That's incredible. Just imagine . . .'

'How valuable it would be to you humans? Yes, and how it could be misused. The technology aboard this ship would represent a quantum jump forward for the human species. If it were available to you.'

'And it's not?'

'Not yet.'

'Then why am I here?'

'You've been chosen to receive a message.'

'Chosen by whom?'

'By thousands of years of evolution. You possess a recessive gene which appears to its fullest only once or twice in a generation – let's call it a "psi-gene". You inherited it from your remote ancestors, the Anaq. Many have possessed it over the millennia – in a few it manifested itself strongly – those were the legendary great *amnirs* of your people. In many, though, it appeared only feebly, as in your uncle, Mukhtar. Over the ages, of course, the gene has spread to other families, other races, but only in the Hawazim does it appear in its most undiluted form.'

'What's the significance of this "psi-gene" anyway?'

Instead of answering, she beckoned me through more tunnels of 'fusion sculpture' into a chamber filled with huge stacks like atomic piles or enormous generators. There were slender columns with fins at the base like the buttresses of jungle trees, giant bell-jars, crystals cut in irregular shapes, and waist-high pylons. The roof was supported by more squat, fluted pillars, all of them decorated with symbols and hieroglyphs, and the walls seemed to be covered in massive metal shields, which close-up looked more like manhole-covers with raised openings to fit a giant's hand. The chamber was lit in patches by what looked like luminous flat strips along the ceiling, but there were no obvious instruments or controls – no handles, levers, dials, gauges, clocks or computer-screens as you'd expect to find in an aircraft or on the bridge of a sea-going ship. In the middle of the hall was a domed chamber like a tiny chapel with open sides, under which a globe-shaped helmet like a goldfish-bowl had been carved in an opaque, greenish crystal, over the bare slab of a seat. 'Sit,' Maryam told me, gesturing to the seat. I stepped inside the open chamber and saw that the inside of the dome was painted with stars – Orion, Sirius A and Sirius B.

'What's this?' I asked.

'This is the Recorder,' she said, 'the message we've been waiting to give humans for a long time about the origin of your civilisation. You are the Chosen One.'

'What about Wingate?'

'Wingate had the psi-gene, yes. He was almost but not quite an *illuminatus*. We led him here, but in the end he failed. Then, before we could prevent it, he let his companion try – the result was madness.'

'How do you know the same won't happen to me?'

'You are an *illuminatus* – the psi-gene has never shown itself so strongly in anyone for generations. Your potential is enormous – as yet you've only glimpsed the surface. If you only open yourself to it, you are capable of holding ten thousand years of human memories in your own head. With the right training you could look deep into the future, even communicate across space.'

'What do you mean, *across space*?'

'Sit. All your questions will be answered.'

I sat down on the cold slab, ducking under the inset 'goldfish-bowl'.

'You must put your head inside,' 'Maryam' said. 'Don't worry. You'll be able to breathe.'

Cautiously I placed my head inside the globe. For a moment there was darkness, and then I felt a prickling sensation as if my scalp was being probed by a million tiny wires. Suddenly my head exploded with a shock of light that smashed the breath from my body and almost knocked me over. I was rushing through a light vortex at blinding speed. I heard myself screaming, but the scream was distant, remote. 'I' was somewhere far away, absorbed in visions of the night sky, stars, constellations – there was Orion and under its wing, Sirius A with its dark sister, Sirius B near by, orbiting it on an elliptical path, once every fifty years. Images and bytes of information zapped through my mind like streaks of lightning. I was in the distant past – *Zep-Tepi*, the First Time – twelve thousand years ago. I saw a traveller from a planet in the Sirius B system landing on earth using some kind of teleportation-drive. The figure was a blurred, out of focus image, because, I realised, he was without definite shape – a shape-shifter, appearing now as a terrifying monster, half-hominid, half-fish, with a scaly body and a tail as well as legs, now a globe-headed man, now as a man with the head of what looked like an ibis, but was not. It was Thoth, the pathfinder of five more travellers from Sirius who landed later, the five *Neteru* of ancient Egyptian mythology – Osiris, Isis, Horus, Nepthys and Set – the *Nommos* of the Dogon.

I saw them through the eyes of my ancestors, the Anaq, a stone-age tribe of hunter-gatherers living on the plains of what is now the Western Desert of Egypt. I saw the Anaq bowing to them, offering them sacrifices. But something had gone wrong; the *Nommos* were troubled. They could not get home. They'd lost contact with the parent race and were stranded on an alien planet with no way of sustaining their technology. They were inventive; they used local materials, employed the natives, taught them the basics of civilisation – the reckoning of time, measurement, astronomy, medicine, engineering. The great monuments of Egypt, the Sphinx, the pyramids, the temples had all grown out of their teachings. By manipulating their own DNA code, they even managed to mate with humans and produce offspring. Over the centuries, the original 'landing party' merged with the natives and its original technology degenerated.

Images and sounds poured into my mind with incredible detail, a maelstrom of voices merging together, some of them speaking ancient Egyptian, others languages which I didn't recognise at all. The information streamed through my head like a river of light, pouring into the sump of my unconscious. It was thousands of years after the original landing, now, and the *Nommos* had been immortalised as the gods of ancient Egypt – gods who were said to have once walked the earth. There had been quarrels between their descendants, and a great struggle between the followers of Set and Nepthys and those of Horus, Osiris and Isis. They had given birth to an advanced civilisation, the first civilisation of earth. I tried to pause, to take a mental respite, but the images were crowding in on me faster and faster. It was as if I was getting a matrix of thoughts recorded from everyone who'd lived through the events I was experiencing. The sheer volume of information streaming into me was colossal. I sensed suddenly why others had failed in this task; their minds must simply have balked at the endless streams of thought. I saw temples dedicated to the falcon-headed god Ra – the supreme godhead – and a corps of shaven-headed priests in white robes conducting ceremonies of sacrifice, studying the stars, writing papyri, supervising vast building projects, performing medical operations, dedicating tombs, examining human beings. These activities and thousands of others went on over a vast span of time, but gradually it dawned on me that these priests – the priests of Ra – had maintained a single obsessive purpose which had never faltered. They were selecting and testing human beings with the object of isolating a rare gene – the 'psi-gene' – and of breeding an individual with the power to transmit telepathic messages across the parsecs of space. With a shock, it struck me that the whole edifice of Egyptian civilisation had been constructed as a complex long-term rescue-plan for the *Nommo* landing-party, which had been stranded here in 12,000 BC!

Suddenly the face of a pharaoh flashed into my mind. It was Amenophis III – supposed by some to be the father of Akhnaton. I knew with certainty that Amenophis was a Chosen One – an *illuminatus* – the end product of the psi-gene programme, which had lasted more than seven thousand years. By Amenophis's time, the programme had devolved into a ritual. The original *Nommo* strains had long since been absorbed into *Homo sapiens*, the *Nommo* parent-race from Sirius had lost all record of any contact with earth, and had anyway evolved into something quite different. The teleportation-drive that had brought the explorers to earth was to the current *Nommos* a failed experiment from the depths of ancient history, which had long ago been replaced by an anti-matter drive. Amenophis III's telepathic messages into space did not bring a rescue mission. Instead they brought the creature that would become Akhnaton, a renegade *Nommo* with objectives of his own. He landed his craft in the Western Desert, forced himself on the pharaoh, killed him and his son Thutmose, abolished the Ra priesthood whose painstaking work had brought him here, and usurped the throne. The images in my head accelerated again, assaulting me with a shocking flow of visions and voices. There were glimpses of torture – human beings being herded into enclosures like cattle-pens, dismembered and examined by the creature calling himself Akhnaton and his minions. I knew suddenly what Akhnaton's purpose had been: to produce an alien-human cross that could be used as a stepping stone to some higher dimension, a hybrid creature devoid of all human characteristics. But something went wrong. There was resistance. Unseen forces intervened. I saw scenes of savage fighting – fires, guards being overthrown by crowds of people and palaces destroyed, and everywhere I looked I saw men carrying a secret symbol – the Eye of Ra. I saw Akhnaton fleeing across the desert. I saw him arriving back at his ship with a small band of followers and their frantic attempts to get the great thing space-borne. All in vain. They were trapped on earth just as their ancestors had been. Finally, there were shadowy eminences – The *Guardians* – laying Akhnaton in his sarcophagus and sealing the doors.

The vision faded suddenly, a mote of light dying away like a shooting star. I felt as if I was rising through space, like a bubble in water. There was a moment of utter darkness during which I groped to find myself – Omar James Ross – buried under the accumulated psychic rubble of twelve thousand years. I wondered if I still existed, if I could ever be the same individual with all that information inside me – information no other individual had ever had from the beginning of time. 'Omar!' my mother's voice called and I dipped out of the 'helmet' to find 'Maryam' still watching me. I stood up, staggered and almost fell. I felt drained of every ounce of energy, burned up as if a million volts had just buzzed through me. I was at the end of a long journey across space–time – I'd been further and seen more than any human traveller in history. Yet I could remember only fragments. I held on to the wall. 'Shit!' was all I could say. 'Holy shit. What *was* that?'

'Call it a history lesson for the human species.'

'I was being bombarded by the memories of millions of dead people!'

'The Recorder works through your genes, it plugs in to the collective unconscious and liberates it. That's why it could only work with an individual with an advanced psi-capacity. Psi-capacity is the ability to experience the collective unconscious of a species on a conscious level. The ability to call up a million years of human experience is power.'

'But I can't remember more than a few fragments; no one could.'

'Nevertheless it's there. You have to develop a way of gaining access. It would be recoverable under hypnosis.'

'Am I supposed to *believe* all this?'

'Look around you. Your civilisation came from the *Nommos*. Tribes such as the Dogon and a few others – descendants of the ancient Ra priesthood – managed to preserve bits of the tradition. You discovered the secret when you found the Siriun Stela, but your rational mind didn't want to accept it. Part of you still doesn't. That's understandable. It's disturbing to realise suddenly that the universe is not the predictable place you'd like to believe. It's like becoming an adult again – except for a whole species, a whole system.'

'What was the point of the "lesson"?'

'The point is simple. Human beings are no longer alone in an empty universe. You belong to something much bigger than yourselves. You are on the brink of a vast transformation – the human race is about to grow up.'

'Or destroy itself.'

'There is that possibility.'

'How was Akhnaton overthrown?'

'You know it already: humans did it with a little help from us. They created an organisation they called The Eye of Ra, which not only overthrew Akhnaton but dedicated itself to ensuring that nothing like him would ever threaten the earth again.'

'Was it the Eye of Ra who killed Julian, Doc, Nikolai and the others?'

She smiled inscrutably. 'Unfortunately there's no time for answers. Not if you wish to live. The ship has performed its task and it will cease to exist in ten minutes' time.'

'What?'

'The ship was programmed to self-destruct as soon as the "lesson" was delivered to a competent member of your species. The lesson has been delivered. It will self-destruct in precisely ten minutes' time. We programmed it to give just enough time for you to escape. I advise you to leave now.' She touched a panel which slid back to reveal two five-litre demijohns of water, made out of a transparent ceramic material that looked neither like plastic nor glass, and a container of fruit. 'Take these,' she said, 'our final gift.'

'But . . .'

'There's only one other thing I have to tell you. Your mother, Maryam, was not lost in the *ghibli*, as you believe. She had the psi-gene too. We brought her here, but, like Wingate she wasn't powerful enough to use the Recorder. Unfortunately, she wasn't able to make it back home either. I'm sorry. It was never our intention that she should come to harm. You'll find her remains in the cave where you left your friend. Now you must go.'

'Maryam' disappeared abruptly, and almost at once I felt the ship tremble. A booming began almost like the boom of Raul's drum, but deeper and even more threatening – a dreadful sawing drone like the bass note of a great organ pipe. I picked up the water and fruit and dashed for the lift. By the time I made it back to Akhnaton's chamber, the whole place was crumbling. A terrifying thunder filled the ship and as I ran, the walls began to split into shreds and collapse. I ran for the exit, scrambled up the stairs two at a time and staggered breathlessly into the desert. I picked myself up and began to run. I hadn't gone more than a hundred yards when the air was rocked by a violent explosion. That was the last thing I remember before I blacked out.

PART III

NEAR KOM OMBO, UPPER EGYPT 1995

47

THE MAN IN THE COFFIN WAS myself.

Consciousness came in flashes, spurts of light alternated with long spans of darkness, and each time my eyes opened I seemed to be in a different place, but always in some kind of dark box, sometimes at the centre of a spaghetti of wires and junctions, of banks of screens and blipping instruments, of tubes feeding some substance into my veins and of conductors draining me. There were voices, soft, whispering, suggestive, voices, cajoling, threatening, probing into the very core of my psyche like needles. I heard myself blubbering like a lunatic, but had no idea what it was I was rambling about. Sometimes there were figures – once or twice a man with a beard, wiry hair like a brush, and gold half-moon spectacles, who seemed to be wearing the habit of a monk. Once, it seemed that I was in an arched and vaulted chapel, alive with flickering shapes, with a horde of hooded shadows hunched around me in semi-darkness – figures with yellow slits for eyes and orange gashes for mouths, whose voices sussurated subliminally.

'You see he *was* an *illuminatus*. And you wanted to eliminate him.'

'OK, you were right, Master. But did we get everything?'

'As much as we'll ever get. It's all in his memory cells. We can't access memory like a hard disk. It's remarkable he could carry so much data.'

357

'What happens to him now?'

'That depends on how much he's worked out. We can't have him giving that message to the world – too dangerous for us. If he *knows*, we'll have to get rid of him. Such a waste, though, after we waited so long to find one. Through him we could finally talk to *them*. . . No more disasters like Roswell.'

'We can't keep him like this for ever, and we can't risk letting him go. Look what happened with Wingate. I say we get rid of him, Master.'

'No. We've got to find out what he remembers before we do anything drastic. We might never get another one like him.'

'What about *her*? Should we put her down?'

'No. Not yet. There might be an interesting development with *her*.'

'His eyelids are flickering. You don't think he can hear us?'

'No. Even if he could this would only be a dream.'

'Hey, I think he's coming round . . .'

I opened my eyes wide to show them that I really was awake, but they were gone, and I was no longer in a chapel but a brightly lit hospital room. There was a gangly young police trooper in a black uniform and beret, with an AK-47 draped from his arm, standing by a glass-panelled door. The room was large and clean-scrubbed – phosphorescent walls, chrome, white enamel and padded plastic, a mad-scientist's tangle of life-monitor screens, computer terminals, wires and tubes. One of the tubes was attached to my arm feeding my veins white fluid from a soft IV bottle suspended from a frame near by, and there were electrodes attached to my chest and head. There was a tubular-steel chair by the bed and a table bearing an anglepoise lamp, a tin ashtray brimfull of cigarette-butts and a pocket cassette-recorder. My gaze rested for a moment on the ashtray. It seemed the only anomaly in the state-of-the-art sterility of the place – a tiny oasis of atavism in a hi-tech desert. There was a smell of surgical spirit, disinfectant, and fibre from the wall-to-wall carpet, mostly dispelled by the cool breeze issuing almost silently from a grille high up the wall. On a bedside desk stood a plastic jug of water with a cover, a paper cup, and my John Lennon spectacles.

I tried to shift my position and felt my body respond sluggishly, as if the synaptic messengers had grown fat and lazy. I was exhausted, I realised, completely drained, aching, as if I'd just run a marathon. My head felt swollen like a balloon and there was phlegm and grit in my throat. I coughed suddenly, and the policeman looked at me startled and disappeared hurriedly while I tried to pull myself up. 'Elena!' I cried, looking round desperately. But there was no one else in the room, only my vital statistics blipping on dark screens. Then I remembered – I'd left her *out there* in a cave, dying of thirst. Jesus Christ, I'd never gone back! I'd just *left* her there! My heart began to pound in my ears with the sound of a basket-ball being bounced on a sprung floor, and I tried to jerk myself out of the tight sheets, wrestling feebly until the IV needle slipped out of my arm and fluid spilled across the carpet. The blipping on the heart-monitor increased to a frantic level. Just then the swing door burst open and a strapping nurse in a polyester uniform came bustling in with the trooper. Her kindly, well-fed peasant face carried an aura of almost palpable competence. As she bent over me I smelt soap and surgical spirit. 'Now look what you've done!' she said, tut-tutting. 'Why couldn't you leave him alone?' I realised suddenly that she was addressing the policeman.

'I didn't do anything,' the guard protested.

The nurse ignored him, 'You need plenty of rest,' she said, tucking me in maternally, and hooking the needle back in my arm. I didn't try to fight her; my tussle with the sheets had shown me it was a waste of time. She smiled at me. 'You almost died, you know,' she said, 'you and your friend.'

'Don't talk to the prisoner,' a voice rapped from behind, and I looked up to see a torpedo-shaped man blocking the light in the doorway. The nurse stared back at him, peasant's solid chin jutting, like a lioness protecting her cub. 'He's a patient, not a prisoner,' she said tersely. 'This might be a police facility, Captain, but there are rules. And one of them is no smoking.'

The figure advanced and stubbed out the cigarette emphatically in the tin ashtray.

'May I have my glasses?' I asked the nurse. My voice sounded hoarse and limp – a voice from far away. She smiled again and put them on for me.

'Thank you,' I said. The world snapped into tight focus. The figure resolved into Hammoudi, wearing his close-fitting suit, white shirt and tie, his great bulb of a forehead wrinkled with lines of brooding, and his sand-bagged eyes burning with silent menace.

'Stand outside,' he told the trooper.

'Now only five minutes, Captain,' the nurse said, wagging a plump finger. 'Don't overtax him. He's still very weak.'

'I won't,' Hammoudi said, half smiling. As soon as she was gone he swore obscenely after her and lit a fresh Cleopatra furtively, like a disobedient boy. The smoke made me cough.

'Well, well,' he said, 'Omar James Ross, back in the land of the living.'

'I shot you,' I panted.

Hammoudi guffawed. 'Actually you did,' he said, 'zapped me right in the belly-button. Nine milly wasn't it – punch like a steam-hammer!'

'You should be dead.'

'Probably would be if it weren't for my trusty body armour. I was wearing the full steel-plate rig – weighs a ton but saves you from the knacker. Your bullet knocked me down but I got up pretty sharpish. I could have zapped you off your camel any time.'

'Why the hell didn't you?'

He ignored the question.

'Someone tipped you off,' I said. 'Who? Not any of the Hawazim.'

'You love asking questions, don't you, Ross?'

'Where is she?' I said.

'There you go again.'

'Where's Elena?'

'Safe.'

You and your friend almost died. Almost. Safe. I closed my eyes. Was it the truth? I prayed it was.

'If you've harmed one . . .'

'You are not in a position to make threats, Ross. You're lucky to be alive. You and the girl were spotted by a police helicopter five days ago wandering in the dunes near the Libyan border. When the crew picked you up you were delirious, and suffering from extreme thirst. They had medical gear and put you on the IV straight away, but it was touch and go. Another couple of hours in the *khala* and you'd both have croaked. We saved your lives.'

'Why can't I see her?' I said.

'Because I say so. You're in a special government facility, and you do what I tell you, OK. You want to play mister tough-guy, you'll never see her again. You keep your nose clean, toe the line, and you might just get to meet. Are you with me?'

'You should have shot me.'

'Plenty of time for that. There's the little matter of Sergeant Mustafa to account for, as well as the other corporal and two troopers at Kwayt, not to mention the attempted murder of your favourite police captain.'

'I haven't killed anyone.'

'Maybe not, but your dirty Hawazim have, and you're collectively guilty.'

'What about an innocent baker's boy? What about David Barrington, a mixed-up kid who had nothing to do with it? And a harmless old share-cropper? Who's going to account for them?'

'We can trade atrocities all day, Ross, it won't change anything.' He jabbed the cigarette out and sat down, shifting the tubular chair closer to the bed. For a moment I had a close glimpse of his face – a tired face, unhappy, worn out.

'I've been sitting here most of the time since you came in,' he said. 'By God, you've been spouting some gobbledygook – drumsand, dunes, *Jinns*, *Guardians*, Akhnaton, aliens, the Lost Oasis of Zerzura. I got most of it on tape. Maybe you'd like to hear it some time?'

How much had I let slip, I wondered? Had I revealed where the Hawazim were hiding?

'Where did you think you were going?'

'To Zerzura,' I said.

Hammoudi smirked, but he didn't seem surprised. 'That old chestnut!' he said. 'There's no such place as Zerzura, Ross. It's just a Bedouin fantasy. Palm-trees and cool water in the midst of desolation. It's just a dream.'

'No it's not. I found it.'

'Yeah, and did you find a pool of water and date-palms with delicious fruit?'

'It was all there.'

'And the treasure?'

'Zerzura was Akhnaton's tomb. I found him and Nefertiti and a hoard of treasure – stuff that makes Tut's tomb look like a one-room stall in Khan al-Khalili.'

Hammoudi clearly wasn't impressed. He watched me sardonically while he lit another cigarette. 'All right,' he said, 'then where is it?'

'It was destroyed.'

'Just like that, eh? Puff! God, what a shame! And you could have become a famous man, too. All gone up in a cloud of smoke just as you happen to find it!'

I coughed. It must sound ludicrous, I realised. 'It was there,' I said, 'I saw it and felt it. I ate the fruit – I even took some fruit and water away with me.'

Hammoudi was shaking his head in silent wonder. 'Listen, Ross. You're in serious trouble. You're going to be asked a lot of questions over the next few days by guys who make me look like Santa Claus. I advise you not to go on with this crazy story, or they'll slam you up in a nuthouse and throw away the key. You ever been in one of those places, Ross?'

'So you're concerned for my future all of a sudden? If I'm certified insane I can't be held guilty for anything, is that it, and you've got to have your pound of flesh?'

'Ross, what were you really doing out there?'

'I've told you what I was doing.'

'You haven't told me the whole story.'

'You wouldn't believe the whole story. I found the Lost Oasis of Zerzura, which also happened to be Akhnaton's tomb – the last great mystery of Egyptology. Only it was destroyed.'

'What about the rest of the insurgents? Where'd you dump them?'

'They're not insurgents, only tribesmen who've been persecuted by the government for centuries simply because they want to be free.'

'They're dangerous rebels who've killed government officers. Where are they?'

'I don't know. If you're going to interrogate me, I have a right to be charged, and to consular representation.'

'I've told you before, I'm not running a fucking kindergarten.'

'So what're you going to do? Fry me like Mustafa was going to fry Elena? I don't think so. You could have shot me and you didn't. I think it's in your interest – or somebody's interest – to keep me alive.'

'There's alive and alive, Ross. This is your last chance – what did you find out there?'

'I told you. I found Zerzura.'

Hammoudi shook his head again and sighed. 'While you were under you kept repeating – ''It's remarkable what thirst will do'' – kept saying it over and over. You're not the first person I've met who's come back from the edge of death by thirst. Five years ago a police convoy was crossing the desert from Siwa to Cairo and one of the trucks got separated and lost in the Qattara Depression. There were twenty trained men aboard. It was summer. Took the rescue-team three days to find the truck, and half of the men had already croaked. Four or five had tabbed off to look for water and fried to death on the way. The five or six survivors were barely conscious, but when they came round they all told fantastic tales. One had seen a whole army with chariots and soldiers in armour rising out of the desert. Another had found a fabulous city with running water and orchards and beautiful *houris* – cried like a baby when he woke up because he wanted to go back there. That's why your story doesn't surprise me. It's par for the course. I can see you believe it, Ross, I just know it isn't true.'

'How?'

'Because the Anasis girl told me everything.'

I tried to sit up, but the sheets trapped me like a strait-jacket. 'She's here?'

'I didn't say she was here. I said she was safe, and I've talked to her. She told me the whole story. Camel going into quicksand, water running out – you slaughtering a camel to survive. But there was no Zerzura, Ross, no Akhnaton's tomb. Anasis swore to me that you never left her side for a moment.'

'But the cave. I left her in a cave – a huge cave near Zerzura.'

'When the chopper crew spotted you, you were dragging her across the dunes. No sign of a cave.'

I blinked and tried to concentrate. This was another lost episode of my life. I remembered the explosion and after that my mind was a complete blank. Then I thought of something.

'The fruit,' I said, 'and the water I got from Zerzura – in ceramic demijohns. That's what must have saved us. We must have had it with us when we were picked up.'

'You had nothing on you but your vicious little Hawazim stinger, which is now in a safe place. No water, no sign of fruit, not even a pip. It was a delusion. While I've been sitting here waiting for you to come round I've taken the trouble to read a dozen reports collected from Bedouin who claim to have found Zerzura – funny thing is that almost every one of them mentions bringing away with them water and delicious fruit which had vanished by the time they got home.'

48

FOR THE REST OF THE DAY I swam like a diver in and out of limbo. Hammoudi went off and didn't come back. The police guard sat outside now; I couldn't see him but sometimes I could hear his deep-moulded soles tramping impatiently up and down a corridor. I didn't rate my chances of escape. I'd have bet money the small windows beneath the shutters were barred, even if I could have mustered the strength to get out of bed, which I couldn't. The nurse bustled in and out, bringing bed-pans, checking the drip, administering tranquilliser and vitamin B shots in the arm. Her name was Thalwa as-Safawi – I knew that much from the little plastic badge pinned on her chest – and her accent told me she was from the south. She had the broad-bottomed, thick-ankled figure, and the directness of a *Sai'idiyya*. She fussed, made cheery comments, clucked like a mother hen, but she wouldn't talk. 'Where am I?' I asked a dozen times.

'Don't ask,' she whispered urgently, 'they're listening.'

Often I strained for sounds and caught only snatches of conversation outside – guards dropping comments as they changed over, nurses passing the time of day. The walls must be soundproofed, I thought, but I'd have expected to hear at least faint traffic sounds if I'd been in a city. There was nothing. Absolute silence. Either I was still in the desert, or somewhere on the moon. I floated half-conscious through the day, and in my lucid moments I thought about Elena, then about my uncle and cousins. Five days since

I was picked up. Were they still riding across the Desolation? Hammoudi had mentioned the *Guardians* and I tried to recall the message they'd given me. Mankind was no longer alone. I'd been chosen to bring that message to my species, and I had no right to keep it secret. But Wingate must have wanted to tell the world about what he'd found at Zerzura, too – or why would he have brought the *ushabtis*? Something had stopped him. His escort had ended up in the quicksand of Abu Simm. The *Guardians* claimed to have benevolent intentions towards humans, but who were the *Guardians*, anyway? What were they? I'd never seen one, only an image of my mother. And what had her shadow meant when it told me Maryam had been unable to get back home? Everyone who'd come near to the secret had been eliminated, why not me too? Sometimes the dream-voices crept into my head again: 'We've got to find out what he remembers before we do anything drastic. We might never get another one like him.'

I had no idea whether my memory was playing tricks – whether these voices were real or imaginary. I thought back to the star-ship, Akhnaton's body, the artificial oasis – the events and images were blurred, and I couldn't tell for sure any longer where reality began or ended. Something told me there was no dividing line and never had been, no subject and object, no eye of consciousness in the void, no *lux in tenebris*.

With ten thousand years' worth of history in my head, I ought to have had a few answers, but instead I had only questions. Akhnaton had been overthrown by an organisation called the Eye of Ra, a secret sect made up partly from priests of the disbanded Ra brotherhood, which went back to the earliest times. Sha-Tehuti had told Doc that the Eye of Ra Society had been in existence under different guises since 'time immemorial'. The question that kept on popping up in my head was whether Doc's Eye of Ra and the one that got rid of Akhnaton were the same? Was it possible for a sect to retain integrity of purpose over five and a half millennia? The Christian church had only been in existence for two thousand years, Islam for only one and a half. But the *Guardian* had claimed that the Ra Priesthood had retained its goals intact for *ten* thousand years. Was it the Eye of Ra Society who murdered Carnarvon and the people associated with the opening of Tut's tomb? Was it responsible for the death of Nikolai Kolpos?

> Let the Eye of Ra descend
> That it may slay the evil conspirators.

Who were the 'evil conspirators'? Kolpos? Me? Julian Cranwell? Conspiring against what? *Ma'at?*
   The twentieth-century guardian of Ma'at.
   I had nothing to do but think, and steadily a shape began to emerge. At last I was beginning to glimpse the outline of the great edifice hidden in the sand – only faintly, maybe, but to glimpse it nevertheless. I wished suddenly that I had Rabjohn here – I was certain he'd be able to help me. But where was Rabjohn? Had he been eliminated too?

I dozed in snatches at night, but in the morning I felt a little better. The nurse gave me a vitamin shot and plumped my pillows so that I could sit up. When I asked for pen and paper, books, newspapers – anything at all to occupy me – she shook her head. 'Sorry,' she said, 'against instructions.' Apart from the nurse no one came near me all day, and I began to hope Hammoudi would return – at least he was someone to talk to. I stared at the whitewashed ceiling, listened to hollow footfalls outside, the occasional murmur of voices, the distant warble of music from a radio. I longed to get up and look out of the window, but I still felt weak, and I guessed they'd be in here before I even reached it.

The following morning a different nurse, called Huda – a Cairene with a hard, sour face – stalked in and gave me a heavy-handed bed-bath. She sat me up and left without a word. A bit later a white-coated lab assistant with a crew-cut shuffled in lugging a steel safety-case, from which he unpacked an expensive cassette tape-deck with a multi-directional microphone.

'What's all this for?' I asked him. He ignored me pointedly, as though I was invisible or already dead. Five minutes afterwards, he brought in four tubular steel chairs and arranged them carefully along the side of my bed.

Visitors, I thought.

They came half an hour later – Hammoudi and two uniformed officers – a major and a colonel – and a civilian in a lab-coat. The major was a heavy man, wearing a hand-tailored black uniform with campaign ribbons. His face was broad and gangsterish, ravaged by chicken-pox scars and by good living – an onion of a nose and a moustache like barbed wire. I guessed he was Hammoudi's superior, Rasim. The colonel was an oldish man – nearing retirement age I'd have thought – with bronzed, wrinkled features and cropped silver hair. There was something almost Slavic about his high cheekbones – he might have been Albanian or Czech, but in contrast to Rasim whose face looked raffish and vulgar, he was dignified and withdrawn. It was the civilian who caught my attention most of all, though. He was small and slight, with a prickly salt-and-pepper beard intended to conceal the fact that his face was almost totally devoid of a chin. His hair was an unkempt wire-brush, and his eyes gleamed in the strip-lighting, peering over gold-framed half-moon glasses. I noticed with astonishment that under his lab-coat he was wearing the robe of a priest – no, I thought, a monk. I'd seen this figure before, leaning over me in my dreams. The colonel and the 'monk' removed their chairs from the military line and sat together at the back of the room. Rasim leaned forwards, while Hammoudi occupied himself with operating the tape-deck. It wasn't difficult to guess who my interrogator would be.

'Omar James Ross,' the major said lifting his chin imperiously, 'you're accused of conspiracy against the government of Egypt, of inciting a rebellion by a tiny minority group of which you are a member, and which has already been responsible for the deaths of several police officers and others. You were arrested with your accomplice five days ago trying to escape across the border into Libya, having separated yourself from the rest of the conspirators. Where are they hiding?'

'I don't know,' I said.

'You're a liar.'

'I wouldn't tell you anyway.'

'Why were you trying to escape to Libya?'

'I wasn't trying to escape to Libya. I have no interest in Libya. I was returning from an expedition to find Zerzura, the Lost Oasis that's been mentioned since the time of the ancient Greeks. It was a successful expedition.'

'I see.' There was utter silence. The tape-deck blinked and creaked. I'd been expecting some kind of reaction, but these dead-pan expressions threw me. Hammoudi lit a cigarette and looked away.

'No smoking, please,' Rasim said. Hammoudi stubbed it out sullenly.

'How come you returned to Egypt?'

'I came in answer to a call from a friend of mine, Dr Julian Cranwell. Three days after I arrived he was found dead at Giza. The police said it was a heart attack, but they didn't know that Cranwell'd rung me a few days earlier saying that he was in danger and being pursued by the same people – he actually said "Devils" – who killed Lord Carnarvon, Orde Wingate and Tutankhamen. It seemed like the rambling of a nutcase, I know – Tutankhamen died about three and a half thousand years ago, Carnarvon in 1923, and Wingate in 1944. How could there be a link between them? I realised in the end that unless the people Cranwell meant were over three thousand years old, he had to be talking about some kind of organisation or institution. He was, and I now know what it is – it's called The Eye of Ra.'

I paused for breath. There were the same dead-pan looks. The tape-recorder creaked on.

'If it's a conspiracy you're after, there it is,' I went on. 'The Eye of Ra has been responsible for the deaths of scores of people over the last century, not only of Carnarvon and twenty-odd others, but also of my grandfather and my best friends Julian Cranwell and Evelyn Barrington, her husband and son and a whole lot more.'

'And how do you happen to know this?'

I took a deep breath, removed my glasses, then put them back on without thinking.

'A few days ago I got access to what you might call privileged knowledge and I've made some deductions from it. The information was that the so-called heretic pharaoh, Akhnaton – father of Tutankhamen – was deposed violently by a popular uprising orchestrated by the Eye of Ra organisation, which was formed mainly from unfrocked priests of the Ra brotherhood. The Eye murdered Smenkhare and later got rid of Tut. It made sure that the names of Akhnaton's dynasty were excised from history and swore that it would continue to exist to protect earth against the likes of Akhnaton for ever.'

'Privileged knowledge?' Rasim scoffed. 'Where did you find it?'

I halted and took another deep breath. So many ways-in offered themselves. I decided to start at the real beginning.

'I'm an Egyptologist,' I said, 'and all my working life I've had a theory that ancient Egyptian civilisation was inherited from an older, more advanced civilisation – you might call it Atlantis. To conventional scholars this labelled me barmy: I was assigned to the lunatic fringe. Dr Abbas Rifad, who so readily supplied you with a report stating that I'd been sacked from the Antiquities Service for illegal trafficking, actually used my "lunatic" theories as an excuse for sacking me. But neither of those was the real reason I was sacked . . .'

'I don't see the relevance of this.'

'Please, give me a second and you will. I was really fired because I turned up a unique artefact that proved beyond all reasonable doubt that the ancient Egyptians – or some other culture they were in contact with – had a knowledge of astronomy that could only have come from advanced physics. The artefact in question showed a star called Sirius B – a star which as it happens can't be seen with the naked eye – and dated back at least three thousand years, probably more. But Sirius B wasn't discovered until the middle of the last century and not properly identified until quite recently.'

'So what *is* the point?'

'The point is that my theory of foreign origins was correct in one way but quite spurious in another. In fact, ancient Egyptian civilisation did come from far away, but not from anywhere on this planet.'

'From where then?'

'From space.'

There was a sharp intake of breath from Hammoudi, who was looking at me with amazement. The monk and the colonel exchanged glances and seemed to be struggling to preserve their poker faces. 'You mean *outer* space?' Rasim enquired, squinting as if he simply hadn't heard right.

'Yes, in fact it came from a planet in the constellation Canis Major, a planet orbiting the white dwarf Sirius B – the one, if you remember, which was shown in the stela I found, despite being invisible to the naked eye. The artefact I found was a record of that origin, but one which had been deliberately hidden in a special cache.'

'You haven't answered my question: what was your privileged information and where did it come from?'

'All right. Five days ago – at least I think it was five days – I discovered something buried under the sands of the Western Desert: a star-ship built more than three and a half thousand years ago. It was this ship which brought an alien to earth from Sirius B.'

There was an unrestrained snort from Hammoudi. Rasim glared at him.

'Excuse me,' said a lisping, almost camp voice from the rear, and I looked up to see the 'monk' in the lab-coat with his hand up like a school-kid in class. 'Sirius is roughly 8 light yearsh from earth,' he said. 'That would mean a voyage of shenturies. How could any living thing survive that?' He stared at me over his half-moon glasses with eyes that were interested and alert.

'It's 8.6 light years to be exact,' I said, 'and yes, it would have taken years, but the aliens developed an anti-matter drive that could convert ninety per cent of its fuel to energy and approach ten percent of light speed.'

The 'monk' looked satisfied. There were expressions that might have been awe on everyone's face but Hammoudi's. His features registered disgust.

'So what happened to this alien from Sirius?' Rasim asked.

'He became the pharaoh Akhnaton.'

'*Akhnaton?*'

'Yes, Tut's father. His – or I should say it's – body was on the ship. It wasn't human, but an alien masquerading as a human. Had the ability to manipulate its own DNA code. It arrived during the reign of Amenophis III, killed the pharaoh and his crown prince and set up in his place as Amenophis IV and later Akhnaton. It revolutionised ancient Egyptian culture, but it was involved in some sort of breeding experiment with human beings, trying to develop a hybrid species. It didn't work though – humans got the better of it. That was why the Eye of Ra was formed, that was why it murdered Tut – Akhnaton's hybrid son. That was the secret it has worked for millennia to preserve.'

Rasim shook his head pityingly. 'I just don't understand how you could know all this. Did the space-ship come complete with a history manual?'

Hammoudi chuckled. The colonel and the monk looked on, expressionless.

'In a way it did,' I said. 'The whole story was written in perfectly recognisable hieroglyphs and stelae inside the ship. But that wasn't all; I was guided by a projection . . .'

'What do you mean?'

'I don't know. It was like a sort of ghost. A ghost of my mother – at least that's how it appeared. She – it – explained everything. Then the ship itself gave me some sort of message – a fantastic review of ancient history – things I'd never even dreamed of. The essence of the message was that mankind is no longer alone. The species has come of age; it's time for us to grow up.'

The thing that surprised me most was how unshocked they seemed. True, Hammoudi seemed to be wavering between pity and repulsion, snorting under his breath, but the others seemed singularly nonplussed. Either they'd heard it all before, or they'd already made up their minds I was a psycho.

372

'I'm beginning to lose the thread,' Rasim said testily. 'How does all this connect with your alleged conspiracy?'

'The Eye might have begun with a noble ideal,' I said, 'but I think it came to value its secret more than human life itself. When Howard Carter and Lord Carnarvon opened the tomb of Tutankhamen in 1923, they came across something there that let the cat out of the bag. Carnarvon was rubbed out for it together with a bunch of colleagues. Carter agreed to keep his trap shut. In 1933, Orde Wingate actually ferreted out the ship, but his party, my grandfather among them, was massacred. Wingate escaped with his headman, and hid the proof of his discovery, a set of Akhnaton *ushabti* figures, with my relatives. He never divulged what he'd found, but his personality became more and more skewed. He was blown up in Burma in 1944.'

I paused. Their faces were riveted on me now, but whether in fascination or incredulity I couldn't tell.

'Nothing much happened until Space Shuttle Columbia buzzed the Western Desert by accident in 1981, with its SIR-A system, a sort of radar-camera that could photograph hundreds of metres under the earth's surface. The SIR film analyst, Lynne Regis, probably picked out the huge unidentified metal object under the sands, but she died in a mysterious accident before she could publish, and the film itself was trashed in a fire at the Jet Propulsion Lab in Pasadena. The point is that the Eye will stop at nothing to preserve its secret: it's killing its own species to protect us from an alien threat.'

'Who are its members?'

'I don't know, but I do know they're all around us. I was sacked from the EAS because I'd found something that threatened their secret and scared them. That means they're in the government and they've got power. And they've had it for some time. Ibrahim Izzadin, the former DG of the Service, was pulped by a runaway car, just as he was about to investigate alleged misconduct in the Tutankhamen project. I suspect that was their doing, too.'

'So your claim is that Cranwell and the dealer Kolpos were both murdered by this Eye of Ra organisation, is that right?'

'I don't know.'

'You don't *know*? But you've been so cocksure of everything else up to now! You're sure you found a space-ship from Sirius, sure Akhnaton was an alien, sure there's a massive conspiracy going on, yet when we come down to the mundane level of your friend's death – the thing, you say, that brought you back to Egypt – you haven't even decided whether he was a victim!'

'I don't know if Cranwell's dead. That night I was arrested at Giza by the Captain here, I'd arranged to meet him.'

Hammoudi snorted even more loudly. 'That's two ghosts so far,' he chuckled. 'Ghosts, voices and aliens! The full head-banger's repertoire!'

Rasim glared at him again and Hammoudi went silent reluctantly.

'I said I don't know if he's dead,' I went on. 'Someone was there and he sounded like Cranwell, but I don't know if it was him or not. Same at Kolpos's shop. I caught a glimpse of someone who *might* have been Cranwell, but I'm not sure.'

I stopped suddenly, realising I'd come round a full circle. All four men were staring at me like mandarins, their faces completely expressionless. I'd been expecting derision like I'd experienced in the years when I'd been expounding my Atlantis theory, only worse. This silence was more intimidating. I realised that I'd just said enough to get myself certified.

Suddenly, the old colonel cleared his throat. Hammoudi and Rasim looked at him deferentially. 'This space-ship you claim to have found,' he asked in a voice that was surprisingly soft, gentle and cultured – not your average *Mukhabaraat* colonel by a long shot. 'Where is it now?'

'It was destroyed,' I said. 'Some kind of self-destruct device.'

'Then there'd be debris wouldn't there – I mean, if it was as big as you say?'

'I suppose so.'

'Then we can easily prove or disprove your story by taking a look out there, can't we?'

'Of course.'

He stood up and the 'monk' followed. They filed out as quietly and solemnly as a funeral cortege. Hammoudi walked a few steps behind the others but as he reached the door he turned. 'Nice going, Ross,' he whispered, grinning. 'They'll give you thirty years in the cuckoo-house for this!'

49

IT WAS THREE DAYS BEFORE I had another visitor, and the time dragged on endlessly. As soon as I was off the drip and allowed to get up, I made a bee-line for the window. I pulled up the blinds and saw through the bars that I was on the first floor of a modern two-storey building looking straight out into the Western Desert. The landscape was a featureless ripple of ridges – sun burning on flint, shale, and amber sand stretching on as far as the pre-Nile escarpment – the banks of a much older, wider Nile Valley, the Ur-Nile of prehistory, whose ragged lines faded into the dust-sheen on the horizon. Nothing moved out there apart from phantom lights and purple shadows, and the occasional kite, falcon or sulphur-headed vulture. It was desolate but its desolation called to me. A thousand times better to be out there in the bigness than shut up in this cell. Still, I gained something from the view – I recognised the shattered canine protrusion of Jabal Barqa, slightly to the north, which told me I was on the edge of the Nile Valley, a little below Kom Ombo. This place seemed to be a high-security establishment, ringed with razor wire, replete with 'keep out' signs and patrolled by black-suited guards. In front of my window, about fifty yards away, was a steel gate opening on a packed gravel drive. The gate was manned by a sentry, but was rarely opened, it seemed; at least during the time I watched it was never opened at all. Within the perimeter someone had busied themselves in laying out a garden – the Egyptians of the Nile

Valley turned the desert a homely, familiar green anywhere a trickle of water could be found. There were acacias, bougainvilleas, palm-saplings wired against goats, and fast-growing pencil cedars. A young Arab boy in a torn black headcloth and cast-off dungarees was working amongst the shrubs, moving methodically from tree to tree with a hosepipe. There was a track outside the gate, but I saw no asphalt roads and no motor-vehicles. There must have been an airstrip nearby, though, because the occasional light plane flew low overhead, and once a helicopter.

The cheerful nurse called Thalwa returned on the second day with a white towelling dressing-gown that I could walk about in, and instead of bed-pans let me use the bathroom in the corridor outside. At least this was a change. The corridor was painted brilliant white with spotless lino floor, and the only living soul there apart from the nurse and myself was the police guard on duty. I kept my senses alert for any sign of Elena, but though there were rows of glass-panelled doors, there seemed to be no activity in any of the rooms. I guessed I was the only patient on the floor, and that worried me. I reasoned that she had to be in the building somewhere. *You and your friend almost died. You and your friend. Almost. . .* Thalwa had said that, so the odds were she'd actually seen her. The question was how to ask her in secrecy. She'd said they were listening, so the room was bugged, and even going to the bathroom I could hear the clump of the guard's boots close behind us. When Thalwa was away I searched the room silently for any trace of writing materials, without success. They hadn't left so much as a paper clip lying around, and the eating utensils they gave me were of brittle plastic. I began to feel claustrophobic and to stump aimlessly round the floor. I would spend hours dreaming, staring at the desert horizon. My Hawazim relations would have been half demented by now, I knew, but I'd lost my fear of confined spaces to some extent as a boy in England. Never completely, though. In desperation I picked up the telephone, to be told sharply, 'Put the phone down, Ross.' It didn't take much to guess that was where their bugging device must be.

*   *   *

The next time Thalwa came in I decided to take a chance. As she was bending over me to remove the eating things, I suddenly snatched the ball-point and notepad out of her top pocket. She tried to snatch it back, and mouthed silent warnings. One peep from her could bring the guard, I knew. It might result in me being handcuffed or even strait-jacketed. But it was worth the risk. I fought her off long enough to scribble in Arabic '*Wayn sadiqati?*' 'Where is my friend?' on the paper. She grabbed it, took the pen and waggled her finger at me. She slipped the pad back into her pocket, unread. Her next move might be to go straight to Hammoudi with it. If so, there might be repercussions, but the situation couldn't be that much worse, I reasoned. At least I'd done something to assert my independence, no matter how futile.

The following morning, after I'd washed and eaten breakfast, the same crew-cut lab-assistant came in carrying a small Korean TV with built-in video-player, which he set up on the table and plugged in. 'Now this is what I call a change for the better,' I said. He ignored me just like the first time, and cleared the table. A moment later Hammoudi flung open the door and marched in briskly carrying a battered briefcase under his arm. He dismissed the assistant, opened the briefcase and dumped a pile of documents and a video-cassette on the table. He removed his jacket and hung it from a hook on the wall and laid out a pack of Cleopatras and a lighter on the table, side by side with his pocket cassette-recorder and a pile of tapes. This looked as though it was going to be a long session. 'Sit,' he told me, and I settled in the upright chair opposite the table, while he took another behind it. An aircraft drummed in to the airstrip over our heads. 'Smoke?' he said, offering me the Cleopatras, 'you don't, do you?'

'I'd be very grateful for my pipe,' I said.

'If you keep your nose clean we'll see what we can do.'

'Thanks.'

He lit a Cleopatra and snorted smoke, pushing himself back against the chair back until it creaked. For a moment I thought the backrest would shear off – these hospital chairs weren't designed for six-foot-three, seventeen-stone giants. The great domed head puckered into what was meant to be an attitude of sympathy, and he smoothed his small moustache with his finger and thumb.

'I've been wrong about you three times, Ross,' he said. 'First I had you down as a murderer and a racketeer, second I thought you were some kind of foreign infiltrator, and third, I thought you were a head-banger. That's the received wisdom right now after your little performance the other day. I warned you to play it straight, but would you listen? See that little guy wearing the dog-collar?'

'The monk?'

'Yeah. He's a Benedictine, Father Mikhaelis, but he's also a Ph.D. in head-shrinking with a list of qualifications as long as your arm. If he says you're nuts, you're nuts – and right now he swears you're a head-banger of the highest order.'

Hammoudi pulled a slim file with a transparent cover from the pile of documents.

'You can read it yourself, Ross ... Paranoia, delusions of persecution, hallucinations, talking to the dead ... classic symptoms of schizophrenia. And you know what they do with schizophrenics here, Ross? They lobotomise 'em, that's what. Turn you into a bloody zombie for the rest of your days.'

I think I actually smiled at the absurdity of the notion. It was a relief to talk about something – anything – and for some reason I found this new gambit highly amusing.

'But you think he's wrong?' I said.

'The more dirt I've dug out the more I'm certain that you were just a dupe. You've been had, and I feel sorry for you.'

'Oh, by whom?'

'By Karlman and Wingate.'

'What are you talking about?' I said.

'I'm talking about your conspiracy theory – the Eye of Ra business. It was a hoax invented by Karlman and Wingate back in the 1930s.'

'You're the head-banger not me.'

The domed head furrowed again, this time in irritation. I could see he wanted to snap something, maybe even lash out, but he was keeping a tight rein on himself. He was trying to be Mister Nice Guy – and I wondered why.

'Look Ross, you better take note, because if bloody Rasputin there has his way you'll be in the funny-farm until your hair turns white.'

'And you want to prove I'm sane so I can go to the hangman, I suppose.'

'Right now I'm the best friend you got, OK. Let me tell you, I've really done my homework these last few days. I've had my people working round the clock. Look, all the shit is here: times, dates, places. Karlman was a real loony-toon right from the start, a pervert who got off watching young boys whacking it in each other's asses. Karlman ran across Wingate in Egypt when he was on leave from his posting in Khartoum, and they hit it off. Wingate was another one who wasn't quite the full tea-service, and they must have recognised each other as brother weirdos. You should see Wingate's medical record: a manic depressive and misanthropist who hated society and had an inclination to violence. Anyway they were both misfits with a grudge against the establishment and they decided to concoct a massive hoax that would really set the cat among the pigeons. Akhnaton's tomb was the last great mystery of Egyptology, like you said, and they had a clever idea – they knew the old legend of Zerzura, where there was supposed to be a pharaoh and his queen asleep on a hoard of treasure, and they decided that Zerzura would be Akhnaton's tomb. It just about fitted, because since Akhnaton was a hated heretic it was possible he might have been buried far out in the desert as a way of protecting his mummy. But there was another layer of hoax too – the suggestion that Akhnaton was an alien and that the ancient Egyptians had contact with the stars.'

'How do you know all this?'

'There's stuff on file about both Karlman and Wingate going way back.'

'But I've *seen* the *ushabtis* Wingate brought back from Zerzura.'

Hammoudi stubbed out his cigarette-butt and stood up, stretching his arms and rolling up his sleeves to reveal powerful forearms covered in coarse black hair. He looked out of the window for a moment, then he turned back to me and shook his head.

'You disappoint me,' he said, 'I thought a sharp guy like you would've known that a whole heap of Akhnaton *ushabtis* was discovered in 1931, in Akhnaton's official tomb at Amarna. They were dug out by a Brit called Pendlebury who was working for the Egypt Exploration Fund on behalf of the Antiquities Service. September 1931 – note the date – only eighteen months before Wingate set off to find Zerzura in January 1933, and pretended to have found the *ushabtis* there.'

'You mean Wingate got hold of these Amarna *ushabtis*?'

'There's no record of them after the 1931 excavation until they turned up this year. I reckon they found their way into the hands of private collectors, one of whom was Wingate. The point is that the *ushabtis* were genuine, but they didn't come from Zerzura.'

'What about the Missing Journal?'

'Oh yeah, that was smart. I've seen it – gives you just enough to sell you on the idea that there's a link between Tut's tomb and Zerzura, and that Zerzura was Akhnaton's tomb, without providing the details. Bits apparently missing and torn out to whet your appetite. A very astute bit of forgery.'

'Look, my uncle told me that Wingate hired my grandfather and a lot of other Hawazim to take him to Zerzura in 1933. They never came back. We found the remains of my grandfather's camel at Abu Simm, a quicksand in the Desolation. There were human skeletons, too.'

'Your uncle? That old bag of bones we arrested at Khan al-Anaq? He's already got one foot in the grave and his mind is playing tricks. As it happens we've got a detailed report of Wingate's trek in January 1933. He employed only five men, all of them from Dakhla, except for Hilmi who was from Kharja. I can even tell you their names. They found bugger all out there, but that wasn't the point. At the end of the trek, Wingate sent his four Dakhla men home and turned up at al-Maqs with Hilmi frothing at the mouth like a rabid dog and the *ushabtis* which he'd had with him from the beginning. Seems your relatives were too superstitious even to question him.'

'How do you explain the fact that Hilmi came out of the desert completely wacko?'

'Hilmi was bloody wacko long before Wingate met him. I pulled the files of the local administration office at Kharja for the late twenties and his name turned up. Seems he'd been mixed up with the Senussis – a fanatic religious brotherhood back in the twenties – and had a reputation for inciting people to attack the government or go on mad escapades. In December 1932, Hilmi got a lot of Hawazim interested in the idea of Zerzura. Those were hard times and he persuaded them there was treasure to be found and they'd all be rich. So off they toddled on their camels, not having the least idea where Zerzura was, and stumbled into the quicksands. Hilmi was the only one who made it back, and by then he really *was* raving mad. Wingate heard the story when he arrived the same month and used it. He even took Hilmi on to make it more convincing. Your grandfather died in Abu Simm all right, but not with Wingate.'

'But the sand around was full of spent cartridge-cases – .45 calibre bullets.'

'Did you find any .45 bullets actually embedded in the bones?'

'No, but . . .'

'Then how do you know those cases didn't belong to some other event entirely? You wouldn't make a very good detective, would you, Ross!'

I watched Hammoudi light another cigarette. I had to admit his story didn't sound implausible. It was just possible that a couple of twisted souls might have launched a hoax – after all, it had happened plenty of times before: the Piltdown Man case was an excellent example. The only thing was that I'd *seen* the ship and Akhnaton's remains.

'Look, I *saw* Akhnaton,' I said, 'and he wasn't a human being.'

'You *thought* you saw him, but you found what you expected to find. You were dying of thirst and suffering from hallucinations. Akhnaton can't have been in any space-ship in the desert, because as Karlman well knew, his mummy'd been found by a

Yank called Theodore Davis in the Valley of the Kings in 1907.'

He dug another folder out of the pile and waved it in front of me. 'Read this. It's the Davis Report. He dug up a tomb known as ''55'' and found in it the mummy of a man with an elongated skull and bisexual features which he was certain belonged to Akhnaton. The coffin itself was engraved with Akhnaton's name, but someone'd tried to scratch it out.'

'I know all about it, but it's old hat. The Davis theory has been disproved – the age of the mummy in Tomb 55 at death was shown to be no more than twenty-three. We know Akhnaton reigned for seventeen years, so if the body in Tomb 55 was Akhnaton, he could only have been five or six when he became pharaoh.'

Hammoudi shrugged. 'Ross, scientists are like everybody else. They believe what they want to believe. All your life you wanted to believe that ancient Egyptian civilisation came from Atlantis, and you leapt at anything that seemed to fit your own ideas. You were easy meat for Karlman. Read the anatomical reports – I've got the lot here, and the weight of the evidence suggests that the Davis mummy *was* Akhnaton. Only no one wanted to believe the evidence.'

'Why shouldn't they?'

'Because everyone likes a mystery, and a lot of people wanted to believe Akhnaton had never been found. The truth was that the ''Great Heretic'' had been shoved into an insignificant grave without any of the treasure and trimmings that everyone dreamed of finding. It was a big let-down, so the Egyptologists just ignored it and went on hoping they'd find the ''real thing'' some day. Karlman knew that, of course, and he played on it. Wingate let drop in the journal that the search for Akhnaton's tomb – i.e. Zerzura – was started by something they'd found in Tut's tomb. That's poppycock too. You ever hear of Hassanein Bey?'

'Yes. Discovered Kufra Oasis with Mrs Rosita Forbes in . . . 1920, was it?'

'Spot on. Well this Hassanein was an Egyptian nob – well in with the *Khedive*, educated at Oxford University – and he was the first to start looking for Zerzura. He set off with a caravan of camels from Mersa Matruh and crossed two thousand miles into the Sudan in December 1922 – that's *before* Tut's sarcophagus was opened in February 1923. Never found Zerzura, of course.'

'So you're saying that proves there was no connection?'

'There was a connection. Hassanein admitted that to the *National Geographic* magazine when they did a write-up on his jaunt. But it wasn't literal. The discovery of Tut's tomb in 1922 made him wonder what other treasures might lie undiscovered in the desert sands, that's all. There was no direct link. The link was made up by our boys Karlman and Wingate. ''The Mummy's Curse'' spiel had been concocted by the press back in the twenties. Karlman dug it up in the thirties and worked in the idea that there was some secret organisation wheeling and dealing behind the scenes. But look at the facts: Carter didn't croak till 1939, and a stack of those mixed up with Tut's tomb pegged out much later. Carnarvon's daughter, who saw the tomb opened, popped off in 1980, aged seventy-eight. Pierre Lacau – a French guy involved in the opening of the tomb, croaked in 1965, at the ripe old age of ninety-two, and there was even an ex-Brit military cop called Adamson whose job was to sleep in the tomb itself, and who bit the dust in 1980 aged eighty-one. And those weren't the only ones. If it was my case, I'd say any conspiracy to murder theory was unproved, but the brilliant Cranwell swallowed it hook, line and sinker – so did you.'

I tried to picture Julian Cranwell and found I could hardly remember his face any more. I'd long ago ceased wondering if he was alive. 'You're suggesting that all this was set up just for Julian Cranwell to find?'

'Look at it like this. Cranwell might have been a maverick, but he was highly respected. He'd taken up causes that everyone pooh-poohed and been proven right time and time again. He was just the person Karlman needed as his patsy. If Cranwell swallowed it, everyone else would and the hoax would be on.'

'It doesn't add up. I mean we're talking about a sixty-year gap here. If it was a hoax, it was a long time brewing.'

'The war and the Nasserite revolution put the kibosh on any digging from the late thirties till the sixties.'

'It's still a long time.'

'Maybe Karlman had dropped the whole scheme. Wingate'd been killed accidentally in a plane crash in Burma in 1944. Karlman was in the States at Harvard until the 1970s, then he got appointed to a post back in Egypt. It went well for a while, but then he got the heave-ho for porno-trafficking and all the old bitterness came back. He realised the *ushabtis* and the journal were still there, and Cranwell was the ideal man for the job. But Karlman didn't reckon with Cranwell's nose. When Cranwell found the *ushabtis* and the Missing Journal he got very enthusiastic: then he began to smell a rat. He got too close too quick, and Karlman whacked him.'

'Oh, please! That feeble old man murdered Julian?'

'Cranwell had a heart condition. Perhaps you didn't know that?'

'No, I didn't.'

'Well Karlman probably did, and I suspect he put the screws on Cranwell – deliberately gave him the jitters. Maybe sent some thugs dressed up in Halloween costumes to knock him about a bit, cut the phone, rough him up. Cranwell ended up having a massive coronary – splat – that was the end of him. They dumped him at the pyramids, carried him in at night and disguised their own tracks. Made it look like he'd materialised out of thin air.'

'So you spotted the absence of Julian's footprints.'

He tapped his nose with a finger. 'I wasn't born yesterday,' he said.

'But Julian was missing for three days. Where was he?'

'His *ghaffir* told me he'd left with two nasty-looking types. They probably kept him holed up somewhere. Cairo's a big place.'

'What about his body? It was missing from the morgue.'

'I told you the truth. The stiff went to the British Consulate at the request of relatives before the autopsy could be performed. If you'd enquired at the Consulate they'd have told you.'

'I did, or rather Dr Barrington did. They wouldn't talk.'

'I expect they have their own rules. Always been tight-arsed with information, the Brits.'

'That night at Giza, the time you jumped me, I met Cranwell. He was my secret contact.'

'You saw him close up, made positive ID?'

'No, but he rang up Dr Barrington earlier and she identified his voice.'

'Dr Barrington was another one with paranoid delusions. I've turned up her file too – taken off the active list with the Brit MI6 because she went scatty and hit the bottle.'

'Still, there *was* somebody there – at Giza. And he had a voice like Cranwell's.'

'Karlman probably sent him to give you goosebumps. The rest was your imagination working overtime. You've had plenty of exercise in imagination just recently, Ross.'

'OK, but what about Kolpos? I saw him nailed to his desk with a garotte round his neck.'

Hammoudi sighed and sifted through his files. He brought out a pink folder and slapped it down on the table. 'Read,' he said, 'I told you we'd had our eyes on Kolpos for years. Perhaps you thought I was swindling you. Kolpos was a villain. He had his thumbs in all sorts of pies, especially smuggling antiquities. This is the confession of a guy called Abdallah Foulah, a professional hit man, who admits to having rubbed out Kolpos and blitzed his shop with a grenade. Foulah said he was paid for the job by a rival smuggling-gang Kolpos had double-crossed. You with me?'

I nodded. 'I know you were at the scene, Ross,' Hammoudi went on, 'but Foulah thought you were part of the operation. How you got out, I don't know. The girl Anasis says she knew nothing about it, but Kolpos must have known he had it coming when he sent her away.'

Elena's face came into my mind suddenly – the tortured, ravaged face I'd last seen in the cave. I'd abandoned her without even thinking and wandered off following a phantom of my mother to Zerzura, the Lost Oasis. Only it wasn't a lost oasis, it was also Akhnaton's tomb and a giant star-ship hidden under the desert, that had been preserved by some mysterious angel-like race for some three and a half thousand years. Just so I could get there and receive a message for all mankind. Which sounded like the ramblings of a maniac, I had to admit. Was it more plausible, I wondered, than a hoax devised by two cracked and embittered souls sixty years ago?

But I'd *seen* it. I'd *touched* it.

Remarkable what thirst will do.

'Let's face it,' Hammoudi said, as if reading my thoughts, 'you've been bamboozled. You never found Zerzura, or Akhnaton's tomb, or a star-ship under the desert. It was a delusion brought on by fatigue, thirst and hunger. I suspect that's true of everyone who claims to have seen Zerzura: for the Bedouin it was a lush oasis, for the Greeks a white city. For you, the modern scientific man, it was some miracle of high technology, a space-ship.'

'And I suppose I just imagined that Akhnaton was an alien? That idea wasn't given to me by Karlman or anyone else.'

Hammoudi chuckled and his dome crinkled again. 'It's a pretty daft idea, you've got to admit. OK, I'm convinced you believe it, I mean, nobody would *invent* a story so wacko. First, Karlman definitely tried to suggest some connection between the ancient Egyptians and outer space. He used the Dogon stuff recently dug up by Dieterlen and Griaule and forged the Siriun Stela you found at Medinat Habu. You were convinced the stela was authentic, so it was only one more step to imagining Akhnaton was actually an alien. It's true, Akhnaton does look like something from the twilight zone but there's a rational explanation for that. He probably had what they call Fröhlich's Syndrome – a condition that gives you a head like a balloon, thighs like sides of beef, and shrinks your prick.' He paused and handed me a typewritten sheet. 'Read,' he said.

'Fröhlich's Syndrome may arise from several different causes,' the report ran, 'but the most common is a tumour on the pituitary gland. There may be a fugitive over-stimulation of the pituitary which results in distortions of the skull and the elongation of the jaw. After puberty the voice remains high, body hair does not develop and the sexual organs remain infantile. In a later stage, there is the plumping out of abdomen, breasts, buttocks and thighs.

The condition may also result in hydrocephalus manifesting itself by the bulging of the parietal areas of the skull.'

I handed the paper back to Hammoudi. 'Poor old Akhnaton was a mini-prick,' he said. 'He just couldn't get it off with the girls. Poor bloody sod – and you called him an alien.'

'But we know he had a whole string of daughters as well as two sons.'

'Children can always be adopted. There's no proof they were actually his, is there?'

'No, I suppose not.'

He chuckled again. I have to confess that for a minute I began to doubt. Hammoudi's explanation made more sense than mine. The more I thought about it the less certain I was that I'd seen Akhnaton or the ship. I'd had bits missing out of my life before – like the time the Kolpos shop went up. I didn't remember seeing Elena after I'd left her in the cave, but they'd found me wandering around with her, and Hammoudi claimed she'd said I'd never left her. The only thing that nagged at me was Hammoudi's manner – anxious, as if he desperately needed to sell me something.

'What about the Space Shuttle Columbia?' I said.

'I thought that question would come up. I've got here a report by the FBI, concluding that the SIR-A mission analyst, Lynne Regis, was killed accidentally in a car-smash in California in 1983. The film was damaged in a fire at the JPS Labs in Pasadena, sure, but it was also proved to have been accidental, started by a faulty electrical circuit.'

'Just like the fire in my room at Shepheard's.'

'It does happen.'

'But the Siriun Stela ... I'm certain it was genuine.'

'Are you? Then I think you'll be interested in this ...'

He stood up and fed the video cassette into the machine. There was a fuzz of grey static and then a slightly blurred colour picture – obviously an amateur job – flashed on to the screen. I blinked and then realised I was watching the last moments of a committee-meeting at the Antiquities Service, chaired by Rifad. In fact I even recognised the conference table as one standing on the top floor of the Egyptian Museum. I'd sat at it myself plenty of times. The faces looked tired and slightly bored as if they'd already sat through an endless debate – the table was covered in ash-trays, teacups, and half-empty bottles of Perrier. Rifad, in shirt-sleeves, sat at the head of the table, and before him, standing on a cardboard base, was the Siriun Stela I'd found at Madinat Habu. I suddenly realised that these men were deciding my fate. The soundtrack crackled. '. . . So,' Rifad was saying, 'your conclusions on the so-called Siriun Stela are generally unfavourable, gentlemen?'

The camera passed to a squat man with popping eyes and a goatee beard. It was Holzmann, a Swiss professor who sometimes worked for the EAS. 'It's a very interesting notion,' he said, 'that the ancient Egyptians had the technology to see a white dwarf that wasn't identified until 1915, but there seems to be no corroborating proof whatsoever. If it were true it would revise all our accepted concepts about ancient Egypt – indeed world civilisation.'

'Agreed,' said another voice, then the camera switched belatedly to a deep-jowled, clean-shaven Egyptian, whom I recognised as Abd al-Bakr Guwaira, an epigraphy specialist known for his uncompromising views and his pompous delight in airing them. Guwaira and I had tussled on many occasions; he was just the sort of long-winded pedant that Julian and I had loved to hate. 'We have to evaluate all evidence as objectively as possible,' Guwaira droned, 'not just in terms of our accepted ideology, since then it becomes simply dogma. If evidence is valid, we must change our dogma accordingly.'

'Yes?' said Rifad, a tad impatiently.

'This stela cannot be easily dated – not organically obviously. That is why it falls to me to try and date it stylistically. We have the hieroglyph for the Dog Star Sirius, and an ellipse consisting of fifty dots around it. The ellipse is most unusual. Indeed, I'd venture to say it's never been seen before in ancient Egyptian epigraphy.'

'Ye-es?' said Rifad again, with obvious impatience this time.

Guwaira looked entirely unruffled. 'It does however appear in Dogon mythology,' he went on, 'in which this ellipse is known as "the Sorghum Female". It was recorded by Dieterlen in 1930, and described as representing the orbit of the star Sirius B around its sister-star Sirius A. The question thus arises as to how a pre-literate people could have known of the existence of Sirius B, an invisible white-dwarf, which actually does orbit Sirius A every fifty years.'

There were audible groans from the rest of the committee. Rifad's voice said, 'Could we keep to the stela?'

'The point is,' Guwaira continued, 'that this ellipse on this stela bears so close a resemblance to the Dogon drawing recorded by Dieterlen that I can only conclude that it has been carefully copied from his book. That would seem to me to date the stela as post-1930. Moreover, when I examined the hieroglyph of Sirius, I concluded from the depth and technique of incision that it was a careful copy of an 18th Dynasty hieroglyph. My general conclusion is that this stela is a forgery and almost certainly a contemporary one.'

'Who is the likely forger?' Rifad asked.

'In my experience, the most likely perpetrator of a hoax is the supposed finder – in this case it was Omar James Ross.'

There was a long silence and mumbles of 'disgrace' and 'inexcusable' as the camera panned swiftly along the faces of the committee. They'd selected it very carefully, I realised. Julian Cranwell wasn't present, and there was scarcely one of them I hadn't disagreed with violently at one time or another. Suddenly I had a sense of something out of place – a glimpse of familiar features in the wrong background. 'Could you rewind?' I asked Hammoudi.

He grunted but pressed the controls. There was a whirr of tape and I watched the sequence again. This time I was sure of it: the face belonged to Robert Rabjohn. Hammoudi flicked the TV off.

'There you are,' he said, 'Karlman saw you coming. He planted the stela and along you came and found it, right on cue.'

He stood up again and began packing away his materials. If nothing else, I thought, he'd exonerated me from the charge of forgery, and I had to admit to myself that he'd sown the seeds of doubt. 'Look,' I said, 'if you're so sure it's a hoax, why don't you let me confront Karlman himself? If I was unfairly dismissed from the EAS, then at least you owe me that.'

Hammoudi grimaced. 'Nothing would give me more pleasure than to put that twisted old bastard on the rack myself. But no can do, Ross. Karlman was found dead in his flat at Imbaba a week ago, strangled to death. His Nubian servant and some of his most valuable books are missing.'

50

EVEN BEFORE HAMMOUDI LEFT I'D NOTICED a blemish at
the edge of my retina – a tiny, dense star that I knew would
expand within half an hour until it obliterated my peripheral vision
entirely. Then the searing pain would start. 'Nurse!' I called,
banging on the door. The guard outside stood up and peered
through the glass at me uncertainly. 'Call the nurse!' I shouted,
clutching my head, play-acted a little. He dithered for a moment,
then dashed off down the corridor shouting and disappeared round
the corner. The door wasn't locked and for a moment I thought
about making a run for it. Then I remembered that I didn't yet
know where Elena was, and this time I wasn't going anywhere
without her. A moment later Thalwa arrived, anyway. 'What is
it?' she asked anxiously.

'Migraine,' I said, 'I get terrible attacks.'

'I'll bring you paracetamol.'

'It's no good,' I said, 'it doesn't work. I need something
stronger.'

She hurried off and returned five minutes later with a tiny
paper cup and a larger one of water on a tray. 'Valium,' she said.
'Take two now, and another two every four hours.' There were
six capsules in the cup. That, I thought, was slip number one.

I took two of the capsules with a gulp of water, and as soon
as she'd gone I spat them out again. I had six Valium caps as
ammunition – enough to make someone groggy. I didn't have a

plan, but at least it was something. The migraine was jabbing a fiery lancet through my skull, though, so I relented. I took one capsule anyway, and hid the other five inside my pillow-case. Then I lay down on my bed and tried to think clearly through the migraine aura and the growing Valium-induced numbness. Hammoudi had given me a lot to think about, and I wasn't completely sure any longer that I'd really experienced what I remembered. I'd started to recall seeing 'things' out there in the desert before I'd found the ship – yellow slit eyes behind me, demonic shapes on the dune-tops. Perhaps I'd merely passed into a shadow-land inside my own head, where all sorts of fantasies were playing themselves out. There seemed to be no collateral for anything I remembered – no water, no demijohns, no fruit. Elena had told Hammoudi I'd never left her side. I'd always been a clear and logical thinker – Oceam's Razor, slicing away the illusions, and this time there was a great deal at stake. If I could believe what I'd seen and heard was true, I was carrying a valuable message for my species – the news that we were no longer on our own. Now, I realised, it came down to one thing: faith. Did I believe in my own senses or not?

By late afternoon the migraine had gone, and in the slightly euphoric state induced by the Valium I stood staring out of the window at the desert. The sand mist had shifted and the crags of the limestone plateau were in sharp focus across the great beach of pebbles. This plateau divided the Nile valley from the oasis-chain of Kharja–Dakhla–Farafra–Bahriyya – about two days' fast journey away – and was criss-crossed by a network of routes known only to the Bedouin, marked by cairns, stones and ancient piles of broken pottery. The Bedouin had brought their herds to market at Isna, Idfu and Aswan this way for centuries. The sun was drifting towards the plateau, turning the pebble beach to soft gold, expanding the shadows of the saplings in the garden. A couple of black-jackets slouched along the wire perimeter casually, their AK-47s slung from their shoulders. They halted by the gate and lit cigarettes, watching the young Arab gardener who'd just come into view with his hose-pipe, moving from tree to tree, giving each what seemed to be a well-measured dose of water. The boy didn't have a watch, and the sureness with which he measured out the water-flow impressed me. There was something familiar in it, as there was in the way he moved – that springy quality to his step that seemed to be an expression of boundless nervous energy. I watched him closely, taking in the angular shape of the face, the wedge-shaped torso, the jaunty way he tied his headcloth. As he leaned over a bush, his headcloth snagged suddenly on a thorny limb and was pulled back. I saw the *fidwa* earring sparkle clearly for a fraction of a second before the boy, with a nervous glance at the smoking guards, hastily covered it up. He was not my clan – probably from one of those more settled along the rim of the oases – but he was a Hazmi nevertheless, and a Hazmi was the sworn ally of any other.

I had a sudden idea. I strained at the hem of my hospital gown and tore at the cotton. It was hard work and I was still feeble, so instead I worked on one of the bed-sheets and managed to rip off a thin strip of material. I removed my silver earring, threaded the cotton through it, then tied it. Then I opened the ventilating window as far as it would go – which was no more than a crack. I watched the boy for a long time, until the police guards had moved on, waiting until he was almost directly beneath me, then I dropped the earring through the crack and saw it fall to the ground. The boy noticed it at once. I saw his body tense. He looked at it, then stooped to pick it up, turned it over in his hand and put it away quickly. Only then did he look up. Our eyes met and he smiled. I pinched my upper right ear between finger and thumb and tweaked it exaggeratedly. He nodded. Then I spread my hands out, palms towards him, fingers spread, thumbs touching – signifying that I was about to talk *Yidshi*, our ancient sign-language. He mirrored my gesture; he was ready. Then I began to move through my limited vocabulary of signs as quickly as I could, while he watched in concentration, occasionally looking around him warily. I was still a bit rusty, and several times he shook his head with the palms-down sign that meant 'I don't understand.' It was hard work, palm on palm, fist on fist, finger, thumb, finger. I spelled out my name, Omar wald Maryam and signed 'I am a prisoner here.' The boy looked alarmed – to the Hawazim the word 'prisoner' signified lingering death. Suddenly he crossed his wrists, with palms closed – signifying 'stop.' He went about his watering again and a moment later I was astonished to see a knot of five or six riders trotting along outside the perimeter fence on big-boned camels. The riders wore khaki uniforms and trim camouflage *shamaghs*, carrying automatic carbines in leather sheaths slung from their military-style saddles. The camels weren't of the small Hawazim breed, but thoroughbred racers from the Sudan. It was a government Camel-Corps patrol, the *Hajana*, and I knew its riders were all picked men from the 'noble' Bedouin tribes – blood enemies of the Hawazim. They looked formidable, and their presence was as unwelcome as it was unexpected. The boy followed them with his eyes and after they'd gone, gave me his attention once more, with the shaken fist sign meaning 'Be hasty!' I began to work through the symbols again, appealing to him to send my *fidwa* to the *amnir* of the al-Maqs Hawazim, Mukhtar wald Salim, and have him meet me here in six days. I knew it was a tall order – only the very fastest of camels could do it – but I was desperate, and if it was humanly possible, Mukhtar wouldn't let me down. The boy gave me the thumb and forefinger circle meaning, 'I will do as you ask.' A moment later he'd vanished.

51

FOR THE NEXT TWO DAYS I looked out anxiously, morning and afternoon, to see if there was any sign of the Hazmi gardener. There wasn't, and that should have been a good omen, but I couldn't help feeling anxious that he'd been caught – that we'd been spotted talking *Yidshi* by the guards.

Then, on the second afternoon, as the guard changed over outside my room, I caught the word 'camel' and pricked up my ears. 'You hear what happened yesterday?' one of them was chortling. 'The *Hajana* had a camel pinched from right under their noses!'

'No, by God!'

'Yeah. They were out on the sands about a day's ride from here and someone sneaked up quiet as a fox, and went off with a camel, saddle and all. Worst thing was that there was a sentry on guard.'

'So much for the *Hajana*.'

'It had to be a Hazmi, they say – no one else could have done it. The leader said he wouldn't have minded, only the thief picked the best camel in the patrol.'

'Why didn't they track him down?'

'Are you joking. Once they get in the desert those Hawazim are like fish in water – even the *Hajana*'d have a hard time tracking him out there.'

I smiled to myself – my watering-boy had shown initiative to be proud of.

*   *   *

I waited anxiously for news of Elena, but Thalwa was no longer on duty and Huda, the sour-faced one who'd replaced her, looked unapproachable. On the third morning after my interview with Hammoudi, Huda marched in with a hypodermic, swabbed my arm with iodine and shot me up with something which burned slightly. 'What was that?' I asked.

'Phenobarbital,' she said begrudgingly.

It was a truth drug, administered to sap the will, and it had already started to work on me when two broad-shouldered orderlies bumped a trolley in through the door and dumped me on to it roughly. They wheeled me down the corridor and into a lift. We descended two floors, to a windowless basement where air-coolers hummed and where the corridors seemed darker and more claustrophobic. They pushed me into a tall, arched cellar done up like an operating theatre, with banks of instruments and guttering computer-screens, where they transferred me brusquely to an operating table. I stared about me. I'd been here before – in my dreams. This was the 'chapel' in which I'd been surrounded by hooded figures. Another figure out of my dreams was standing by the table – the monk, Father Mikhaelis – flicking a hypodermic he was holding up to the light. Both Mikhaelis and the nurse grasping the kidney-tray wore operating-masks, I noticed.

He turned to me with the syringe poised. 'Nursh,' he said, his voice almost parodying the words, 'Nursh, the swab.'

The nurse swabbed my arm again.

'I just had a jab there,' I said, and noticed that my voice sounded slurred and drunken.

'That was phenobarbital,' Mikhaelis lisped, 'thish is a stimulant to help you talk.'

I sensed more figures near me, and I turned to see Rasim and the colonel settling themselves on tubular-steel chairs.

This time it was Mikhaelis who did the talking. Instead of sitting, he hovered around me, insinuating his chinless face into my vision, examining me with eyes that were stony and fish-like behind the half-moon glasses, as if I was a specimen on a dissecting-board. 'All right, Mr Rosh,' he said, 'could you pleash tell me where your Hawazim people are hiding?'

'No,' I said, but I could feel his eyes boring into me, willing me to speak, and I could feel the drugs working, prompting me to answer, to help him, to cooperate.

'Rosh, you will help us in the end, you know?' he lisped. 'You do know that, don't you. Why can't you help us? It doesn't matter, you know, just relax, let yourself go. It doesn't matter. Nothing matters. We are your friends really – we saved your lives – we only want to make sure everything is all right. You really do owe it to us to tell us after all the help we've given you.'

'I can't . . .' I said, groaning with anguish.

The monk looked at me with concern and plucked up my limp hand. His palms felt soft and plump. 'Oh, but you can, my dear, dear Mr Omar Rosh. It doesn't matter. After all, what do the Hawazim mean to you? Your mother left you when you were only a little boy, didn't she? Went off and left you to face the big world alone. It's her fault you grew up so awkward that nobody would accept you. Poor Jamie, always a misfit. But you're not a misfit to us – we accept you for what you are. We saved your life. Why don't you do something for us in return.'

'What do you want to know?'

'Where are your Hawazim?'

He leaned over and his eyes drilled into me. I wanted to tell him, I really did. I needed to tell him, not just because of anything they might do to me, but because I genuinely wanted to help. The trouble was, I just couldn't. There was a barrier inside me, a psychic obstacle forged by my childhood which was too strong to break and too difficult to cross.

'I can't,' I said, 'I . . . just can't.'

The monk shook his head at Rasim and the colonel.

'Very well,' he said, 'could you perhaps describe to us again what you found in the Sand Sea.'

'I've already told you,' I said, and this time my voice came out less like a protest than a child's whingeing complaint.

'Would you please tell us again.'

For hours, it seemed, we went over the same old ground: Zerzura, Akhnaton's tomb, the star-ship, the *Guardians*, the Eye of Ra, round and round in circles, and the more confused I became the more I stumbled. OK, I was no longer so certain about what I thought I'd seen, I admitted. OK, Captain Hammoudi *had* introduced some points I hadn't known about, like the fact that Akhnaton *ushabtis* had been found by Pendlebury in 1931. OK, it was possible Karlman had made the whole thing up as a hoax. All right, I couldn't deny that someone had confessed to the murder of Kolpos. Perhaps I hadn't really found a star-ship that was Akhnaton's tomb – all right, it could have been a hallucination. Maybe I hadn't talked to a projection of the ship in the form of my mother. Maybe it'd been just my imagination, induced by a combination of thirst, fatigue and hunger. Probably I just saw what I wanted to see. Occasionally, Mikhaelis would peer over his half-moons at me happily. 'Good,' he would coo, 'very good indeed. If we continue like this I think we shall have you cured very soon.' On and on went the lisping, insinuating, mock-sympathetic voice, probing, questioning, doubting, teasing out inconsistencies I'd never thought of, but which suddenly seemed so obvious. Round and round we went, the sparkling predator's eyes, the hypnotic voice, the drugs, the monotony, the repetition, combined to create a mesmeric trance in which I was no longer fully conscious but merely answering questions by rote – giving the answers another part of me knew he wanted. Meanwhile the rest of me was floating somewhere up above it all, running in the body of a spectral jackal – Anubis – through a white desert. I had become the spirit of the Shining, my ancestral spirit, the desert-jackal, running effortlessly, heart pounding rhythmically, feet cutting the sand in a crisp percussion of strikes. Far in the distance was a dark, hooded figure by a rock. As I approached in my jackal-form, the figure turned. It was Maryam, without her *burqa* – the beautiful, sparkling face I'd seen in the star-ship. I stopped running and sat down in front of her, studying her face.

'Are you my mother or one of the *Guardians*?'

'Both,' she said.

'How can you be here?'

'I'm not. I have no material existence, just a mote in your mind's eye.'

'They say I didn't really see you, didn't really find the ship.'

She laughed refreshingly, showing perfect white teeth. 'You can control your body by will,' she said, 'their pathetic potions can't chain down someone of your power. Believe in yourself, Omar. You're an *illuminatus*.'

'What about the Eye of Ra?'

'I give you a name, Omar: Jibril. Three men called Jibril.'

'What do you mean . . .' I asked, but she was already fading, merging with the desert sands. Then I was back on the operating table with Mikhaelis leaning over me, looking worried. 'What did you say?' he asked.

'I said you're wasting your time,' I told him, clearly this time, 'I know what I am and I know what I saw. You're all involved in it. I'm carrying a message from the *Guardians*, and as soon as I get out of here I'm going to make sure everyone knows about it, and about your squalid little plot to keep it under wraps.'

52

THE NEXT MORNING I WAS LEFT alone, and Thalwa came back on duty. I immediately bombarded her with so many complaints about migraine that she brought me six more Valium caps. I went through the same pretence as before, taking them and then spitting them out after she was gone, and hiding them with the rest in my pillow-case. Near sunset, I settled by the window. The guards were doing their rounds, and as I watched a troop of *Hajana* pounded around the perimeter again on their magnificent camels. They looked good, I had to admit. They weren't Hawazim, but they were Bedouin, after all, and they knew the desert – the only section of the armed forces that my people held in any esteem at all. I watched as the guards opened the steel gate and the camels walked in file up the drive with their tasselled saddle-bags swinging.

Just after sunset I paid a visit to the bathroom, while the nurse and the guard waited outside as usual. I showered and dried myself thoroughly, and was about to open the door when I thought I heard the whispering of voices. I shook my head violently, remembering the ghost-voices I'd heard in the desert; I didn't want a repetition of that. The voices weren't in my head though – they were coming from behind the tiny window. It sounded as though there might be another room beyond it, but there couldn't be, I told myself – no one built a bathroom with a window opening on another room. I glanced back at the door. There was no lock on it; the nurse and guard coud burst in at any moment. The window was the sash-type, barred with white-painted steel. I tried it. It came up with more ease than I'd expected and there was a sudden bang. 'Everything all right in there?' came the nurse's call from the corridor.

'Fine,' I shouted back cheerfully, 'just lost the soap!'

The window didn't open to another room or to the outside, I saw, but to an internal shaft. The same voices came again – much clearer and more distinct now it was open. I realised the shaft must pass by an office on the lower floor, in which two men were standing by an open window talking. I listened again: the two men were Rasim and Hammoudi, and they were discussing me.

'What more are you hoping to get out of him?' Hammoudi was demanding with his usual insistence, despite the fact that he was talking to a superior rank.

'Nothing,' Rasim answered testily. 'We want to make sure he keeps his mouth shut. If he believes that what he saw in the desert was a delusion that'll be easier.'

'But it *was* a delusion, wasn't it?'

'You don't need to know. Keep your nose out of it.'

'Why not let him go?'

'Conspiracy. Have you forgotten police officers died?'

'He's not guilty of conspiracy. Source Jibril set the whole thing up – if anyone ought to be charged it's him. Jibril has knocked us down every time, and you're still playing ball with him.'

'OK, let's just say Ross has something that we might need someday. Something that could be very valuable to us. Only he has to keep quiet and to cooperate. Otherwise we can't use him.'

'Who the hell is this "us" and "we" – not the *Mukhabaraat*.'

'This is big – much bigger than your bloody piss-pot *Mukhabaraat*.'

'Oh, so it isn't dead policemen that count! This piss-pot *Mukhabaraat* exists to defend the state against foreign powers not to do their dirty shit for them. Who decides what happens to Ross. You?'

'Policy.'

'Whose bloody policy? Ours or someone else's?'

'Just do your job, Hammoudi, or you'll get your hat. We still have a chance with Anasis, but Ross is getting more and more resistant. We're giving him two days' grace and if he doesn't come round by then, he gets wiped out.'

'On what grounds?'

'On the grounds of national security.'

53

WHEN HAMMOUDI WALKED INTO MY ROOM next morning, I was shocked by his appearance. He looked as though he'd aged overnight; certainly he hadn't slept. His eyes were red, his skin looked sallow and deeply lined, and his great dome head was puckered into permanent creases. I didn't believe it was squeamishness at the thought of killing me. Hammoudi wasn't that type. It was something else, summed up in that last phrase I'd overheard – 'national security'. Hammoudi was a man who'd just had his lifelong values crushed. He slumped down in the chair, switched on his pocket tape-recorder, then switched it off, and lit a cigarette. 'Well,' he said wearily as I sat down opposite, 'our search-team came back from the Western Desert. There's no trace of debris, no wrecked space-ship, not even a sniff of an explosion. So I think that we can wipe out the aliens theory, don't you.'

'All right,' I said, 'then why are you keeping me? Why not let me go?'

The same question I'd heard him ask Rasim the day before.

He looked troubled. 'It's not as easy as that, Ross. Policemen have been killed thanks to you.'

'Thanks to me, or thanks to Source Jibril?'

The effect was electric. Hammoudi turned pale, swallowed hard and a tremor went through his cigarette-hand. He stubbed out the butt and half stood up as if he would lunge at me, but he didn't.

'Who told you about Jibril?' he snapped.

'You're slipping,' I said, 'you mentioned him at Khan al-Anaq. You said you had a feeling in your bones we were mixed up with a Source Jibril. You're not so sure now are you?'

He hauled himself to his feet and walked over to the window. He stared out of it for a few moments then turned on his heel and faced me. 'Ross,' he said, 'do I need to tell you you're on record here?'

'No,' I said. What did he mean – did I know the place was bugged? What did that matter now?

'Your story the other day omitted something . . .' I said.

'Ross!' Hammoudi said again. 'You're on record here!'

'Good, because what I have to say is for the record.'

'You're steering very close to the wind, Ross.'

'I know.'

'Maybe you do, maybe you don't, but whatever it is you've got to tell me I don't want to hear.'

'I think you ought to, Captain, because as I was saying what you told me the other day is as full of holes as a tart's stocking . . .'

He turned to the door as if considering walking out, then turned back and sat down heavily again in the chair, watching me with narrow, defeated red eyes.

'There was a curious omission from your data,' I said. 'The Zerzura Club, formed in 1930 with the objective of finding the Lost Oasis of Zerzura. One of the members of the Club was Aurel Karlman, whom they used to call "The Monk" because for some reason he used to waltz round in Benedictine togs – by a great coincidence, the same order as your friend Dr Mikhaelis who has such an interest in the anti-matter drive.'

Hammoudi revived slightly. 'I told you Karlman was behind the hoax,' he said.

'OK,' I said, 'but did you know the Club was actually a front for British intelligence, MI6 – it was run by a cabal of MI6 officers – and only they knew what was really going on. The boss of the outfit, a guy called Ralph Bagnold, deferred to Karlman, who was evidently the Big Effendi. Now, I don't believe Karlman was capable of fooling British intelligence, so the question is, what were MI6 doing in the Western Desert? More than looking for some legendary lost oasis, you can bet. And who was Karlman working for? Not CIA – it didn't exist in those days, and not FBI – too far out of their territory.'

Hammoudi scowled and bowed his head. For once, it seemed, he had nothing to say.

'MI6 kept a file on the comings and goings of the Zerzura Club,' I went on. 'You know what it was called? "Operation Eye of Ra". Now, why do you suppose they chose such a weird name? In 1989 a keen MI6 officer called Ronald Barrington got a sniff of something that wasn't quite pukka and opened the file. Before he could get his teeth into it, the file suddenly disappeared and Barrington found out that it had been transferred to a set-up called MJ-12 – an American outfit that apparently deals with UFOs and alien contacts, so secret that it's not even supposed to exist. Barrington was killed in a car crash the next day – and by the way that was his kid you shot dead at Kwayt. Now, why should an MI6 file be passed on to a Yank outfit, *unless that outfit had been running the show from the beginning*?'

Hammoudi screwed up his eyes dismally. 'What does all this have to do with Source Jibril, anyway?' he said.

'Somebody's been tipping you off from the start. We've been set up at every step of the way. There's no conspiracy charge for us to answer, Captain, because the whole thing has been incited by Source Jibril, and it's no coincidence that Jibril also happens to be the name of the guy running a little outfit of "rich loony-toons" known as the Eye of Ra. Only they're not rich loony-toons, are they, Captain? They're a bunch of deadly killers, just as I said they were.'

'If all you've got to go on's a name, forget it – Jibril's as common as muck in this country.'

'A man known as Jibril was spotted by Hawazim spies at Kharja, overseeing the unloading of police troops. It sounds to me as if he's run the whole operation.'

'Bullshit!'

'OK, but let me try a what if? What if your Source Jibril and the Jibril of the Eye of Ra are the same person? What if the Eye of Ra isn't just a society that goes back to ancient times, but a facade, a front for something rich, powerful and foreign, which has managed to infiltrate the government of this country – something foreign which is deciding *policy*.'

I spat the word out with all the venom I could muster – it had been Rasim's reason for keeping me prisoner without charge.

'Ross, you're off your trolley,' Hammoudi said. 'All this because three men have the same name! It means nothing at all.'

'OK, why did MI6 name their Zerzura op, "Operation Eye of Ra"?'

'They can call an op any damn thing they want.'

'Right, then tell me why the British Consul Melvin Renner and Abbas Rifad, the DG of the Antiquities Service were spotted entering the Eye of Ra Society's office within half an hour of each other.'

'By whom?'

'By my friend Doc Barrington, who was found dead in her flat the same day.'

'Suicide.'

'What?'

'I read the report on Dr Barrington's death. Suicide. She was a paranoid, as I told you. There's no proof for any of the things that you're saying.'

I felt the anger rising now. I removed my glasses and rubbed them slowly on the hem of my dressing-gown, breathing deeply. *Ronnie, Doc* and *David*, I thought.

'OK, there's no proof,' I said calmly, 'but there are three implications. One, that British intelligence was searching the Western Desert in the 1930s for something big enough to sling a lot of cash at. Two, that the operation was being run by the Yanks, possibly by an outfit called MJ-12, whose agent, let's say, was Aurel Karlman, and whose interest wasn't in ancient tombs or lost oases at all.'

'OK, that's two, what's the third?'

'The third is that you're not receiving your orders from your own government any longer, but from some foreign power, possibly the United States, possibly their proxies, most of whom you consider to be enemies.' I stopped and fixed him in the eye. 'And *that's* what's really bothering you, isn't it, Captain Hammoudi?'

He glared at me and stood up. 'That's enough,' he said. 'You're going to fry for this, Ross.'

'I know,' I said, 'national security.'

He gave me a last mystified glance, then turned to go. At the door, though, he stopped suddenly and turned back, leaning his long shanks against the door-frame. 'Oh, I forgot to tell you something,' he said. 'Our search team *did* spot a largish cave half hidden in the dunes not far from where you were picked up. They cleared it – found a drinking bowl, Bedouin type, a blanket, a saddle-bag and odd bits of junk. They also found a human skeleton there, female, they thought. Wasn't much left – been there for years and the rats had been at it, but they found this among the bones.' He held out a shiny object. It was an inlaid Agadez cross of the type worn by Tuareg nomads in the Sahara. I took it, turned it over and realised I'd seen it before. Often. It was the one my father had given Maryam when they'd got married. She'd worn it almost every day.

You'll find her remains in the cave where you left your friend.

I smiled and suppressed an urge to leap with exultation. My mother had just given me back a bit of my life. Several bits, actually.

'You know what it is?' Hammoudi growled.

'An Agadez cross. Worn by nomads in the Sahara.'

'What would it be doing in a cave in the Western Desert?'

'Maybe a stray Tuareg. Refugee from Libya or Chad. The Hawazim find their bodies sometimes.'

I stroked the piece affectionately. 'Can I keep this?' I asked.

'Suit yourself,' he said.

54

I ACTUALLY FELT A TOUCH OF pity for Hammoudi as he slouched away defeated. And I knew he was right. It would have been better for everyone if I'd swallowed the hoax story. That was probably the way their predecessors had done it with Wingate, and Wingate had been wiser than me. He'd just pretended to accept the whole thing was a delusion and they'd left him alone. But the experience had never left *him* alone. It had tormented him for the rest of his life, and I'd have bet money it was them who whacked him in the end. I began to pace round and round the room restlessly, trying to think. What was it they wanted from me?

'Such a waste, though, after we waited so long to find one. Through him we could finally talk to them. No more disasters like Roswell.'

I hadn't imagined those voices, I'd heard them, heard them discussing my fate while they thought I was unconscious.

'We can't keep him like this for ever, and we can't risk letting him go. Look what happened with Wingate. I say we eliminate him.'

They'd made their decision. They were going to kill me. But they hadn't done it yet, and I still had fight in me. What really worried me, though, was what they planned to do with Elena.

* * *

I trod my room in circles, wondering desperately if my Hazmi gardener had managed to get the message through to my uncle. If I was going to fight this, I'd need help, and there wasn't much time. I'd almost given up on Rabjohn – there'd been silence from him so long I was afraid he might be on the casualty list himself. Failing him, only my uncle and the Hawazim could help me now. I stood and watched the desert sunset until Thalwa brought the dinner. She smiled at me and nodded to the water jug, then walked out without speaking. When I lifted the jug, there was a hastily scribbled note underneath. *'Your friend is on the Ground Floor room 23. Her condition is good.'* Ground floor! This building only had two storeys, which meant she was right below me! I had the impulse to run out of the room straight away, drop the guard and dash downstairs to find her, but I held myself in tight check and calmed myself with deep breathing exercises. It might be a trap – an excuse for someone to shoot me whilst attempting to escape. I tore the note to small shreds and stuffed it inside my pillow case with the Valium caps. Then I sat down to think. The only real problem was the guard. The Valium might be the solution, but it wouldn't be any kind of a weapon without something to disguise it in, I thought. I mean I couldn't just walk up to the guard and say 'Excuse me, would you mind taking this handful of Valium'. It had to be administered in some kind of drink – preferably hot and strong. Tea would be ideal. When Thalwa came in with tea, I begged her for my own kettle – it would save her so much trouble, I explained. She looked doubtful and clucked over it; 'Bless me, I don't know,' she said, 'what with boiling water and everything . . . I mean what would Captain Hammoudi say?'

'No need to tell him.'

'Sssh – they're listening.'

'Look, I'm not asking for a gun or something, and I'd really appreciate it.'

'Well, I'll see what I can do.'

I didn't really hold out much hope. After all, boiling water, even electric flex, might easily be converted into weapons. When she came back with an electric kettle, paper cups, tea, sugar and milk powder, an hour later, I was less surprised than suspicious.

It had gone down way too easily, I thought. I kept my feelings to myself, though, tried to look delighted and kissed Thalwa until she retreated giggling.

When she'd gone, I tipped the Valium caps into my hand and opened them one by one, pouring the white powder into a paper cup. There was enough of the stuff here to stun a horse. I slipped the primed cup in between two others. Then I went to bed, dozed off, and woke at about three in the morning – the ideal time for skulduggery of any kind. I padded over to the door and peered through the glass panel. The guard was sitting opposite, a shambling, heavy-boned young man with an olive-coloured face disfigured by acne. He was sound asleep with his AK-47 across his knees. Perhaps I wasn't going to need the Valium after all. I removed my plastic flip-flops and pushed the door gently. There was no sound. I pushed it harder and it creaked so sharply that the guard opened his eyes wide, grabbed his rifle and jumped up. 'It's only me,' I said, 'I need to go to the bathroom.'

'OK,' he said, rubbing his eyes sheepishly, 'I'll come with you.'

When I'd finished, I found him leaning on the wall, yawning. He looked about twenty, probably a conscript doing his three years of military service. I smiled at him and we walked back towards the room side by side. 'Hard to stay awake at this time of night, isn't it?' I said, 'I wouldn't have your job for anything.'

He glanced at me uneasily. 'Don't worry,' I said, 'I won't tell anyone you were asleep.'

'Thank you,' he said, 'Captain Hammoudi would have me flogged.'

I had his accent, now. He was an oasis-man from Dakhla. Near enough, I thought.

'I know Hammoudi, he can be vicious,' I said, 'but the *Mukhabaraat* are all like that aren't they? You're what? Border police?'

'I'm not supposed to talk to prisoners.'

'Of course, I know that. I wouldn't want to compromise you, believe me.' We halted by the door of my room and I made a show of thinking deeply. 'Tell you what,' I said, 'why don't I make you a cup of tea? That'd help you stay awake.'

'Well, I don't know . . .'

'Come on. You know I'm a Hazmi? You're from Dakhla aren't you?'

He beamed. 'How do you know?'

'I know the dialect.'

'We used to see Hawazim in the market all the time at home when I was small. I never had anything against them. Folk said they were dirty – pardon me – but they were always dead honest. A Hazmi's word is his bond.'

'So you know the custom: to a Hazmi, once you've eaten or drunk together, you're friends.'

'Yes.'

'So you'll have some tea.'

'OK.'

When the kettle was breathing steam, I took the paper cup I'd laced with Valium powder and added a teabag and four large spoonsful of sugar. I left the tea to stew until the flavour was strong, then fished the teabag out.

'God bless you,' the boy said as I handed it to him.

'I won't make things worse by standing here talking,' I said, 'just give me the cup back once you've finished.'

He nodded and I retired into the room, hoping it had all been out of earshot of whatever listening device they'd got switched on. I sat down on the bed and listened carefully. It must have been half an hour before I heard a soft 'thunk' of the guard's rifle falling on the floor. I stood up and padded over to the door in my bare feet. He was sitting slumped in his chair with his eyes closed and his mouth open, snoring. I opened the door and this time the creak had no effect on him at all. The AK-47 lay on the lino at his feet and for a moment I was tempted to pick it up. But no, I thought, the weapon was too bulky to carry, and right now I didn't need it anyway. I just left him where he was and crept down the corridor to the stair-head. There was a lift further down, but I felt safer with the stairs. Only one flight divided me from her, I thought. I descended the double-flight, pushed at the ground floor exit door carefully and peered along the corridor.

*　　*　　*

There was no one about. Evidently, they didn't consider Elena much of a security risk. I padded out along the row of doors until I found 23 and ducked inside. Elena was lying asleep on her side, her long dark hair foaming over the pillow just as I remembered it from Rabjohn's. Her face looked deadly pale in the faint light from outside. I shook her gently. She moaned but didn't respond. 'Elena!' I whispered, shaking her more urgently. Suddenly I caught a movement behind me. I tried to turn but before I could move a cold, hard metal object was shoved against the side of my head. The feel was uncomfortably familiar. 'It's no good, she can't hear you,' Hammoudi's voice grated, 'they've got her heavily sedated. Just like you did with that poor farm-boy upstairs. I approved the kettle myself, and I knew about the Valium, of course. Now, turn very slowly, Ross.'

I turned and looked into Hammoudi's exhausted face. The great dome head was furrowed with pressure and the eyes heavy with bags. 'Sit down, Ross,' he said, gesturing with the muzzle of his Ruger at a chair. 'Don't try anything. Believe me I'll zap you if I have to.'

I sat down. Shafts of light through the blinds illuminated his massive body in strips – but now the eyes lay in darkness. There was a rustle as he held out a slip of paper to me. I took it and lifted it into a beam of light. It was my note to the nurse: '*Wayn sadiqati* – Where is my friend?'

'She did the right thing, of course,' Hammoudi said, 'she brought it straight to me. It was foolish, Ross. But in your position I suppose I'd have done the same. If you'd left it much later you wouldn't have found her, though. In three days she's going to be moved to a new facility in Israel.'

'*Israel?*'

He put the gun in his lap and lit a cigarette with unsteady fingers, the flick of flame encircling his great head for a moment in a halo of orange light. 'Oh, yes,' he said, blowing out smoke, 'it's called *détente*, I believe. But you are a damned fool, Ross. I warned you. You should have kept your nose clean.'

'What will they do to me?'

'Since you've rumbled them, you're expendable.'

'And Elena?'

'No, she's very special now.'

'Why?'

'Because she's pregnant.'

The word hit me like a bombshell. Elena was carrying our child, after all we'd been through, after everything! I remembered the night of the Shining. I'd sensed somehow it had been no passing thing, but a moment of true connection with eternity.

'If you're lying . . .' I said.

'I've no more reason to lie to you, Ross. Whether you believe it or not won't change a damn thing.'

'Why are they so interested in her?'

'They reckon that this – whatever it is you're supposed to have – will be passed on to your kid. They've given up on you, Ross. You're too strong for them. So they'll get what it is they want out of the kid.'

'What *do* they want?'

'I don't know. They had you under for five days before you came round properly, and they were doing something with you in that damned operating theatre – had you strung up to God knows what machines, and pumped you full of drugs. You can bet your ass that whatever they want, it's something worth more than a few *ushabtis*. Something that could change everything – or more likely keep everything the way it is for ever with them on top. They want to make sure they've got it and no one else.'

'How come you don't know?'

'Listen,' he said morosely, 'all my life I've fought for this country. I was a parachute sergeant in the Yemen fighting the royalists, did you know that? Led a special night-patrol they used to call "The Night Butchers". I was wounded six times and won six bravery citations. When I joined the *Mukhabaraat* they called me an unbelieving Copt and a stupid *Sa'idi*. I never was one of them, but I endured it because I believed that this country was more than just them – it was all of us. I worked hard; there was no special recommendation for me. I outshone the lot of them. I caught terrorists and smugglers. I killed some, tortured, yes, but all for this country. My country. I'm an Egyptian. We were a great nation once, but for hundreds of years we've been raped by foreigners. I thought that was all finished. I was proud. But at the end of twenty-five years' faithful service what do I find? I'm being given orders by superiors who've sold out to the damned foreigners.'

'So the Eye of Ra is a facade?'

'I don't know, but whatever *is* behind this doesn't give two shakes of a monkey's arsehole for Egypt. If I thought whacking you would serve my country, I'd do it willingly, Ross. But I'm not going to be a hit-man for my country's enemies, that's for sure.'

He paused and stubbed his cigarette out on the floor. Elena stirred slightly and gasped in her sleep.

'Jesus,' I said suddenly, 'they shouldn't be knocking her out with tranquillisers. It'll affect the foetus.'

'How do you think the rest of her life's going to be?'

'Not while I'm around.'

Hammoudi looked as if he'd made a decision. 'I'm giving you a chance, Ross,' he said. 'Tomorrow you'll find a package outside the window of your bathroom. It's all I can do for you. I'll make sure the girl isn't sedated. Take her and get out. If you ever mention this conversation to anyone, I'll deny it, and whenever we meet again I'll appear to be doing my damnedest to kill you. Go back now, and I'll sort out our friend upstairs.' The chair creaked as he stood up. 'Oh and Ross, one more thing,' he said, 'I told you I was wrong about you three times – actually it was four.'

'How?'

'When I said you were nothing, I was wrong then, too. You've stood by your people, stood by what you believed, and in the end no one can do more than that.'

55

I AWOKE TO BRIGHT SUNLIGHT, WITH a sense that something
was terribly wrong. It was the same feeling I'd experienced the
night Kolpos was killed. I felt panic symptoms. My heart pumped
and my hands trembled. Suddenly, I remembered that this was
the day Rasim said he'd have me wiped out, and I knew with
absolute certainty that I was about to encounter the man who'd
been sent here to kill me. I sat up in bed, put on my glasses and
made a powerful effort to control my body. I spent almost twenty
minutes at my deep-breathing exercises, clearing my mind of all
thoughts, until my heart-rate settled. Then I stepped out of bed,
put on my dressing-gown and went to the window. It was mid-
morning and the sun was already high – I'd slept far more than
I'd meant to. The beach of flints that spread as far as the escarpment looked like a field of jewels – emeralds, rubies, sapphires –
sparkling in the raw sunlight. As I watched, a black insect detached
itself from the background – a many-legged spider, which grew
and grew until it became a dozen camel-riders, carrying spills of
light that glittered on the stocks of holstered carbines. As they
came closer, I recognised the brawny camels and khaki uniforms
of the *Hajana*. They must have been out early, I thought, to be
returning at mid-morning. Or perhaps they'd been out all night.
There was a weariness about them. The patrol I'd seen the other
day had ridden stiff-backed and in strict military formation, but
this time the riders seemed to loll in the saddle, and the camels

trotted at irregular intervals. Their uniforms were unkempt as if they'd been put on hastily – in fact there was a general air of untidiness about them that I found surprising. They came right up to the gate and I watched as the guards opened it to admit them. At that moment the sour-faced nurse marched into the room and distracted me. 'You overslept,' she said, 'and that's a pity because you have an important visitor today.'

A pulse of fear swept over me again, and I turned away from the window.

'Oh?' I said. 'Who?'

'Do you think they tell *me*?' she said. 'Come on now. Time for your shower – and be quick about it.'

Outside in the corridor, I noticed that my sleeping guard had gone. He hadn't been replaced, either. I thought about Elena – I'd seen her and she was alive. Hammoudi had said she was pregnant, but could I trust Hammoudi after all the things I'd seen him do? I knew he was right about one thing, though. Today was our only chance. Tomorrow they'd be moving her and besides, I might be dead by then. I closed the bathroom door, hung up my dressing-gown and reached to turn on the shower. It was then that I noticed the string. It was nothing remarkable, just ordinary cheap jute string that you might find at any stationers, but it had been deliberately trapped under the sash of the small window. Suddenly Hammoudi's promise came back to me. '. . . *you'll find a package outside the window of your bathroom.*'

First I held the string tentatively between thumb and forefinger, then, with the other hand I began to lift the window-frame. One hand wasn't strong enough alone, so I took the string in my teeth and shifted it up with both hands, then pulled at the string. At the end of about two metres of line there was a little brown paper package weighing a kilo or less. I hauled it in, laid it on the toilet seat and closed the window as cautiously as I could. There was a rap on the door, and I jumped. 'All right in there?' came the sour nurse's voice.

'Don't come in,' I said, 'I'm not decent.'

I undid the package as quickly and as quietly as I could. Inside were two smaller packages wrapped up in plastic bags. One contained my passport and Elena's, and a thousand Egyptian pounds in twenties. The second was heavier, and I weighed it in my hand for a second before opening it. Inside was my *khanjar* with its sheath.

'. . . *your vicious little Hawazim stinger, which is now in a safe place* . . .'

I stared at it for another long second. It might be a trick, but Hammoudi had given me the means, and if I was fast enough, decisive enough, ruthless enough I still had a chance whatever the case.

There was another knock on the door. 'Just a minute,' I said. I ripped the brown paper into shreds and flushed the pieces down the toilet, then coiled the string and put it in the pocket of my dressing-gown. I put the passports and money in the other pocket and strapped my blade to my left wrist. I waited ten more seconds, then flung open the door.

'I did say be quick,' the nurse said testily. 'You'd better hurry. Your visitor will be here in a minute.'

The first thing I noticed when I entered the room was that the telephone-bugging device was conspicuous by its absence. What was that about, I wondered? I went to the window and gazed out. The *Hajana* patrol had dismounted just inside the gate as if they were waiting for something. The camels were hobbled all over the place and were chewing the cud and leaving droppings like piles of smooth black balls. A uniformed sergeant was talking to a *Hajana* corporal and seemed to be remonstrating with him, probably about the mess. A gaggle of *Hajana* patrol-men had gathered around the sergeant and were watching him slightly menacingly, I thought. I had a momentary impression of unease about the figures. The gate, I noticed, was still open.

I sat down at the table, and the chill feeling that had been waiting in the wings suddenly emerged and hit me like a cold wind. The man who was to kill me was on his way to my room at this very moment. He was stepping out of the lift. He was walking along the corridor. I heard soft footsteps coming closer and closer, and suddenly the door opened and I was looking into the face of the British Consul, Melvin Renner.

'Ah, Ross,' he said, 'hear you've got yourself into a spot of bother.'

'What are you doing here?'

'I've made a special journey here from Cairo.'

'You needn't have bothered.'

He smiled blandly as if humouring a cranky old person, or someone not quite right in the head, slicking back his wayward lock of hair. 'Aren't you even going to ask me to sit down?'

'Why? I didn't think you believed in such niceties.'

He sat down on the upright chair opposite. He looked around with feigned interest, putting on his best boyish charm act. He was dressed immaculately in a tailored white suit, blue shirt, club tie, suede desert boots and held a panama hat – the perfect image of what imaginary British Consuls in the tropics were supposed to wear but never really did. 'They're looking after you, then?' he said in that jolly-good-old-boy voice that was palpably false.

'Why have you come?'

'Well, I'm told you're in quite a bit of trouble. There have been incidents in which police officers have been killed – oh, I don't say you killed them, but you're involved as an accessory, so to speak. They want certain information out of you, such as where the er . . . insurgents are hiding and other details.'

I stared at him, noticing the intense eyes. A trickle of sweat ran down his brow. He was nervous despite the jolly tones.

'I advise you to say nothing.'

'You do?' I said suspiciously.

'Yes, I do. You have British citizenship and you're not obliged to breathe a word. You're entitled to Consular presence and a good lawyer as well as an interpreter . . . not that you need one, of course. By God, I wish I'd known about all this before. I mean, they haven't even *charged* you with anything yet . . .'

'So you think I should keep my mouth shut?'

'Oh, quite definitely. At least to them. But between us, if you can give me an idea of what this is really all about, it'd put me in a stronger position. Just between us of course. No farther than these walls.'

My eyes fell involuntarily on the place where the telephone had stood. His gaze followed mine. 'Don't worry,' he said, 'it's all kosher. I insisted that they remove any bugs before I agreed to talk to you. Anything you say's for my ears only.'

For a moment I wavered, and he saw it in my eyes. All my childhood I'd wanted to be him – a Melvin Renner, or the sort of person I'd imagined he was. I'd never been accepted by them though – to the Renners of this world I'd always been a 'bloody wog'.

'I really am your friend, Ross. You can trust me. If I don't know the story from your point of view, I can't help you much. This is what HM government pays me to do. To look after the interests of British citizens like yourself.'

'You mean like you looked after Doc Barrington?'

His eyes narrowed. 'I was so sorry to hear about Evelyn,' he said. 'Such a tragedy – but well . . . everyone knew she'd always been slightly dodgy . . .'

The image of Doc swinging from the ceiling struck me suddenly, and something inside me splintered like fragile wood.

'You two-faced shit, Renner,' I said, 'you deliberately obstructed Doc Barrington's enquiries about Julian Cranwell, and even if he's not dead, Doc is, and so is her son David. You could have helped avoid the deaths of at least two British citizens, and probably a lot of others, so don't come round here talking about people's interests. I know what interests you've got. If they sent you to do their dirty-work for them they really must be scraping the barrel.'

For a split second the boyish facade slid and I glimpsed beneath it a vicious, bigoted little toadie hanging on outdated imperial delusions. Another dribble of sweat ran down his forehead. I looked at him closely. Why was his jacket so thoroughly buttoned? There was an almost imperceptible droop of the neck, a minuscule displacement of the shoulders forwards. I looked at his face again, the narrowed, beady eyes which betrayed the boyish laugh, then I reached across and ripped open the front of his suit.

A small black tape-recorder hung round his neck on a string.

'For your ears only, eh?' I said. 'What did they tell you to do? Find out where my relatives are then put a bullet through my head?'

He pulled back powerfully, setting me off-balance, knocking my hand away with a snapping karate block and slid a Walther PP smoothly out of a holster at his waist with his right hand. 'You fool, Ross,' he said pointing the pistol at me with both hands, 'you could have been one of us. You could have had it all. Now you're dead meat.'

I felt along my left wrist for my blade, but I knew it was too late. I'd save it for the very last resort.

'You know, Renner,' I said, 'I grew up respecting people like you, or the people I thought you were. Now I realise all that hope and glory bullshit wasn't worth tuppence. How much are they paying you to kill me?'

'This isn't about money, Ross. With *their* technology we could rule the world. No more wars, no more squabbling. No one could oppose power like that.'

'Still the same old story, eh? Not developing human potential, but rule, control, power. Anyway I'm glad to say there is no technology. The ship's gone.'

'You poor bloody idiot. You think it's to do with ancient history? Something that happened thousands of years ago? It isn't – they're still here, Ross . . .'

'Shut up!' a voice cracked out like whiplash, and I looked up to see two beefy police troopers with their AK-47s at the ready. Behind them, pistol in hand, stood Major Rasim. 'That's enough, Mr Renner,' he said.

'What does it matter now?' Renner said.

'It matters,' he said, staring straight at me, 'we can do this two ways, Ross. The hard way, or with dignity.'

'All right,' I said.

'That's better. Follow me.'

He led me silently along the corridor, with the guards and Renner following. I swung my arms loosely. At least I still had my *khanjar* – a small hope, perhaps, but battles had been decided by less. The door of the lift slid open and we entered. Rasim pressed a button and we lurched down to the ground floor. The door opened into a small lobby with automatic plate-glass doors, where a corpulent police-sergeant stood behind a desk. 'Open the doors,' Rasim commanded him. As we walked out into the blazing sunlight, I smelt camels and looked up to see the *Hajana* mounts hobbled around the gate, with their riders still milling about uneasily. Rasim looked annoyed.

'Sergeant!' he bellowed, and the guard-sergeant I'd seen arguing with the *Hajana* corporal came running up. 'What are these *Hajana* doing here?' Rasim demanded. 'Why aren't they in their quarters? And why is the gate open?'

The sergeant began to explain, but Rasim cut him short, 'Get them out of here now. I don't want every Tom, Dick or Harry watching us.'

The sergeant saluted. 'Very good, Sir.'

Rasim pointed to a high concrete wall like a triptych of panels with the wings folded slightly inwards, standing in a sand-bank about a hundred metres from the gate. It was a shooting-range, I realised. That was where they were going to kill me.

'Let's get it over with,' Rasim said.

As they marched me towards the wall, I glanced along the ground-floor windows, hoping for a glimpse of her. There was Hammoudi, standing in the shadows by an open window, his face pale, his eyes standing out like gaping sores. A little further along I caught a glimpse of Elena's face for a fraction of a second, ghostly and drawn, before someone pulled her away. I had the fleeting impression of Mikhaelis's face behind her. We were at the wall now, and I stood facing it. Who would do it, I wondered, Renner or Rasim? It was Renner. I felt the cold hard snub of his Walther suddenly in the back of my head. 'Turn round,' he said. I turned and faced him, unblinking. He was about a metre away, I judged. Too close for his own good.

'Any last words?' he asked, sneering.

'Yes,' I said, folding my arms, feeling for my blade. 'You're a traitor, Renner, and you make me ashamed to have English blood.'

'Fuck you!'

The Walther came up and my blade came out in a sweep even faster. I lunged at him with all the power in my calves, caught his head in the crook of my left elbow and jabbed the knife into the cleft just below his right ear. 'Drop it!' I hissed. 'This is your jugular. I'm sure you've read my CV, Renner! I almost killed a boy at school with a cricket bat. I can do even better with a knife.'

The Walther tumbled into the sand. Rasim and the guards reeled away with their weapons up, 'Shoot!' Rasim said.

'No!' Renner screamed, and at that moment Rasim's immaculately uniformed chest disintegrated into slivers of bloody flesh and he fell over like a wet sack.

Everything went haywire. *Hajana* riders were racing towards us firing their carbines, not at me, I suddenly realised, but at the two guards who dropped their weapons and raised their hands frantically shouting 'Don't shoot!'

'Always pulling your fat out of the fire, you pipsqueak city-boy!' a bass voice said, and I glanced round to see my cousin Ahmad's broad, laughing face, out of place in the khaki uniform and camouflage headcloth of the *Hajana*.

'Khaki doesn't suit you,' I said. No wonder the *Hajana* patrol had seemed so unmilitary – they were Hawazim tribesmen. I saw the slim, hard figure of Mansur behind him, his blank eye flopping comically to one side. 'Peace be on you!' said another voice – and I recognised my uncle, Mukhtar, advancing with his six-shot ready and a grim smile on his face. It was just then that Renner kicked me backwards in the groin with his heel, broke free of my grasp, snatched his Walther from the sand and fired point-blank at Mukhtar. The old man groaned and fell. I brought my blade down hard into the pit of Renner's back, almost at the same time as Ahmad's carbine cracked out, blasting him in the chest. One of the guards grabbed his AK-47, turning its muzzle on Mansur. I sprang on him, boiling with fury, wrenched the weapon from his grip and smashed his jaw with the stock so hard that the whole butt broke off. The trooper dropped and grovelled in the sand next to Renner's inert body, sobbing, choking blood and teeth. Mansur and I had stooped to pick up Mukhtar, when there was a crackle of gunfire from the main entrance, and we looked up to see black-jackets pouring out of the doors with Hammoudi in the lead. He hadn't yet twigged what was happening, I realised, because he was yelling at the *Hajana* to fire on us. Instead they let rip a ragged salvo at Hammoudi, their rounds smashing the glass door and tearing the woodwork to shreds. Hammoudi and his men retreated swiftly. We had my uncle on his feet now, and Mansur supported him while I picked up Renner's pistol.

'Elena!' I shouted. 'She's still inside!'

'Let's get her out, then!' Ahmad said.

Suddenly the shooting stopped. I looked up to see that more figures had emerged on the steps outside the main door – one of them was the monk Mikhaelis in his white lab-coat. His arm was clamped tightly around Elena's neck and he was holding a pistol to her head. At one shoulder stood the quiet colonel and at the other stood Hammoudi. 'Drop your weapons!' the monk shouted. 'Put them down, or the girl dies.'

56

FOR AN INSTANT NOBODY MOVED. I felt the Walther heavy in my hand. Mansur and Ahmad glanced at me expectantly – I'd always been the best pistol-shot in the family. The monk and Elena were a hundred metres away, a long shot for a Walther PP, but Mikhaelis's attention was concentrated on the Hawazim at the gate. I lifted the pistol in an arc up to my eye, and for a moment time seemed to skid to a halt. Elena's head covered the monk's almost completely – there was no window for a clear shot. He hadn't seen me yet, but his eyes were beginning to slew towards me when suddenly Elena tilted forward, leaving a fraction of a degree between them. I squeezed the trigger. There was a dull thunk and Mikhaelis's head snapped backwards. A scarlet aureole appeared just below his ear, and blood from the exit-wound splashed Hammoudi's suit. The monk crumpled and Elena jumped free. 'Run!' I screamed. She dashed towards the gate, and I saw Hammoudi raise his Ruger, then lower it again. 'Shoot her!' the colonel bawled, drawing a pistol from his belt. Out of the corner of my eye I saw Ahmad fire a snap-shot from the shoulder, then another. The colonel screamed, dropped the pistol and clutched at his hand. The Hawazim, grouped round the gate, behind shrubs, posts and palm-saplings, began pumping rounds at the policemen with their quick-firing *Hajana* carbines. 'Get back inside!' I heard Hammoudi yell. I looked down at the Walther in my hand and realised that I was shaking uncontrollably. Then I saw something that really shook me. My John Lennon spectacles were lying in the sand at my feet. I'd made the most important shot of my life without them, and without them I couldn't hit a barn door.

It was Mansur who pulled me out of it. 'Come on,' he shouted in my ear, 'help me with Mukhtar.' I put on my glasses and together we dragged my uncle towards the gate. I recognised the tall gaunt figure of 'Ali among the uniformed tribesmen, carrying his favourite rifle, Hawk's Eye. He was already getting the camels on their feet and urging the Hawazim to leap into the saddle. Mansur mounted while 'Ali and I passed Mukhtar's limp and bleeding body up to him. Mansur urged his camel up, his good eye glittering with rage.

Elena half turned towards me and I pulled her to me tightly. 'Thank God!' she said.

'*Yallah*!' Ahmad shouted, sprinting past. 'There's no time for canoodling now!' I took the nearest camel, swarmed up its neck and pulled Elena on after me. Then I kicked its withers with my feet and we charged out of the gate, a tight knot of men and roaring camels, out into the vast pebble beach, where in ancient days the great Ur-Nile used to flow.

We rode in near silence. By sunset we'd reached the limestone plateau and just had time to climb the tortuous pass of Naqb before full darkness set in. At the top we came to a sandy fissure between crags and overhangs of limestone, where more than a dozen camels were hobbled. A guard hailed us out of the night as we arrived. We couched the camels amid grumbling and spitting, and as soon as I'd slipped out of the saddle, I held Elena silently. 'Thank God, Jamie,' she said. 'They kept on promising to let me see you if I talked. I told them little bits to keep them happy but they were never satisfied. They kept coming back for more. I told myself that whatever they did I'd never tell them where Mukhtar's people were hiding. Then that disgusting creature, the monk, told me they'd found out I was expecting a baby.'

'Elena, it's wonderful.'

'Yes. Once I knew that, I was even more worried about you.

After that they began to treat me as if I was somebody special. It was all false, really sick. That beast – the monk – kept on giving me tests, slavering over me as though I was a prize pig.'

'It's over now. I left you once. I'll never leave you again.'

She was about to say something when Mansur called us over to look at Mukhtar. They had laid him out on a blanket, and Ahmad was cutting away his shirt, while 'Ali held a torch and Mansur watched. I examined the wound in the torch-light. It looked bad. Renner had shot him at almost point-blank range and the entry wound was huge and edged with powder-burns. The round had probably missed his heart but had punctured his lungs. He was barely conscious and his breathing was laboured. Ahmad shook his head sadly. I guessed there'd be a full medical kit in one of the saddle-bags of the *Hajana* camels and I ran to look for it. When I came back with some vials of morphine, Mukhtar's eyes were wide.

'Don't try to talk, Uncle,' I said. 'I'm going to give you something for the pain.'

'Don't stick needles in me,' Mukhtar croaked, 'I know it's over. The Divine Spirit has given me a long life. I've led the tribe as best I could – the best of a poor bunch.'

He shifted himself a little and gulped. 'I can't see the stars,' he said suddenly, 'I can't see your faces.'

'We're all here, Father,' Mansur said.

'My sons, I love you all, but the tribe needs an *amnir* to guide it. Omar's the only one with the Shining power. Omar, promise me you'll stay with the family after I'm gone.'

'Uncle!' I said, 'I don't know if I can . . .'

'The tribe needs you. You belong. Promise me you will be *amnir*.'

'Uncle, I don't know . . .'

'Promise!'

I looked at Elena in the starlight. She nodded. 'I promise,' I said.

The old man closed his eyes. 'Then it's done,' he said.

A few moments later, he was dead.

* * *

After we'd wrapped Mukhtar's body in cotton shrouds, we dug a shallow trench in the floor of the wadi with our hands and knives, and buried him there. This small crack in the plateau's skin would be remembered as Mukhtar's place – he would be part of the landscape for ever. The night cold had fallen on us like a breath of ice, and we lit a fire and hoped the crackling flames would cheer us. Ahmad made coffee, his face an orange smear with black holes for eyes. The stars were out and the Milky Way spread across the night sky like a gossamer cloud. I stared at the fire, burrowed into the flickering flames, trying to separate myself mentally from my companions. I already sensed an almost imperceptible change in their attitude towards me. How could I tell them I'd only promised to make the old man happy in his dying moments? I couldn't resign the rest of my life to being a hunted tribesman in the Egyptian deserts.

'The Divine Spirit works in strange ways,' Ahmad said suddenly. 'Now we've got a pipsqueak city-boy as an *amnir*. Remind me to give you pistol-shooting lessons some time!'

'I will, preferably with my glasses on.'

'The thanks is to God, Omar,' Mansur cut in, 'you saved my life down there.'

'How many's that I owe you now?'

'Look,' he said, 'I know you only promised to make the old man happy. But will you stay?'

I sought out Elena's face, a trembling vapour of light and shade in the flames. 'I don't know . . .' I said.

Ahmad concentrated on the coffee, flicking the lid of the hornbill-spouted pot open, sniffing the steam, stirring it with a stick.

'I think you should stay,' said Mansur, his one good eye sparkling like the Pole Star, 'The family needs a proper *amnir*. We can fight and herd camels, but we don't have the Shining power.'

'Mansur's right,' Ali said.

'I just don't know,' I said.

We all stared at the flames in silence for a moment. Then Elena asked, 'How did you find us?'

'Only by God's will,' Mansur said, 'we thought you'd died in the Sand Sea. We waited four days. On the third we spotted a helicopter, but we saw nothing else. We waited another day, then we headed back to the Jilf. God help us! Finding our way through that drumsand on hardly any water almost killed us. But we lost no one and made it by the skin of our teeth. God bless the camels – they saved us. Not one of us could stand upright by the time we sighted the Jilf, let alone walk!'

'So you waited for us at the Jilf?'

'Yes, we'd just about given up on you, when Mohammad wald Salam – our third-degree cousin, who lives in Baris – arrived from Kharja on a half-dead camel carrying your *fidwa* and saying you're a prisoner near Kom Ombo on the edge of the town. "Prisoner!" Mukhtar said, "Then he's half dead already!" So Mukhtar picks a dozen good men and the very best camels – it's a wonder we had any after the Desolation – and we set off. We hardly stopped till we got within a day of the prison.'

'Actually it was a hospital, a special police facility of some kind.'

'Hospital, prison, it's all the same. Anyhow, we send a couple of scouts out and they see this *Hajana* patrol coming and going. Yesterday night, they camped under the plateau. We left our own camels here under guard and crept down the pass as quiet as snakes. They didn't hear a thing till we jumped on them. We tied the lot up and left them there with a boy to keep an eye on them and give them water. They struggled a bit when we took their uniforms. They've been lying in the baking sun all day in their underpants!'

There was a ripple of laughter around the campfire.

'I saw you coming,' I said. 'I thought you looked a bit ragged for a military patrol.'

'I suppose we did, but at the gate they didn't turn a hair, just opened right up. The guard sergeant said "You lot look a bit rough!" I said, "So would you if you'd been riding all night." It was when we barracked the camels inside the gate that he cut up rusty. Said they were messing the place up with their droppings. I said we'd had orders to wait for a special convoy and the gate was to stay open. We're hanging around there getting a bit nervous, when they bring you out looking like they're about to shoot you.'

'What would you have done if they hadn't brought me out?'

'We'd have gone in.'

'Thanks.'

'The thanks is to God.'

'Did you find Zerzura?' 'Ali asked.

I paused. I knew I wasn't ready to explain everything. There wasn't even a word for 'star-ship' in the Hawazim vocabulary. I would have had to call it a ship or a plane – but since most of them had been in neither, that wouldn't have meant much more to them. Then I thought of my mother's Agadez cross, and I brought it out. 'You remember this, Mansur?' I asked.

Mansur took the cross and examined it in wonder. 'It's Aunt Maryam's,' he said, 'she used to wear it all the time.'

'Well, my mother showed me a place where there were palm-trees and water. It was Zerzura.'

Mansur shivered and his blank, wayward eye seemed to pop out of his skull. 'A ghost?' he whispered. He made the sign against the evil-eye. The rest of the tribesmen copied him. 'No evil!' they exclaimed.

'Ghost or no ghost, all I know is we're both alive. A police helicopter picked us up – I guess that was the one you saw on the third day – but I don't remember that.'

'I was barely conscious,' Elena said, 'I remember them putting us on a drip. Then they gave me a jab and I passed out.'

'What happened to Dhahabiyya?' Ahmad demanded suddenly.

'I'm sorry,' Elena said, 'she foundered.'

His face dropped. 'My grandfather, my father and my two best camels,' he said, 'by God, Zerzura has a lot to answer for. What now, *amnir*?'

Amnir. It was the first time anyone had called me that. I'd promised Mukhtar only to ease his dying, but somehow the title seemed to fit. It had no connotations of authority, only guidance, and I realised suddenly that the word meant 'enlightened one', the direct equivalent of the Latin word *illuminatus*. These men had risked their lives for me; for my sake they'd undergone incredible hardship, non-stop rides across the harshest of landscapes, fatigue, thirst, hunger. For me they'd made certain that they'd be outlaws for the rest of their days. Mukhtar had sacrificed himself, the watering-boy whose name I didn't know had risked death, Mohammad, a third cousin I'd never even met, had almost killed himself to take my *fidwa* to the Jilf. True belonging wasn't just acceptance, I thought, it meant responsibility too.

'I think we should send these camels back to their owners for a start,' I said, 'and set them free.'

Ahmad looked troubled. 'That's going to be like letting a hyena out of a trap – very dicey work.'

'No – just hide their weapons and free only one of them. Tell him not to move until you're out of sight. They won't want to follow us in the dark with no guns, that's for certain.'

'Yes. Good thinking, Omar.'

'And we split up. The government will be sending aircraft after us. We'll stand a better chance in small parties. Mansur – you and 'Ali take the camels back to the *Hajana*, then divide into two parties and make for the Jilf double quick. If any planes come over use your camouflage nets.'

'Right, Omar.'

'Ahmad, you stay with Elena and me. I think we should start right now, to make use of the darkness. They'll be out looking for us at first light.'

57

WE SKIRTED KHARJA NOT LONG BEFORE dawn, and the sunrise found us in the sand-plains beyond. A long plume of red dust decorated the eastern horizon, and it was from that direction that the helicopter came, falling out of the sky like a falcon – almost on top of us before we even saw it. 'Get the cam-nets out!' I said.

'No use,' Ahmad said, 'they've spotted us already.'

The chopper swooped over us, its rotors licking up the sand, its engines deafening, frightening the camels. 'It's a Scout,' I shouted over the din, 'not more than four men.'

'We can take them,' Ahmad growled, reaching for Renner's Walther, which I'd given him, knowing that in Hawazim superstition the weapon that has killed a relative is imbued with tremendous power.

The aircraft settled in a vortex of dust a hundred metres away and two men, their faces muffled by red *shamaghs*, jumped out. The rotors ground slowly to a halt and the men stood waiting casually, unthreateningly. They didn't appear to be armed. In the helicopter itself I glimpsed a pilot and a third crewman.

'Who is it?' Ahmad said.

We couched and hobbled the camels and walked towards the chopper. Apart from their headcloths, the men wore zipped khaki flying overalls, and bomber-jackets, but their figures were as different as Laurel and Hardy. One was pear-shaped and small, built like a barrel, his face covered by his headcloth except for slits for the eyes. The other towered over him, lean and wiry, and when he removed his *shamagh* we saw he was an old man with shaven stubble for hair, suncured skin and bright blue eyes.

'It's *Robert*!' Elena cried suddenly, rushing towards him. 'Robert! Thank God! Where have you been.'

Rabjohn smiled and hugged Elena. He shook hands warmly and kissed me on both cheeks. 'I thought I'd lost you,' he said.

'I thought you were dead,' I replied. 'What happened?'

'I'll explain everything,' he said. 'But first, where are you going?'

'To the Jilf,' I said.

'Is that where the rest of the Hawazim are?'

'Yes, but . . .'

He turned towards the pilot. 'Send this message to *Whisky Zero*,' he snapped. 'The rest of them are hiding out in the Jilf.'

'Who are you talking to?' I asked.

'To Colonel Fahad of the *Mukhabaraat*,' he said calmly. 'Of course, he only knows me as Source Jibril.'

I must have taken a step backwards. For a second, I just stared at him. There was a scuff of dust behind me and suddenly the other man whisked out a 9mm Browning pistol with amazing speed, and fired twice. I ducked instinctively, and turned to see Ahmad, pistol in hand, slowly toppling over into the sand. Elena and I ran over to him. He was still conscious, but blood was pumping out of his thigh. I pulled off my *shamagh* and bunched it, holding it over the wound to staunch the flow. I looked up to see that the little man had unveiled himself. I saw an obese pink baby's face with dark piggy eyes and a half-moon mouth upturned with satisfaction as though he'd just done something very impressive indeed. It was Dr Abbas Rifad.

'You fucking little shit,' I said, standing up.

Rifad smiled nervously. 'You're next, Ross,' he said, 'I wouldn't bother with your friend if I were you. None of you are going to live that long.'

I stared at Rabjohn. 'I should have known,' I said. 'It had to be you, didn't it? You met Doc at the Eye of Ra Society office as "Sha-Tehuti", knowing that she wouldn't recognise you, then you had her murdered. You reported to the *Mukhabaraat* every step of the way. How else did Hammoudi know we were going to al-Maqs?'

'Dear Hammoudi – he knew nothing except what Rasim told him. I used him as a catspaw all the way through, but you should have listened to him, Jamie. If you'd accepted that the whole thing was just a hoax concocted by Karlman you might have got away with it.'

'I'm not a bloody fool, Rabjohn. You would never have run the risk of the message reaching the world – too dangerous for you. You wanted to use me, but you realised you couldn't. Either way I'd have been snuffed in the end. Elena would have been treated like some kind of brood-mare and killed as soon as the baby arrived.'

Rabjohn shrugged. 'It's all academic now, anyway. We got the message you received from the *Guardians* by subliminal probes while you were unconscious. Of course, I knew you were an *illuminatus*, but I couldn't have you giving my secrets to the world. In short, you know too much. Now you'll pay the penalty. A body could lie in these wastes a century without being found.'

'So you're the Eye of Ra.'

'Yes, Jamie, essentially I am. Of course, the Eye of Ra has existed for thousands of years – sworn from the beginning to protect the earth from the likes of Akhnaton and his kind. The Eye got rid of Tutankhamen in 1430 BC. He was an alien hybrid with some of his father's characteristics, including an ability to hypnotise and control people that became increasingly effective as he grew up. Oh, they thought they could control him, but they were wrong. After his murder Ay took over, but he was still tainted with Akhnaton's heresy, so four years later Horemheb had him killed and went about wiping any trace of the aliens from history. The Eye of Ra passed down the secret from mouth to mouth over the millennia. Sometimes only a single person knew the truth. Then in 1922, Carter and Carnarvon came along, meddling, found Tutankhamen's tomb and learned the secret. His Lordship had a big mouth and he wasn't easily frightened – the product of generations of aristocracy used to getting their own way. He told a lot of his cronies before the Eye got him, and they all had to be put down – at least the ones the Eye considered a security risk.'

'How?'

'You know as well as I do how skilled the ancient Egyptians were in toxicology, Jamie. The Eye used *soba*, a poison derived from a hallucinogenic fungus whose use had been shrouded in mystery for centuries. The poison varies in its effects, sometimes brings on horrific visions, sometimes the symptoms of illness, fever, cramps, heart failure. In small doses it can cause deep depression over a number of years. Thing is, it leaves no trace; that's what mystified the medics in every case. Carnarvon got a horse's dose of the stuff.'

'Why didn't they kill Carter?'

'Carter knew what was going on, but he cooperated – agreed to keep quiet and work for them. But they insured against him changing his tune by administering the poison in tiny, cumulative doses over a long period, causing periodic bouts of depression. Only the Eye had the antidote, so they had Carter by the short and curlies until he died.'

'So I was right. The Eye was behind the deaths linked with Tut's tomb.'

'Yes, we tracked them down and killed them, some in Egypt, others in London, Paris and other places. Walter Morrison, the Reuters man who'd seen the *anachronae*, for example, was slipped a massive dose of *soba* in a drink at his club in Piccadilly. Carter'd originally persuaded him to lie in his report, but he'd decided he was going to write another one telling the true story. We had to nip that in the bud very quickly. Of course, there were the awkward ones who couldn't be tricked into taking the poison, like Ali Fahmi Bey. The Eye had him shot outside Tut's tomb. Needless to say, the gunman was never found.'

'What about Julian and Nikolai?'

'Julian's obsession with Zerzura and Nikolai's cupidity proved a fatal combination for them both. Julian nosed about with Nikolai's text until he came across Wingate's little hoard. When he brought me the *ushabtis*, I guessed what had happened and that it would only be a short time before he got his intuition into gear and worked the whole thing out. I sent a couple of boys round to put the frighteners on him, and they abducted him and kept him hidden for a few days, while you were scouring Cairo and chatting with our man Renner. When they let him go, he came straight round to my place and told me the whole story. He was an incredible man, Julian. Brilliant really. Within a few short weeks he'd worked out that there was some long-term conspiracy that connected Tut, Carnarvon and Wingate. I realised things had gone too far. I tried to get the whereabouts of Wingate's souvenirs out of him, but he wouldn't budge on that. So I spiked his whisky with a few milligrams of *soba* and when he collapsed I had him taken to Giza by night. I got the police to stay out of the way, got hold of a ticket and had an expert cover up the tracks. I admit it didn't occur to me that the absence of his own tracks would look odd. Hammoudi noticed but wisely he kept quiet about it.'

'What about Julian's body? I saw him *alive!*'

'Renner requested the body, then disposed of it. There were no relatives, as you well knew. We didn't want anybody poking around with it. As for Cranwell's "appearances", we had an out-of-work actor on our books who posed as Cranwell. If you thought he was alive you wouldn't waste much time searching for the body. Our Cranwell look-alike also dealt with Nikolai, and rolled a grenade into his flat.'

'Nikolai!' Elena shrieked. 'You bastards . . . you killed him too!'

'That was a regrettable business. Nikolai was so wary after Julian's death that we couldn't get near enough to give him the poison. We had to resort to more primitive methods. The Eye on the mirror in blood was a nice touch though, added by our actor-friend. No, I'm sorry, but Nikolai knew too much. He had to go.'

'Why?' Elena said, tears in her eyes, 'What was so important that they had to die? What was it they found in the tomb?'

Rifad scowled. 'We shouldn't be wasting time talking to this scum, Master,' he said. 'Let's kill them and be done.'

Master. The word sounded strange coming from someone as

arrogant and egocentric as Rifad. It was almost as if Rabjohn had some profound power over him – some deep-seated means of control.

Rabjohn looked at him as if a flea had spoken. 'I want to explain it all to Jamie,' he said, petulantly, 'I'd like him to know why he and all his family have to be liquidated.'

Elena bit her knuckle and gasped.

'So?' I said.

'There were three things in the tomb. There was a papyrus and a map, just as your newspaper said, but it was no ordinary map and no ordinary papyrus. The map was the original of the Piri Reis portolan. Are you familiar with that, Jamie?'

'I've heard of it.'

'It was a navigation chart discovered in Istanbul's Topkapi Palace in 1929 showing part of the southern hemisphere – bits of Africa, South America and Antarctica. It was only after the US Hydrographic Office had studied it that it was realised the map actually showed Antarctica *before it was covered in ice*. That caused a sensation. For a start, the map was dated 1513, while Antarctica wasn't discovered till 1818. But more important, the Antarctic hasn't been ice-free since 4000 BC, which meant that the chart had to be based on something at least six thousand years old, and would thus precede the accepted era for the invention of writing. Actually, the Hydrographic Survey never knew that the original had been found in Tut's tomb in 1923. It was made of a synthetic polymer so strong it was indestructible even by fire, and so fine that the whole map, covering the entire globe, fitted into a large pocket. Moreover, those who studied it later proved conclusively it could only have been made by a culture capable of flight, probably space-flight. So you see, you were almost on the right track from the beginning, Jamie. You just didn't have the data.'

'Where is the map now?'

'Why the hell should we tell him?' Rifad said.

'Shut up. I want to tell him. It's kept with the other artefacts at a secret research site called Area 51 in the New Mexico desert.'

'What about the papyrus?'

'That was an artefact made by Akhnaton himself to record the location of his star-ship in the desert. The Eye wanted to find the ship, but the map system Akhnaton used was too difficult and they never cracked it. It was also made of some indestructible material that is still being studied.'

'What was the third thing?'

'The third thing was pieces of a very ancient machine – our technicians believe it was a teleportation-drive of some kind, dating back to at least twelve thousand years ago. It wasn't functional, of course – it had been kept by the Ra priesthood as a sacred object until Akhnaton came along. After Tut's execution they buried it with the other things in his tomb. Horemheb was aware the artefacts couldn't easily be destroyed, and he didn't want anyone else to know about them – ever. That's why the people who broke into the tomb were silenced.'

'And I suppose that fragment of ancient machinery is not on display at any public museum either.'

'Such secrets are not for the masses, Jamie. Surely you understand that.'

'What about the star-ship? Why didn't you study that?'

'We couldn't. It was guarded by some kind of protective field which had the power to destroy it if its integrity was threatened. Wingate found it by intuition, like you did, but unlike you he failed to get the Message. We had his party ambushed at the quicksands on their return in January 1933, and whacked the lot – your grandfather included, though I didn't know that at the time.'

'But Wingate and Hilmi escaped.'

'Yes, Wingate was another brilliant man. He gave us the slip with Hilmi, and made it to al-Maqs, where he had the *ushabtis* hidden in a place even we didn't know about. We soon traced him there, though. Hilmi was a mental case, so no one was going to believe him, anyway – but we were worried about Wingate. We interrogated him, and from his description we figured out that the star-ship's instruments couldn't be operated except by someone with special telepathic ability.'

'And then you bumped him off, of course.'

'Of course. He was always unstable. In 1944, he started threatening to let the cat out of the bag, so we put a bomb in his plane. Lost the pilot and co-pilot too, of course, but that couldn't be helped.'

Rifad was looking more and more impatient. 'Why bother with these fools, Master,' he said again, 'let's do them now. If I'd had my way I'd have squashed you like a roach years ago, Ross, just like I had that interfering fool Izzadin squashed when he tried to dig up the dirt on Carter. I disliked you from the start. I knew it was only a matter of time. I wanted to have you killed when you found the Sirian Stela, but I was overruled.'

'There would be chaos if people found out what's really out there,' Rabjohn said solemnly. 'Imagine it! We have a duty to protect the human species from such a threat.'

'You're lying, Rabjohn! I've seen the leeches you've got working for you. People like Renner and Rifad here. I can see how concerned you are about the human species – so concerned that you're willing to murder me and my entire family just to protect it. The Eye of Ra is all hocus-pocus. Who are you really, Rabjohn?'

Rabjohn glanced around at the desert horizon. 'You're going to die here, Jamie, so you might as well know. MJ-12 – Majesty – and its predecessor the Jason Scholars infiltrated the Eye of Ra when it was reactivated in 1922 as a result of Carter's find. We soon realised what this was all about – not lost tombs or mummies, but technology so advanced we couldn't even imagine it. We wanted that technology, and we wanted it before anyone else got it. Majesty's original objective was to gain access to the star-ship and to contact the aliens who constructed it. The Zerzura Club was formed through Majesty's proxies, the British Secret Intelligence Service. Unfortunately they didn't find it, so Karlman fed the idea to Wingate, who did.'

'Who was Karlman?'

'Karlman was another failed *illuminatus*, whose genius was tempered by an unfortunate desire to watch young boys having sex, which eventually obliged him to leave his order. Originally he was a Benedictine, and as a young man, in the forgotten library of a monastery in Cairo, he'd come across the lost Books of Thoth, the accumulated wisdom of the Ra brotherhood over ten thousand years.'

'Good Lord!'

'Yes. The set wasn't complete, but the texts gave Karlman an inkling of what had really been going on behind the scenes. He became fascinated and formed a little ring of like-minded clerics, which is still going. Our Father Mikhaelis was a distinguished member until you murdered him.'

'He had it coming.'

'So do you, Ross,' Rifad spat.

'Karlman orchestrated the search for Zerzura, which came to an end when Wingate found the star-ship. When we realised we couldn't use it, we tried other methods. Our first contact was made at Roswell in New Mexico in 1947. Things went wrong: neither side understood the other and the alien shuttle-craft crashed. We picked up a couple of the crew, but they weren't much use to us dead. They're now at Area 51 with the Piri Reis Map and the Akhnaton Papyrus. We realised that we had a communications problem. We needed a sort of "interpreter", if you like. We'd found out about the psi-gene, and we guessed that to talk to the aliens we needed an individual with this gene – an *illuminatus* as the ancient books called it. They were very rare. Karlman had a touch of it. Wingate had had it a bit but not enough, and by then he was dead anyway. I knew that it ran in the Hawazim, and that one facet of it was precognition, so when I heard the stories from your father I wondered if you had it. Of course, it was pure chance that you turned up like that, and at first I saw you as a threat. That's why we bombed your room in the hotel. Then I realised you were Calvin's son, and remembered the stories about your childhood. Anyway I decided to give you a little test – your experience at Nikolai's. You passed.'

'It's like a game to you, isn't it, Rabjohn?'

'I admit it's amusing.'

'What about the Barringtons?'

'You really do like to dot the "i"'s and cross the "t"'s don't you?'

'Let's blast them now, Master!' Rifad said.

'I said shut up!' Rabjohn snapped. 'Ronnie Barrington was just what I said he was – one of those plodders who seem dopey on the surface, but who never let go once they get their teeth into something. He realised what the Zerzura Club had been up to, and then he found out their Eye of Ra Operation file had been transferred to MJ-12. Fortunately he reported it to a superior who was one of us, and we arranged to have his brakes tampered with. By the way, the same happened to Lynne Regis, the Space-Shuttle analyst, in California. Your friend Evelyn – such an amusing lady. Of course, when she came to visit us at the Eye of Ra Society, I knew who she was from the start; I just played along to find out how much she was aware of. Luckily she'd never seen me, so she didn't know I was ''Rabjohn''. As soon as she'd gone I called Renner and Rifad, who got rid of her and made it look like suicide.'

'Why did you try to persuade me to leave the country?'

'I wanted to get you out of the way, where we could examine you more closely, but since you were determined to go to al-Maqs, I decided to let you find the ship. It would be a good test of your abilities, I thought, and we'd learn something if you were able to operate the instruments. I was right; you succeeded where Wingate had failed and brought out a message, twelve thousand years of data. The ship was destroyed, of course, but we still had you and your message, and a great deal of what we wanted to know about technology would be in it. After we'd got that, the question was what to do with you. We still needed someone to help us communicate with the aliens, but you proved uncooperative. So now we're here.'

'Let me kill him and get it over with, Master,' Rifad said.

Master. That word again. For a second I let my senses go out of focus. I removed my glasses and took three deep breaths. I summoned up all the mental energy I could and concentrated on Rabjohn. Then suddenly I saw it: the photo of Carter and Carnarvon in the Valley of the Kings in 1923. The third person in the picture – it *was* Rabjohn, looking exactly as he looked now. But if Rabjohn had been seventy in 1923, that would make him over a hundred and forty years old! It was impossible. But it was him all right. Then in a flash of intuition, I saw the whole thing. It was a lie from beginning to end. I slapped my glasses back on my nose and grinned triumphantly. Rifad raised the gun. 'All right,' I said, 'maybe I'm going to die, but before I do I want to tell you that you haven't fooled me, Rabjohn. At least one human being saw through you, and even when I'm gone, someone else will too. They'll get you in the end.'

'What?'

'It was you from the beginning, wasn't it. You're stuck here just like they were. Ha! ha! What cosmic bloody fools you must be! Twelve thousand years and in the same predicament! There was no Eye of Ra, not this century. You killed the lot, set up cranks like Montuhotep, created Majesty for your own purposes, set up the Zerzura Club. You have a special skill in persuading people to do what you want – some kind of mental control. Look at Rifad here – ''*Master*''. I suppose that's what Akhnaton had; that's how he was able to handle an entire population of humans alone. You thought you could control me in the same way, but I was too strong for you. You collected all the remnants of the old technology and all the debris of the psi-gene programme like me and Wingate, everything you thought might give you that vital little piece of knowledge to allow you to escape, but none of it helped. At least you managed to get your act right since Akhnaton's time and actually *appear* to be human. I feel sorry for you, Rabjohn, or whatever it is you really call yourself, you *dirty shape-shifter*!'

'Damn you to eternity!'

'About time!' Rifad said, raising the gun. I watched his lids narrowing, and felt for my blade, too late. There was a whistle and a thud, and his eyes suddenly opened very wide indeed, his face creased in agony, and a gout of blood spurted from his mouth. As he collapsed forwards, I saw Ahmad's stiletto growing out of his solar plexus. I snatched the pistol from his stubby hand and turned it on Rabjohn, catching a glimpse of Ahmad out of the corner of my eye, lurching towards us holding his bloody thigh, roaring, 'That's for my father and my grandfather!'

After that it seemed I was watching the whole sequence of

events from somewhere above my own head. I saw the third crewman emerging from the back of the chopper with a sub-machine-gun, saw Elena catch the pistol that Ahmad threw to her, aim with both hands, fire twice, three times, saw the wisp of smoke, smelt the powder, saw the crewman fall into the sand. I saw Rabjohn ducking down to pick up the fallen sub-machine-gun, saw myself squeeze the trigger, saw how Rabjohn's arm twisted and shattered, splashing blood on the fuselage. I saw Rabjohn squirm with anger, saw him shaking, shaking, shaking, until his whole body was vibrating so fast that it seemed to go out of focus, until I could no longer make out his features or even his figure. It seemed that he'd gone into a sort of cocoon of vibration, his whole body disintegrating and spinning in a wild vortex. There was a terrifying howl, like the howl of an injured animal and suddenly the vibration slowly wound down until a creature with a feral, ferocious face, an unnaturally elongated cranium, an ape-like body that was neither a man's nor a woman's, screeched once and, with a last terrified glance at me, leapt up and ran off into the desert. I will never forget the last glimpse of that face. The eye-sockets were large but narrowed to slits, and behind the slits the eyes looked yellow, like the eyes of a cat.

58

ELENA HAD THE PILOT IN HER sights with his hands up, but his attention was not on her weapon, it was on the desert and the creature that had just disappeared into it. 'God protect us from the devil!' he said under his breath. 'What was that thing?'

'That was a *Nommo*,' I said.

'A what?'

'A cosmic idiot,' I said. 'For twelve thousand years they've been trying to use human beings for their own purposes one way or another, and yet they've failed every time. That creature was like Robinson Crusoe on a desert island, making the best of it, trying desperately to find a way to get home. It assumed human form, collected the old texts, got people working for it, built up institutions and organisations for the sole purpose of getting off this planet.'

'Are you just going to let it go?' Elena said.

'Whatever it is, it won't last long out in al-Ghul.'

Ahmad hobbled up to us. '*Jinns* live for ever,' he said. 'I've seen plenty of them, even more ugly than that! Should have known that was a *Jinn* in disguise.'

I examined Rifad and the injured crewman. Rifad was dead, but the crewman was still breathing. Elena's rounds had gone low, into the thigh and groin and he was bleeding profusely. I opened the helicopter's medical kit and staunched the bleeding with field-dressings. 'He'll be OK,' I said.

A burst of sound came over the radio – a fuzzy voice demanding answer.

'You answer that and we'll leave your body here for the vultures,' I told the pilot.

'Too late,' he said, 'they're already on their way.'

I helped Ahmad into the back of the Scout. 'Will those camels find their way back alone?' I asked.

He nodded. 'They'll be all right. Our camels can find their way home over twenty days' ride. Elena and I hurried off to unsaddle them while Ahmad kept an eye on the pilot. We stripped them, pointed their heads towards the Jilf and slapped their haunches to set them off. Then we brought the saddles and gear over and loaded them into the Scout. 'What are you going to do?' the pilot asked.

'Nothing. You're going to take us to the Jilf.'

The rotors started, gyrating faster and faster until a great cloud of sand and dust wheezed through the open port. A moment later the Scout leapt off the sand like a grasshopper and was airborne. I craned out of the open side, seeing the desert going on and on, a pattern of black and amber – silicon sand-flats, alkali playas, ridges of sand, great mountain-dunes like fairytale pinnacles. Somewhere down there was a *Nommo*, an alien who'd become stranded in a foreign place, had moved mountains to try to get back home, and had failed.

The Jilf came up with what seemed like incredible speed, from afar a great rock island in a pastel sea, its wadis traced with green, a patina of verdancy against the nothingness that surrounded it to infinity. In the far distance I could see the plains of the *Khuraab* – the Desolation – which we'd crossed on our way to Zerzura. On the very edge of my vision lay the labyrinth of the Sand Sea where the creature Akhnaton had once landed his star-ship. From up here, far above the desert, the whole landscape looked like the board of a massive game played by children. Perhaps that was how it had looked to the *Nommos*, but the game had ceased to be a game when they'd found themselves stranded inside it for ever. For the original landing party, back in the First Time, I thought, it would have been a bit like the crewmen of the *Bounty* stranded on an island in the Pacific. They had been worshipped as gods at first, been regarded with awe for their superior technology. As they intermarried with the natives and the generations passed, though, they had become more and more like them, and though their new ideas had influenced the native population profoundly, their own technology had been lost. Year after year, though, the descendants of the sailors had lit a great bonfire in the hope of attracting a rescue-ship, even though they no longer needed to be rescued, and indeed had probably forgotten the purpose of the signal-fire. The *Nommos* psi-gene programme had been like that, I reflected, and just as the signal-fire might have brought down on the island a pirate who'd robbed the crewmen's descendants of power and taken over the place for himself, so the psi-gene programme had ultimately brought the rogue alien Akhnaton. How Rabjohn fitted in, I'd probably never know – another *Nommo* refugee stranded on earth more recently, perhaps, the victim of some new experiment. There was one thing I was certain of, though. As Renner had said, they were still with us. I was certain, because suddenly I could feel them, there just beyond the veil of consciousness, pushing like barbarian tribes to come in.

The pilot put the craft down in front of the Cave of Pictures and even before we landed, scores of Hawazim came running out with their rifles, ready to open fire.

'Don't shoot,' Ahmad yelled, lolling out of the open side, 'it's us!' Mansur and 'Ali were among our reception committee. 'What happened?' Mansur asked.

'We met a *Jinn*,' Ahmad said, 'a real one.'

'God protect us from the Stoned Devil!'

'Are the camels loaded?' I asked.

'Yes, *amnir*.'

'We'd better get moving. The government are already on their way.'

'What about this thing?' Mansur asked.

'Stand back,' I said.

I took his rifle from him, cocked it and put five rounds through the fuel tank which exploded with a clap and a whiplash of smoke and orange fire. Mansur and the other tribesmen ducked as bits of debris whistled over their heads.

'Throw a cam-net over the hulk and take the pilot and the wounded man to the Water Cave. Leave them food.'

Within minutes, the caravan was winding out of the cave-mouth, a great train of camels, an entire tribe on the move. Within the hour we were streaming out of the *Siq*, heading south towards the Sudanese border. It was thrilling to be among these people, moulded by the desert, who fitted the landscape like a hand in a glove. First came the warriors, the men of the tribe on their fast camels in their russet *jibbas*, wearing their scarlet headcloths, or merely letting their great plumes of fat-smeared hair blow in the wind. Then the women and children in their litters mounted on bull-camels, carrying rolls, tents, grinding-stones, cooking-pots, gourds, baskets and waterbags, the entire worldly possessions of their people. Finally came the true wealth of the tribe, the milch-herd – fine fat camels, being driven by ragged herdsboys on camels that seemed to dwarf them. The camels lifted their heads proudly, stepping out towards the desert horizon, and the men began to sing, softly at first, then louder and louder, the deep-throated chorus of the tribe. Mansur rode close to me at the head of the caravan, and fixed me with his good eye. 'Omar,' he said, 'I know you only promised to stay to ease Father's going. We won't hold you to your promise if you want to go.'

I looked at Elena whose camel was pacing near me. 'We couldn't go back even if we wanted to,' she said. 'And you know, the desert would be a fine place to bring up a child.'

'I'm not sure I want to go back,' I said. 'Back to what? Human beings are made to belong, and I belong here, in this place, with these people. My ancestors wandered the desert for millennia; this life is good enough for me.'

What of the Message I was carrying? What of the *Guardians*? The Message would have to wait, I thought, at least for now. Without collateral many wouldn't believe me anyway – in the end it just came down to faith.

'There's just one thing puzzling me,' I said to Elena, 'Hammoudi told me Zerzura was a delusion. He said you told him I'd never left your side, not even for a moment.'

She regarded me with liquid eyes, shining in the full sunlight. 'That's what I wanted to tell you,' she said. 'He's right – you never did.'

It was almost sunset when we came to the frontier – a line on a map somewhere without much significance to the Hawazim. We halted the caravan for a moment to drink, then mounted up. We were just about to start forward, when Mansur's eye blazed. 'Look!' he yelled, pointing to the sky. A helicopter gunship was racing towards us like a vulture; even from ground level I could see that it was bristling with machine-guns and cannons. There was a figure – a tall, powerful-looking man leaning out of the open port at the back, secured by a belt, with his feet on the landing-ski, and both hands on the stock of a heavy machine-gun mounted on a brace. I pulled a pair of binos out of my saddle-bag and scanned the craft. 'It's Hammoudi!' I said.

The Hawazim cocked their rifles in unison and trained them on the chopper. A couple of rounds from its cannon would have wiped every man, woman and child out, I knew, but no one thought of running away. If this was it, we would fight. I watched the chopper as it dropped closer and closer. The tension mounted almost perceptibly as fingers tightened on triggers. 'No, wait!' I snapped suddenly. 'It's not coming.'

The aircraft buzzed over our heads, kicking up dust, stirring the camels, and banked sharply east, flying in a direct line along the imaginary frontier. 'It's the border,' Mansur said suddenly, 'that's the legal limit of Egyptian authority.'

My eyes followed the retreating aircraft. The last thing I saw was Hammoudi grinning and waving as the aircraft turned again to the north, and spun off low into the distance leaving only a pattern of ripples on the blowing sand.

AUTHOR'S NOTE

The Hawazim, the Ancient Egyptians and Their Traditions

The ancestors of the Hawazim belonged to two separate strains. The first strain may be traced to the Anaq – stone-age hunter-gatherers who spoke an unknown language and who inhabited the regions west of the Nile in prehistoric times. This tribe, who had no domestic animals except for dogs, lived by hunting the abundant fauna – elephant, giraffe, wild oxen, zebra, antelope, and other species which roamed the lush prairies of what is now the Western Desert, the most arid area on earth. Like most hunters they possessed an animistic religion which attributed to everything – each tree, hill, stream, rock and valley – its own characteristic spirit. The Anaq also worshipped the stars, and the sun in the form of the sacred sun disk, which was later to become the symbol of the ancient Egyptian sun-god, Ra.

The second cultural and genetic strain among the Hawazim came from the Bedouin – Semitic camel-herding nomads whose origin lay in northern Arabia, and who began to wander down the Nile with their herds and black tents around the 8th century AD. These Arabic speaking Muslims who worshipped the One God, Allah, originally roamed the fringes of the Nile Valley, but were so persecuted by successive waves of stronger tribes and by governments during times of stability, that they were pushed farther and farther out into the margins of the desert. Here they met and fused with the descendants of the Anaq, producing a hybrid culture, Arabic speaking, superficially Muslim, and yet with strong influences from traditional Anaq religion and culture. The Hawazim are unique among Bedouin, for example, in referring to 'The Divine Spirit' in addition to 'God', and the use of the sacred mandrake and the Shining ritual are examples of religious practises amongst them surviving from prehistoric times.

Because of their hybrid nature, the Hawazim were traditionally looked down on by the so-called 'noble' Bedouin, yet they were also feared for their seemingly supernatural ability to survive in the arid desert.

*   *   *

The Hawazim language is Arabic, with the addition of a small stratum of Anaq words. For Westerners, the tongue appears extremely logical in its construction since almost every word is based on a sequence of 3 consonants ('roots'), each set conveying one idea. Thus the sequence K-T-B conveys the idea of 'writing', and no matter what prefixes, suffixes or infixes are added, any word having these consonants in this order must be connected with the idea of writing. Thus, KiTaB means 'a book', maKTaB means 'an office', KaaTiB means 'a clerk', KaTaBa means 'he wrote', yaKTiB means 'he writes', KiTaaBa means 'handwriting' etc etc. The language contains some exotic sounds not found in English, the most common of these being the consonant 'ayn, pronounced by producing a slight retching noise in the throat, and usually signified by a' in English texts. This sound exists in names such as 'Ali, 'Abdallah, Sa'udi-Arabia, Sa'idi, and even in the word 'Arab itself when properly pronounced.

Arabic forms plurals differently from English, often changing the form of the noun itself. Thus, in Arabic, the word *bedawi* (a Bedouin man) usually becomes *bedu* (all the Bedouin), in the plural. There is also a feminine form, *bedawiyya* (a Bedouin woman). In the case of the Hawazim, the masculine and feminine singulars respectively would be *Hazmi* (a Hawazim man) and *Hazmiyya* (a Hawazim woman). The possessive in Arabic is usually formed by what is known as 'the construct', which expresses belonging. Thus one would not normally say 'a Hawazim camel' in colloquial Arabic, only 'a camel belonging to the Hawazim' or 'a camel belonging to a Hazmi' (*jamal hagg al-hawazim/ jamal hagg hazmi*). For this reason the English forms 'a Hawazim camel' or 'A Hazmi camel' can be used interchangeably, having no direct counterpart in Arabic.

Like other Arabs, the Bedouin generally do not possess family names. A child has a given name which is then followed by the word *wald* (son of) and then the name of the father. The son of a man called Ali, for example, might be called Hassan wald Ali, (other forms of 'wald' are 'wad' 'bin' and 'ibn'). In the case of a girl it might be Fatima bint (daughter of) Ali. A full name usually includes 3 generations, so, if our Ali's father was called Sayid, his son's full name would be Hassan wald Ali wald Sayid. Among townsmen, though, the 'wald' or 'bint' is assumed and therefore generally missed out. A townsman named Daud whose father was called 'Rashid' would merely be called Daud Rashid.

The primitive ancestors of the Hawazim probably belonged to much the same stock as the original inhabitants of the Nile Valley, and thus there is a common stratum in ancient Egyptian and Hawazim (Anaq) mythology. To both, the star Sirius, in the constellation Canis Major, was of great importance. Sirius is the brightest star in the sky, and throughout much of the early period of Egyptian civilisation its heliacal rising (that is its first rising after a period of invisibility), happened to coincide with the beginning of the annual inundation of the Nile – the most important event in the Egyptian calendar. Since the 12 lunar months fell just short of an actual year, the regular rising of Sirius therefore enabled the ancient Egyptians to regulate their calendar by introducing a 13th intercalary month every 2 or 3 years. The Egyptians identified Sirius with the goddess Isis, one of the *neteru* who founded ancient Egyptian civilisation, and the Hawazim had also inherited a parallel tradition that Sirius was the birthplace of human culture.